Turn to Me

Books by Becky Wade

My Stubborn Heart

THE PORTER FAMILY NOVELS

Undeniably Yours

Meant to Be Mine

A Love Like Ours

Her One and Only

A BRADFORD SISTERS ROMANCE

True to You

Falling for You

Sweet on You

A MISTY RIVER ROMANCE

Stay with Me

Let It Be Me

Turn to Me

Turn to Me

A Misty River Romance

BECKY WADE

BethanyHouse
a division of Baker Publishing Group
Minneapolis, Minnesota

Published by Bethany House Publishers
11400 Hampshire Avenue South
Minneapolis, Minnesota 55438
www.bethanyhouse.com

Bethany House Publishers is a division of
Baker Publishing Group, Grand Rapids, Michigan

Printed in the United States of America

Library of Congress Cataloging-in-Publication Data
Names: Wade, Becky, author.
Title: Turn to me / Becky Wade.
Description: Minneapolis, Minnesota : Bethany House, a division of Baker Publishing Group, [2022] | Series: Misty river romance ; 3
Identifiers: LCCN 2021056246 | ISBN 9780764235627 (paper) | ISBN 9780764240089 (casebound) | ISBN 9781493425235 (ebook)
Subjects: LCGFT: Romance fiction. | Christian fiction. | Novels.
Classification: LCC PS3623.A33 T87 2022 | DDC 813/.6—dc23/eng/20211119
LC record available at https://lccn.loc.gov/2021056246

Cover design by Jennifer Parker
Cover photography by Todd Hafermann Photography, Inc.

Author is represented by Linda Kruger.

Baker Publishing Group publications use paper produced from sustainable forestry practices and post-consumer waste whenever possible.

22 23 24 25 26 27 28 7 6 5 4 3 2 1

In memory of my beloved Writer Dog, Sam
2010–2021
You were beside me
while I wrote the PORTER FAMILY series,
the BRADFORD SISTERS series,
and the MISTY RIVER ROMANCE series.
Your love and companionship
made my life so much richer.
Thank you, sweetheart.

PROLOGUE

NOVEMBER

Finley Sutherland's father had left her several things in his will, the most surprising of which was a clue.

"But . . . I don't understand," she said to Rosco Horton, attorney-at-law.

"Your father planned a treasure hunt for you." Mr. Horton leaned forward over his impressive potbelly, huffing at the exertion, to extend a white envelope to her across his desk. "He stipulated that you be presented with this, the first clue in the treasure hunt, at the reading of his will."

She accepted the envelope, instantly recognizing her father's handwriting and the thick flow of black ink from his favorite fountain pen.

For Finley, he'd written on the outside.

"He asks that you store the envelope in a safe location," Mr. Horton said, "and wait until the morning of your next birthday to open it. When is your next birthday?"

"January."

"Do you think you can resist peeking until then?"

"Absolutely." It felt sacrilegious to even consider violating a request left for her in her dad's will.

Finley held the envelope carefully, aware of the attorney's attention on her as she looked down at it in her lap. Her father had named Mr. Horton the executor of his will. And since she was the only child of a bachelor, he'd named her his sole beneficiary. After the will cleared probate, she'd inherit his property, bank accounts, investments, and assets. And yet this—a simple envelope—was the thing stirring both grief and wonder within her.

Her father had died suddenly in prison one month ago.

She hadn't expected him to speak or write another word to her. Yet through this mysterious, surprising letter, he'd found a way to continue communicating with her. *For Finley.*

"Your father told me that he used to create birthday treasure hunts for you when you were growing up," Mr. Horton said.

She raised her face. "Yes. Every single birthday before I left for college, he'd send me on a treasure hunt to find my gift."

"Sounds like a nice father-daughter tradition."

"It was." Memories rushed like a film reel through her brain. Her gasps of discovery when she'd solved one of his clues. His deep chuckle. The patter of her feet as she'd race to see if she'd guessed the location of the next clue correctly. Tearing away shiny pink paper to reveal the dollhouse he'd given her when she turned seven.

Astonishingly, her father was reaching out from the grave to give her one final gift.

CHAPTER ONE

JANUARY

This wasn't the first time that Luke Dempsey had been burned by his belief in the concept of honor among thieves.

This was only the most recent time.

When he'd been burned in the past, he'd told himself he wouldn't put himself on the line again. But in time, his conscience would butt in where it wasn't wanted. He'd put himself on the line. Then pay the price. Then tell himself all over again that he'd learned his lesson.

This time he really *had* learned his lesson. For the final time.

On this cold, overcast Wednesday morning, Luke set his jaw and walked from his parking space toward Furry Tails Animal Rescue Center. A black metal roof topped the dark gray modern building that occupied several acres on the road leading east out of Misty River, Georgia.

He'd waited a long time to be free. In fact, he'd spent all seven years of his incarceration meticulously planning his future. The second he finished his obligation here, he'd move to Montana and build a house with a view of mountains and big sky. From his home office, he'd launch a career in software and website development.

He'd walked through the rooms of his Montana house in his

imagination so many times, furnishing every square inch, that those rooms had become more real to him than the rooms of his childhood home. He *needed* to get to Montana and begin work. His old life had been stripped away, and his new start was the only thing left that mattered to him.

But thanks to his inconvenient sense of honor, he first had to keep his promise to Ed Sutherland. Until he made good on that, he'd be stuck here, in the hometown that reminded him a hundred times a day of the worst thing that had ever happened to him.

He let himself inside the building.

No one waited in the foyer. The Furry Tails logo—a stylized dog inside a circle—had been painted in white on the slats of wood covering the wall opposite him. Four chairs surrounded a coffee table. On top of that sat a few small pots of cacti and a stack of *ASPCA Action* magazines. The air smelled like pears and dog. A baby gate guarded the bottom half of a door that led to a concrete hallway and the distant sound of barking.

Frowning, he tapped the bell resting on top of the magazines. He hadn't even started his first workday here, and irritation was already infecting his mood.

He waited. No one responded to the bell, so he punched it with his fist. It rang loudly.

"Coming!" a feminine voice called cheerfully from the back.

According to Furry Tails' website, Finley had started the non-profit eight years ago out of her house while working a full-time day job. Six years ago, a local farmer had donated the use of his barn as her headquarters, and she'd become the organization's first paid employee. Two years ago, Furry Tails had built and relocated to this facility—

A woman sailed into the room. She was young, beautiful, and dressed like a hippie in a strange felt hat with a wide brim. "May I help you?"

"My name's Luke Dempsey. I'm here to see Finley Sutherland."

She smiled. "I'm Finley Sutherland."

His body tensed in surprise.

She extended her hand. He shook it.

"It's great to finally meet you," she said.

How could this be Finley?

"Welcome to the Furry Tails team." Stepping away, she stuck her fingers into the tiny front pockets of her bell-bottom jeans. Her head tilted. "Were you expecting someone older?"

"Yes." Much older.

"That's a common response when people meet my dad before they meet me."

"He was in his eighties."

"I was born when he was fifty-two. You'd think that more children would have resulted from all of those passionate love affairs of his." She shrugged. "But no. He only had me. And fairly late in the game."

Ed's nickname had been Mountain Man. He'd had thick white hair. A white-gray beard. His features were strong and even, but his skin had been deeply lined and permanently tanned.

Luke would never have expected Ed's daughter to look like this. Skin as pale as the moon. Bright blue eyes. Long black hair. Around five foot eight with slender limbs. Her beige sweater looked like it had been knitted by a person instead of a machine. She wore brown clogs and gold rings on almost every finger.

Why would anyone wear a hat indoors to work with animals? Her body was perfect, though. And those lips—

Stop it. He needed to think straight. It's just . . . How could *this* be Ed's daughter? "How old are you?" he asked bluntly.

"I'm about to turn thirty." She beckoned him to follow. "Come. Let me give you a tour."

They walked past the baby gate, which she clicked closed behind them.

"This is a big day for us because you're Furry Tails' fifth official employee," she announced. "For the most part, we function thanks to a large number of volunteers." She gestured right and left. "Our offices are through there. This is our meeting and training room.

This is the classroom for the after-school program. Here are the restrooms. This is the equipment room. This is where we bathe the dogs."

Through a doorway, they entered a wide space lined with kennels on both sides. About half were occupied with dogs.

"Hello, sweethearts," she said to them as they made their way toward a door marked with an exit sign.

Luke had only had one dog in his life, when he'd been in elementary school. A golden retriever named Caramel. She'd been very laid-back and he'd gotten along with her fine. But he definitely hadn't been an animal-crazy kid and wasn't an animal-crazy adult.

"The rest of the dogs are outside having recess," Finley told him as they stepped into a large fenced yard. Beyond, forested hills arched toward the sky. Here, toys littered the ground. So did short tunnels and equipment for the dogs to climb.

Dogs of all ages ran around, yipping. One of them was missing an eye. Another had three legs. Another had wheels strapped to his hips, which functioned in the place of his limp back legs.

Mentally, he tried to count how many hours he'd have to work here before he could fulfill his promise and quit.

"When I started Furry Tails, I rescued all kinds of animals near and far," she said. "But I quickly figured out how important it was to concentrate my mission. Now we focus on dogs in Rabun County. Specifically abandoned puppies, senior pets who've been surrendered by their owners, and dogs with special needs. As you probably noticed, several of the dogs here are pugs."

He hadn't noticed, nor cared.

"I'm very involved with pug rescue," she said.

"I see."

One of the pugs approached, and she knelt to scratch under his chin. "Hello, Harry, you gorgeous dog. You're gorgeous, aren't you? So gorgeous!"

Harry was not gorgeous. And Furry Tails was a lame thing

to call a shelter. The pugs' tails weren't even very furry. They reminded him of pigs' tails.

"Do the dogs . . . get along okay?" It couldn't be a good idea to put a lot of rescue dogs in a yard together, could it?

"We can accommodate sixteen animals here at the shelter. The animals who stay here all have the ability to play nicely with others. We release half of them to the playground at a time. We know from experience that these eight, and the eight who are inside and will have the next turn, get along great." Harry reached his nose upward to give her better access. Based on Harry's breathing, it sounded like he suffered from allergies. "The large majority of the dogs in our program don't stay here."

"Where do they stay?"

"Foster homes. We have a wonderful network of foster parent volunteers who support our primary mission."

"Which is?"

"To place every dog in a loving forever home."

An old dog waddled over and put her paw on Luke's shin. Awkwardly, he gave her a couple of head pats.

"Our secondary mission," she continued, "is to stop the needless killing of animals. We do everything we can to keep them out of the pound. We offer a food pantry for owners struggling to afford the cost of dog food. We also organize spay and neutering clinics." Harry and the old dog lay down near their feet. Finley straightened, rattling off statistics about how many dogs and cats were euthanized each year.

Luke crossed his arms. Expressionless, he watched her cheeks turn pink as she got riled up about her topic. She moved her hands to underscore what she was saying. Clearly, it made her furious that senior, special needs, shy, stray, and aggressive animals didn't stand a chance at the pound.

"We rescue as many as we can off death row."

He'd always thought bleeding-heart animal activists were eccentric, and Finley was proving him right. She was odd. Probably entitled, if her dad had handed her everything in life. Soft. Idealistic and naïve. A dreamer.

She finally paused long enough to take a deep breath. "Do you have any questions about our mission?"

"No."

"Well, when questions occur to you, feel free to ask." She met his eyes. "My dad really wanted you to work here while you're getting back on your feet. It's fulfilling to see his plan come to fruition."

He didn't tell her that he didn't need this job to get back on his feet. He had both plenty of money and plenty of direction. "How much do you know about my friendship with your dad?"

"He talked about you a lot, so I know quite a bit. I know that you arrived at the penitentiary not long after he did."

"Right."

"How long had he been there when you got there? A year or so?"

He inclined his chin.

"Dad's fellow inmates knew that I lived in Misty River. So they told Dad you were from here. He made a point of introducing himself to you and liked you from the start."

"He was a good man."

"Yes, he was." Above, the clouds shifted. The first sunbeams of the day moved across the yard, sparkling against her rings. "Last summer, he told me that you'd be coming up for parole in the fall. He knew that you'd gotten a bachelor's degree and master's degree in computer science while in prison. He also knew that Furry Tails was in the market for a new website. You see, we need a more sophisticated way of matching available animals with people looking for certain criteria in a dog. We want to sell merchandise from our site. We want a platform for online fundraisers. We could really use more effective SEO, newsletters, ads, and social media. In my dad's eyes, you're a tech genius."

"Your dad was over eighty. I think he viewed everyone my age as a tech genius."

"No. He was hard to impress. If he thought someone was a genius in an area, he or she probably *is* a genius."

He grunted.

The small dog with three legs stopped and gave Finley begging eyes. She scooped it into her arms. "Are we agreed that you're enough of a genius to handle Furry Tails' tech needs?"

"We're agreed."

"Excellent." Carrying the dog, she led him back inside. After she pushed open the door marked *Offices* with her foot, they walked into a room with three desks on one side, facing windows. An island with storage below and a worktop above was positioned at the center of the space. A printer, copier, fax machine, water cooler, coffee bar, and mini fridge filled the wall across from the desks.

"This is our central work area. And this desk will be yours." Supporting the dog with one hand, she indicated the desk farthest from the hallway with the other. "Do you have a computer, or do you need me to supply one?"

"I brought my own desktop computer. It's in my truck."

"Perfect. These two desks belong to Kat and Trish. They're working today, but not in the office. They're out doing home visits for prospective adoptive parents."

Home visits? Was the bar to adopt a one-eyed dog high? He couldn't imagine how she found homes for any of these animals.

"Kat handles adoptive parent training, volunteer committees, grants, the spay and neuter clinics, and all the paperwork and financials. Trish is the liaison for veterinary care, fundraisers, and the pet food pantry."

"And what do you do?"

"I communicate with everyone who reaches out to us, which takes quite a bit of my time. I get more than a hundred daily emails and phone calls. I speak at events. Meet with donors. Stay in contact with the county pound. We all split the care and training of the animals."

"You said I was the fifth employee. Who's the fourth?"

"Akira, who runs our after-school program." The dog with three legs sneezed. "I'm anticipating that you'll spend most of your time at the computer. The rest with the animals."

"I'm not experienced with animals."

"Not a problem."

Maybe not for her.

"We'll teach you everything you need to know," she said. A door at the end of the work area led to a smaller room. "This is my office. Please, have a seat."

She'd painted the walls dark turquoise. Her shag rug seemed like a weird choice for a building that included dogs who might not be house-trained. More cacti were grouped on her Lucite desk next to a lamp, a mug, and an alabaster statue of a pug.

They sat.

It was hard to take her seriously while a dog was draped across her lap like a blanket.

"You make that chair look small and uncomfortable," she said, obviously amused.

"That's because it's both." Her chair was large and yellow. His was little and patterned, with shiny metal armrests.

"It's neither," she countered warmly. "I think it's just that you're large and predisposed to discomfort."

He held her gaze but didn't reply.

Finley did not subscribe to stereotypes.

That didn't mean that she failed to note the characteristics of the people she met. She did note them. She just refrained from sticking people into boxes based on those characteristics.

She'd grown up running free across her father's acres. With a tangle of hair flying behind her and a pack of animals dancing at her heels. It hadn't been a conventional childhood, and she viewed herself as open-minded.

So, despite the fact that Luke Dempsey fit neatly into a box marked *Ex-Con*, she steadfastly refused to place him there.

His barricaded hazel eyes were thrown into prominence by his light tan. He had a regal nose that would have suited a nineteenth-century Italian prince. His lips formed a straight, serious line. Thick scruff covered the lean angles of cheekbones and jaw. His hair was a beautiful shade of dark brown. He'd cut it in a masculine style that had grown out so much that some of the strands were almost long enough to catch in his eyelashes. He wore a gray hoodie beneath a black leather jacket. His black jeans ended at lace-up boots.

She didn't often feel short around men, but he was several inches taller than she was. Six foot two, maybe? His muscular body moved with both defensiveness and the smoothness of an athlete. Had she not already known him to be thirty-three, she'd have guessed him to be slightly older.

Luke reminded her of slabs of slate. Craggy. Unyielding.

Typically, she surrounded herself with calming music, calming herbal teas, calming smells, calming poetry. He was not calming. He was quiet, but in the way that a volcano is quiet while magma rises dangerously below the surface.

Fortunately, silence didn't make Finley uncomfortable. She'd spent a lifetime talking to pets who couldn't talk back. In fact, few things—other than the killing of animals, nuclear weapons, injustice, war, the destruction of natural habitats, and the banning of books—made her uncomfortable.

"When did you get out on parole?" she asked.

"November."

"Oh?" The sound communicated her surprise. "I told Dad months ago that I'd hire you as soon as you got out. Why did you wait until last week to contact me?"

"Because the promise I made to your dad doesn't go into effect until this weekend."

If her brain had been a runner, the runner had just hit a brick wall. "Hmm?"

"What did they tell you about your dad's death?"

She scrambled to understand. He'd made a promise to her dad? Connected in some way to his death? "Everything I know about my dad's death came from the report the prison gave me. It said that Dad was in the common area, playing checkers. He stood up, swayed, and collapsed. His friends called for help, and he received treatment quickly. But there was nothing that could be done. He'd suffered sudden cardiac arrest. Within just a few minutes, he was gone."

He'd died on an especially golden October day. She'd been driving back to work after lunch out with donors, windows down to let in the beautiful weather, when she'd received a call from the prison. "Both Sides, Now" by Joni Mitchell had been playing. Immediately, she'd pulled to the shoulder of the road, rolled up her windows, and turned down the sound system so she could concentrate on the conversation. Thus, she'd heard loud and clear the news that her father—the one who'd loved her, defended her, believed in her, and placed her at the top of his priorities—was gone.

Every time she thought back on that moment, she heard the strains of the song she'd been listening to when the call came in. *So many things I would have done. But clouds got in my way.*

"I was the one playing checkers with him before his cardiac arrest," Luke told her. "Everything happened just like you were told."

"You were with him when he died?"

He dipped his chin.

"Was he in pain?"

"Some pain, yes."

Grief stabbed her, clean and deep.

"But he wasn't panicking," he added. "He was speaking clearly—"

"Wait. Can you tell me exactly, word for word, what was said? I really . . . I just—it would help me to know every detail." Luke had been beside her father—where she wished she'd been—during his final moments. She needed the details.

"After he collapsed, I bent down and asked him what was the matter. He said that it was his chest."

"Okay."

"I yelled for help, but I could see that the other guys and the guards were already on it. I tried to tell Ed to take it easy, but he interrupted me. He said that if he didn't make it, he needed me to do something for him."

Foreboding circled her ribs and squeezed.

"He was short of breath," Luke continued, "but he managed to tell me that he'd set up a birthday treasure hunt for you. He said you'd open the first clue on January ninth. He said that he needed me to start work here before that date, then keep you safe during the treasure hunt because it might put you in danger."

"Danger?"

"That's what he said."

She slid the ring on her middle finger up a few millimeters, then back down to meet the ring below it. *Click*. Up and down. *Click click click*. Dad had confided in Luke about the treasure hunt. He'd done so before she'd known of its existence, and he'd added a detail she hadn't received: potential danger. "So, you told Dad that you'd work here and . . . keep me safe?"

"Not at first. I had—*have* things I want to do. But he pleaded with me. I didn't know if he was dying, but I could tell it was bad. So I agreed. He made me promise him. After that, it was like he had permission to go. He closed his eyes. A few seconds later, he was unconscious."

She pulled her mug of peppermint tea in front of her, wrapping her hands around it as if it could offer comforting warmth. It couldn't. It had long since grown cold. "Thank you. For being with him. For making that promise. There's not a doubt in my mind that you eased my dad's final moments."

After she'd told her dad she'd be willing to hire Luke, Finley had educated herself on prisoner reentry and acclimation. With every page she'd read, her enthusiasm had grown. Following incarceration, men and women often had a hard time finding employment. She'd wanted to fill that need and, in doing so, benefit a man like her father. Plus, animals were therapy. What could be more ideal than parolees helping animals and animals helping parolees? She'd viewed Luke's new job here as his lifeline.

Now she saw it might be his albatross.

"Please know that I won't hold you to your promise," she said. "You don't have to work here. You don't have to help me with the treasure hunt. You can go."

"No, I can't."

"You said you have things you want to do. Feel free to go and do them, with my blessing."

He was not a man who wore his emotions on his sleeve, but she saw a subtle flash of longing on his hard features.

"You're free," she told him. "I'll hire someone else to redesign the website."

"The promise wasn't between you and me, so you can't free me from it. It was between me and your dad." His body language communicated stubborn resolve. "I'm going to keep my promise."

She considered him, lining up what she saw before her with what she knew of his past.

Once upon a time, a group of middle school kids had survived more than a week buried in the rubble of an earthquake that had struck while they were on a mission trip in Central America. They'd become known as the Miracle Five, and they were Misty River's best-known and best-loved sons and daughters.

Luke was one of the five.

Almost twenty years had come and gone since that fateful earthquake. The former middle school kids were all adults now, and Luke remained the most reclusive of the five. After their rescue, he'd immediately retreated from the spotlight and never consented to interviews or public appearances.

The other four had gone on to become successful. Natasha MacKenzie, an attorney and mother. Genevieve Woodward, Natasha's sister, a Bible study author. Ben Coleman, high school teacher. Sebastian Grant, pediatric heart surgeon.

The day Luke had turned eighteen, he'd dropped out of high school and left home. He'd worked for a chop shop in Atlanta until he'd been arrested for stealing a car and sent to prison.

It didn't take much intuition to discern why Luke had gone off the rails while the other four were living constructive lives. The earthquake had resulted in two thousand fatalities, but only one Misty River resident had died.

His name had been Ethan. He'd been twelve years old. And he was Luke's younger brother.

Finley had moved to this town after college, so she'd had no interaction with Luke when he was young. But everyone who'd known him then agreed that he'd been a golden boy before his brother's death. The natural disaster had ripped from Luke both his brother and his promising future.

And now she was struggling to absorb the realization that this injured, complicated, infamous man knew about her birthday treasure hunt. Even though Luke was hard as slate, he was also, apparently, compassionate enough to grant her father's dying wish. Which was that Luke . . . protect her?

From what?

She'd been envisioning the hunt as a very personal journey between herself and her father. Perfectly safe, just like all the prior hunts. Resistance was pushing upward inside her at the idea of embarking on this hunt with a stranger.

Gradually, though, an opposing force matched and then surpassed her resistance.

The tug to rehabilitate.

Luke Dempsey was a tragic and thorny case. Many would say he was a lost cause.

Thing was, she had a soft spot for lost causes. It ran contrary to her nature to abandon any creature to its lostness. Over the years, she'd come face-to-face with numerous ferocious animals. Dogs who'd been beaten. Feral cats. Unbroken horses. There'd even been the memorable case of one very angry raccoon.

So many times she'd sensed, at the deepest level, that God had entrusted a certain wounded creature to her care.

That's exactly how she felt now. About Luke.

Not a single one of her past "lost causes" had remained a lost cause. No one—no animal or person on earth—was beyond redemption. If she and Luke worked together here at Furry Tails and on her treasure hunt, she'd have double the opportunity to assist in the Restoration of Luke.

"Can you explain the treasure hunt?" he asked.

She told him about their annual birthday tradition during her childhood and how her father had left the first clue in his will.

"How did he plant the rest of the clues? He was in prison for eight years."

"He must have prepared the hunt, hidden the clues, and gotten his will in order after he'd posted bail and before he went to trial."

Luke held himself with uncommon stillness, his strong hands resting on the ends of the armrests. "Where's the first clue now?"

"It's been in a safe-deposit box for the last couple of months. My birthday's on Saturday, so I just went the day before yesterday and picked it up. At the moment, it's sitting on my kitchen table."

"I'd hide it."

She nodded. "I'm completely stumped as to how or why this hunt could put me in danger."

"My guess is that he hid something valuable for you this time. So valuable that other people might want it."

"If so, I can't fathom what the treasure might be."

"When on Saturday will you open the clue?"

"In the morning, right after I finish eating breakfast. Just like old times."

"I'll meet you then."

"Thanks for the offer, but I'd like to be alone when I open the envelope."

He looked displeased. Luke did displeased very well.

"I won't go in search of the treasure," she added. "I'd just like time to . . . process." Absently, she stroked the warm head of the dog still snoozing on her lap. "How about you come over for dinner on Sunday night? I'll show you the letter then."

Another serving of Displeased Luke.

"If you're going to be involved with this treasure hunt—" she began.

"Which I am."

"Then you're going to have to enter into my life at least a little. And compromise with me. We'll need to do this on my schedule. Both my literal work schedule and my emotional grieving schedule."

"How long do you think it will take to finish the hunt?"

"When I was young, the hunts were quick and easy. I could finish one in thirty minutes. During my teenage years, they became more and more elaborate. The last one took me a couple of months to complete. He had me crisscrossing North Georgia on weekends."

Luke looked like she'd just informed him they'd have to go to the town dump and sort through every item of trash. "In order to protect you, I'll need you to share all the information you have about the hunt, your dad's arrest, his career, his family, his friends, his mistakes, his money. Will you do that?"

"I . . . guess?" She hadn't had to answer to anyone in years.

"Finley."

"Fine."

"Who else knows about the treasure hunt?"

"Just my dad's attorney."

"Name?"

"Rosco Horton."

"We can't trust anyone," he said. "No one other than you, me, and Rosco can know anything about this."

"I haven't told anyone. And I won't."

"Good." He moved as if to rise.

"Not so fast."

He returned to his seat.

"Since you're asking for concessions," she said, "it's only fair for me to ask you for something."

"I'm listening."

"Furry Tails really does need a revamped website. So if you're going to stay on, I'd ask that you complete the site, regardless of how quickly we complete the hunt."

"I'll finish your website."

No one had ever mistaken her for a hard-nosed capitalist, and talking about finances made her itchy. That said, she was a businesswoman and transparency was one of her highest ideals. "Also, Furry Tails can afford to pay your salary, but I didn't budget bodyguard payroll into my monthly personal expenses."

His hazel eyes could cut diamonds. "I don't want you to pay me anything extra."

"Okay then. You and me. Treasure hunt partners?" This really was the most unlikely pairing ever.

"Partners," he agreed.

CHAPTER TWO

Luke's life fell into four categories.

Category One: Life before Ethan died.

Category Two: Life after Ethan died.

Category Three: Life in prison.

Category Four: This new life on the outside.

He punched off his alarm on Friday morning and cracked open his eyes. Five a.m. Still black outside.

Many of the details of his four selves were different.

For example, before Ethan died, Luke would pull a shade over his window every night and sleep in total darkness. After Ethan died, total darkness had no longer been his friend. He hadn't been able to sleep at all unless his closet light was on and the closet door wide open. Even so, sleep became a battle he never won. In prison, lighting choices hadn't been up to him. When the lights went out, they went out. But never to total darkness. Since he'd been released on parole, he'd been sleeping with light filtering in from the bathroom. He also kept one curtain pushed to the side and the window behind it cracked open a few inches, regardless of the weather.

No one knew when an earthquake might strike. If one struck, you didn't want it to trap you.

He shoved the covers away and sat on the edge of the mattress. Cold air snaked over him.

For years he'd been looking forward to regaining control over his life. Then he'd gotten out of prison and realized he no longer knew how to choose among a wide range of options or how to fill a day.

It had taken him hours to make his first trip through a grocery store. He'd stared at the huge number of soap choices for ten minutes. Then stared at the cereal choices. Then the apple choices and the yogurt choices—overwhelmed.

Finally, he'd returned home and unpacked his groceries. But then he'd had no idea how to spend the rest of his hours. Not that day or the days that followed. For long periods of time, he'd forgotten to eat.

In prison, his choices had been minimal, his schedule regulated. The sudden lack of a schedule had, to his disgust, caused him stress. He'd felt like a boat carried by the tide because its line to the dock had been cut.

Out of necessity, for the past two months since his release, he'd gone back to following the structure he'd followed on the inside. He woke at five. Ate at six. Exercised. Started work at eight. Lunch at eleven. Back to work until three. From three to five, he focused on projects. He educated himself on all the cultural advances he'd missed—the rise of social media and the polarization of Americans was hard to believe. He did maintenance on his truck, attended meetings with his parole officer or financial planner. He purchased, then linked together a desktop computer, secondary laptop, and smartphone. He installed the best Wi-Fi and TV package available. At five, he ate dinner. Followed by free time on the computer, watching TV, or reading. Bed before eleven.

For more than eight weeks now, he'd been living in a rented apartment on the top floor of one of Misty River's industrial buildings. And still, every morning, he was struck by the amount of space surrounding him. The square feet of flooring and the cubic feet of air felt enormous. The windows alone—rectangular and divided into square panes—were ten feet tall.

Wearing black flannel pajama pants, he padded across his bedroom and pulled on a zip-up hoodie. When he reached his kitchen, he stared dully at the coffee maker while shoveling tablespoons of ground coffee into the filter. He'd never been a morning person—that detail had remained true through all four of his selves.

The first time his landlady had shown him this apartment, the bones of the one-bedroom, one-bathroom space with its large living area had been hiding beneath ancient carpet, shredded paint, and decaying wood. He'd asked her if he could renovate the place if he did so on his own dime. Since the apartment was already in the worst possible condition and there wasn't anything he could have done to ruin it further, she'd given him permission.

After moving in, he'd dedicated all his daily "work" hours to construction. Drawing on the money he'd invested before entering prison and the experience he'd gained working construction in high school, he'd ripped up the carpet and refinished the hardwood floors. He'd smoothed the surface of the walls and ceiling and repainted them off-white. Whenever he'd been unsure about how to do something, he watched how-to videos online or checked out books from the library. In the end, he'd gutted the kitchen and bathroom, keeping nothing but the sinks and tub. He'd installed new unfinished cabinetry and painted it dark gray. After tossing the old countertops in the dumpster, he'd taught himself how to pour concrete counters. He'd installed new appliances and fixtures.

Early on, he'd gone to where he'd stored the belongings from his second life, intending to transfer them here. But as he'd stood, surrounded by the dusty evidence of the person he'd been, his stomach had turned. He was no longer that person with that life.

He'd told the owner of the storage facility he was welcome to the items inside. Then he'd furnished this place with pieces he'd chosen in his mind long ago for his Montana house.

If he'd been in communication with his family or if he'd had friends, no doubt they'd have asked him why he was spending his money and sweat on a place he didn't own. The benefit of not having friends and not being in communication with his family was that he'd only had to explain his actions to himself.

He'd fixed up this apartment because after seven years in prison he'd needed a good place to live and something to occupy his time. Doing so had kept him sane while stuck in this purgatory between incarceration and Montana.

He carried his coffee to the table, woke his laptop, and opened *The Wall Street Journal* online. Instead of seeing the headlines, he saw how Finley had looked sitting across from him in her office. Deep blue eyes. Dark shiny hair slipping forward over one shoulder.

Since meeting her, he'd been unable to get her out of his head. He'd existed alone in this apartment before starting work at Furry Tails. Now she existed in these rooms with him.

He no longer did transitions well. So, on his first workday and all day yesterday, he'd struggled to adapt to his new job. Almost fiercely, he'd focused on his responsibilities. He'd done his best to tune out the other employees, the volunteers, the animals, and, most of all, Finley.

She'd emailed him a list of the things she wanted for the website and a link to a design board that included Furry Tails' logo, color schemes, inspiration photos, and fonts she liked. Otherwise, she'd mostly left him alone.

Why hadn't his thoughts returned the favor and left her alone?

Having to look at pugs and listen to barking in the workplace was bad enough. The complication of Finley on top of that?

Too much.

Many years had passed since he'd been intimate with a woman. In his self-destructive second life, he'd been a heavy drinker who'd run through women more often than loaves of bread. Love had never been a factor. But that hadn't stopped him from experiencing the pleasure.

In this, his fourth life, he wanted freedom, quiet, and simplicity.

He was finished with breaking the law, with heavy drinking, and with using women for sex.

Finley was a temptation he couldn't afford. Ed had been a rusty nail, but his daughter was white as snow. Had she been a singer, actress, or model, that face and body of hers would have made her famous.

Being near her forced him to remember the pleasure he was no longer willing to chase.

And want it again.

Can you lend me a hand bathing a couple of the dogs?" Finley asked Luke later that day. "Arthur is large and can be challenging to control."

He didn't answer right away. His posture informed her that he dearly wanted to tell her no. However, she'd made it clear that his job would require some animal care, so she was reasonably certain that he'd comply.

He gave an abbreviated nod. Without enthusiasm, he followed her down the hall. For the past few days, Luke had been sitting at his desk, working intently on his computer, rarely getting up for breaks, and driving off in his old truck for exactly one hour each day at lunchtime.

Deliberately, she'd been giving him space.

For one thing, he clearly wasn't the type who'd accept micromanagement. Everything about him broadcast a very headstrong brand of independence.

For another thing, it had taken her a few days to adjust to his account of her dad's death and to accept that he'd be accompanying her as she tracked down clues.

Finally, she'd needed time to ask God what He would have her do regarding the Restoration of Luke. Whenever new animals came into her universe, she assessed them and formulated a plan.

She'd now confidently arrived at a five-step program that had worked well with wounded canines in the past.

1) Meet Luke's physical needs. In this case, provide a safe and healthy work environment, food, and water.
2) Show him extreme patience.
3) Introduce him to daily quiet time, which was, to her way of thinking, the human equivalent of crate time.
4) Carefully condition him by exposing him to all the things he'd been avoiding. Including, but not limited to, the town of Misty River, close connections with others, and God.
5) Train him how to behave constructively.

Bathing dogs fell under numbers four and five. This would give her a chance to expose him to interaction with her and some of God's beautiful animals. Plus, what behavior could be more constructive than that of serving dogs in need?

Finley released Arthur (two-year-old German Shepherd mix, loves Milk-Bone dog treats) from his indoor pen and snapped a leash onto his collar. Currently Furry Tails' largest dog, Arthur wasn't technically due for a bath until next week. But thanks to Arthur's size, it certainly was true that they had their hands full when bathing him, so Luke wasn't likely to become suspicious regarding her request for assistance. She handed Arthur's leash to Luke and picked up Hazel (nine-month-old pug, strains to chase cars).

Together, they entered the pristine bathing room. Here, tile lined the floor and climbed four feet up the walls. Finley stuck her phone in the dock. "I have a music playlist for the dogs' bath time."

Before five seconds of the first track had passed, Luke said, "That's not music."

"It certainly is."

"It sounds like a bad wind chime."

Her lips quirked. "What qualifies as music in your book?"

"Linkin Park."

"Goodness no. I think bath-time music should be relaxing. How about Enya?"

"Worse than the wind chime."

"Sinead O'Connor?" He didn't immediately shut that down. "I'm taking your lack of a growl as consent." She put several of Sinead's slowest and most lyrical songs in the queue and let them roll, then placed Hazel in the standing sink. Luke guided Arthur into the floor-level tub for large dogs.

"We keep a kneepad there," she pointed, "that you can kneel on."

"Why would I kneel?"

"You don't have to, but several of us find it more comfortable than leaning over."

"I'll lean."

She talked him through the procedure. They began by using handheld sprayers to wet the dogs' coats with warm water. Arthur tolerated the water agreeably. Hazel, whose collar she'd attached to a short tether affixed to the wall, whined and scrambled around in circles.

Finley squirted shampoo into her palm. "Our shampoo is natural and organic. Non-toxic, free of parabens and sulfates. It has honey and oatmeal in it, among other things. The dogs smell like oatmeal cookies after their baths."

He didn't reply, but he did start smearing shampoo onto Arthur's back. He seemed to be enjoying this about as much as he'd enjoy smearing mud on asphalt.

She had to bite her bottom lip to keep from laughing.

Today, Luke had on a simple white T-shirt with a pair of old jeans. His waist was lean and sleek. His upper back and shoulders, broad.

It was cold out, and the rest of them dressed in winter clothes each day. He must be hot-natured, because he came in wearing a jacket and a hoodie, then quickly peeled them off.

"What type of work did you do while in prison?" she asked.

"I don't want to talk about my time in prison. Or any other part of my history."

"Why not?"

"I just don't."

"Because . . . ?"

"Because I don't like thinking about it."

Ah! Proof that Luke needed a great deal of number four—conditioning. "Refusing to think about difficult experiences isn't the best approach, psychologically."

"I've never pretended to be a poster child for psychological health."

She eyed the play of muscles in his sudsy forearms. "Sometimes it's therapeutic to confront the hard parts of our past."

"Are you a psychologist?" He spoke the words without any heat, yet his meaning was clear. He was questioning her right to lecture him on this topic.

"No, but I've been through some stuff. One brutal thing in particular that resulted in years of therapy."

He paused to give her a skeptical look that said, *Oh? What brutal thing? You weren't elected homecoming queen?*

"I've spent a lot of time soul-searching with psychologists," she said, "and discussing matters of the heart with friends. I could talk through the ins-and-outs of personality and behavior for hours."

"Not with me."

"Well. If you ever *do* want to talk about anything, including your time in prison, I'm here. I visited my dad a lot while he was incarcerated. I've read books and watched documentaries about life inside. I follow a blog that elevates prisoners' voices."

He grunted as if unimpressed.

"For those reasons," she continued, "I might be able to listen with more informed ears than some people. Also, I'm not easily scandalized." She adjusted Hazel. "Time to wash the dogs' hind legs."

When Luke moved to do so, Arthur's soggy tail caught him in

the shoulder, spraying him in the face with droplets and leaving a dark wet stain. He froze, his aristocratic profile iron hard.

She bit her lip again.

"You're enjoying this," he said without looking at her.

"If I say that I am, will you take it out on innocent Arthur?"

"I'm not in the habit of taking out anything on innocents."

"In that case, yes. I'm enjoying this."

"My irritation?"

"Mostly your company."

She worked soap into Hazel's paws. "What time would you like to come over for dinner on Sunday night?"

"Dinner's unnecessary. I'll just stop by, take a look at the clue, and go."

"I'd like for you to stay and eat. It's important to me to get to know the person who'll be joining me on the treasure hunt." It was true. Also, feeding him fulfilled step one and would give her an opportunity to dig around in his psyche. "Will seven o'clock work?"

"Yes."

"Do you have any food intolerances, allergies, or preferences that I should know about?"

"No."

"Just so you're aware, I'm vegan."

"Of course you are."

She arched her brows, amused. "What does that mean?"

"It means you look like a vegan."

"What does a vegan look like?"

"A flower child."

"You think I look like a flower child?" she asked with delight.

"Yes."

"My fashion choices must be succeeding, then, because that's exactly the vibe I'm going for."

They rinsed the dogs. Arthur licked Luke's face from the bottom of his cheek all the way up to his hairline. Luke winced.

Good boy, Arthur.

"Please tell me what other characteristics you think a flower child has," she said.

"No."

"C'mon," she cajoled.

"A flower child walks around barefoot. Burns incense. Wears"—he circled his fingers around his head—"daisies in her hair. Talks about profound mystical crap."

"Hmm." Humor laced her tone. "I don't go around barefoot because I have a sensory issue about grit on the soles of my feet. However, I do wear sandals all the time in warm weather. I never burn incense, but I do burn candles constantly. I've been known to put flowers in my hair. The only mystical thing I believe in is God, but I do talk to Him and about Him a lot. And I've already admitted how much I adore discussing the profound. Surface conversations become boring after a few minutes."

"In that case, conversations with me will always become boring after a few minutes."

She liked his dry sense of humor. "No, they won't. There's nothing boring about you." All that control and sorrow! He was *fascinating*. Without even trying, Luke absorbed her attention as if she were sitting in a dark theater and he was lit by stage lights.

They placed the dogs on the mat and toweled them off. Arthur shook his coat vigorously, spraying Luke again. Luke stilled for a moment, then continued to dry the dog so gently that it warmed her heart.

She herded both dogs into the room's small gated area, then activated the pet hair dryer.

"You're not going to do anything about the first clue until we talk about it." He folded a wet towel over his forearm. "Right?"

"I told you I wouldn't, and so I won't. You can trust me." Even as she spoke the words, she knew they weren't enough. "In time, I'll show you through my actions that you can trust me."

He considered her before tipping his head toward the door. "Are we done here?"

"We're done here." To his retreating back, she added, "I'll text you my address."

He came to a stop halfway through the door. "How about you just write it out for me?"

"Hesitant to give me your cell phone number?"

"Yes."

"But I have access to it, remember? It's on your employment documents."

"Yeah, but flower child–types don't like to use cell phone numbers without consent."

He was one hundred percent right. "And here I was, getting all excited about my plan to text you cute dog pictures twice a day."

"Start doing that and I'll have to get a new number." Then he was gone.

Luke was tough, but she was an expert on tough cases. He did not scare her. And no doubt, she did not scare him. Which was to her advantage.

Luke would never guess that he'd just met his match.

CHAPTER THREE

The next morning, Finley settled at her round kitchen table with the exact birthday breakfast her father had made for her so many times. Vegan buttermilk pancakes. Two strawberries sliced to look like rosebuds. Hot tea. Glass of icy lemon water.

For the first many years after she'd founded Furry Tails, she'd worked whenever duty called. She'd spent weekends dashing around Georgia and beyond to rescue abused and abandoned animals. Eventually, she realized that if she wanted to sustain her job over the long haul, she'd need to set boundaries and rely on the help of others a few days a week so that she could unplug from the constant stream of entreaties.

Nowadays, she typically slept late on Saturday mornings. But on this particular morning, the questions drifting through her mind had woken her early. What was inside the envelope? If the hunt led her to something valuable, what could that something be? Why had her father told Luke the hunt might be dangerous? The man who'd spent his life protecting her wouldn't endanger her. She couldn't imagine why his last words to Luke had indicated that he'd done just that.

She placed a lavender cloth napkin in her lap and doctored her pancakes with plant-based butter and maple syrup. A few minutes ago, she'd retrieved her father's clue from the spot where she'd hidden it after her conversation with Luke on Wednesday. At present, it rested on the table next to her place setting.

"Wish you were here, Dad. Cheers." She raised her mug and imagined him clinking his mug to hers. This breakfast belonged to the two of them. Her dad and her. After a sip of tea, she took a bite of pancake. Then nibbled a strawberry.

Her father was the eldest of two sons who'd been raised by farmers outside of Hartwell, Georgia. When he'd graduated high school, there'd been no discussion of higher education. There'd only been the necessity of working the family land. He'd done just that until the age of twenty-four, when he'd been drafted into the Vietnam War. After serving two years, he returned home in the late sixties and went to work for the railroad.

The profession suited him. He'd lived nomadically, traveling across the country, chasing new horizons, saving the lion's share of his earnings. He rose to the role of engine driver. Read book after book. Romanced women both single and married. Played his guitar. Penned the occasional poem. Whittled wood. Sketched. Protested for causes he believed in. He'd fancied himself to be a renaissance man, a freethinker who didn't subscribe to anyone's code but his own.

He only ever splurged on one thing: electronics. He'd been reading issues of *Popular Mechanics* from cover to cover since he was a boy. Though he'd remained loyal to the record player all his life, he loved to purchase the newest gadgets in every other category. During her childhood, he'd been the first person she knew to adopt the DVD player, the use of flash drives, the Blackberry, the Kindle, the Wii, and the iPhone.

Thanks to his fascination with tech, he did something in the eighties that no financial planner would have advised. Ed Sutherland funneled every penny of his savings into the IPO of a single stock.

For a little-known company named Apple.

Much later, when she'd asked him why he'd taken such a risk, he'd shrugged and said, "*I could tell you that I'd been following the market or that I'd done quite a bit of research. Those things are true. But that's not why I did it. I invested in Apple because I had a gut feeling. I knew they were going to be a success.*"

Quickly, his shares escalated in value. Content with his rambling life, he hadn't parted with a single one.

It wasn't until he was in his early fifties that his life had taken a dramatic turn. He'd had an affair with a married woman named Jade, whose military husband had been deployed at the time. Jade hadn't wanted to keep her husband. Or her baby. Or—as it turned out—Ed. She and Ed struck a bargain. Jade would have the baby if he'd agree to become the baby's sole parent. Her commitment took nine months. His, the rest of his life.

Every time Finley had talked to her father about Jade, he'd told Finley it was the best bargain he'd ever made and that he'd make it again a hundred times over.

Since he'd recognized that he couldn't raise a baby on a pair of railroad tracks, he'd retired and sold just enough stock to purchase a mid-century modern house on a big piece of land near his hometown. He'd gone to work crafting model train cars in his home studio and raising Finley much like he'd been raised—with freedom, space for adventures, and animals.

Her dad loved her. And she loved her dad.

Yes, he got grumpy when he had to pay taxes, when he disagreed with politicians, or when she didn't do what he asked. But he never lost his temper. He volunteered with the PTA, brought food to class parties, and clapped for her at every school performance. He'd parted ways with organized religion, but he'd never lost the faith in God that his mother had instilled in him. He'd sent Finley to church with his brother, Robbie, and Robbie's wife, June, every time the sanctuary doors were thrown open. They were thrown open a lot. Finley's relationship with God had grown in the soil of that small-town church and ended up changing her life.

Her junior year of college she'd been horribly blindsided when her father—the man who'd been such a reliable source of security for her—had been arrested for manslaughter. By then, he was in his seventies. After his arrest, she'd come home on weekends and school vacations. However, he'd ordered her to remain at college the rest of the time as he dealt with lawyers, hearings, and eventually, his trial.

She'd been significantly more naïve then than she was now. Maybe she'd been in denial, too, because she'd believed there was no possible way her father could be guilty. She'd trusted that he'd be acquitted and that her happy life could continue unfettered.

Instead, he'd been found guilty, sentenced, and sent away. Certain that the legal system had betrayed her father, she'd pursued appeals, all of which had gone nowhere. As a girl, she'd gone to him when scared or angry or sad, and he'd made everything better. She'd been powerless to make his conviction better.

He'd tried to salvage the situation for her by liquidating his remaining stock, placing it in a trust for her, and appointing his brother as the trustee.

Robbie, an accountant, had advised her. She'd used some of the money to purchase this cabin. They'd invested the rest in a portfolio. She hadn't dipped into that portfolio until she'd been sure that Furry Tails was a viable non-profit. Only then had she used another portion of the money to help bankroll Furry Tails' new building.

Other than his land and his house, her father hadn't owned anything of great value. From his parents, he'd inherited a couple of antiques. He'd driven used trucks for their utility. He'd happened upon a few small historic finds—coins, a metal vase, arrowheads—during metal detector expeditions with Robbie. He'd acquired three well-made guitars and some quality art supplies.

But, to her knowledge, none of those items came with the type of price tag that would stir the interest of dangerous people.

Breakfast finished, she ran her fingertip over the shallow dips and ledges of the writing on the front of the envelope.

For Finley.

While her father hadn't spent his wealth on exorbitant things, he had proven his willingness to give her extremely generous gifts through the trust he'd arranged for her.

Was that what he was doing via this treasure hunt? Giving her another extremely generous gift? If so, why? He'd already done so much to ensure her financial stability.

A scuffling sound from the floor drew her attention. Sally (twelve-year-old pug, snores loudly) shifted from lying down to sitting up. She peered at Finley with sweet round eyes. Sally's frequent sidekick, Dudley (four-year-old hedgehog, loves apples) stood beside her, tiny nose twitching.

"Should I go ahead and open it?" Finley asked them.

Dudley gave her a poker face, but Sally panted happily.

Finley took that as a yes. She turned the envelope and slid her thumb between the flap and the backing.

Nostalgia curled tentacles around her. She'd experienced this same wistful squeeze whenever things she'd valued had begun to reach their conclusion. When her best childhood friend had been about to move away. When her high school years had wound down. During the waning days before Dad left to serve his sentence. When her years at Furry Tails' first location had drawn to a close.

This was the beginning of another end. Once she reached the treasure—*if* she reached the treasure—she'd receive no more communication from her father. Not for the rest of her life.

Don't be ridiculous, Finley! Change is the drumbeat of life. You know this.

She slid out a piece of ivory cardstock. A photograph drifted to the tabletop. She turned it right side up, revealing an old picture of her and her dad. She tilted the letter to the light.

Finley,

If you're reading this, I'm gone. I'm sorry if I left you sooner or more suddenly than you wanted. If I could have, I'd have stayed alive as long as you needed me.

I want to make sure you know that you're my sun, my everything. My daughter. My joy. My source of significance. Before you, I thought I knew what it meant to live, but I was wrong. It was only in you, in my role as your father, that I found out what it meant to truly live. My wish for you is that in loving someone, you, too, will discover what I did.

Thank you, sweetheart.

You made me so happy. I have no regrets when I look back on our time together. Only endless gratitude. You're my legacy, and I couldn't be prouder.

If I have to go out, and it seems like I do, then why not go out big with one last birthday treasure hunt? For the next clue, return to your roots and to the place shown in the photo.

Happy birthday.

I love you.
Dad

Tears blurred her vision, but she reread the letter anyway. Sniffed a few times, then studied the picture.

She'd been maybe four years old when this picture was taken at the home they'd shared. She wore a long-sleeved, long-skirted red-and-white dress she still vaguely remembered. The living room bookcase that held his record collection spanned the wall behind them. A small pile of gifts waited on the coffee table in the foreground. This hadn't been snapped at Christmas, because the gifts were wrapped in shades of pink, yellow, and light blue. It had been taken on her birthday, then.

Dad had hoisted her onto his hip. He'd dressed his fit, rangy body in the type of clothing he'd always worn. Comfortable jeans and a lightweight plaid shirt, worn thin over time. He was grinning at her, and she was looking at the photographer, a wide and genuine smile creasing her face.

A lump formed in her throat. Thankfulness and loss swirled to the tips of her fingers.

The part of her life that his living, breathing presence had occupied would from now on remain vacant. Yet the part of her heart that had and did belong to him would always remain full.

"What in the world," she whispered to her father, "have you hidden for me to find?"

"You're finally here!" Meadow called as Finley approached her friend Bridget's front door. Meadow pulled Finley inside the condo. As always, Meadow was the more exuberant of the two. Bridget waited serenely in her foyer, then gave Finley a hug.

Both her friends were wearing cardboard crowns that spelled out *Happy Birthday!* Meadow slipped one into Finley's hair, then they both exclaimed "Happy Birthday!" and blew noisemakers, unfurling them into Finley's face with a honking noise.

"Thank you." Her birthday morning had been important and emotional but also serious. It felt like a vacation to come here, to this condo she knew so well, to the company of her best friends.

"Ready for a day of celebration?" Bridget asked.

"Ready," Finley answered.

"I printed out our itinerary." Bridget handed them both papers.

Bridget and Meadow had planned lunch at a winery, followed by a visit to the spa, where they'd each splurge on two treatments. Then back here for dinner, a movie, and cake. Finley knew what had motivated her friends to book such a long day of activities: They didn't want her spending the bulk of her birthday alone now that her father was gone.

"We're running eleven minutes early," Bridget said. "Come in, sit down, and tell us all about your new employee."

Meadow guided her into the living room the way a sheepdog guides a sheep.

Bridget's condo had become their default hang-out spot. Finley's and Meadow's houses were located outside city limits on opposite sides of Misty River. Bridget's house was located in the middle, tucked into a cute neighborhood downtown. Plus, it was always tidy.

Finley had met Bridget her freshman year of college, when they'd lived on the same floor in the dorm at the University of Georgia. Bridget was shy, sweet, supportive, and highly organized. She'd invited Finley to her hometown of Misty River one weekend, and thank goodness Finley had said yes, because two momentous things had happened on that trip.

One, Bridget had introduced Finley to her hometown friend, Meadow, who was three years ahead of them in school. Two, Finley had fallen in love with the town and announced to both Meadow (whom she'd known for two-and-a-half minutes) and Bridget (whom she'd known a couple of months) that she'd move here as soon as she graduated.

She'd followed through on that promise. And when Finley had left her first job at the art gallery to work at Furry Tails full time, Bridget had taken her position at the gallery—and proved herself far better at it than Finley had ever been.

Meadow sat on the edge of her chair, practically vibrating with energy. Despite her name, nothing about Meadow brought to mind peaceful green expanses of grass. With a firm face and compact body, Meadow resembled the singer Pink. She'd played up the resemblance by cutting her hair in a short upswept style and dying it fuchsia. Today, she wore her usual uniform—a tank top and cotton pants designed with a crotch that hovered at mid-thigh.

Meadow's hair, outfits, nose ring, and upper-arm tattoos might not scream "successful entrepreneur," but that's exactly what she was. She'd started working for her family's struggling peach orchard immediately after college. She was thirty-three now and had turned the orchard into a thriving company. Thanks to her, they shipped peach candles, peach pies, peach jam, and much more across the United States and beyond. Their orchard had become one of Misty River's most popular tourist attractions.

"So?" Meadow prodded. "How's Luke? Is he a jerk?"

"No. He's gruff and . . . aloof. But I like him."

"Finley!" Meadow exclaimed. "You're fanatically determined to see the best in every person and dog alive."

"Not *fanatically* determined," Finley corrected. "Just determined."

"Do you *like him* like him?" Bridget asked in her calm way. "Or just like him as a person in a general way?"

"Are you asking that because you're interested in Luke Dempsey?" Meadow demanded.

Bridget's hands folded in her lap. "He's a handsome single man in his early thirties who is new to town. Of course I'm interested."

Bridget's pale hair nearly matched the color of her elfin face. She had a long nose, a nearly invisible upper lip, a closet full of Gap dresses, and the soul of a seventy-year-old married lady. She'd yet to find a man, so when she wasn't working, cleaning, or making spreadsheets, she was daydreaming about men, checking online dating sites, and struggling to boost her confidence enough to risk a blind date.

"You can't seriously imagine that you're going to pair well with an ex-con," Meadow said to Bridget. "It's like . . . like trying to pair peanut butter with a steak."

Bridget sniffed. "I happen to think that combination sounds promising."

Meadow fell back against her chair, wrist to her brow. "Bridge. Just no! You're a lady. You need a gentleman."

"A gentleman would be lovely," Bridget returned primly. "If you'll kindly point me in the direction of the nearest one, I'll head that way immediately."

"Men are pigs. You're better off without." Meadow's volatile on-again, off-again relationship with the father of her twelve-year-old daughter had dragged on for years before finally blowing up. Ever since then, she'd been pessimistic about men.

They were very different—Finley, Meadow, and Bridget. Yet their differences paled in comparison to their loyalty and affection for one another. In the magical way that sometimes happens, their trio clicked.

"The statement that men are pigs," Finley said, "might be a tad too broad."

"Name one who's not a pig."

"Your father," Finley answered.

Meadow smiled sheepishly. "Fine. Point taken. *Most* men are pigs."

"To answer your question," Finley said to Bridget, "I don't like Luke romantically. Nothing about my stance on dating has changed."

"Is he as good-looking as I've heard he is?" Bridget asked.

"Better," Finley acknowledged.

Bridget laid a hand on her heart.

Meadow squawked. "Finley! Don't encourage her!"

"I don't think Luke's right for you," Finley said to Bridget. "But I promise you that if a wonderful man who *is* right for you ever wants to foster or adopt one of my dogs, you'll be the first to know."

CHAPTER FOUR

Finley claimed that she didn't go barefoot or burn incense, but her house looked like the type of house where a flower child would live.

Luke parked in front of the address she'd given him, peering through darkness at her cabin. Nothing around it but forest, so the only light came from the two fixtures on either side of her front door. She'd painted the wooden two-story gray and the trim around the eaves, windows, and door green. Not the color combination he would've chosen. The upstairs rooms must have slanted ceilings because the roofline came to a peak at the center.

He let himself out of his 1974 Chevy C10 and walked up the steps to the landing. Pots of white flowers, ivy, and cabbages waited like doormen.

Fulfilling his promise to Ed shouldn't require dinners with Finley. He was a fool because he'd somehow let a cream puff of a woman rope him into this.

He knocked. Immediately, he heard answering footsteps within. As the door swung open, he tried to brace himself for the sight of her.

It didn't do any good. The power of her appearance hit him hard in the chest. She was color and life and warmth.

"Welcome," she said. "I'm so glad you're here."

He figured remaining silent was better than saying, "*I'm not glad I came.*"

"Come in."

He entered her house just as a pug came to a stop at her feet.

Great. More pugs.

"Right this way." Her clogs thumped against the hardwood floor as she walked past an office, stairs, and a bathroom tucked under the staircase.

She wore a loose white tank top and leggings beneath a silky robe-thing in a blue print. The robe-thing was open down the middle and ended near her knees. He guessed it wasn't a robe since she was wearing it for dinner over clothes. Still, it seemed weird. She had on two necklaces—a short one and a long one that dangled a metal feather. Her black hair was down tonight and slightly wavy. She and her house smelled like orange blossoms.

He followed her to the living room, dining room, kitchen space at the back of the house that overlooked a rectangular deck.

She picked up a spoon and stirred one of the pots on the stove. "This is Sally." She motioned with her elbow toward the dog. "And there's my cat, Rufus." A scraggly cat with one ripped ear curled on a living room chair. He eyed Luke suspiciously. "He's antisocial. I have a hedgehog named Dudley, who's currently napping in his cage in the office. And I have Gloria here." She indicated the fishbowl on the half-wall separating the dining room from the kitchen. "She's a Siamese fighting fish."

"*I'm not easily scandalized,*" she'd said to him on Friday. She had no idea what she was talking about, living out here in her little house in the woods with her pets, listening to soundtracks of wind chimes, eating tofu, and viewing herself as worldly.

"Are your pets all rescues?" he asked.

"Yes." She took a sample bite from the pot, then added seasoning. "Sally was grossly overfed by her first owner. Rufus and Dudley came to me back in the days when Furry Tails was taking in all types of animals. Rufus was feral and brought to the vet half dead. Dudley was abandoned in the middle of Misty River's central park. I received Gloria from a vendor running a ring toss game at the Apple Festival." Her lips pursed as she twisted the salt grinder aggressively. "I do not approve of giving animals away as prizes or gifts. After several volunteers and I organized a sit-in protest, the ring toss vendor agreed to sell the fish to us."

He really hoped she wasn't going to spend the whole meal ranting about the treatment of animals. He wanted to cut to the chase and demand, "*Show me the first clue,*" but he held the words back.

For a long time he'd been caged apart from society. On the outside, guys who'd been raised on the streets were low in the social hierarchy. But inside, the hierarchy was flipped. Those guys were the kings. To survive, Luke had learned their ways. In prison, every interaction was about respect. He'd become more self-controlled, cautious, and socially withdrawn. To his surprise, however, the manners his mom had taught him when he was a kid hadn't been fully erased. They were rusty, but still there. "Do you need any help?"

"Thanks, but I've got this. I just need to chop up the last few ingredients for the salad. Would you like anything to drink?"

"Not yet."

The bones of her house were neutral. Off-white paint and wood floors. But then she'd added bright rugs, throw pillows, and lots of other . . . stuff. On the wall behind her sofa, a strand of lights glowed above some woven baskets and several pieces of modern art in dark pastel colors. Dozens of cacti filled a ladder-type thing set to the side of the sliding doors. Potted plants on tall stands took up every corner.

He neared a set of floating shelves. They held books. Folk art. Framed photos, many of her with Ed. Some of her with female friends. Some of animals.

He picked up a photo of her with a guy who wore his blond hair in a ponytail. "Who's this?" He tilted the frame toward her.

She glanced up. "Oh." Her features softened. "That's Chase. My fiancé."

Just like that, his gut hardened into a knot.

Her fiancé.

All-American and blond, Chase had a square jaw and blue eyes lighter than Finley's blue eyes. He wore an olive-colored T-shirt and a leather necklace.

In the photo, Chase was embracing Finley, and they were laughing. Their love for each other was obvious. Clearly, they belonged together.

"We met and started dating the fall of our junior year at UGA. He was selfless. A musician. Loved the Lord. He went to seminary and became a youth pastor."

Ah. She'd fallen in love with a saint. A perfect match—

"He died five years ago."

He stilled, frowning. The fact that Chase had died so young was a tragedy. So why had her words loosened the knot in his gut?

She carried a tray of vegetables toward the backyard.

He replaced the frame and opened the sliding door for her that led to the deck. "How did he die?"

She set the tray on the edge of her barbecue grill. "How would you feel if I told you that I don't want to talk about any part of my history?"

She was quoting him. "Irritated."

"Huh," she said meaningfully.

"If you don't want to talk about it, I'll respect that."

"Actually, I'm more than happy to talk about my life. All of it. Any of it. I'm an open book." She lifted the barbecue's lid, displaying flames. Quickly, she set rows of vegetables on it. Peppers, onion, giant mushrooms, asparagus.

"How did he die?" he repeated.

Her body slanted toward his. She crossed one foot over the other, her toe pointing down. "He was driving home one night and lost control."

"How?"

"We don't know for sure, which has been one of the hardest things. We think he might have swerved for some reason. He drove off the side of the road. His Jeep hit bushes, went airborne, overturned, struck a tree. He was thrown from the vehicle. When the ambulance arrived, he was unconscious but alive. They rushed him to the hospital. He died of his injuries shortly after, without ever regaining consciousness."

Luke didn't say any of the empty things people had said to him about death.

"Five months before he passed away, he proposed. I said yes. We were so happy as we planned our wedding. It was . . . devastating to lose him."

"You mentioned that you'd been through something that resulted in years of therapy. This was what you were referring to?"

"Yes. For the entire first year afterward, I felt as if I'd died, too. For two more years after that, I was mired in grief. All my hopes and dreams for the future had died along with Chase. I didn't know how to move forward."

"What helped?"

"My psychologist played a key role. Also, I continued working because the animals needed me. I spent a lot of time with God. Instead of focusing on what I lost, I tried to cultivate gratitude for what I had." She pulled the flaps of the robe across her chest. "Most people never get to experience what Chase and I shared. It was a once-in-a-lifetime love." She sighed. "Since his death, I've heard God calling me to embrace singleness. And I have. My life is good. Full."

"Let me get this straight." He scowled. "You haven't had a boyfriend since Chase?"

"No."

"Have you gone on any dates since Chase?"

"No."

"You've become a nun for the Church of Chase."

"I've embraced singleness."

"Because you're a nun for the Church of Chase."

"Because singleness is what God has for me."

No. That's not why she was avoiding relationships.

"How come," she inquired pleasantly, "you're looking at me like that's the silliest thing you've ever heard?"

"Because it is. There's no such thing as a once-in-a-lifetime love."

"Of course there is—"

"And it's a cop-out to blame God for the fact that you haven't dated anyone."

"I acknowledge that God's call on my life might be hard for you to understand. But it's my truth."

"If you haven't dated anyone, it has nothing to do with God. It's because you're scared."

They locked eyes. Physical awareness hammered through him. He watched her pulse thrum in her neck.

"It's my truth," she repeated stubbornly.

Who did she think she was kidding? He was no stranger to grief.

After what had happened with Ethan, he'd never let himself love anyone. He couldn't. Because if he lost another person he loved, he knew it would break him. The difference between him and her was that he was man enough to admit that.

Gracefully, she turned toward the barbecue and flipped the veggies.

Smoke rose past the lights strung back and forth above her deck. Past trees alive with breeze. Up beyond, to a pitch-black sky.

She tilted her profile to watch it disappear.

It had been an unusually warm January day, reaching all the way up to a temperature of sixty-five. It was cooler than that now. Goosebumps lined her forearms. "You're cold," he said.

"A little."

"Where's your coat? I'll get it for you."

She gave him directions to her coat closet, and he returned within seconds. He handed her a long pale denim coat with a huge sheepskin collar.

She slipped it on. It appeared two sizes too big. "Thank you."

He could look at Finley for hours from every angle and still want to look at her longer.

Purposely, he averted his focus to the woods.

"Even when it's cold, I love it out here." She went to stand at the edge of her deck. "I practically live in my backyard when the weather's nice."

He came to a stop next to her, but not too near.

"Misty River runs right through my property," she said. "You'll have to come back in daylight so that you can see how pretty it is." Wind lifted the edges of her hair. "Listen."

He heard water rushing over rocks.

"Beautiful, eh?"

He made an affirmative noise.

One minute expanded into the next. "Would you like to see the first treasure hunt clue?" she asked.

"Yes."

She pulled a piece of paper and a photo from the pocket of the robe and handed them over. He had just enough light to read the note and study the picture.

"The photo was taken," she said, "at the house where I was raised."

"Which is where?"

"Near Hartwell. It takes me a little over an hour to drive there."

"Who owns the house now?"

"I do. Dad kept it while he was in prison. Then I inherited it."

"'For the next clue,'" he read aloud, "'return to your roots and to the place shown in the photo.'"

"Yep."

"He doesn't say where to look once you return there."

"I'm guessing that the setting of the photo is a clue. Knowing him, he's hidden the next envelope in the bookcase you see there. Or maybe it's taped to the underside of the coffee table. Or the rug."

"When can we go?"

"I'll have to juggle my schedule a bit, but I might be able to leave work a few hours early on Thursday afternoon."

He'd have preferred they drive there now, tonight. But she'd made it clear that she didn't want him to rush her. "Okay. Do you have a safe here at the house?"

"No."

"I'll buy one for you. Then you can keep this and everything else that has to do with the treasure hunt inside."

"You think that's necessary?"

"I'm not sure. I only know that I probably won't regret it if we're too careful. But I might regret it if we're not careful enough."

She blinked at him.

"Which reminds me," he said, "before I go tonight, I'd like to take a look at your security."

"No problem."

"Do you have an alarm system?"

"Yes. And deadbolts on the doors. That's about it." She wrinkled her forehead. "Luke, my father might not have been in his right mind in his final moments. He was in pain . . . having a heart attack. Who knows how much oxygen was getting to his brain? I don't think we should set too much store on what he told you when he said the hunt might put me in danger. He's always been concerned about my safety. Maybe his generalized worry got tangled with thoughts about the treasure hunt and blown out of proportion."

"I don't think so. His words were clear, and he was looking right at me."

"Well, even if he was lucid, it's still possible that we won't encounter any threats. Dad might have been wrong about the danger. Or maybe we won't be able to solve the hunt. In which case, danger won't be a factor."

What? "There's a chance we won't be able to solve the hunt?"

"During my teenage years, it wasn't unusual for me to get stuck on a clue. When that happened, I'd ask my dad for a hint."

His jaw hardened. He *needed* a new start in Montana like he needed air. There, he could live exactly how he wanted: alone, on his own terms, surrounded by rugged nature. He and Finley had to solve this hunt. "Ed created this particular hunt knowing he wouldn't be around to give hints."

"Even so, I'm afraid I might get stumped."

"We'll cross that bridge if we come to it."

They worked together to set the outdoor table after she announced that she enjoyed eating outside more than inside, even if it meant "bundling up."

Again, weird. But her house, her decision.

Back in the kitchen, she spooned food into serving bowls, then handed them to him to transfer outside. A yellow-colored rice dish. Beans. Bread rolls. Then the grilled vegetables.

They sat across from each other at the table on her deck. More food than the two of them could eat and five little cacti filled the surface between them.

Awkwardly, he waited for her to pick up her fork and begin.

"I'll pray over the food," she stated.

Oh. That was the hold-up.

"Father God, thank you so much for Luke and his willingness to honor his promise to Dad. Praise you for sending him. I ask that you protect us both, should there be any need for protection. I ask that you bless us both as we make our way through the clues. May this become a beautiful journey."

He stayed still, eyes respectfully closed. Good grief. How much longer was this flowery prayer going to last?

"Thank you for this earth, all your creatures, this food, and this grace of yours that goes beyond all understanding. Amen." She smoothed her napkin in her lap and took a bite of bread.

In prison, the meals had been so bad that chips and candy bars purchased at the commissary became prized possessions. Since his release, food had been the best thing in his life because he now took his time with it, tasting and appreciating it.

Maybe it was her company or the setting or the fact that some of the food had come right off the grill and onto his plate, but every item burst with flavor in his mouth. "This is really good."

"Thank you. Are you surprised that vegan food can be tasty?"

"Yes."

"What were you expecting?"

"That you'd make me sit cross-legged on the floor and eat nuts and seeds out of a bowl with my fingers."

She laughed. "I don't cook much on weeknights, but I find it relaxing on weekends."

He wasn't good at small talk and was extremely out of practice at having dinner with a woman. It was like his hands were suddenly double the size and he'd forgotten how to coordinate their movements.

The worst thing, though? The worst thing was that his physical attraction to her distracted him. He kept fixating on details of her. Her clavicle bones. Her wrist. The delicate skin beneath her ear. Her cheekbones. The indent above her upper lip.

What would it feel like to touch her there?

Ed would roll over in his grave if he could see into Luke's mind tonight.

From his earliest memories, Luke's worst fear had been his own worthlessness. After Ethan died, Luke had blamed himself, and his fear had come to fruition. He *was* worthless. That's the conclusion he'd come to at fourteen.

When life meant nothing, it wasn't difficult to throw it away. He'd numbed the pain with danger, defiance, and bad decisions. In some twisted way, the rush he'd gotten from that had at least made him feel partly alive. Jail had finally put a stop to his downward spiral. But Luke knew he'd never be good enough for Finley. Ed would agree.

He took a drink of water, struggling to get his head straight. What he'd promised was to keep her safe. His best shot at that was to hold on to his objectivity. So long as his emotions and hormones weren't involved, he'd remain clearheaded enough to make decisions.

Finley set her fork on her plate and pulled her coat sleeves over her hands. "I've been thinking about the treasure hunt, and something has occurred to me."

"I'm listening." He took a bite of rice seasoned with herbs.

"I'm going to sound as if I have a very suspicious nature. Understand that my dad did *try* to develop some street smarts in me."

"Understood."

"It has occurred to me that my dad might've told you—at any point over the last several years—about the treasure hunt and the valuable thing he'd saved for me. And that you want it for yourself. So you concocted the story of my dad's dying wish."

Gradually, a wolfish grin overtook his face.

"Why are you smiling?" she asked. "I just accused you of potentially having evil motives."

"I'm smiling because I respect that accusation. It's clever and logical." Also painful, because he deserved her suspicion. He was an ex-con who had not been wrongly convicted. In fact, he'd stolen many more cars than the one he'd been arrested for stealing. "You shouldn't trust me."

"Does that mean that you *do* have evil motives?"

"In this situation, no."

"I believe you."

"What?" he barked. "Don't believe me so easily."

"But I do believe you. My intuition about people is sound."

"Clearly not, if you're so quick to accept my word. I'm a criminal."

"It's not that I'm gullible, Luke. It's that, if my intuition tells me a person is good, then I make the conscious choice to see them as good. Regardless of their past. I see you as good."

How was he supposed to reason with a person like this?

"If you lied to me just now and your motives are evil," she said, "it's all right. You won't have to take the treasure from me. I'll just give it to you."

He paused, disbelief surging. "Are you out of your mind?"

"I have everything I need." She shrugged. "If you don't have everything you need, you can have the treasure."

"First, I do have everything I need. Second, you don't even know what the treasure is. Now is not the time to give it away."

"I know myself, and I'll only feel attached to it if it's something that has emotional significance. But even then, I could just take a picture to remember it by. I won't keep it because I don't want to own anything that could bring me harm."

"In that case, you can sell it. And put the money in your retirement account."

She didn't look impressed.

"Or donate the money to the Center," he said.

"I've already funneled some of the money my dad gave me into Furry Tails. At this point, Furry Tails needs to be self-sustaining."

He'd misread her. She was not a cream puff. She was unusual. Too honest and too generous for her own good. But she was also, in her way, very determined.

He didn't want her to blindly put her faith in him, yet . . . he did want to show her that, this time, her faith hadn't been misplaced.

He leaned forward on his elbows. "For the record, your dad's last words were exactly what I told you they were. Things between him and me went down like I said they did, and I'm here for the reason I told you I was."

"But just in case you're not—"

"I am," he said roughly. There'd been a time when he robbed people. But he was not a liar. If he'd failed to keep his word in prison, he wouldn't have lasted long. "A few other guys heard what your dad said to me at the end. I'll give you their names, and you can double-check my story."

Seconds passed. She held his gaze. "That won't be necessary."

His blood carried a premonition through his veins. Finley represented trouble for him. Terrible trouble.

The most dangerous thing he'd have to deal with on this hunt . . .

Was her.

CHAPTER FIVE

Akira had a dreadful habit.

Three times in the past, she'd fallen in love with men at first sight. Three times, love at first sight had not worked out well for her.

Thus, when she and Finley settled in at Pablo's on Tuesday for lunch with a prospective volunteer, she had no intention of falling in love at first sight. Today or ever again.

But then she glanced up and actually *saw* the male volunteer making his way toward their table.

Her internal shields trembled.

Finley waved to the stranger. He strode through the casual interior of the restaurant, which smelled of pulled pork and frying tortillas.

"Finley?" he asked as they stood up.

"That's me."

"I'm Ben Coleman." They shook hands. "Nice to meet you."

"The pleasure's mine." Finley gestured to her. "This is my coworker Akira Wells."

"Hi." He turned an easy, confident smile on her. His hand was dry. His handshake—exactly the right temperature and firmness. "I knew a girl named Kaya Wells in high school. Any relation?"

"Kaya's my oldest sister. She's now an investment banker in New York."

"Good for her."

"My other sister, Suki, would have been a few years behind you in school."

"Oh yeah. I remember her, too."

"She works in LA for a very successful consignment fashion start-up."

"Great."

Akira was, by far, the most unremarkable sibling and always took the opportunity to make that clear to new acquaintances.

They lowered to their seats. A server hurried over and claimed Ben's attention, which gave Akira an opportunity to observe him.

Her own father was Black, her mother Japanese. Ben was the son of two African-American parents. His coloring was smooth and warm with a copper undertone. He had eyes of deep, rich brown. All those straight white teeth! All that laid-back kindness.

He was *handsome*. The kind of handsome that usually came with aloofness and superiority. Yet she didn't catch a whiff of either of those things in Ben.

"Have you already ordered?" he asked.

"We have," Finley answered.

He requested the taco special without needing to look at a menu, and their server moved off.

Don't give him moony eyes, Akira! She was twenty-eight years old, yet her sisters claimed she *still* gave moony eyes to men she found attractive.

"Thanks for inviting me to join you," he said to Finley.

"I'm glad you were able to get away from the high school long enough to meet us for lunch."

"It's an in-service day."

"Are you a teacher?" Akira asked.

"I am. I teach eleventh-grade science."

Inwardly, she swooned. Ministering to children was her life purpose.

Finley straightened her flowy print blouse. "Akira's the head of our after-school program. At present, that's the area of our operation most in need of volunteer support."

"That would be a good fit for me," he said. "I love kids."

She imagined the sound of police sirens. *Do not fall in love with him, Akira!*

This was a terrible time for one of her ill-fated crushes. The last nine months had been the worst of her life health wise, as well as mental health wise.

Having Ben as a boyfriend would be the best possible kind of self-care, her heart stage-whispered to her.

No, it wouldn't, her mind hissed back.

What were the chances that *he* would like *her*? But even if he did, she couldn't ignore the hulking shipwrecks of her three past love-at-first-sight endeavors.

"Can you tell us a little about why you're interested in volunteering at Furry Tails?" Finley asked.

"Luke Dempsey."

Akira's eyes rounded. Back when Finley had informed the staff that she would be hiring a parolee, Akira had been concerned. Meeting Luke hadn't reassured her. When he was working at his desk, he gave off a don't-bother-me vibe. Her interactions with him so far had been brief and uncomfortable.

Intimidating. That was the best word to describe Luke. She counted it a blessing that he'd yet to mug her.

"Did Luke recommend Furry Tails to you?" Finley asked Ben.

"No."

"I was going to be surprised if he had," Finley admitted. "He's not yet Furry Tails' number one fan."

"He's an old friend of mine. It's been a long time since we were close, but I'm not ready to give up. If I volunteer at Furry Tails, I'll have an in with Luke. Plus, I really like what I've heard about the work you're doing."

"You and Luke are both part of the Miracle Five," Akira said.

She'd long known *of* Ben, in the way she'd long known *of* Elvis. Ben was the Misty River equivalent of a celebrity.

"Yeah," he replied. "I knew Luke before the earthquake. I was with him during. And it's no secret that he's never been the same since."

Finley gathered her hair forward over one shoulder. "I read a book that claimed Luke told Ethan to go to the back of the line just before the earthquake. Then the five of you went downstairs to store sports equipment in the basement of a building near the camp you were running. The earthquake hit. Everyone except Ethan, who was at the back of the line, made it to safety. Is that true?"

"It is. Ethan was an awesome kid. Talkative. Happy. Eager, you know? Like a puppy. He was pestering Luke with a million questions. Luke got annoyed. But actually, he responded patiently for a fourteen-year-old. He didn't shove his brother. He didn't lash out. He just told him to go to the back of the line so that he could have some space. Any other time, it would have been nothing." Ben gave a small shake of his head and took a sip of his water. "I have three siblings. We irritated one another constantly growing up. We treated one another worse than Luke treated Ethan that day. The only difference is that an earthquake didn't strike in the middle of any of my disagreements with my siblings. The timing was incredibly unfortunate for Luke."

"Other than in that one book," Finley said, "I've never seen it mentioned that Luke asked Ethan to go to the back of the line."

"After what we went through together, there was unspoken loyalty between Luke, Sebastian, Natasha, Genevieve, and me. We never would have told anyone that we'd heard Luke send Ethan to the back of the line. Luke was the one who told his parents. Then they told the author who interviewed them. They're wonderful people. They wanted to free Luke from the weight of having to keep what he'd done a secret. Plus, they wanted to publicly state that they in no way blamed Luke or held him accountable for Ethan's death. They hoped that might lessen Luke's guilt."

"But it didn't," Finley said.

"No. Imagine going through life with your sibling's death on your conscience."

Akira could feel the weight of Finley's empathy for Luke. Her boss had a big heart.

"I'm so encouraged to hear that you want to rebuild old bridges with Luke," Finley said. "I'm really hoping his job at Furry Tails will spur a metamorphosis in him."

Entrees were deposited in front of Akira and Finley. Ben encouraged them to begin eating, but Akira desperately did not want to eat in front of this man. Especially not a salad bigger than a hat box that included dripping meat and gooey sour cream.

Finley had no such qualms. She picked up her fork and took a bite.

Akira broke off a corner of the fried shell and scooped up one morsel of ground beef. She had a very colorful thought life. Her verbal life sometimes reflected that and sometimes didn't. Either she was overly quiet, like now, or she overshared. She struggled to find a happy medium.

"Sebastian, Natasha, Genevieve, and I," Ben said, "are all in support of a metamorphosis for Luke. Please let me know if there's anything we can do."

"Thank you. I will."

Finley was incredibly good at rehabilitation. Amazingly so. Akira had told her more than once that she should have her own TV show. If she'd let cameras record the miraculous work she did with dogs, she'd have a hit on her hands.

"In case it's not already extremely obvious," Finley told Ben, "I'd be delighted to have you volunteer at Furry Tails."

"Awesome."

"We'll run a background check and have you undergo some training. Once you finish that, you can assist Akira with her program."

Ben moved his attention to her. "How many kids are in the after-school program?"

Her stomach twinged with self-consciousness. "Ten. A sweet eighty-five-year-old gentleman volunteers with the program several times a week, but I'm the only staff member, so ten is as many as we can accommodate. The kids all attend East Side Elementary. I pick them up at three in the Furry Tails van. They spend part of their afternoon doing homework, part on enrichment activities, part with the dogs, and part exercising. Their parents pick them up between five thirty and six."

"What can I do to help?" he asked.

"We can work together to organize a science unit for the kids. I'm always looking for ways to stir passion in them for the different subjects."

"Sure," Ben said. "When can I start?"

"Next week," Finley answered.

On Wednesday, Luke sat at his desk trying to decide which of his co-workers he liked less.

Too close to call.

Trish was middle-aged with a soft body and a sugary face. She stuck headbands into her frizzy brown hair, which was something he'd thought only ten-year-old girls did. Green holly leaves decorated today's red headband.

Trish's two grown children had yet to marry and have kids, so she'd told him at least ten times that, for now, the shelter dogs were her grandbabies. She was obsessed with Christmas for unclear reasons, viewed everything as "adorable," and her favorite word was *aww*. She had less backbone than a jellyfish.

Kat was probably only thirty, which hadn't stopped her from appointing herself the boss and chaperone of Trish. She had the wiry body of a distance runner. Short red hair, light skin, orange freckles. No makeup.

Luke knew that he had the ability to drain the fun from a room, but at least he did so silently. Kat did so by one-upping everyone.

The two women were a mismatch, and Finley should give him a raise for the pain and suffering of having to listen to Kat throw wet blankets on top of Trish every time they talked.

"I'll have to order two new doggy figurines for my nativity set," Trish said. Though seated in front of her computer, she was doing zero work.

Kat, on the other hand, was typing so fast and hard that her keyboard trembled.

He glanced at the time. 10:40 a.m. Why wasn't Finley back? At this time of day, she often went on a bike ride—like she had this morning—in order to exercise their four most athletic dogs. It was taking her longer than usual to return.

Clearly, riding a bike attached to the leashes of four big dogs seemed like a recipe for death. If Finley had any sense, this would have occurred to her.

Think about coding.

Under normal circumstances, he could concentrate fully when writing code. He could lose himself in it, which he liked. He also liked that, as the author of it, he could make a website or a piece of software or a program do exactly what he wanted it to do. In the real world, things sometimes didn't add up or couldn't be controlled. But in the world of coding, they did. And could.

"Luke, have I told you about my nativity set?" Trish asked.

"No."

"It's the most adorable thing ever. Several years ago, I found this website where you can order wooden pieces for your nativity set to represent your family members and pets. Then you paint them to personalize them even more. Right after I started working here, I began ordering dog figurines that look like each of Furry Tails' dogs." She laughed happily. "As you can imagine, it's been a full-time job to keep my nativity set up-to-date. It's also been a pure, pure joy. My set includes three hundred animals at this point."

Luke grunted.

"I don't own a nativity set," Kat said.

"Oh, but they're such a precious reminder of the reason for the season. Of little baby Jesus in the manger. Emmanuel, God with us."

"I don't need to be reminded of anything," Kat stated. "I have an excellent memory. Plus, I refuse to be a victim of holiday commercialism. For Christmas, I put up my artificial tree, wrap it in white lights, and hang identical ornaments. It's more than adequate."

"But—" Trish tried to interject.

"I spent less than one hundred dollars on all of that seven years ago and haven't spent a dime on Christmas decorations since."

"I keep my Christmas decorations up year-round." Trish tilted back her chair and whispered to Luke behind Kat, who sat in the middle desk. "I have about thirty nativity sets and at least one tree in every room, including the bathrooms. It's getting to where there's hardly any flat surfaces left in my house. I just about have to push Christmas knickknacks to the side in order to set a mixing bowl on my kitchen counter."

"I don't have a single thing on my kitchen countertops," Kat informed them. "Not even a toaster or a utensil holder. All of that is best stored in cabinets."

"What about a coffee maker?" Trish asked.

"I don't drink coffee, remember? It's full of caffeine and terrible for you."

Sounds reached him from the hallway beyond the closed door. A commotion of panting and dogs' nails against concrete. Finley had returned. His chest eased with relief.

As intrusive as Trish and Kat were, Finley was worse. All day long, he'd pass her in the hallway, smell her perfume, or hear the murmur of her voice as she talked on the phone in her office.

Those small things shouldn't have registered with him. Instead, he *noticed.*

Then, right when he'd succeed at settling his attention on work, she'd arrive at his elbow. She'd ask questions about the Center's social media, website, or email. Or request his help with the dogs. Or—strangest of all—she'd drop off a bottled water, a vegan protein bar, a bag of nuts, a piece of fruit. It's like she was worried he'd starve.

He'd gained weight after entering prison because he'd put on muscle. He didn't look like a starving man.

The door to the workroom opened, and Finley entered like a ray of sun, brightening a space that had been dim and dull. Her hair was tangled from the bike ride. She wore the hat from the day they'd met, a black patterned dress with a long, wide skirt, and tall boots. The rolled mats they used for their doggy yoga classes filled her arms.

He set his jaw. She'd worn a dress to ride a bike?

"May I have everyone's attention, please?" she asked.

The women swiveled toward her expectantly.

"The work we do is stressful and emotionally draining. It's difficult to advocate for animals with those who won't listen to reason or accept new and better methods of population management. It can feel like trying to move a redwood tree with your bare hands. And then, of course, there's the sorrow that comes from seeing the plight of animals in need. And the helplessness of the realization that the four of us in this room can't rescue them all. Compassion fatigue is real."

This job was a pain in the butt for Luke. But not for any of those reasons.

"So," Finley continued, "I think it would be healthy to add quiet time to our work routine so that we can all enjoy a few moments to pray or meditate. It's centering to take a mental break."

"No," Luke said, impressed with himself for not using an expletive before the *no*.

"Not a problem," she said without missing a beat. "This is absolutely voluntary."

"I love to pray," Trish said.

"I already meditate for twenty minutes a day," Kat announced. "It enhances self-awareness and promotes emotional health."

"Exactly." Finley smiled. "I love prayerful meditation." She handed mats to the women, then flicked off the lights.

Finley, Trish, and Kat sat cross-legged on the floor.

"Luke," Finley said, "this posture is great for focusing on your breath."

"You know what I like about my breath? The fact that I don't have to focus on it."

She selected a track on her phone that sounded like monks slowly singing *uh-oh* over and over again. In a calm voice, Finley talked about closing the eyes and expanding the ribs and emptying the lungs and a lot of other mumbo-jumbo.

Luke stared at her incredulously, wondering if he was being pranked. Maybe Finley was a YouTube celebrity who recorded herself fooling unsuspecting people.

He did his best to return to work and even tapped on the keys to let Finley know that at least one of them was spending time productively.

In truth, he wasn't spending it productively. Because how was he supposed to follow a thought under these conditions?

He could tell by Finley's earnest expression that she was praying.

He'd done the whole church thing when he was a kid. He'd gone to Sunday school and sung songs in worship services. His parents had driven him to youth group events and Bible studies. He'd been on a mission trip when the earthquake struck.

It's not that he didn't think there was a God. He still did. It's just that Luke had lost his faith in Him, along with everything else in his life, when Ethan died.

In the years since, his decisions and mistakes had pushed him further and further from God.

He had the disorienting thought that maybe this wasn't his real, actual life. Maybe he'd lost his mind while in prison and his body was still there. Just a few months ago, he'd been wearing a jumpsuit and waiting in line at the penitentiary's cafeteria. That had been real. That had been his life.

Now he was at an animal rescue center in Misty River, surrounded by women on yoga mats, one of whom was so beautiful she stole his breath.

How could this be real? How could this be his life?

CHAPTER SIX

I'm going to turn off up here," Luke said to Finley the following afternoon.

"It's not time quite yet." They were driving to her dad's property in Hartwell to investigate the first clue. She knew every mile, farmhouse, and sign of this route.

"A blue sedan has been behind us for a while. I just want to make sure it's not following us."

"Okay." Finley twisted in her seat. She had to squint to see the sedan.

Luke slowed, exited, and pulled up to a stop sign.

The sedan continued on, zooming past.

"I guess the sedan wasn't following us," she said.

"I guess not."

He waited a bit, then merged back onto Highway 51.

She'd noticed him checking his rearview and side mirrors often. She appreciated his vigilance. She did. At the same time, it seemed slightly over the top.

Ten minutes later, they passed over the boundary onto Sutherland land, the land that had nurtured her childhood.

Emotion took root in her belly and expanded outward, building pressure. She was coming home. But the man who'd made this her home wouldn't be here.

She bumped around on the old-fashioned seat of Luke's truck as he drove them along the familiar winding dirt road. The warm temperatures of last weekend had plunged almost enough to convince today's drizzle to turn to snow. The sky hovered close, the gray color of dove feathers.

They rounded a bend, ascended slightly, and then the house came into view. It was low-slung and linear, positioned on a wooded plateau.

"When was the house built?" Luke asked.

"In the early fifties. It needed a lot of work when Dad bought it. He renovated it before I was born."

"How many acres are there?"

"One hundred. With lots of lakeshore."

Moments later, Finley unlocked the front door and they stepped inside. Raw, frigid air greeted them. It smelled of dust and loneliness.

Finley switched on lights, turned the heat on, then faced Luke.

He seemed impervious to the cold or, really, to any other stimulus that affected lesser mortals. Hunger. Worry. Family. The need for love.

Brown-gold starbursts surrounded his pupils, sending flecks into his green irises. His face—the serious lips, the straight nose, the creased forehead—still reminded her of an Italian prince. But the rest of him—the clothing he wore like armor, the tense posture, and the unruly hair destined to make women yearn to run their fingers through it—was all pirate.

A pirate prince. Her employee was a pirate prince.

How long had she been staring at him? She cleared her throat. "This is the setting of the photo included with the first clue." She indicated the furniture captured in the picture. Everything was exactly as it had been then, except that the shades of red, brown, and beige in the antique rug had mellowed.

Shivering inside her coat, she gave him a quick tour. They walked through the kitchen and dining room, the three bedrooms and two bathrooms, the garage Dad had converted into his model train studio. The simplicity of the floorplan and the placement of the large windows whispered of top-notch architectural design.

Back in the living room, she set her hands on her hips. "I'll begin by searching the rug and coffee table, which shouldn't take long. Do you want to start with the top shelf of the bookcase?" Dad had neatly arranged a lifetime's worth of record purchases—all of them still in their original album covers—on the shelves.

"Sure."

"When I finish with the rug and coffee table, I'll start with the bottom shelf. We'll work toward meeting in the middle."

"What are we looking for?"

"I'm hoping Dad left the second clue in an envelope identical to the first one. He may have placed it inside an album cover or between records or on the base of a shelf. Perhaps even behind the bookcase. There's a chance, though, that the clue could be more subtle than an envelope."

"What do you mean?"

"He doesn't always write out the treasure hunt clues. Sometimes the clue is an item."

"Explain."

"On one of the last birthday hunts I completed before going away to college, he sent me to a botanical garden. There were several sculptures there. One of them was a father fishing with his daughter. Which reminded me of all the times I'd fished with my dad. I found the next clue waiting for me at our favorite fishing spot."

"If this clue is like that, do you think you'll recognize it when you see it?"

"I hope so, though I admit I haven't *always* recognized the object Dad intended as a clue. Once, he sent me to a wing of an art museum, and I failed to comprehend that a painting of a milkshake was supposed to point me to the diner where he and I sometimes stopped for milkshakes after school."

He did not look amused.

"We need to pay close attention to details," she plunged on. "Basically, if you notice anything at all—a newspaper clipping, an album with a corner cut off, a sticker—speak up."

They went to work while the musty scent of a furnace that hadn't been active in months rose around them.

She placed the coffee table on its side and ran her fingertips around every corner and crevice. She searched the underside of the rug. Nothing there. She scooted over to the bookcase and began making her way through records.

The nearness of his strong body grew more and more impossible to ignore. Over the past several days she'd become . . . aware of him as a man, despite the fact that she hadn't been aware of anyone in *that kind of way* in years.

He stepped behind her, not touching her at all. The skin of her back flushed with heat.

She was his employer!

Yet her body had a rebellious mind of its own.

It was unseemly to notice the physical attributes of a man she was genuinely trying to assist in his new lease on life. Not to mention, it was a betrayal of Chase.

Chase had been perfect for her in every way. Kind, creative, devoted to animals. He'd loved music and dreamt of bringing the gospel to unreached people groups. So chill, so altruistic.

Luke had scoffed at the idea that Chase was her once-in-a-lifetime love because he couldn't fathom what she and Chase had shared. Her relationship with Chase had been singular. Irreplaceable. Chase was the husband and life partner who'd never had the chance to be either of those things, yet he would always be both of those things in her mind.

Luke had accused her of refusing to go on dates with other men because she was scared. That wasn't it. She'd thrown herself at God when Chase died, and God had caught and carried her. At first, He'd carried her through flames and smoke and pain. Later, He'd carried her to meadows filled with clear air and hope.

God had shown her He was all she needed. Naturally, He'd removed feelings of desire from her life because romance was no longer what He had for her.

Besides, how could anyone stir her the way Chase had? How could anyone be as supportive and self-sacrificing as Chase? They couldn't.

Luke was nothing like Chase.

Luke had an unapologetically bad-boy vibe. He was hardened and cynical. To be fair, he also had several sterling qualities. He worked hard. He was ferociously smart with computers. He adhered to a code of honor. That he was beside her today, attempting to fulfill his promise to her dad, proved it.

Chase had taken part in peace demonstrations.

Luke could probably kill someone with his bare hands.

The woman who'd been drawn to Chase should not be drawn to Luke. Really, since God had called her to singleness, she shouldn't be drawn to anyone. But, *please Lord*, definitely not to Luke.

Surely this . . . consciousness of him . . . was a passing whim. He had the appeal of a destination like Morocco. You'd see pictures of Morocco, and it was so different from anywhere you'd ever been or planned to go that you'd feel a tug of fascination. But then reality would set in and you'd realize, no, no. You didn't want to go to Morocco. When the time came to put down a deposit for your trip, you'd put your money down for a European vacation. Because, of course, Europe was the place you'd always wanted to visit.

Time would sort this out. She made a mental note to ask the Lord to keep her thoughts toward Luke honorable and to show her how to rehabilitate him. *That* must remain her focus.

"The day we met . . ." Luke said.

She jumped at the sudden sound of his deep voice.

" . . . you told me that, as far as you know, only you, me, and your dad's attorney know about the treasure hunt."

"True."

"Do you think the attorney, Rosco Horton, poses a threat?"

"No. He's a grandfatherly type."

"I'm not ruling him out as a suspect, but let's assume you're right. If there's danger coming, that means someone else knows about the hunt. Who were Ed's enemies?"

Adroitly, she slid several records back into their slot and pulled free the next batch. "Dad was a vocal critic of Hartwell's mayor and his policies. He told off one of the pastors at the largest church in Hartwell for caring more about how much money the church brought in than the people in it. He confronted a business owner who was running waste into the river."

"I'm going to need all those names."

"If you'll give me your cell number, I'll text them to you."

"Fine. Was your dad involved in anything illegal in the years leading up to his arrest?"

"Not as far as I know."

"Did he have a long arrest record?"

"Not very long, no. When he was in his early twenties, he was charged with drunkenness. Several years later, he was charged with unlawful assembly while protesting against nuclear proliferation. All of that happened before I was born."

"Who was Ed closest to, other than you?"

"Definitely his brother, Robbie. Robbie's two years younger."

"Were they alike?"

"No. Robbie's more careful than Dad. More conventional. Also harder to read. Robbie can mask what he's thinking and feeling."

"But Ed never did."

"Precisely." Warm air from the vent drifted over her. She set her coat aside and straightened her oversized ivory knit turtleneck. She'd worn her red corduroy leggings beneath it in a nod to the red-and-white color scheme of her birthday outfit in the old photo. She crossed her legs. "Dad was protective of Robbie. Back when they started to draft soldiers to Vietnam, he rushed Robbie and June to the altar because if you got married before August twenty-sixth of 1965, you wouldn't be drafted. Dad paid for their wedding flowers, reception food, honeymoon."

"Did the plan work?"

"It worked great. Robbie didn't get drafted, and he and June have been happily married ever since."

"But your dad did get drafted."

"Yes."

"How come he didn't marry before the deadline like Robbie did?"

"He was fond of saying he preferred taking his chances in 'Nam to taking his chances in marriage." She shot Luke a small smile.

"Where does Robbie live now?"

"Here in Hartwell. When Dad and Robbie's parents passed away, they left their property to their sons. Dad already had this place, so he gave Robbie his share of the family land and Robbie moved there."

"Has Robbie ever been arrested?"

"No. He's very upstanding."

"What can you tell me about your dad's friends?"

"That he had lots of them. And lots of girlfriends."

"Any that were criminals?"

"No."

"I'm also going to need the names of his friends and girlfriends." He took a step to the side, moving farther down his shelf. "What led to your dad's conviction?"

She paused her search, her heart heavy. "How much do you know?"

"Not much. When you're on the inside, you don't ask about the other inmates' crimes."

If he was going to figure out who might be after this treasure, he'd need facts. "Almost ten years ago, Dad started dating a woman named Carla. Dad was in his early seventies, she was in her early fifties. She'd been married four times. No kids. She dressed like Stevie Nicks and looked like her, too, except that she had dark hair." Finley pulled a record from its cover and peeked inside. "Carla owned a store that sold posters and art prints."

"Did you like her?"

"I was in college when she and Dad were together. I only spent time with her when I was home or on the few occasions when they came to visit me."

"Did you like her?" he repeated.

"I strive to like everyone."

"Except Carla," he guessed.

"She had her strengths. She was a passionate, artistic person. She wrote songs that she performed at bars around town. She was independent."

"But?"

"There were times when I thought I spotted something a little bit . . . predatory behind her eyes. It felt like she was assessing me while she was smiling at me, which made me uneasy." She gave a *tsk* sound. "I feel badly for saying that. I might have read her wrong. But if I did, it's because she never gave me a chance to see or know the real her."

"What happened to Carla?"

"Dad and Robbie went over to her apartment one evening. They planned to pick her up, then go to a sports bar for dinner and shoot some pool. When they arrived at her apartment, she brought out a secondhand semi-automatic handgun she'd purchased. She asked Dad to show her how to clean it." The pine tree outside shuddered in the wind, causing the tip of one branch to dance against the window. It took effort, but she continued, speaking each word evenly. "As Dad showed her how to clean the gun, it accidentally discharged. The bullet went through Carla's chest."

"I doubt that's what happened," Luke said.

"Run a search for accidental injury and death caused by people attempting to clean guns. You'll see that it happens often."

"But usually to younger people. More careless people. Ed must have known his way around guns after serving in the military."

"He did. He'd grown up with guns on the farm."

"What did Ed and Robbie do after the gun went off?"

"They called 9-1-1 and started CPR. Tragically, they couldn't save her."

"Had your dad been drinking?"

"No. There was no alcohol or drugs in his system. Robbie saw everything. He testified at Dad's trial that it was simply a terrible accident."

"But was Robbie an impartial witness? He'd have said anything, wouldn't he, to protect his older brother? The one who'd protected him from Vietnam?"

"The circumstances are fishy," Finley conceded. She'd always had the sense that more was involved. "Neither Robbie nor Dad ever budged on a single detail. We talked about it a lot, and they told me that's how it happened."

Luke grunted.

"You think Dad wanted to kill Carla?" Finley asked.

"Probably."

Her pulse pounded. "Why would someone with no history of violence suddenly kill his girlfriend? And why would he do it with his brother present?"

"I can't answer the first question. But having his brother present meant he had a chance of making a jury believe he'd killed her accidentally while cleaning her gun. He was convicted of involuntary manslaughter?"

"Yes."

"Which comes with a much lighter sentence than murder."

"But I knew him. Better than anyone." She fidgeted with the edge of Pink Floyd's *Dark Side of the Moon* album. "My father was not a murderer."

"Tell me more about Carla."

"She's from the town of Toccoa. Her mother and her three younger brothers still live there. They hold a fundraiser in her honor every year. It's coming up, actually. I always go, but anonymously, since I don't think they'd be delighted to see me."

"Her family members might be the ones who pose a threat to you."

"If they wanted to take revenge on me, they'd have done it by now. Also, there's no way for them to know about this treasure hunt. Dad arranged this hunt while he was awaiting trial for killing Carla. Her family members are the last people he'd ever have told about this."

She peeked at him. He was frowning.

"Her mother and brothers all have great reputations," she said. "They're active in the community. Centered on their families. Well-respected."

Luke didn't press the line of questioning further. However, she could almost hear the gears of his brain grinding as he thought about who might be chasing after her treasure and why.

After a time, he handed her a receipt he'd found inside an album from the seventies. "Is this anything?"

She studied the receipt and album. "Maybe. Let's set all of the possibilities to the side." She laid the items on the hardwood floor adjacent the rug.

Later, she noted that one of the songs on the back of an album cover had been circled.

Later still, he discovered a Snoopy bookmark inside an album of kids' songs that had belonged to her.

By the time they'd completed a thorough investigation of every shelf, and even the bottom, sides, and back of the bookcase, they'd found three more records that either had markings on the outside or something stashed inside.

What they had not unearthed?

An envelope.

"Dad," she whispered, sitting back on her heels. "You scoundrel. I can't help but imagine you're cackling over how hard you made this."

"I'm still trying to figure out why you and your dad thought this was fun."

"Didn't you ever go on a treasure hunt when you were a kid?"

"A few. I don't like games."

Shocker. He seemed to have made dissatisfaction into an art form. "I challenge you to name five things you *do* like."

"Cars. Food. Solitude. Technology." Pause. "Not being in prison."

"I was an imaginative girl. I loved the treasure hunts because they were whimsical. Adventurous. Challenging."

At the moment, though, she wasn't sure that she still liked the challenge. What if she couldn't solve this hunt? What if she'd dragged Luke all the way here for nothing? She could *feel* his impatience pressing down on her. "That look you're giving me is adding additional pressure that might stymie my ability to figure out the next clue."

"What look?"

"That glowering one."

He shrugged as if to say, *I don't know what you're talking about*. "Thirsty?"

"Yes. I know I left a box of tea bags here." If he made tea, that would buy her a few minutes to think. "There's a kettle on the stove."

He departed, taking away his impatience but also the energy and sizzle that had been charging the room.

She carefully considered each of the albums and objects they'd set aside. She read the song titles, the names of the artists, the lyrics, hunting for even slight points of connection that might guide her to the discovery of the next clue. Nothing jumped out.

She was going back over them yet again when Luke handed her tea. He'd poured it into a Grand Canyon mug Dad had purchased on the road trip they'd taken when she was thirteen. "Thank you."

"Find anything?"

"Still looking." She took a sip of peppermint tea and lifted a record called *Theatre of the Mind* by Mystery. "It occurs to me that the band's name—Mystery—might be a clue. Dad's mom grew up in the thick of the Great Depression. She found a lot of joy in the books she checked out from the library. Her favorites were about unsolved real-life mysteries. When she'd tuck her sons into bed at night, she'd tell stories of missing people and artifacts."

"Did she ever solve any of the real-life mysteries?"

"To my knowledge, the only mystery she cracked was how to fry okra to perfection. Every time my dad saw okra on a menu anywhere, he'd reminisce about his mom's okra, because he'd never tasted better." She rested the album cover on her lap. "She did succeed, though, in capturing her sons' imagination concerning mysteries. The bedtime stories Dad told me were also all real-life mysteries. Dad loved to do his own amateur detective research. Like his mother, he never made any actual headway."

"If 'mystery' is the clue, what is it leading us toward?"

"Nothing springs to mind." She picked up the record with the circled song title. This LP was titled *Barton Hollow* by The Civil Wars. The song of the same name had been circled.

Wait.

Dad hadn't circled the full title. The circle centered around the second word. Hollow.

A small seed of inspiration sprouted in her memory. She pointed to the circled word. "There's a hollow tree here on the property that I used to go to all the time."

"Did your dad know about it?"

"Yes. I'd make up stories about animal families who lived in the tree. From time to time, he'd surprise me by placing something in the tree for me to find. Doll furniture. A piece of fabric for a squirrel to wear as a coat. That kind of thing."

"Let's check it."

Excitement battled with doubt as she buttoned her coat. She dug her mittens from her pocket and tugged them on.

They walked a path through the forest that seemed to transport her back in time. She recalled the bark of her first dog. The *thwap* of her flip-flops as she ran. The riffle of her dress against her legs.

"Here." Finley stopped before the hollow tree. It stood near the lip of a washout, surrounded by a regiment of brother oaks, looking as if it had been undisturbed for decades.

Luke went to his knee next to the large triangular opening in the base of the trunk. He extended an arm as if to begin clearing the drift of leaves that had accumulated, then paused. "Do you want to do this without me? If there's a clue here, it's yours to find."

The pirate prince was thoughtful. "Let's work together. To my way of thinking, it's ours to find."

She knelt and they both swept aside leaves.

He had on his battered leather jacket but hadn't put on gloves. The cold whitened his face and hands. The tips of his ears stained pink.

Their digging brought their profiles into close proximity. She timed her motion to ensure that her hands didn't hit his.

They cleared a few inches of dirt. Nothing. They'd reached hard-packed earth. "I'm second-guessing this," she said. "That circled word might've been a coincidence. The Civil Wars album might not even be the album he wants me to pay attention to."

Luke pulled out his key ring and jabbed the largest key into the ground, breaking it apart.

Crunch crunch scrape. Crunch crunch scrape.

His mouth set in determination, he didn't complain and he didn't let up. At this pace, however, they might be here all evening. Perhaps she should go back to the house and return with a shovel—

Crunch crunch scrape.

Crinkle.

At the new sound, Luke stilled. He leaned back, silently giving her access.

She pressed aside handfuls of soil and caught a glimpse of something white. Her breath snagged. She moved faster, knees aching as she fought to excavate what her dad had buried.

Finally, she slid out a telltale envelope sealed in a Ziploc. On the front, her dad had written *For Finley*.

Amazement moved through her like a cascade of droplets.

Scrambling to her feet, she brandished the envelope high. "I can't believe we found it."

Luke rose. She thought she detected a hint of warmth in those steely eyes.

"Dad," she called to the sky, "I hope the rest of the clues aren't this tricky. If you want me to figure this out, I'm going to need for you to give me more obvious direction." She opened the plastic bag, broke the seal on the envelope, and pulled out the cardstock within.

> *Do you remember the train depot we visited together, Finley? I never enjoyed trains as much as I did when seeing them through your eyes.*
>
> *I love you, Dad*

Her exultation swooped into dismay.

She handed the note to Luke.

He read it. "Do you remember the train depot?"

"I have a vague memory of him taking me to a depot. Maybe when I was in high school? But I have *no idea* where the depot's located."

A blue sedan waited on the main road near Ed Sutherland's property. Its driver had parked in the lot of a mini mart across the street and a good distance away. Several other cars occupied the lot. There'd be no reason for Luke or Finley to notice him when they exited Ed's land.

Killing time, he listened to music. He patiently ate the food he'd brought and drank the soda he'd purchased when he'd arrived.

When Luke's Chevy truck finally pulled back onto the road, he saw it clearly through the binoculars held to his eyes.

CHAPTER SEVEN

The following Monday afternoon, Ben Coleman entered Furry Tails Animal Rescue Center for the first time.

After checking his ID to verify he was an approved volunteer, the woman at the welcome desk directed him toward a room down the hall.

Furry Tails would give him something he'd wanted for a long time: a connection to Luke. Bonus: It would also give him a way to spend some of his free time. Which meant he'd have less time to sit around mourning Leah.

He reached the door labeled *After-School Program* and knocked.

"Come in," a feminine voice called.

He let himself into a large sunny space. Quiet fell as ten kids and two adults swung toward him from their standing and sitting positions. The room looked a lot like an elementary school classroom. Tables with small chairs. A whiteboard. Artwork displays. A computer station.

Akira, whom he'd met at lunch at Pablo's, approached. "Hi."

"Hi."

She was an attractive woman but so soft-spoken that he hadn't gotten a good read on her. Today, she'd chosen a pale pink sweater, dark jeans she'd rolled up at the hem a few times, and sneakers. Her straight black hair ended a few inches below her shoulders. Her face held sweetness. Her body, curves.

She turned toward her kids. "This is Mr. Coleman, who will be stopping by occasionally to lend a hand."

None of them spoke.

"Can you say hello to Mr. Coleman?" she prompted.

"Hello, Mr. Coleman," they said in unison.

A confident-looking white kid with brown hair cut in a trendy style raised his hand.

"Yes, Maxwell?" Akira said.

"What's your career?" Maxwell asked him.

"I'm a high school science teacher."

"He's going to help plan a science unit for all of us," Akira said, "among other things. Won't that be great?"

None of them appeared to think that would be great.

"Is it all right with you if I give them your mini bio?" Akira asked him under her breath.

"Sure."

"Mr. Coleman grew up here in Misty River. Those of you who love sports will be interested to know that he played baseball in high school and college. Do you still play?"

"Casually. In a local league."

"And all of you," Akira continued, "will be interested to know that he is one of the astonishing Miracle Five."

People mentioned the Miracle Five so often that, in a way, it no longer surprised him. In another way, it still *always* surprised him.

He was a normal guy. He liked to eat his mom's pot roast. He let his nieces and nephews climb on his back to play fighting horses with pool noodles. He watched sports on TV. He went to church on Sunday mornings and graded papers at night.

Yet he often came into contact with people who identified him with the one *abnormal* thing he'd experienced. The earthquake had happened almost twenty years ago, during his childhood. News of the five kids trapped under the rubble had spread around the world, and so people remembered it still. He'd had no control over any of it. He'd done nothing extraordinary.

But God had. So as long as people kept asking him about it, he'd gladly keep answering.

"Raise your hand if you know about the Miracle Five," Akira said.

About half the kids raised their hands.

"Maybe," Akira continued, "Mr. Coleman will be kind enough to tell the rest of you about it. Or," she said with amusement, "maybe he prefers to keep it a secret."

"No," moaned the kids who'd never heard of the Miracle Five. A few gave *That's not fair!* expressions.

He'd told the story so many times it often felt like he was delivering a monologue in a play he'd performed a thousand times before. He gave the short version, modified to kid level.

Hardly any of the kids moved. They simply listened with round eyes.

"So," he said, to wrap up, "we'd been stuck down there for eight days when we heard big machines digging their way toward us. We were sitting under two diagonal concrete slabs. They formed the top of a triangle above us. We thought it would be safer to sit under one of them, but we didn't know which one, so we flipped a coin. There was a lot of noise, a lot of vibration. And then, *boom*."

The kids flinched.

"The wall across from us crashed down," he said. "But the wall above us stayed in place. It protected us from the chunks of the building that were falling. The rescue team reached us and loaded us into a helicopter. As soon as we were safe, that wall crashed down, too. Later, we learned that there was no explanation as to why that wall stayed in place as long as it did."

"Which is why they're called the Miracle Five," Akira said.

"What did you eat for those eight days?" asked a blond girl with a neat braid.

"We didn't eat. Food you can go without for a while. But we would've been in serious trouble without water. We managed to crack an exposed pipe. It turned out that it had water inside. We drank from it, and that's how we stayed alive."

"Do you have nightmares about it?" Maxwell wanted to know. "I never have nightmares."

"It would have been normal to have had nightmares after being that scared. But for some reason, I never did." He pushed his hands into his flat-front khakis. "I've lived every day feeling fortunate, because I shouldn't be alive, but I am because God protected us."

For the most part, living a life of gratitude had served him well. The only exception to that came when he faced something hard, like he had this last fall when Leah had broken his heart. He was used to feeling optimistic, joyful, calm. But sad? No. Sadness made him feel like a schmuck. He should've died when he was thirteen. So what right did he have now to grieve a broken heart?

Maybe he was flawed or selfish or low on faith. Or maybe, like his friends told him, he was simply human. Because yeah. Right or wrong, he was grieving.

"Okay, kids, that's enough questions for Mr. Coleman right now. Finish your art projects, please," Akira said. "If you have any questions, you can direct them to Mr. Wrigley."

Mr. Wrigley's short gray hair had receded to the top of his head, so that it sat there like a tiara. He had glasses as big as his smile. Clearly, this was the volunteer Akira had mentioned at lunch.

"Right this way," she said to Ben quietly.

He'd learned early in his teaching career that he had to stay on top of his classroom. If he let it slide, even for a couple of days, he'd find himself buried in mess. It looked like Akira had learned the same lesson. She kept this place organized . . . except for her desk. Stacks of loose paper took up most of the space. Two empty mugs sat on top of a calendar. One mug said, *It takes a village!* The other one said, *One child, one teacher, one book, one pen can change the world.—Malala Yousafzai.* Mechanical pencils lay everywhere, like trees fallen in a forest.

He took the chair she'd placed next to hers.

She opened a document on her computer titled *Science Unit*, then set her fingertips on the keyboard. A moment passed. Then several more.

He filled the silence. "What did you have in mind for the science unit?"

"Oh . . . What did *you* have in mind? I'm open to your superior knowledge on the subject."

"What aspects of science are the kids learning at this age?"

"Um . . ." She regarded him with kindness but didn't answer. It was as if her mind were a hundred miles away.

He finally repeated his question. "What aspects of science are the kids learning at this age?"

Again, an unusually long pause. "I really . . . um . . . don't know."

"But you're the director of the after-school program here." He grinned. "Right?"

A merry laugh broke from her. Gently, she leaned her forehead on the top edge of her computer, then shook it from side to side. Straightening, she met his eyes. "I'm going to confess something to you, and afterward you're going to think I'm weird."

He already did think she was weird, but he said, "No, I won't," because that was the reassuring thing you were supposed to say.

"Did you notice the other day at lunch that I hardly spoke?"

"I don't have any problem with quiet people. If you met my family of loud talkers, you'd know why."

"And now I'm acting like a space cadet in front of you. The truth is . . ." She drew in a breath. "I think you're very handsome. So much so that it's scrambling my brain. I apologize in advance for any further awkward behavior that is probably forthcoming. Even presently forthcoming."

Her words surprised him so much that he didn't move or blink.

Her presence at lunch had been small, and he hadn't taken much notice of her.

But after that little speech, she had his full attention.

Her skin was a beautiful shade of light brown. The apples of her cheeks were round and defined. Thick lashes surrounded intelligent eyes. The large silver hoops in her ears matched the two silver bracelets she wore next to her smartwatch.

"You . . . think I'm handsome?" he asked.

"Don't sell yourself short. I believe I said *very* handsome."

He chuckled. "Thanks."

Before he fell for Leah, he used to go out a lot, and not just with women he was into romantically. He could have fun with just about anyone because he liked getting to know people. It was way past time for him to get back out there. "If you want to hang out sometime, then let's do it."

"It's nice of you to offer that, even if the offer was motivated by pity."

His brows lifted. "Have you looked in the mirror? I don't think any man has asked you out because of pity."

"Unfortunately, I can't accept."

Again she'd surprised him. "Why?"

"Last spring, I had some really severe complications from the flu. I was almost one of those people they talk about on the news when they mention how many the flu kills annually."

"I'm sorry."

"My recovery was slow at first, so I got serious about self-care. Dating is the opposite of self-care for me. My health can't take any more heartbreaks."

"I understand." And he did.

"People who survive serious diseases often talk about how it was ultimately the best thing that happened to them because it shifted their priorities. And it *did* do some of that for me. But I'm definitely not in a place yet where I can say it was the best thing. It was a long, scary, painful tunnel."

His respect for her grew. "You're a survivor."

"A shaky one."

"An honest one." An *interesting* one. "If you want, we can do something together as friends."

"I'd love to have a new and very handsome friend." She turned to the computer, then back to him. "However, if I fling myself at you, you must resist."

"All right."

"And you'll do everything in your power to keep this relationship strictly platonic."

"Absolutely. Yes."

"Because we cannot let our time together become date-like."

"Definitely not."

Her face shone. The points of her smile dug into those expressive cheeks. "Now that we have *that* out of the way, maybe I can concentrate enough to talk with you about science."

When Luke arrived back at the Center after lunch the next day, he found Finley waiting for him in the hallway. She was biting the side of her bottom lip, phone in hand.

His stomach knotted. "What's the matter?"

"A woman just called to report a litter of abandoned puppies underneath her back porch."

When he'd seen Finley, he'd worried that something was wrong with *her*. But, of course, this was about animals.

"Would you be willing to head over there with me to retrieve them?" she asked.

"Yes."

Finley led him into the supply room and handed him a travel crate. He watched her add clean towels to it. She had on loose army green overalls with a white top. Modest. Yet the overalls' sides were open down to her waist and he couldn't look away from the glimpses that gave him of the shirt beneath. The cotton followed the lines of her slim body as she moved.

He carried the crate to his truck and followed the directions she provided.

Since his release from prison, he'd enjoyed every minute he'd spent driving. He'd fallen in love with cars as a kid. He'd liked them even more when he'd started learning about their mechanics. Through all the changes in his life, his passion for cars had remained.

This V-8 engine, thanks to all the work he'd done on it, sounded like a dream. His truck had an incredibly strong chassis. Two-axle drivetrain. Front and rear bumpers made of steel. He'd perfected the tightness of the suspension. His truck drove like a classic truck should—

Finley gasped and braced a hand against the dashboard as a car pulled out in front of them.

"It's okay," he said, smoothly braking before building back up to speed.

She balled her hands in her lap.

She was not an uptight person. But on their trip to her dad's house, her body language in his passenger seat had sometimes been tense. "What's with you and cars?"

"Ever since Chase's accident, I'm . . . jumpy when driving. Cars, well, they can be deadly."

He shot a look at her and registered dark bangs and uncommonly blue eyes. His focus returned forward. "I'm a defensive driver. You'll be safe while I'm driving you places."

"You can't promise that."

"I just did."

"No one can promise that."

"I can promise you that you're safer with me behind the wheel than when you drive yourself places. No telling what you'd do if a deer ran in front of your car, or if you saw a skinny dog on the side of the road."

He caught a glimpse of her smile. "Point taken."

They pulled up in front of a run-down house that had once been white. A dead-eyed older woman escorted them around the side yard while listing the reasons why this situation wasn't her fault and why she could not care for puppies. Apparently, the mother dog was a Chihuahua who occasionally ate the kibble the woman left out for her.

"The puppies are under there." She pointed to the crawl space beneath the raised foundation, then went indoors.

"Why would a mother dog abandon her puppies?" Luke asked Finley.

"She might be part of the roaming dog population. If so, it's possible she was killed or injured while out scavenging for food. It's also possible that she may have weaned them and simply moved on."

Beneath the house he saw spiderwebs, mud, rusty nails. Since the earthquake, he no longer went underneath structures. No basements. No below-ground parking garages. But he heard himself say, "I'll go."

Finley laughed.

"What?" he demanded.

"How many litters of puppies have you rescued?" She got down on her hands and knees to peer into the opening.

"None."

"Exactly. So I'm going." She'd gasped when a car pulled out in front of them, but now she shimmied under the house without hesitation. "You stay here. I'll hand the puppies to you and you can place them in the crate."

"Have you had a tetanus shot?" he grumbled.

She didn't answer.

Soon after, her white wrist extended from the crawl space, holding a ball of light brown fluff.

"Um." Since he had no other option, he lifted the baby animal from her hand. The fluff eyed him impatiently, wiggling. It had a pointy nose and eyes like brown Skittles. Its ears folded down and its tail folded up. It reminded him of a dirty brown dandelion with a face and legs. He stuck it in the crate. It pawed the door, whining.

Concerned about Finley, he squinted into the hole under the house.

He wasn't getting paid enough to do this job.

Near the end of Luke's workday, Finley carried the four puppies into the workspace and carefully set them on the floor. She'd placed them in an open-topped container that looked like a laundry hamper padded with sheets. Immediately, Trish knelt to cuddle them.

Hours ago, after Finley had scooped the dogs from under the house, she'd crawled from the foundation with a cobweb on her shoulder, dirt on her hands and streaked across one cheek, and stains on the knees of her overalls. Why all of that had made her look even prettier, he couldn't explain.

He'd dropped Finley and the puppies off at the vet. Later, Kat had given them a ride back to the Center, where volunteers had fed and bathed the puppies.

"They look to me like Pomchis." Kat stood over them with her hands on her hips.

"What's a Pomchi?" Luke asked.

"A mix between a Chihuahua and a Pomeranian."

"Adorable!" Trish beamed.

"While they're in our care," Finley said, "they'll be called Oscar, Agatha, Felicia, and Steve."

"Are you trying to give them the worst possible names?" he asked.

"I love those names!"

Trish lifted a puppy, rocking it like a newborn and singing "Away in a Manger."

He turned toward his monitor.

"Luke," Finley said.

He reversed his chair just enough to meet her eyes. The cobweb was gone. Her hands and face were clean. But stains remained on the knees of her overalls.

"You'll be fostering Agatha," she said.

"Come again?"

"Our vet confirmed that these puppies have been weaned. When we receive puppies of an adoptable age, we share the work of fostering them until we can place them in forever homes. There are four of us. And four puppies."

He was having a hard time comprehending. "You expect me to take a dog home tonight?"

"I do."

"What about Akira? She works here."

"Her role is different than ours. The only pet care she's responsible for is the pet care she oversees during the after-school program."

"I'd love to cuddle Agatha and Steve all night," Trish cooed. "I have two pairs of matching Santa jammies in puppy sizes."

"I can housetrain a dog in three days," Kat announced.

"And yet we're going to share the workload like we always do," Finley said stubbornly.

"You don't want"—no way was he saying the name *Agatha*—"that puppy going home with me. I don't know how to take care of a puppy."

"We'll give you pointers and provide supplies."

"No thanks."

She lifted her shoulders. "It's a duty that comes with the job."

Trish eyed him nervously. Kat smirked.

The confrontation pulled the air tight. He didn't care. He had more experience with confrontation in his pinky finger than all three of these women combined.

"Chat with me in my office?" Finley asked him lightly.

He nodded. Just before he shut Finley's office door behind him, he heard Trish singing "round yon virgin" to the puppies.

He turned on Finley. "Trish said she'd be willing to take two puppies."

In one graceful movement, she lowered into her chair and crossed her legs. "Yes, but we're all going to take one."

"Are you doing this to punish me?"

Her lips parted with surprise. "No! I have no reason to punish you and even if I did, I'd never use an animal to do so. There's an order to the way we do things around here. Very young puppies that need round-the-clock feeding go to specially trained volunteers. Weaned puppies stay at Furry Tails during the day. At night, we divide them evenly among us."

He scowled.

She cocked her head the way she did when she was trying to psychoanalyze him. "Why would you think I'd want to punish you?"

"I don't know."

"I earnestly want for you to enjoy working here."

"Yet you just told me that I have to take care of a puppy against my will."

"Yes, because puppies require a lot of care—"

"Which I am not qualified to give."

"—which any kind, mature adult is qualified to give."

"I'm not a kind, mature adult. I'm an ex-con."

Finley took his measure. "You're a kind, mature adult. All that's left is to line up your actions with the nobility that's always been inside."

"Finley, it irritates the crap out of me when you say things like that. Blind optimism is not in your best interest." He'd never met anyone so determined to see people and animals as better than they were. She'd have followed along behind Billy the Kid, smiling.

She stiffened, and he could tell he'd rubbed her the wrong way. "I've buried my fiancé and my father. I am not blindly optimistic. I'm an experienced, eyes-wide-open optimist."

Several seconds passed. So much of what he felt toward her—admiration, frustration, physical desire, defensiveness—was confusing and contradictory.

"I'll take the puppy home," he said, "if you'll agree to move on to the next clue sooner rather than later."

"During our initial discussion, I told you that I needed to do this hunt on my timeline."

"Yeah, but procrastinating isn't going to make anything better. It's only going to increase your stress. And it's definitely going to increase my stress."

She twirled one of her many rings. "Take Agatha home, and I'll start researching train depots to see if I can figure out which depot my dad was referencing in the new clue."

"When will you start researching?"

"Tonight."

"How long before someone adopts Agatha?"

"Female puppies go fast."

"How fast?"

"Almost always in less than a week. And you'll only have Agatha to yourself in the evenings. Others will take over when you're here."

"Fine." He moved to the door, eager to be free of the closeness of the small office and the scent of her perfume. That scent made him think of spending a day in bed with her, surrounded by twisted sheets that smelled like an orange grove in spring.

Finley trailed him into the workroom, giving him an earful on puppy care 101.

A superior glint in her eye, Kat handed him a piece of paper that said, *How to Love Your Puppy.*

Trish sang "Deck the Halls."

Luke's mind flicked off when Finley started talking about products to use to clean up puppy accidents, but his attention snapped back when Ben Coleman stopped in the open doorway.

Inwardly, Luke cursed. Just when he'd been sure this day couldn't get worse, here was Ben.

"Ben!" Finley said warmly, beckoning him in and introducing him to the others as the Center's newest volunteer.

Ben greeted the women, then turned to him with a smile. "Hey, man."

"Hey."

"Luke is going to be doing some puppy-sitting for the next few days," Finley told Ben. "It's possible that he could use a hand from an old friend." She sounded like a mom arranging a playdate between two preschool boys who didn't like each other.

Luke wished, painfully, that Ed had never asked him to come here and protect Finley. He wished he'd never entered the doors of this place. He wished he'd never met Finley.

Most of all, he wished she didn't stir up feelings in him that he'd never wanted to feel again.

CHAPTER EIGHT

Foreboding jolted through Finley the moment she stepped into her house that night after work.

She froze just inside her front door, senses straining. Sally ran up to her, panting and wagging her tail. Usually Sally woke from sleep to greet Finley, so the panting was somewhat unusual.

Finley waited, testing the environment. The sun hadn't yet set. Though the house was dim with coming dusk, there was still plenty of light, and she didn't see anything suspicious.

So what had set off a clang of warning in her?

Oscar the Pomchi puppy shifted sleepily inside the sling Finley wore diagonally across her body. She registered the soft squeaking of Dudley the hedgehog's wheel, but that was normal. She peeked into her office and, sure enough, saw him running on his wheel inside his cage.

She made her way deeper into the house. In the living room, her cat sat on a shelf, regarding her with irritation. That, too, was unusual. Not the irritation, which was his default expression, but the fact that Rufus had jumped onto that particular shelf.

"Everything okay here?" she asked him.

Rufus scowled.

The items surrounding her were exactly as she'd left them. Even so, she set down her purse, then peeked into one room after another, checking to see if anything was amiss.

Nothing was.

The front door had been locked and the sliding door was locked, too. A strong gust of wind sent the trees in the backyard shuddering. A storm front was sweeping across the mountains, which likely explained her pets' odd behavior. From time to time, harmless things like shifts in the weather, the noise of the trash truck, or the sound of a car backfiring unsettled them.

She was being paranoid. Maybe her dad's concerns about the dangers that might be wrapped up in the treasure hunt had burrowed into her subconscious.

She let Sally outside, then filled her tiny watering can. Caring for her miniature cactus collection always calmed her.

For years she'd been adding to her stash of cacti. In the winter, they lived on this sunny shelving unit. In the warmer months, they lived outside. Methodically, she watered each of the fifty varieties in turn.

By the time she finished, she felt more like herself. She opened the door for Sally and stashed the watering can. She'd have preferred to spend her precious after-work hours on reading, music, movies, or a bubble bath. However . . .

"I feel obligated to spend time looking at pictures of train depots," she told her pug.

Sally peered at Finley the way tourists peer at the *Mona Lisa*.

"Why do I need to look at pictures of train depots, you ask?" She dropped to her haunches and gave Sally a belly rub. "Because Dad's clue is pointing me toward a train depot we once visited together. Ask me how much I remember about the depot."

Sally snuffled happily.

"It was pushy of Luke to force me into researching the treasure hunt ahead of my wishes."

Her conscience niggled. It had been pushy of her to force him into caring for Agatha.

She headed toward her office. She'd insisted Luke take a puppy for two reasons. One, they truly did divide the puppy care duties exactly the way she'd told Luke they did. Two, she couldn't have scripted a better way to make progress toward points number four and five in the Restoration of Luke: *Carefully condition him by exposing him to all the things he'd been avoiding including, but not limited to, the town of Misty River, close connections with others, and God. Train him how to behave constructively.*

So far she'd been meeting his needs by bringing him plenty of food and water while he was at his desk. She'd been treating him with great patience. She had to admit that her attempt at point three in her plan, *introduce him to daily quiet time*, was not having the desired effect. But maybe she'd win him over to that soon.

Little Agatha would expose Luke to a close connection with a puppy who needed him. And caring for Agatha would train him to behave constructively. This, she knew.

Long ago, she'd rescued a beagle mother dog and her puppies. They'd been kept inside a plastic box with a lid. The conditions had been hot and suffocating. Two of the puppies had been dead when she'd arrived. They'd done their best to save the third, without success. Only the mother survived, but her spirit had been broken.

A few months later, the police department had brought in motherless terrier pups. Finley had placed the pups with the beagle and, in caring for those puppies, that mother had found purpose and joy. The change in her had been remarkable. Inspirational. She'd come back to herself.

Perhaps the same metamorphosis would occur in Luke.

She thought of his forceful nature. How he suppressed his emotions. How he isolated himself. He'd been avoiding showing love to others. But he couldn't avoid it now.

In her office, she fed Dudley a bit of dried apple and opened his door in case he wanted a jaunt-about.

Settling at her desk, she pulled out a drawer and contemplated the small home safe Luke had purchased. She tapped in the code, opened its door, and pondered the two treasure hunt notes they'd found so far.

Do you remember the train depot we visited together, Finley? the most recent one read. *I never enjoyed trains as much as I did when seeing them through your eyes.*

Did the second sentence have a hidden meaning? Was he hinting at something when he said *through your eyes*? Eyeglasses? She'd never worn any.

She tugged on her earlobe.

If that second sentence held a hint, she couldn't figure it out. She opened her laptop. Best to look at photos of depots in this region to see if one of them sparked a memory.

Agatha had a death wish.

Every time Luke placed the ball of terror down in his apartment, she went straight for the nearest electrical cord or darted for the space under the oven.

He'd trap her and stick her in the "playpen" Finley had provided—a circle of short metal gates attached to the open side of her crate. Agatha would cry, so he or Ben would pick her up. She'd stay still for a minute or two, then squirm to get down. They'd go through the whole cycle again.

"Aren't puppies supposed to sleep a lot?" Luke asked irritably.

"I think so, but I really don't know." Ben went down on all fours to shovel her out from beneath the oven again. "You go ahead and eat. I'll handle this."

Back at the Center, Luke had agreed when Ben had offered to pick up dinner for them both. Then Luke had driven the dog here and taken her to the patch of grass and trees between his building and the parking lot.

She hadn't liked the leash. She'd either plant her tiny legs, pull, or try to get herself flattened by rushing beneath his boots while he was walking.

Finley had tried to send him home with a pink leash and pink collar. He'd flatly refused. The dog had ended up with a black leash and black collar. Even so, it insulted his masculinity to be seen with such a sad excuse for a dog.

He'd waited and waited for her to go to the bathroom. Instead, she'd chewed leaves and acorns. As soon as he'd taken her upstairs, she'd immediately peed on his newly refinished hardwood floors.

Luke now sat on his sofa, hunching forward to eat from the take-out container on his coffee table. Ben had bought a rice dish with egg, meat, bean sprouts, and carrots from the Korean restaurant. Luke opened a second packet of sriracha with his teeth and squirted it on top.

For two decades, the other four of the Miracle Five had never stopped reaching out to him, even though his refusal to be a part of their group hadn't changed. He'd been forced together with them in that crushed basement in El Salvador. He hadn't had a choice then. Ever since, his choice had been to distance himself from them. It hadn't worked.

Natasha and Genevieve had written to him in prison. Ben had visited him there every few months.

Now that he'd returned to Misty River, they were ramping up their efforts. He'd walked out of the gas station shortly after arriving in town to find Sebastian waiting next to his truck. Genevieve and Natasha had each come by the apartment a couple of times back when he'd been renovating. Ben had showed up at his workplace.

Ben set the dog in her playpen. Right away, she started whining.

"Can you see if she'll eat something?" Luke asked.

Ben stepped inside the fencing, took a seat, and held a few pieces of dry food on his palm. She trotted in the other direction.

Finley had told him how important it was for puppies to eat and drink. She'd described the steps he should take if the dog wouldn't eat due to the "trauma" she was currently experiencing. She'd recommended softening her dry food and mixing it with wet food. If that didn't work, feed her liquid oatmeal with a syringe.

He was not going to make oatmeal and squirt it down the throats of puppies. At the same time, his puppy hadn't eaten one bite of food since he'd taken over her care, and concern had started to darken his thoughts.

Why wouldn't she eat like a normal dog? He'd feel better if she'd eat.

Ben kept trying to entice her with food, and she kept ignoring him.

Ben picked her up and walked her back and forth in front of the wall of industrial windows, murmuring endearments and patting her. It was the kind of thing parents did with babies on TV shows.

The puppy calmed, so Ben continued.

Ben was better with the dog than he was. Luke was torn between wanting Ben to leave so he could be alone in his apartment and not wanting Ben to leave because then he'd lose his puppy-sitter. "Feel free to go anytime," Luke said.

"I'll eat here, if you don't mind. Then head out."

Luke shrugged.

Still holding the puppy, Ben sat at Luke's table in front of the remaining take-out container.

"Do you want me to hold her?" Luke hadn't finished his dinner, but it didn't seem right to make Ben deal with a dog that was Luke's responsibility.

"Nah. She's finally settled down. I learned the skill of eating one-handed while taking care of my nieces and nephews." He grinned, reminding Luke forcefully of the kid that Ben had once been.

Luke was a year older, but he'd known Ben throughout his childhood because they'd grown up in the same church youth group. Of the Coleman family's four kids, Ben was the nicest, the one who was always in a good mood.

The day of the earthquake, the people on their mission trip had held a sports camp for local kids on inner-city soccer fields. At one point, Luke had seen Ben jogging down the field, passing a ball back-and-forth with a young boy. Eventually, the boy had kicked the ball into a portable net. Ben had thrown his fists in the air and given the same smile he'd given just now.

A few hours after that, their lives went from normal to near death. Down in that dusty dungeon, Ben had been hopeful and supportive. Luke had been neither of those things. It had taken all his effort to continue to breathe in and out in the face of his overwhelming terror and remorse. He'd been gripped with the worst type of shock, his mind consumed with one thought.

Ethan.

Ethan!

Over and over, with sickening, gut-punching guilt, he'd recalled the words he'd said to Ethan as they were about to take the stairs to the basement. "*You're last in line.*"

So stupid. So, so stupid. Why had he said that?

All these years later, he still didn't have an answer. He only had regret. And the sharp physical pain that wedged between his ribs every time he put himself back there, even for a few moments.

Luke crossed to the trash and threw away the remains of his meal. "So, you've started volunteering at the Center?"

Ben swallowed his bite. "Yes. I'm enjoying it so far."

"Are you volunteering there because that's where I work?" Luke leaned his hips against the kitchen counter and crossed his arms.

Ben stuck his fork in his rice so that it pointed straight up like a flagpole. "I had several reasons for wanting to volunteer there. But to answer your question, yes. One of them was you. I'd like for there to be at least a little bit of communication between us."

"Why?"

"You were . . . there with us. It's never set well with me, the fact that the rest of us have been close friends ever since but you haven't been a part of that. Our group will never . . . feel complete without you."

"You want to communicate with me so you can feel a sense of completion?"

"Sure. And because I think our friendship can be of some benefit to you."

"You remind me of the worst day of my life. So I don't see how contact between us could be for my benefit."

Ben's mouth formed a grim line. "You saved us the day of the earthquake. I've never been able to do anything for you in return, but I've always wanted to. I still want to."

They'd been kids when the walls of that basement had begun to shake. Luke had been first in line. He'd simply pulled Ben forward, then Natasha, then Sebastian, then Genevieve. He'd turned to race back into the pitch-dark hallway for Ethan when Sebastian had stopped his progress a split-second before concrete crashed down. Luke hadn't been fast enough.

"I didn't save you." It was a joke to think that anybody could have left that pile of rubble feeling gratitude toward him, the boy who'd killed his brother. "You'd all have made it to safety without me."

"No, we wouldn't have."

"Of course you would have."

"That's not how I remember it."

"You don't owe me," Luke stated. He *hated* the patient way Ben was trying to reason with him. People had handled him the very same way after Ethan's death.

He wondered sometimes if that's partly what had spurred his rebellious teenage years—the driving need to take the pitying look out of everyone's eyes. If he was a drinker, a partier, and a drug user who drove too fast and slept around, they couldn't keep looking at him with all that sympathy.

His strategy had failed. They'd still looked at him with sympathy. The day he'd turned eighteen, he'd left town with the urgency of a drowning swimmer fighting for air.

The strangers he'd met in Atlanta hadn't treated him like the brother of a dead kid.

"Even if I don't owe you," Ben said, "I do care. I really liked Ethan. I still think about him often. I'm sorry about what happened to him and sorry about what happened to you and your family because of it."

Based on what Luke's mom had told him, Ben kept in close contact with her and his dad. Ben was perfect in every way.

It was annoying.

"I'm just hoping," Ben went on, "that you might get to a place where spending time with us doesn't *only* remind you of the worst day of your life. It would be great if we could also remind you of the good, at least some of the time."

"What good?"

"The fact that we lived."

"Here's where you and I view things differently."

"How so?"

"For years, I didn't see the fact that I lived as good."

Ben nodded once, solemn. "And now?"

"I'm still undecided."

Luke could see that Ben wanted to say more.

"What?" Luke asked.

"You remember my mom?"

"Yeah." CeCe was a short woman with tall opinions.

"She and Genevieve's mom, Caroline, are going to host a Valentine's party. It's the kind of event they love to do. Big. All their friends and family members will be there, from eighty-year-olds down to teenagers. Mom wants you to come."

"No."

"She talks to me about it every day."

"Still no."

"Will you come if I take this dog home with me for the night?" Laugh lines creased the skin around Ben's eyes.

"No." As little as he wanted to keep the dog overnight, Luke wanted to attend a Valentine's Day party much less.

I *should have taken Ben up on his offer*, Luke thought at 2:40 a.m. What had he been thinking? Lying on his side, he clamped a pillow over his exposed ear. *No Valentine's Day party could be worse than this*. The puppy had more energy than a football fan hopped up on Red Bull.

Finley had said a lot of things to him about crate training, house training, and putting the puppy on a schedule because puppies loved routine.

At this point he could not have cared less about crate training, house training, or a routine. His goal was far simpler. Keep the dog alive until its rightful owners—and he couldn't imagine who'd be idiot enough to adopt this puppy—took it home.

He just wished he knew how to make the job of keeping the dog alive easier on himself.

Before he'd stretched out in bed, he'd moved the playpen and crate into his bedroom because Finley had told him it would be comforting for the puppy to sense his presence through the night.

She'd said nothing about how uncomfortable it would be for him to sense her loud, unhappy presence through the night.

With a groan, he stretched his torso off the side of the bed and rooted around until he caught hold of the puppy in the dark. She easily fit inside the grip of one hand. He gently pressed her into the angle between the mattress and his bare chest.

She tried to scramble away, upset and shaking. No doubt she was searching for Ben, the love of her life.

Looping a finger around her collar, he kept her in place. In his most soothing voice, he whispered, "Ben's not here, which means you're stuck with me, and I really, really dislike you. You're making my life hell, and if I could sell you to a dog meat distributor in exchange for sleep, I would."

She continued to strain against his hold, but not as frantically.

"I hate the way you pee and poop on my floor," he whispered sweetly. "I hate the sound of your crying. And I hate that you still haven't eaten anything. If I never see you again, I'll be glad. Also, your ears are dumb. They don't fit on your head."

Gradually, finally, she stilled. Plopping down on her belly, she scooted as close to him as she could get. Then tried to scoot even closer.

She was a small warmth against his skin, a body mostly made up of fur with fragile bones and a pattering heart underneath. She smelled like dog breath and shampoo.

He hadn't shared a bed with anything or anyone in years, and this wasn't how he would've chosen to break that streak. He was going to have to wash her stink off his sheets.

He closed his eyes, exhaustion creeping over his muscles. If he squished her during the night, or if she fell off the bed and broke her neck, or if she starved, then it would serve Finley right.

An image of Finley took shape in his mind, coming into focus. Her pale skin. Eyes the clear illuminated blue of the most stunning place he'd ever been: a mountain lake in the Tetons on a family trip a month before the earthquake. Her bright and genuine smile.

Finley, passionate champion of underdogs.

Finley, whose dead fiancé had been a do-gooder.

He wanted her—

No.

Don't think about her, he warned himself. *You cannot let yourself care.*

And with every fiber of his soul, he knew it was true.

CHAPTER NINE

The next morning, Finley relocated herself and her laptop to Furry Tails' foyer so that she could keep an eye out for Luke.

He arrived right on time. She watched him approach the building, holding a dog carrier in one hand. He shouldered in the door like an angry north wind.

Lately, pleasure coursed through her every time she saw Luke after they'd been apart. This time, no different. Pleasure swirled, warm and enticing.

No no no. Take away this pull I'm feeling toward him, Lord! Her motives toward Luke had to be sterling.

"How'd it go?" she asked cheerfully.

"Not well." His eyes looked red and tired.

"In what way?"

"Every way. I think you're going to need to shoot oatmeal into her mouth because she hasn't eaten anything."

"Has she been drinking water?"

"Some." He set down the carrier. Agatha wailed.

"Not to worry. We'll take over now."

"Have you figured out which train depot you visited with your dad?" he asked, changing the subject.

"I spent time looking at pictures last night, but nothing clicked."

"What do you remember about the depot?"

"I don't think trains were coming and going, back when we visited. So it might have been a historic site." She sounded uncertain, because she was. "When I checked, I learned that North Georgia has *a lot* of historic train depots."

"What color was the building?"

"Grayish . . . maybe?"

"How long did it take you and your dad to drive there?"

"I don't remember."

His face fell.

She did not want this hiccup to affect the progress he'd made thanks to her five-step plan.

"I don't think my dad would have taken me on a long trip to a train depot," she said quickly. "Hours in the car have always made me antsy."

This did not appear to brighten his spirits.

"I'll keep working on it," she assured him, "and come up with some train depot suggestions soon."

"Very soon?"

"Yes!"

He stalked down the hallway.

"Thanks for taking care of Agatha," she called after him. "I'm sure that you and Ben did a great job."

Luke vanished from sight.

She regarded the puppy. "Affectionate man, no?"

Agatha gave her a look like, *Are you crazy, lady?*

"I'm crazy like a fox," she whispered to the dog. She took Agatha to the empty play yard, released her, then texted Meadow and Bridget.

Finley
I'm experiencing consistent pangs of attraction toward Luke Dempsey. I feel sheepish admitting this because these feelings don't square with my no-dating stance and because Bridget expressed interest in Luke back on my birthday.

Bridget
I officially withdraw my romantic interest in Luke Dempsey! I've never even met the man.

Finley
How do I squelch pangs of attraction?

Meadow
By ignoring pangs at all costs.

Bridget
Feelings are valid. Don't stuff them down. Take time to explore your chemistry with Luke.

Meadow
Um, what? She decided ages ago to remain single.

Bridget
Situations change. God's will for us changes. You have to give yourself permission to change, too, Finley.

Meadow
Because she's feeling hormones for a man? I'd stay committed to singlehood if I were you. Trust me when I say hormones are liars.

Bridget
Whatever you choose to do, we'll support you 100%.

That night, Agatha continued to act like a diva.

Luke spent his whole evening trying to find the set of conditions that would cause her to *shut up*. Or sleep without him holding her. Or eat.

"Look at this delicious piece of food," Luke said from his position inside her cramped playpen. He held out a piece of kibble. She sniffed it. He waited for a chance to stuff it in her mouth.

She turned and padded away.

He pretended to pop the kibble into his mouth and chew. "Mmm."

She tilted her baby head to the side, then poked at one of her toys with her paw.

He extended the kibble to her again. "Please give it a try. Growing dogs need nutrition."

He ended up chasing her around and around the pen with the hand holding the piece of food.

She did not eat it.

Later, when he was about to get in bed, she ran over to his mattress. Placing her front feet on it, she said without words, *Lift me up, sucker.*

He set her on top, flipped off the lights, and lay down.

Immediately, she burrowed next to him as she had the previous night. She yawned loudly, then made a weird little smacking sound. He braced for more frantic movement and noises.

But none came. The holy terror went to sleep. He'd never appreciated quiet this much.

Agatha's new owners were going to inherit a dog who was used to sleeping in human beds. But, for those poor fools, that was going to be the least of their worries.

"Can you close the window?" Kat asked Luke the next day.

"No."

"The optimal indoor temperature in the winter is sixty-eight degrees." She walked over to consult the thermostat.

"It's my window." They each had one in front of their desk. "And it's only cracked half an inch."

"Yes, but it's freezing outside, and the cold air coming in through the crack has lowered the temp to sixty-seven."

"The window stays like it is." In prison, he had almost no control over his environment—other than behaving in a way that ensured he'd never get sent to solitary confinement. Here, he could keep his window open, and so he did. Less claustrophobic that way.

Trish entered, holding Agatha. Finley had led him to believe he wouldn't have to deal with the puppy while at work. Wrong. The gluttons for punishment frequently brought the puppies into their workspace.

"You know, Luke," Kat said in her lecture tone, "it would be best if you could expose Agatha to cars, sounds, different walking surfaces, people of all ages, and retail environments. Pet stores and some home-improvement stores allow animals."

"I will be exposing her to none of those things."

"It would be best—"

"I don't want to hear it," Luke said. "You're welcome to take her and manage her conditioning."

Finley breezed into the space. "Agatha stays with Luke."

Awareness prickled over his skin. *Don't look in her direction.* It was too hard on him if he had to see her smile, the shape of her body, or the way her earrings swung against her throat a hundred times a day.

"The less change Agatha has to deal with right now," Finley said, "the better."

"God rest ye merry gentlemen," Trish sang to Agatha. She attempted to place the dog on her thighs and scratch her tummy, but Agatha was having none of it.

Maybe nice, normal puppies liked to lie on their backs and have their tummies scratched. Agatha wasn't nice or normal, which Trish didn't seem capable of figuring out. Her necklace, which looked like a string of old-fashioned colored Christmas lights, swung forward when she finally set the puppy on the floor.

Agatha ran to Luke like a sprinter toward a finish line and gazed up at him. Lifting his eyebrows in challenge, he gazed back. She turned in a tight circle, lay down, and rested her chin on the toe of his boot.

"Aww," said Finley and Trish in unison.

Could he file a complaint with the city, citing unacceptable work conditions? No employee should be expected to sacrifice his sleep to a puppy, then turn around and keep his foot stationary while on the job so that the same puppy could get quality rest.

Luke spent that evening the way he'd spent all his evenings since they'd forced Agatha on him—going down his building's elevator and escorting Agatha to a patch of grass, where she mostly failed to go to the bathroom. Going up his building's elevator, then cleaning up the messes she made on his floor. He was on his hands and knees more than Cinderella.

"Doesn't this kibble look amazing?" he asked the puppy, his big body once again crammed inside her pen. He placed several pieces of food in the palm of his hand and moved it back and forth in front of her hypnotically.

Hypnosis. Why hadn't he thought of that before? He'd pay thousands for a dog hypnotist to straighten this animal out.

"You're getting hungry." He spoke in a relaxing hypnotist's voice. "You want to eat kibble, like a regular dog. Yummy. Very, very yummy."

To his astonishment, she stuck her nose close to the food.

He held perfectly still. "Yummy," he repeated.

Finally, she took a few pieces, crunching it loudly and eating with her mouth open.

He felt like he'd won an Olympic medal. Grinning, he nodded encouragingly. "Yummy."

She ate the rest of the food on his hand. He scooted her bowl toward her. "Well, go on. You've got a whole bowl there. Go to town."

She simply stared at him meaningfully, waiting.

The fluff expected him to hand-feed her?

He put more food on his hand. She ate it. He kept trying to interest her in the bowl, and she kept refusing. He got up, grabbed a book, and placed it under her bowl, which brought the food up to the height of her chin.

She gave him another meaningful stare.

For the next ten minutes, he endured a cramp in his leg while he fed her small portions from his hand over and over.

When she'd finally had enough, she lay down on the floor, her expression unmistakable. It said, *Gotcha*.

How come she hasn't been adopted yet?" Luke asked Finley the next morning when they were alone in the workroom. As if he didn't already know the answer. Any person with a brain cell would take one look at the pictures they'd posted of Agatha and recognize that the puppy was crazy.

He was sitting at his desk. Once again, Agatha was napping on his shoe.

Finley stood nearby wearing bell-bottom jeans, a wide leather belt, and a gray V-neck shirt. The stone beads of her long necklace dipped to a big piece of turquoise shaped like a teardrop. She'd placed her assigned puppy in a sling across her chest. Her puppy slept most of the time and never made a sound. "We're still getting the word out about Agatha," she said. "She'll be adopted very soon, I'm sure."

"She arrived Tuesday and it's Friday. You said puppies are always adopted in less than a week."

"I said *almost* always in less than a week. It's been three days."

"That have felt like three weeks."

"I'm in conversations with two different families about Agatha. They're filling out paperwork so that we can confirm them to be reliable pet owners."

"Reliable?" he asked, outraged. "You didn't care about proving my reliability when you gave her to me."

"I know you."

"No, you don't."

"Yes, I do." She adjusted the sling. "I have to be diligent about vetting the people I don't know who apply to adopt our animals."

He'd been working here for two-and-a-half weeks. Long enough to know that the animals received outstanding care. The workers and volunteers kept the place extremely clean. They ensured the dogs had food, rest, exercise, playtime, health screenings, and baths.

He'd known plenty of people who were dedicated to their jobs. But he'd never met anyone as dedicated to their job as Finley was. She worked *hard*.

"You might want to be less diligent," he said. "Then you could find homes for more dogs."

Her eyes flashed as she lifted her chin. "I'm not trying to get rid of them. I'm determined to find every one of them a loving, committed home. There's a world of difference."

"Find a loving, committed home for Agatha soon because I'm not doing this for more than a week. I'm tired and irritated—"

"Yes, I see that," she said wryly.

"If she's not adopted by next Tuesday, I'm quitting this job and moving to Montana."

She rolled her lips in, as if trying to keep herself from smiling.

"This is not funny," he growled.

"It is just a very tiny bit funny."

"Aren't you the one who's famous for being so full of empathy?"

"I am! It's just that I'm a complex individual. I can experience humor and feel a sense of empathy toward you simultaneously."

"What am I supposed to do with Agatha all weekend?"

"Tomorrow and Sunday, you can drop her off here in the morning and pick her up around dinnertime. Both Kat and Trish have

Fridays off. But Trish and several volunteers are here every Saturday, and Kat and several volunteers are here every Sunday."

"When were you going to tell me that I could drop her off here on the weekend?"

She shrugged. "All you had to do was ask."

He slid his boot out from under the puppy's chin, causing her to wake with a start. She whined. He slipped his palm under her belly and thrust her at Finley. "I think she needs to go to the bathroom. Again. Which isn't my problem during my work hours."

Finley accepted the puppy and stroked her back. "I'd be glad to take her outside." She moved toward the door, then paused to look back. "I meant to tell you that I'm going to see my uncle Robbie today. He has a doctor's appointment near here and called to ask if he could take me to lunch."

"Where are you eating?"

"The Green Eatery downtown."

"Can I come by? I want to get a read on him."

"Why?"

"Because of the things you've told me about him and your dad."

"If I say you can come by, are you going to be nice to him?"

"So nice."

She regarded him doubtfully. "Just so we're clear, I don't think Uncle Robbie knows anything about the treasure hunt."

Right. Which was why Robbie called her to set up lunch right after she started looking for clues.

"Robbie and June," she went on, "their two kids, and their grandkids are the only family I have left. They've been wonderful to me. I love them, and I trust them. I am *not* suspicious of them."

"You don't have to be. So long as one of us is suspicious of them, that'll be enough."

She rolled her eyes.

"I want to get a read on him," he repeated.

"I'll text you when Robbie and I are finishing up. You can come by and talk with him briefly."

"Afterward, let's walk over to Misty River's visitors bureau. They might be able to help you find your historic train depot."

"Absolutely."

"Good."

"*If* you're nice to my uncle," she added.

CHAPTER TEN

The interior of the Green Eatery smelled like grass and pineapple. Luke immediately spotted Finley and her uncle sitting at a metal table next to a wall the color of peas.

He approached, assessing the older man. Ed's features had been bold and memorable. Robbie's were plainer and less wrinkled. Ed had sported a full head of long white curls. For a man of eighty, Robbie also had a lot of hair. But his was gray, and he kept it short and tidy. Like Ed, Robbie had a lean frame. He'd dressed today in chinos and a striped button-down.

Clearly, Finley and her uncle had already finished eating. Their lunch plates and silverware had been removed. Only two near-empty glasses of iced tea remained.

"Luke," Finley said in welcome, "I'd like to introduce you to my uncle, Robbie Sutherland."

Robbie stood, and they shook hands.

"Nice to meet you," Luke told him.

"Likewise."

By the time they stepped apart, Finley had pulled up a chair for him.

"My brother told me all about you," Robbie said as they took their seats. "Your friendship meant a lot to him."

"It meant a lot to me, too. What was it like to grow up with Ed?"

A sad smile moved across the older man's face. "Great. Always eventful. I was lucky."

"Tell Luke the story about the time Dad talked you into plugging the neighbor's sink and turning the faucet on full blast."

In his measured way, Robbie relayed the story.

"*He can mask what he's thinking and feeling,*" Finley had said about Robbie. Luke could see the evidence of that. Robbie was self-controlled. Distinguished.

Luke had been around plenty of dangerous men and criminals, both at the chop shop and in prison. He'd become pretty good at recognizing people who fell into those categories, even when they were soft-spoken and wore button-down shirts.

He didn't recognize Robbie as dangerous or as a criminal. However, he did have the sense that Robbie might be more complex than he appeared. Most people couldn't keep a secret. Robbie seemed like the type who could take a secret to the grave.

"We'd better head out, Luke," Finley said a few minutes later.

"Certainly," Robbie replied courteously. "I'll let you two get on with your day."

Finley hugged her uncle. After exchanging good-byes, Luke held the door for Finley as they exited. On this late-January day, the bare branches of the trees stretched through thin sunlight toward bands of clouds in a light blue sky.

Their steps turned toward the visitors bureau.

"What did you think of Uncle Robbie?" Finley asked.

"He seems like a good guy."

"He is," Finley said, pulling on her coat. Her clogs thumped, but his boots hardly made a sound as they passed brick buildings almost two hundred years old. Some housed companies. Others held trendy distilleries, restaurants, shops.

Finley's hair swayed against her back as they walked. He watched the strands slide against the fabric, overwhelmed by how much he wanted to pull her into one of these recessed doorways and push his hands into that hair—

He wrenched his gaze away.

She was in front of him five days a week, yet as unavailable as if the walls of a jail separated the two of them. With his current issues and past mistakes, he wasn't even close to being worthy of her. And she was still in love with the person who *had* been worthy of her.

Her dead fiancé.

Misty River's visitors bureau was enjoying a bustling day. Of the four employees behind the granite counter, only a curvy blonde in her late thirties was currently unencumbered with tourists.

"Hi, Melanie," Finley said to her as they neared.

Because Melanie worked for the town of Misty River and Finley kept in close communication with town government on behalf of the county's animals, they often attended the same events.

"Finley!" Melanie brightened. "So nice to see you. And who's with you today?"

"This is Luke Dempsey."

If Melanie's eyes could have bounced out of her head like a cartoon character, they would have. A sighting of Luke was more prized than a Bigfoot sighting. "I'm delighted to meet you, Mr. Dempsey. I'm Melanie Carlson."

"Hi," Luke said.

If he could be counted on for anything, it was monosyllabic responses. *This is good conditioning for him*, Finley reminded herself gamely. Step four of his program!

"What can I do to help the two of you?" Melanie's focus remained firmly on Luke.

"A friend was telling me about a train depot she visited many years ago," Finley said. "She thinks that it might have been gray in color and historic. Somewhere here in North Georgia. She'd like to go back, but she can't remember the name of the town where it's located. So I told her I'd drop by and ask."

"I'm so glad you returned to Misty River, Luke," Melanie said. "I think I speak for the whole town when I say that we've missed you."

It was as if Melanie had not registered Finley's words.

"Have things changed a lot since you were here last?" Melanie asked him.

"Yes."

Melanie laughed, even though he'd said nothing funny. "I can only imagine. I'd be happy to catch you up on the developments of the last several years."

I bet you would, Finley thought darkly. She'd liked Melanie just fine in the past. But didn't at the moment.

"I'm only here to find a train depot for Finley's friend," Luke told her.

"Certainly!" Melanie whipped out a map of North Georgia historic sites and uncapped a green highlighter. "Many historic train depots are still in existence. You said your friend thought the depot was gray?"

"She wasn't sure," Finley answered. "But yes. She thinks so."

Melanie scrutinized the map. "How long ago did she visit?"

"About fifteen years ago."

"Hmm. And how far away was the depot?"

"Probably within a two-hour drive of here."

"In the mountains?"

"I think so, yes."

"Was it in use? For example, as a shop or restaurant or event venue?"

"She's pretty sure it was still in use." It seemed unlikely that her father would have left a clue at an abandoned depot. He'd have had no assurance that it would still be standing when she began the hunt.

"It's hard to know which of the depots might have been gray fifteen years ago. Many that are still in use have been repainted." Melanie's highlighter squeaked as she repeatedly marked the shiny paper. "These are the depots I can think of that fit your conditions."

"Would it be possible to see pictures of these depots?" Luke asked.

Melanie gave him a long dose of eye contact. "I'd love to show you pictures."

"Thanks," Luke said.

Melanie seemed frozen by his attractiveness. "It really is so good to have you back."

"Were you going to pull up pictures of the depots?" Finley prompted. To her own ears, she sounded jealous. She *was* jealous.

Why was she jealous?

Because she wanted Luke for herself.

What?

No. He was her employee.

"Pictures of depots?" Luke asked the woman.

"Yes. Of course." Melanie typed something into a nearby computer, then turned its monitor to show them a photo of a green depot with white trim. "This is the depot in Holly Springs."

Finley didn't recognize it.

Melanie turned back to the computer.

Luke leaned close, bringing a tantalizing whiff of clean skin and leather. "Keep your hand on your necklace," he whispered, "until you see one you recognize."

She nodded.

Melanie, in an obvious bid to please Luke, brought up photo after photo.

Finley kept her fingers casually entwined with her long necklace. No. She didn't recognize that one. Or that one. Or that one.

Melanie consulted the map again. "Could the depot have been constructed of grayish stone?"

Finley weighed the question. "Yes. Maybe."

"They have one in Stone Mountain that's under two hours from here, but it's not in North Georgia." Three more squeaks of her highlighter. "The depot in Chickamauga also comes to mind. As does this one in Ringgold. They're in the mountains, but they're more than two hours away." Again, she showed Finley a picture that didn't ring a bell. Melanie's fingers danced over the keyboard. "This is the stone depot in Chickamauga."

At last, a faint memory buried in the sludge of passing years stirred. Finley didn't clearly recall visiting this place with her dad. But the sight of it *did* cause familiarity to echo within. She dropped her hand from her necklace.

"Do you think one of these might be the depot your friend described?" Melanie asked.

"I think so, yes."

"Thanks for your help," Luke said.

Melanie beamed. "Here." She scribbled her cell number on the back of a business card and passed it to Luke. "Please feel free to contact me at any time."

Honestly. It took titanic restraint to keep Finley from rolling her eyes.

Luke steered her outdoors. The park at Misty River's center faced them. Beyond that, forested hills hemmed in the town on three sides.

"Melanie was hitting on you." She faced him.

One dark brow tilted up. "Yeah. So?"

"Do women often hit on you?"

"I don't get out much these days."

"But when you do, they hit on you?"

"I guess so."

"I really don't think it would be wise to . . . dally with women . . . here in Misty River."

A beat of silence. "Dally?" He appeared amused by her choice of words.

"Dally." She stood beside the verb. "Now might not be the best time to—to take part in casual relationships."

"You think I should take part in serious relationships?" He was being purposely obtuse.

The heat of a blush climbed her cheeks. "Someday! Just maybe not now."

"Really? Because it's been seven years."

Why had she brought up this subject? That had been rash. "All I'm saying is that you're working hard to get back on your feet, and that's the best thing to focus on at the moment."

His attention remained on her.

She jutted her chin and refused to look away. Seconds passed. He was tall and muscular with body language that said *back off* to everyone he came in contact with. Yet she knew she had nothing to fear from him. On the contrary, when he was nearby, it was as if safety encircled her.

"I agree," he said, releasing her from the stalemate. He strode down the sidewalk. "I don't want a casual or a serious relationship. But even if I did, it wouldn't be with Melanie."

She rushed to catch up with him.

"When can we travel to the depot in Chickamauga?" he asked.

She punched details into her phone. "It looks like it will take us about three hours to get there, heading due west."

"Let's drive there now."

"Absolutely not. I have appointments this afternoon." She ran a new search on her phone. "The depot is now a regional heritage and train museum. It's open ten to four, Tuesday through Saturday."

"Was it a museum back when you were there?"

"I don't remember, but that definitely sounds like the type of thing my dad would have taken me to see. He was a museum junkie."

"Do you think he left a white envelope there?"

"Probably not. It would be hard to leave an envelope at a museum in a place where I'd be able to find it but no one else would disturb it. This clue is likely an object. Something that's a part of their collection."

"If so, how do we know the object hasn't been moved or thrown away?"

"We don't. But if the clue *is* in the form of an object, I'm guessing Dad would have had the foresight to choose an object he believed wouldn't be removed."

"Can we go tomorrow?"

Tomorrow was Saturday. "I can't. I'm spending the day in Franklin with Bridget, Meadow, and Meadow's daughter."

Disapproval rumbled in his throat. "Next Saturday, then?"

"Yes." She hadn't been sure at the start if she'd like having Luke as a treasure hunt partner. It turned out that she did like it. A lot. It was good to have an ally. It was also frightening to have this particular ally.

She was inexplicably drawn to him. So much so that she'd experienced actual jealousy over him today.

It wouldn't do.

These feelings belittled what she'd had with Chase and cheapened her plan to assist in the Restoration of Luke.

He was only staying in Misty River until they solved the hunt. He'd just said he wasn't interested in a relationship. And she'd said it was best for him to concentrate on getting back on his feet. Which was true. She deeply wanted for him to reenter society wholly. To let go of his past and his guilt so that he could embrace God and life.

What was best for Luke must—and did—come before her passing fancies.

A man watched from his car as Luke and Finley walked past. At the corner, they turned right.

Smoothly, he let himself out of his vehicle and followed on foot.

CHAPTER ELEVEN

This was what he'd wanted his Saturday to look like, Luke reminded himself the next day. He was stretched out on his sofa, watching sports, feeling the way new mothers probably feel when they finally get to pass their demanding babies off to a babysitter. He planned to pick Agatha up at the last possible moment. Until then, he simply wanted to eat, nap, sit in front of the TV, and eat some more.

So why couldn't he make himself relax?

For one thing, it frustrated him that he and Finley weren't traveling to the train depot today. Ever since he'd spent eight days wondering if Ethan was alive or dead, he didn't coexist well with doubt. Little things like this—not knowing whether they'd find a clue at the depot—caused him low-level stress.

For another thing, while he was really glad to have a day off from Agatha, concerns about the puppy kept sliding into his head. There were plenty of things in the world that people should be anxious about. A puppy in the care of experienced volunteers was not one of them.

He shifted, set one foot on his coffee table, and crossed the other ankle on top.

Worry needled him.

With a growl, he picked up his phone. He'd give Trish a quick call.

"Hello?" she sang into the phone.

"It's Luke. How's Agatha doing?" He sounded like a world-class idiot to his own ears.

"Oh! Very well. She's such a little dear."

He hoped that was a lie because he was going to be angry if she behaved like "a dear" for Trish and like a demon for him.

"I've been enjoying lots of cuddles today," she added.

"Has she been eating? Because she doesn't like to eat out of a bowl. She likes for people to hold her food in their hand. Then she'll eat."

"Well, hang on a minute, and I'll go check to see how much food she's had today. If she hasn't eaten much, I'll be certain to try your technique."

"Fine. Thanks."

"I'll tell her Uncle Luke called to check on her—"

"That won't be necessary."

"Feliz Navidad!"

He ended the call at the exact moment that someone knocked on his door. The only people likely to visit him here—Ben, Natasha, Genevieve—he didn't want to talk to. So he didn't get up.

Half a minute passed. Then came another knock, followed by words. "Open up."

The young female voice didn't belong to either Natasha or Genevieve, which meant this person was probably knocking on his door by mistake.

"It's Blair," she called.

Luke rested his head against the back of the sofa and closed his eyes. As little as he wanted to see Ben, Natasha, or Genevieve, he wanted to see Blair less.

More knocking.

Her arrival was like the arrival of a speeding ticket. Bad news that couldn't be ignored.

He opened the door. Though he kept his expression neutral, shock rolled into him at the sight of her. She was much older than he'd expected. This . . . teenager . . . was Blair?

She'd dressed in military-style boots, camo pants, a long black-and-white graphic T-shirt, and a black leather jacket very much like his own. A knit hat covered most of her medium-length brown hair. "Hello, big brother."

"How did you find me?" he asked.

She raised her chin to a confrontational angle. "Mr. Coleman teaches at our school. I asked him for your address."

Ben was going to hear about this from him. "How old are you?" It came out more like an accusation than a question.

"Almost sixteen. So . . . can I come in or what?"

He answered by stepping out of the doorway. She clomped inside. "Sweet place." She moved farther in, studying the surroundings.

He followed at a distance.

She'd been a kid the last time he'd seen her. A skinny little kid with a ponytail and sparkly shoes.

He hardly knew her or her twin sister, Hailey. So, what did he expect? That they'd remained frozen in time? Still. The girl he remembered and this teenager didn't even seem like the same person. It would have been easier to believe this was a stranger rather than the girl with the sparkly shoes.

Blair and Hailey had been babies when he'd left home. During his years in Atlanta, his mom and dad had repeatedly reached out to him. They'd even shown up on his doorstep with the girls occasionally. Each time, seeing them had made him feel like dirt. The last time they'd forced a family visit the twins had probably been six.

After he'd gone to prison, his parents had insisted on coming to see him there, too. He'd told them that interacting with them was hard for him, but if they had to come for reasons of their own, they could. However, he'd asked them not to bring Blair and Hailey to the penitentiary. It had been bad enough for his parents to see him in a jumpsuit. There was no way he wanted young girls to see him that way, to be brought into that environment. His parents had honored his request.

Since he'd come back to Misty River, he'd talked to his parents on the phone a couple of times, and they'd come by here once. They frequently invited him to their house.

He hadn't taken them up on that.

Estrangement was easier and less painful for everyone. He wished—had wished for a long time now—that they'd let that happen.

The central truth of his life was that he'd let himself down. But he'd also let his parents down. Horribly. He knew it. They knew it. Every time he spoke with them, he was confronted by all his mistakes.

Blair pointed to the puppy pen. "Do you have a dog?"

"No. I'm just fostering one at night for a couple of days."

"Because of your job at Furry Tails?"

"Yeah."

"It seems like a strange job for a guy like you. Why are you working there?"

"I just am." If she was almost sixteen, how come she looked like she was twenty-one?

She finished her surveillance of his apartment and turned to him. "Do you want to do some heartwarming brother-sister activities? We could bake cookies," she suggested with sarcastic sweetness, "or play Chutes and Ladders."

"No."

She stuck her hands in her jacket pockets. "You know, people tell me that we look alike, but I don't see it."

He *did* see the resemblance, and it was unsettling. She was tall, somewhere around five foot nine. Slender and strong, she had a long nose, a sharp jaw. They had the same shade of brown hair, and her eyes were hazel, like his.

"Why'd you come here?" he asked.

"I'm about to get my driver's license. A year ago, Dad told me he'd match the amount I saved for a car. So I've been working at Ingles."

Their dad had offered Luke the same deal when he'd been that age.

"A month ago," she said, "we bought a blue 1970 Pontiac Firebird. He's been trying to help me fix it up, but we've done all we can and it's still not running. I don't have any money left to pay a mechanic, so I need you to help me get it going."

"Why would I want to do that?"

"Because you haven't exactly been a great older brother. You owe me."

"I don't owe you. I did you a favor. I gave you what was better, in your case, than an older brother."

"What's that?"

"No brother at all. If anyone owes anyone here, you owe me."

She swore, kicking his floor with her toe.

"No cussing in front of me," he said.

"What? You don't expect me to believe, do you, that you're as lame and uptight as Mom and Dad?"

The fact that she'd just insulted their parents shocked him more than the cussing. "Our parents are not lame." He struggled for patience. "If you haven't recognized that you won the parent lottery, you're a fool."

"They're lame."

She was a fool. Blair hadn't survived an earthquake. She hadn't had to live through the death of her sibling because she hadn't been born when Ethan died. Blair was a very fortunate girl, raised in a secure home by loving parents.

Yet, she'd come here, trying to impress him with her toughness. She'd probably have thrown back a shot or smoked a cigarette in front of him if either of those options had been available.

In addition to looking like him, she also reminded him of someone he hadn't liked at all in high school.

Himself.

"I think you do owe me," she said. "So. Are you going to help me with the Firebird?"

"No."

"*Shocker*. Big surprise."

"How did you get here?"

"What does it matter?"

"*How did you get here?*"

"Mom dropped me off at a store a few blocks away while she's running errands. She doesn't know that I came to see you."

"You're going to meet back up with her for a ride home?"

"Maybe. Maybe I'll run away. Or maybe I'll hitchhike home. I've heard that's safe."

Blair had been back in his life for ten minutes, and she was already giving him a migraine. He went to his bedroom and pulled on boots. It was cold enough for a jacket, but forget it. He wasn't going to walk around town near her wearing a jacket that matched hers—

Actually, it was *her* jacket that matched his. He'd had his jacket almost as long as she'd been alive.

Without a word, he walked past her to the front door and held it open.

She faked excitement. "Are you taking me to get ice cream cones?"

He didn't like her attitude. At all. "I don't trust you, so I'm going to keep an eye on you until you meet back up with Mom."

"Can we hold hands?"

"I'm not even going to walk beside you. I'm going to follow from several yards away. You won't even know I'm there."

"So . . . pretty much like my whole life so far?" She stomped down the staircase.

Late the following night, Luke had just exited the shower and was drying off when he saw an alert on his phone.

His forehead knit as he wrapped the towel around his waist and stared at the message. The alert informed him that someone had been trying to force a password through his remote access software in order to gain control over his computers. They'd input the wrong information too many times and been locked out.

A bead of water ran down the skin between his shoulder blades.

The alert provided one other piece of information. The hacker's IP address.

Moving quickly, he pulled on pajama pants and a hoodie. He strode to the kitchen table and his laptop. Ignoring Agatha's attempts to steal his attention, he went to work, testing to see if he could use the IP address to learn the identity of the person who'd attempted to hack his system.

Hold up," Finley said to him the next morning when he told her about the attempted breach. She sat behind her desk, beautiful in a loose white shirt and about fifteen bracelets.

He stood facing her.

"I speak Animal," she said, "but I don't speak Computer. What's remote access software?"

"It's a plug-in that enables me to use my phone or secondary computer to check information or run programs on my main computer." Luke nudged his chin in the direction of the workroom. "The one here."

"If they wanted information off this computer, why wouldn't they try to hack into this one directly?"

"With all the firewalls and security these days, it's hard to do that. So they try to get in through remote access software."

"But it turned out that they couldn't get in that way, either."

"Correct."

"Because, like my dad believed, you're a tech genius."

He let that go. "I chased down the hacker's IP address, but they were using a virtual private network. In short, they covered their tracks. I can't use that IP address to figure out who they are."

"So we didn't learn much."

"We learned one very important thing. We learned that your dad's worries about the treasure hunt were valid."

"You believe this proves that someone else is after the treasure?"

"I do."

"But the fact that a hacker tried to snoop inside your computer could be completely disconnected from the hunt."

"I don't think so. No one's tried to do that since I set up the computers weeks ago. Now, right after we start finding clues, they try?"

"The timing could be a coincidence."

"It's not. On my desktop computer, I only store information about this non-profit that's of no value to anyone except the employees here. A person would only go to the trouble of hacking into that computer if they thought I'd saved treasure hunt information there."

She picked up a pen and tapped it thoughtfully against the head of her alabaster pug.

"Your dad brought me into this hunt," he said, "because he suspected at least one other person might get involved. It's now clear that at least one other person *is* involved."

"That's . . . sobering."

Having no adversary in this hunt would have been the best scenario. But since an adversary *did* exist, this was the second-best scenario. At least now, he had proof. His concerns—Ed's concerns—were justified. "Somebody else is on the hunt for the treasure."

"Should we change anything we're doing?"

"We haven't been storing information about the hunt on our computers," he said, "and this confirms that we definitely can't do that going forward. Just to be safe, we both also need to clear our search history every time we look up anything on the Internet that's connected to the hunt."

She nodded.

"I'm going to beef up security around here," he said. The Center's security sucked. The doors leading from the foyer to the rest of the building and from the building to the play yard had key codes. However, the employees and volunteers were too lazy to use them so they'd been deactivated. He'd get them back online. "Make sure you turn your house alarm on. Stay on the lookout for anything unusual. Be aware of the people in your surroundings in case the same face keeps popping up. When you're driving, make sure no one's following."

"Done."

"Most of all, take Agatha off my hands because she makes it hard for me to concentrate."

"I'll be finalizing her adoption soon," she said earnestly. "It's just taking me a bit longer than expected to get the paperwork through."

"Tomorrow I'll have had her a week."

"Agatha's adoption is a high priority of mine, Luke."

"Yeah? Then how come your puppy got adopted before mine?"

"Because Oscar's family requested a male."

"Finley, I'm about to take Agatha to the nearest freeway and throw a dog treat in front of an oncoming car."

"If you're using hyperbole, you really must be desperate." She smiled. "She'll be adopted shortly."

He left her office and settled behind his computer console. After selecting and editing some of the photos that volunteers had taken over the weekend, he scheduled them to go up on the different social media sites. Writing captions was the worst. *Ronald enjoying the sunny weather! Wanda is looking forward to seeing you the next time you visit Furry Tails. Beverly wishes you a very happy Monday.*

The captions sounded maniacally happy to him, as if a clown with a painted-on smile and a white flower in his hat had written them. Even so, Finley kept encouraging him to make them even *more* cheery.

If she wanted them cheerier than this, she was going to have to hire the good witch from *The Wizard of Oz* to write them.

That afternoon, Luke came to a stop in the open doorway of the room housing the Center's after-school program.

Ben stood in front of a whiteboard, talking with enthusiasm about how clouds store water. The kids watched with interest.

Akira, the woman who ran the program, was so busy staring at Ben she hadn't noticed Luke's appearance.

In the middle of a sentence, Ben caught sight of him, paused to nod at Luke, then finished his thought. "Any questions?" he asked the kids.

He called on a pale-haired girl with a braid.

"Rain, snow, sleet, and hail are called precipitation," she said. Not a question.

"That's right," Ben replied. "Good."

"Oooh!" a redheaded boy said. "Isn't hail a bad word?"

"No," Akira assured him. "Hail—H-A-I-L—is a perfectly good scientific word. Who knows what hail is?"

"It's like round ice cubes," another boy answered. "We had hail at our house last year, and I caught every single one in my baseball cap before it hit the ground in my backyard."

"Impressive," Ben said. "Please prepare the ingredients for our storm-in-a-cup experiment. I'll be right back." Ben stepped into the hall with Luke. "Hey. Nice to see you."

"Hey."

"How's Agatha?"

"Terrible."

Ben laughed. "Everything good with you?"

"Blair came by my apartment on Saturday. She said you told her where I live."

"Yeah."

"Do I seem like someone who has the gift of hospitality?"

"No."

"Visitors put me in a bad mood. Just so we're clear, I don't want anyone else to know where I live. It's bad enough having to deal with those who already know. I just want to be left alone."

"Got it." Apology entered Ben's friendly expression. "Sorry."

Luke ran a hand through his hair and saw that several of the kids were peering at them. He moved out of the doorway. Ben followed.

"Just how much of a rebel without a cause is Blair?" Luke asked.

"She's not as wheels-off as you were at that age, but she's challenging. Reckless." Ben massaged one of his knuckles. "She doesn't respect the boundaries your parents have put down to try to keep her safe. She's got a lot of attitude."

"I noticed."

"I'm worried about her, and your parents are worried about her, too."

It sounded like history was repeating itself. His mom and dad had done everything possible to keep him out of trouble during his high school years. But there's only so much adults can do to restrain a teenager who's set on destruction.

After Ethan was born, his parents had attempted to have one more child. They'd suffered a miscarriage, followed by infertility. No luck having a third child, so they'd made peace with the fact that God meant for them to be a family of four. Then Ethan died, and they'd all imploded.

His parents had held tight to each other and God. They'd tried to hold tight to him, too. But Luke had made that impossible.

Three years later, when his mom was forty-one, she and Dad had been shocked to discover they were expecting a baby. Then shocked again to discover the pregnancy would result in twins.

Luke had been glad for them. He'd also been glad for himself, because the girls' arrival made it easier for him to leave. His parents could have a family of four again—with two girls this time instead of two boys. He'd been sure they'd have nothing but happy, carefree parenting days in front of them. They'd been through a lot. They deserved happy, carefree parenting days.

Only Blair wasn't acting according to plan.

"And Hailey?" Luke asked. "How's she?"

"She's a dream. Very sweet and studious. Have you seen her lately?"

"No. Why?"

"Just . . ." Ben shrugged. "You'll know when you see her."

"What's Blair into?"

"So far, I think it's stuff like vaping, smoking, drinking at parties. She doesn't have a boyfriend that I know of, but sometimes kids hide that."

Luke didn't want to remember the things he'd been doing at Blair's age. "Can you get me the name and number of a high school kid who can tell me what's going on with her?"

Ben thought for a second. "Sebastian's girlfriend is named Leah. She's a friend of mine and a teacher at the school, too. Her younger brother, Dylan, is a senior. He and Blair aren't in the same friend group, but I'm positive he knows who she is. No doubt they've hung out at some of the same parties."

"Do you think Dylan would help me?"

"Probably. He's a good kid, and he might be willing to fill you in because of your connection to Sebastian. Not to mention, his sister is all about keeping kids safe. I'll talk to Leah about it. If she's cool with this plan, I'll pass Dylan's number along to you."

"Is Agatha's family arriving today, or am I going to have to take her to a freeway?" Luke asked Finley the following morning in her office. The little dog lay on his forearm like a woman on a spa massage table.

"Good morning." Finley looked genuinely happy to see him.

She'd piled her black hair on top of her head. The style highlighted the back of her long graceful neck and the hinge of her jaw. It made him want to pull on a strand so he could watch the heavy mass fall.

"I'm very pleased to inform you," she said, "that the Gomez family will arrive to collect her in an hour and a half."

"I don't believe you."

"Why?"

"Because it's too good to be true."

I insist that you come out and meet them," Finley said to him once Agatha's owners arrived.

"You don't need me there. You can give them instructions. You're the expert."

"And you're the one who fostered her. The employees here who foster a puppy are always a part of Gotcha Day."

He sat at his desk, staring at his monitor. He hadn't looked directly at her, but he knew she'd placed her hands on her hips.

"Gotcha Day?" he asked.

"That's what we call it around here. It's the day when the new owner says, 'Gotcha!' to their fabulous little fur baby."

"I hate the term *Gotcha Day*. And I hate the term *fur baby*."

"You're coming out to meet them. It's a rule."

He swiveled his chair to frown up at her. "I'd like to see where it's written that the schmuck who fosters a puppy has to be there to hand the puppy over."

"It's a rule if I say it's a rule! You don't want me to tell the family to go away and come back another time, do you? They're in the foyer waiting." She reached down and grabbed his hand, which sent a shock of heat up to his shoulder. "Come on. You are so stubborn. Come on!"

Grumbling, he stood.

Kat was positioned at the central worktable, sorting the papers she'd just printed. "Luke is throwing all of my excellent qualities as an employee into focus. I feel that I deserve an Employee of the Year plaque."

Quick as a flash, Finley dashed behind him. Placing her palms on the middle of his back, she pushed him toward the hallway. As if she could physically force him to go anywhere.

"That's not necessary," he told her. "I'm going." How was he supposed to maintain control around her if she kept putting her hands on him?

When they reached the yard, Agatha raced over, her stupid ears flapping. He lifted her leash from the hook and clipped it to her collar. Together, he and Finley walked toward the foyer.

"You're going to give the family her supplies, right?" he asked.

"Oh yes. We provide every adoptive family with a bag full of the dog's familiar items, plus food, treats, and toys."

"Did you include her stuffed lamb? She likes her lamb."

"I included her lamb."

As soon as Agatha entered the foyer, the Gomez family of four let out gasps of adoration and dropped to their knees to greet her.

The son looked to be around twelve, the daughter a few years younger. Their dark-haired mother explained that she'd kept the kids home from school this morning because adopting a dog was such a big moment for all of them. She said that their fifteen-year-old Pomeranian had died nine months ago. They'd been mourning his loss and struggling to live in a house that suddenly felt too empty and too quiet. This was the first time the kids would have the chance to raise a puppy.

Luke nodded and put on what he hoped read as a pleasant expression.

Finley went into raptures with the Gomezes, clearly delighting in her matchmaking skills. "Luke is the one who's been fostering Agatha."

"It looks like you did a great job," the dad said. "She seems happy and healthy."

She's awful, and she ruined my life.

"You must have had so much fun with her," the daughter said.

If you consider cleaning dog accidents to be fun.

Finley answered the family's questions and gave them encouragement and suggestions. The parents signed the paperwork. As they gathered up Agatha's gear in preparation to leave, the puppy positioned herself between Luke's legs. She eyed the others suspiciously, as if he were her protector and they were her abductors.

When the mom came forward to pick Agatha up, the puppy placed her front feet as high on his pants leg as she could reach, which was only about five inches. Her eyes said, *Save me. I don't want to go anywhere with these strangers.* Which proved how unintuitive Agatha was. She didn't have enough sense to recognize the gravy train that had just pulled to a stop in front of her.

He leaned over and placed her front feet on the ground. Agatha plopped down and rested her chin on his boot.

"Aw," the girl said. "She loves you."

"She definitely does," Finley agreed. "She's such a gifted little dog. I think you'll find that she has the capacity to do a lot of things well—including forming bonds and giving affection. With your care and training, she'll become a treasured member of your family."

Spare him. He didn't like this kind of sentimentality. If he'd just met Finley, he would've concluded that she was faking it, laying it on thick. But she wasn't. Her excitement was genuine. She spent hours ensuring that the adoptions overseen by the Center resulted in what she'd classify as "happily-ever-afters."

Luke lifted Agatha, feeling her slight weight in his hand for the last time. He handed her to the girl.

"Thank you for taking care of her." She cuddled the puppy against her chest.

"You're welcome."

"She's so cute!" she cooed.

If your taste runs to tiny devils. "Enjoy," Luke said, when what he wanted to say was, *I'm very sorry for you all.*

The Gomezes gave another round of gratitude and then goodbyes. Luke knew with certainty that Finley had succeeded at finding Agatha her ideal family. She would be much, much better off with the Gomezes.

The girl turned, stealing the puppy from view as the family ushered themselves outdoors.

What he mostly felt was relief. But a surprising amount of sorrow pierced him, too. It had been what felt like a lifetime since he'd taken care of anyone the way he'd taken care of Agatha.

He was glad to see the puppy go.

But also, a little bit sorry to see her go.

He could feel Finley's attention on him. He looked over at her, and the force of their eye contact clanged in his gut.

He wasn't a fan of messy emotions. He didn't like experiencing grief. Or tenderness for Finley. Or protectiveness of Finley. Or guilt. In no way did he want to set himself up for pain.

He liked simplicity. In the years since he'd left home, he'd been happiest when he'd done his job and spent the rest of his hours alone, free from being taken hostage by his feelings.

"Are you okay?" Finley asked.

"I'm better than I've been since the day that you gave me that high-maintenance rodent."

"But also slightly sad?"

"Nah."

"Hmm," she said knowingly. "It's always bittersweet to say good-bye. I'm choosing to focus on how happy that family will be with Agatha."

"Or not."

She laughed. "Luke. Have a little faith."

CHAPTER TWELVE

Luke and Finley arrived at the Chickamauga train depot at eleven a.m. on Saturday and paid the two-dollar-per-person entrance price.

One look around the Walker County Regional Heritage Train Museum housed inside the depot, and Luke's spirits sank. It was larger than he'd expected and packed with stuff. They were going to be here awhile. "Do you remember this place?"

"Now that I'm here, yes. I remember it in a very hazy type of way." She leaned over the first glass case. Today, she had on a long patterned sweater that opened down the middle with a simple T-shirt and jeans that fit her long legs perfectly—

"I can feel you there," she said. "Your nearness is making it hard for me to concentrate."

"Because?"

"Because waves of impatience are rolling off you. It's menacing."

"What do you want me to do about it?"

"I'll start here. How about you start there?" She pointed to the opposite wall. "And we'll both work clockwise?"

"Fine."

"I need to think on every detail of every item so that I don't miss what my dad intended as a clue."

He crossed the space and began to skim the information in the cases and on wall displays. He glanced at Finley. Fingers interlaced behind her back, she observed a painting.

Ten minutes passed. He wasn't really a museum kind of guy.

Forty minutes passed. What if she didn't recognize the clue? This time, Ed Sutherland wasn't around to give out hints.

An hour and a half passed. What if, in the past eight years, the museum had gotten rid of the object Ed intended for Finley to find?

Two hours passed. What if they'd chosen the wrong depot? What if numerous stone depots existed in this region of Georgia that Melanie at the visitors bureau hadn't known about?

He didn't want to waste their three-hour drive this morning, the time they were spending here, and the three-hour drive home—

"I found it," Finley whispered near his shoulder.

"Thank goodness."

She led him to a piece of sheet music. "'Pat Works on the Railroad' is an old song that my dad used to play on his guitar. When I was little, we sang it together often. This is the clue."

Sheet music didn't seem like much. "You sure?"

"Quite sure."

He wanted to believe that this *was* the clue. But he also needed to think straight because, of the two of them, he was the sensible one. The one who didn't meditate or wear felt hats indoors or ride bikes attached to big dogs. "If this is the clue, where is it leading you next?"

"Dad once gave me a piece of art with the chorus of this song written in calligraphy. It's framed and hanging in the office at my house."

"The next clue is at your house?"

"If I know my dad—and I do—then yes. This has his fingerprints all over it."

"Okay, but while we're here, you should probably continue looking at the remaining items."

"Why?"

"Because what if there's more than one item here with a connection to your dad? Your dad was a railroad guy, and this is a railroad museum."

She shook her head, a grin transforming her face. "No need. I'm certain this is what he wanted me to find. If you knew how many times we'd sung this song together, you'd understand."

"But—"

She walked toward the exit doors.

On the drive back to Misty River, Finley played several renditions of "Pat Works on the Railroad" for him. The song was old-timey, catchy, and Irish. Something about a cravat and a straw hat. Britches and whiskey. Lots of "working on the railway."

Finley hummed along the first few times, then started singing. She wasn't a trained singer, but she wasn't bad, either. Her voice was low and sweet and *why had he been forced into such close proximity with her*?

Finley looked like a cross between a Disney princess and an extra in a movie about Woodstock, but she was deceptively strong. A miracle worker with dogs. Someone who refused to quit. It was as if light loved her. . . . It seemed to gather within her so that she glowed.

Surely, Ed couldn't have imagined that Luke had enough self-control to withstand this many hours with Finley. Luke's defenses were high. But not high enough.

"Sing with me!" she encouraged.

"Not on your life."

They reached her cabin in the bronze hours of late afternoon. She waited for him on her front step before unlocking the door. Finley's pug greeted her with excitement. Inside her office, the hedgehog woke and scurried over to them inside its cage. If hedgehogs could smile, hers was smiling.

"This is it." She stopped before the piece of art hanging on the wall to the side of her desk. Her dad had done a good job of pegging her style. Colorful lettering in a modern font covered the poster-sized rectangle. Delicately, she lifted the artwork from its hook and turned it around. Nothing out of the ordinary about the back of the piece. No envelope taped to the smooth foam board.

Discouraging.

"Don't be discouraged," she said, reading his mind. After placing the art facedown on her desk, she used a pair of scissors to pry up the metal tabs holding the backing in place. When she'd freed three sides, she slowly tilted up the board . . . and revealed a white envelope with *For Finley* written across the front.

Her breath caught. "Good Lord above." With a half-laugh, half-squeal, she flung her arms around him.

Luke froze.

Need rose inside him with the suddenness and force of a snake preparing to strike. And not just physical need. Worse was the overwhelming need for connection. For affection. For forgiveness.

Keeping her arms around him, she looked at him with an expression that said, *Be happy with me, Luke. We found the clue.*

She had to let him go.

He didn't want her to let him go.

"I nailed the clue inside the depot," she said, "and now I give you permission to admit that I'm a skilled treasure hunter. . . ." The sentence slowed as her focus dropped to his lips. Awareness thickened the air. "And that . . . you were smart to . . . trust me on this." By the end, her words were little more than breath.

Time spun out. He held himself totally still.

She went up on her tiptoes and gently pressed her mouth to his.

A rushing vacuum sound filled his ears. Sensations—her warmth, her curves, her scent, her softness—poured in. Her hands slid up and came to rest on the back of his neck.

He felt every detail of every single thing, and glaciers fell within him.

She leaned back.

Don't pull away.

She didn't. She studied him from just a few inches of distance.

His heart drummed, loyal and fast.

"That was spontaneous," she said quietly. "I followed an impulse and didn't . . . necessarily think that through fully. I'm sorry if—"

Luke crushed his mouth to hers. His fingers delved into her hair, registering its silky texture. The rest of the world vanished.

This was the best thing he'd experienced in years. Ever?

Maybe kissing had never been this good before because he'd never kissed Finley before. Never kissed anyone he liked as much as he liked her. Never resisted temptation as long as he'd resisted it with her.

Alarms were blaring inside of him, but he didn't care. He walked backward with her in his arms until his hips came up against a cage. But when he felt a nose nudge the small of his back, he walked her forward until she bumped her desk chair, which clattered and spun.

She gave a huff of laughter and resumed kissing him. Distantly, he heard the small feminine sound of pleasure she made in her throat.

The kiss increased in urgency. It still wasn't enough. He wanted more. Closer. She matched him for a time, but eventually put a gap of space between them.

He stared at her, blood pounding hot against his temples.

"So." She was slightly winded. "That was . . . amazing."

His hands were still in her hair.

"I'm sure it would be best," she confessed, "if I could think clearly right now and say something that makes sense. But my head isn't clear. Yours?"

"No."

"Come outside with me."

Reluctantly, he released her. She picked up the envelope and led him through the living room, across her back deck, and to the river.

His body was raging, his thoughts chaos.

She'd positioned outdoor wooden furniture to one side of her property, beneath the shade of an oak. Finley chose a chair facing the water. She gestured for him to take a seat. Instead, he continued to stand, arms crossed.

"You don't want to sit?" she asked.

"No."

She laid the envelope in her lap and stacked her palms on top of it. "This spot always calms me."

He watched her. She watched the river.

It had been too dark to see the river when he'd come for dinner. Now he dimly registered that it was green-blue, fast-moving, glittering in the sunlight.

Her pug ran around on the cold brown winter grass, chasing a squirrel.

What had he allowed to happen? He'd let emotion overrule caution—something he never did. And now she was going to want to process what had happened verbally.

Verbal processing was not his thing. His thing would've been to leave and work through this on his own. But that would be disrespectful, and he'd never disrespect her.

"It was probably very bad form," she said, "to spring a kiss on you."

She hadn't asked a question, so he gave no answer.

"You work for my non-profit. It might have been more politically correct to ask you to sign a waiver before kissing you."

"I don't care about political correctness."

"Please know that I'd never want you to feel obligated to reciprocate because you work at—"

"Did any reaction of mine make you think I felt obligated?"

"I . . ." She shrugged.

"I kissed you because I wanted to. Don't take the blame for that."

She groaned, then whispered, "I'm rusty at this." Her fingers swept her bangs to the side a few times, then smoothed her hair behind her ears in a gesture that told him she wished she could smooth out the complications of this situation as easily. Finally, she stilled and met his eyes. "I haven't kissed anyone in a very long time. Not since Chase. I thought Chase would be the last person I ever kissed."

"You're still in love with him." He hadn't planned to say that. Or even to care about that.

"I'll always love him. You'd have loved him, too, if you could have met him."

No. He wouldn't have.

She slid the ring on her middle finger up and down, up and down. He was getting better at reading her. She fiddled with her rings when trying to settle herself and pulled on her ear when thinking.

He didn't doubt that she'd enjoyed the kiss while it was happening. She'd responded with passion. But he also didn't doubt that she was now second-guessing it.

"You're feeling guilty because you failed at your role of nun," Luke concluded.

"I'm not a nun. But I *do* feel like I failed at my decision to abstain."

"Was Chase so selfish that he'd have wanted you to make your life a shrine to him?"

"No." She looked offended on Chase's behalf. "He was the most unselfish man in the world. My decision wasn't about Chase's preferences. It was about what God led me to do."

"Your fiancé died. Just because that happened, God doesn't expect for you never to kiss another man for as long as you live."

"I really thought He did."

"Maybe for a while. But not forever. You've held on to this decision for five years. Not for God. Not for Chase. Because it keeps you safe." He glanced at the river, then back to her. "Staying committed to Chase is easy. He'll always remain perfect in your memory, and he'll never let you down. The relationship you didn't have with him can stay on its pedestal."

She sighed.

"It's better not to love anyone new than have them taken from you. Right?"

"I don't know. All of a sudden I'm confused about my motivations . . . about what God's leading me to do."

"People move on after loss, Finley."

"Have you moved on from your loss?" She spoke the question compassionately, yet it found its mark accurately. She was calling him out for being a hypocrite.

"We're talking about you," he answered. "And I firmly believe that you can move on."

Her gaze traveled down to his boots and back up again. "I firmly believe you can, too."

He listened to the sound of cold water rushing past stones.

"I need to sort some things out," she said after a time. "But if you're right and God is giving me the green light to start dating again . . . Would you be interested in dating me?"

Her words kicked him in the stomach with shock. He'd been certain she'd been building up to an explanation of why they couldn't repeat the kiss. "Dating? What? No. The kiss was just . . . one of those things that happens between people sometimes. More wouldn't be a good idea."

"Why?"

"You really need for me to spell it out?"

"Yes."

"When you play with physical attraction as strong as this, you play with fire—"

"We did a good job of holding things in check."

"I'm only here to fulfill a promise to your dad."

"You can still fulfill your promise."

"And then I'm leaving."

"With my blessing."

"I'm not good enough for you."

"I'm not asking you to become an Eagle Scout."

"I can't afford to get involved."

"We don't have to become"—she made air quotes—"involved. If it turns out that I'm going to start dating again, then I'd like to give us the chance to . . . experiment with what's going on between us. That's all."

He glared, fighting to understand.

And then he did understand. Chase was a saint. He wasn't. "The fact that you could never take me seriously means that you can lower your guard and experiment with me. Is that it?"

"No." She scrunched her nose. "Are you angry?"

"I'm not angry." But he was. "I just don't want to be the lab rat in your experiment."

"It wouldn't be like that."

"My answer's no." The idea of her loving Chase while messing around with him made him crazy. "I need to head out. Are you going to open that?" He indicated the envelope.

"I'd like to talk about us more."

"No." He'd dissected this as much as he could stand.

She gave him several long seconds to change his mind. He didn't.

Her body language resigned, she ripped open the envelope and slid out the card. She read it, then slanted it toward him.

He stepped forward.

Ed had written down a number. Nothing else.

306.8752

"What does that mean?" Luke asked.

"I have no idea."

While he looked at the number, his memory kept pulling him back to their kiss. "So the treasure hunt's done for the day."

"I'm afraid so. It's done until we figure this out."

He was already walking toward his truck. "If you think of something, text or call me. Don't search for the next clue without me."

"Luke?"

He paused.

"I like having you as my treasure hunt partner. You can trust me never to take off in search of the next clue without you."

He turned his back on her and continued through the house. For the most part, he did trust her not to search for clues without him. However, he couldn't trust her with more. He couldn't trust her with himself.

Forty minutes later, Finley's friends convened at Bridget's house for an emergency meeting. Topic: Finley and Luke's kiss.

Actually, Luke was the one who'd called it a *kiss*. It hadn't been one kiss. It had been plural. Many kisses, which had added up to one explosive experience. It was astonishing and scary to realize that she was still capable of responding to kisses so powerfully.

The three of them sat on the plush living room rug, Bridget's coffee table between them.

Finley finished explaining what had transpired. "Today's kisses were worthy of banners and marching bands and twenty-one-gun salutes."

"Let's just hope," Meadow muttered, "Luke doesn't make you want to take one of those twenty-one guns and shoot him with it in a few months."

"Don't mind her." Bridget rested her chin on her hand, smiling dreamily. "I'm swooning."

"Just because you shared some fabulous kisses doesn't mean you should revoke your decision to stay single," Meadow pointed out.

"True," Finley agreed. "It's not so much the fabulousness of the kisses that's making me doubt my choice. It's more that the conviction that I once had about my singleness is draining away. I no longer have the sense of certainty and rightness I once had about it."

"You know," Bridget said, "it's understandable that you were led to draw back from dating after Chase's death. What happened to him was just so sudden and so . . . completely devastating."

One day, she'd been part of a stable, wonderful relationship. Cherished. Confident that her wedding to Chase would happen soon and that she'd spend the rest of her life married to him. He was the only man she'd love, the only man she'd sleep with, and that's how it was going to be. The next day, he'd died.

Bridget pushed the mug of tea she'd made for Finley closer.

Finley tasted it, registering the tang of ginger. "Chase's death was incredibly hard to accept. It took me ages to get used to the idea that he was gone. That I wouldn't become his wife. That my future wouldn't look anything like I'd envisioned."

He'd died just three months before their wedding date. By that point, most of the plans for their big day had already been in place. Her wedding dress still hung in the back of her closet, where she'd placed it after a successful day of shopping at bridal boutiques in Atlanta.

Meadow and Bridget had been with her that day, as had Aunt June, her cousin Leslie, and Leslie's daughter. They'd burst into applause when they'd seen her in the gown she'd eventually selected.

In fact, choosing that dress was just one in a long line of perfect moments that defined her love story with Chase. They'd met when she'd entered the animal shelter where she'd volunteered during her college years and seen him feeding a kitten milk through an eyedropper.

He'd told her he loved her for the first time after a day at the beach. They'd been sandy and happy and lying on a blanket under an umbrella, Atlantic Ocean waves crashing in the distance. "*I love you, Finley,*" he'd said, looking deeply into her eyes. And her heart had soared. Unreservedly she'd said, "*I love you, too*."

He'd proposed by bringing her to a rooftop at night. They'd stepped inside a line of flowers and flickering votives he'd placed on the floor in the shape of a heart. He'd played a song for her, then explained how much he loved her and why. Then he'd asked if she'd marry him. She'd cried with joy.

The ring had been perfect. The prayer they'd prayed together afterward had been perfect.

Every aspect of their relationship had felt destined and star-crossed until the story's end, when he'd lost control of his Jeep and shattered his body.

In the days following Chase's funeral, Meadow and Bridget had swooped in and canceled Finley's wedding venue, caterer, florist, photographer, and the rest.

"The path you walked changed you," Bridget said soothingly.

"It toughened you," Meadow said.

"Yes and yes." It had matured her. "It took a long time to envision my future a different way."

"And now it's difficult to consider envisioning it differently yet again?" Bridget asked.

Finley nodded.

"Sometimes," Bridget said thoughtfully, "the Lord can place a temporary call on our lives. Not every calling is forever."

"I thought I was supposed to spend my life as an overseas missionary," Meadow said. "But then I served abroad for that summer in college. Best thing I ever did. I think He called me to that summer trip in order to show me that my actual mission wasn't on the other side of the world. My mission is the family farm."

"When Juilliard turned me down," Bridget told Finley, "I was certain that meant I was never supposed to play the clarinet again. I was so disillusioned. So sick of it and burned out on it that I quit for six years. Then the worship director at church asked me to play, remember?"

Finley and Meadow nodded. They'd been there to support her the Sunday she'd joined the church orchestra.

"It turned out that it really *was* important for me to stop playing," Bridget continued, "but only for a season. All along, God intended for me to play in church. There's none of the stress or pressure or performance anxiety. I love the clarinet more now than ever before."

"I'm wondering if I'm experiencing a similar change in plan," Finley said. What if God was ready for her to open the door to relationships, but she wasn't willing to risk it because she was hiding behind an expired plan for her life?

Or what if she was telling herself God was ready for her to open the door to relationships only in order to validate her own newfound desires? "Gah." Finley rubbed the back of her neck. "Luke thinks I haven't been dating anyone because I'm scared."

"And?" Meadow asked. "Are you scared?"

"I didn't think so at first. But maybe? I mean, I barely made it through the loss of my last relationship. It's been five years, and now I've met someone I want to date, but he's made it clear he's not emotionally available."

"Do not fall for emotionally unavailable men," Meadow said in a serious tone.

"I know. So if I put myself back on the market, it would be to date other people. And that's scary."

"I find the dating world incredibly scary," Bridget admitted.

"Dating is not for me," Meadow announced grandly, as if this was news to any of them. "That said, fear should never be what holds any of the three of us back from something. If that's the only thing left that's stopping you from dating, Finley, you need to kick it out of your way."

Luke had kissed her with raw need. The hands that had supported the back of her head had been fervent and reverent. For the first time, he'd been unguarded with her.

Afterward, she'd thought he might be open to dating her. But no. In floating the proposition of dating, she'd somehow hurt him. Which she would make right.

As far as she knew, Luke hadn't had a close relationship with any woman since his brother died. But honestly, how much did she really know about his years in Atlanta? Almost nothing. Her information about his Misty River high school years was suspect, too, because it was founded on gossip. Maybe he'd had some deep relationships. Maybe, like her, he'd loved and lost.

Before the earthquake, everyone said he'd been friendly, open, self-assured. A straightforward boy so courageous that he'd pulled other kids to safety when the ground of El Salvador started to shake.

Following that event, he'd become something much more complex—a man full of both virtues and vices. Aloof and intense. Disdainful of affection and clearly in need of affection.

She and Luke had experienced tragedy.

Tragedy left scars.

She was the last person on earth who'd criticize the way someone else's scars had formed.

CHAPTER THIRTEEN

Late that night, when Finley couldn't sleep, she clicked on her bedside light and pulled her laptop onto the covers. She ran a few searches until she located a picture of Luke's brother, Ethan, in an old news article. He had dark blond hair, freckles, a contagious smile. He'd been a cute kid. A normal, happy child. Unbearably, unfairly young.

When Ethan had gone on that mission trip, the vast majority of his years *should* have been ahead of him. High school, college, love, travel, career, old age—all of it. So many of the things life offered, he hadn't tasted.

Tears collected in her eyes as she studied Ethan's face. Tears for him. Tears for Luke.

Luke had only been fourteen when Ethan died. Several times since he'd come to work at Furry Tails, she'd tried to imagine the heart of a fourteen-year-old who believed himself responsible for his brother's death. How had he gone on after that? How had he found a way to carry the weight?

Luke had made mistakes, but the fact that he'd survived at all was the unsung miracle of the Miracle Five.

Her friendship with him would continue. She'd pray, asking God to show her the role He had for her to play in Luke's life and asking whether the time had come to put herself back on the dating market.

If it made her sad to think that she'd never again kiss Luke—which it did—then she needed to get over herself.

For one thing, she'd had her one great love. Which was more than many people received.

For another thing, Luke was leaving soon. Even though she'd slightly elongated the amount of time between Agatha's arrival at Furry Tails and the puppy's adoption, she wasn't deceitful enough to knowingly lengthen the treasure hunt. Not even to give the Restoration of Luke its best shot at success.

It wouldn't be fair to keep him here when she knew how much he wanted to go.

On Sunday afternoon, Luke received a text from Dylan, the teenager who'd agreed to keep him informed on Blair.

Dylan
Hey, Mr. Dempsey. I was kind of hoping that
Blair wouldn't do anything to make you upset.
Or that I wouldn't see her doing it.

Luke
Unfortunately, the chance that Blair will start
making good choices is zero.

Dylan
It's not like I know her really well or anything,
but I feel kind of bad telling on her.

Ben had told Luke that Leah could relate so much to Luke's desire to stay up to date on Blair's behavior that she'd told her brother, Dylan, she'd add thirty minutes to his curfew if he'd help out. Dylan had agreed, but now it sounded like he was getting cold feet.

Luke
I understand, but I promise you that you're
doing the right thing. I'm trying to keep her

out of trouble, but I can't do that without information.

Scrolling dots answered, but no words came through.

Luke
Blair won't know who's keeping me in the loop. You're doing this for her own good. Plus, it's not terrible to have a later curfew.

Dylan
You don't know how bad I want a later curfew. My sister makes me come home super early.

Luke
I'm glad this will work out for us both. Where's Blair and what is she doing?

Dylan
She's smoking in the alley behind the shops on Sunset Road, near the school.

Luke
Thanks, Dylan. I appreciate it.

Luke didn't have to wonder which location the kid meant. When he'd been Blair's age, he'd smoked in the same alley behind the same shops.

Fifteen minutes later, Luke parked near the mouth of the alley and followed the sound of conversation and the smell of cigarette smoke. He found Blair sitting with three boys and one girl on the curb—all of them holding cigarettes.

His anger shot to a ten. The twin girls were supposed to have made up for the stress and devastation he'd cost his parents. They were supposed to be sweet, obedient, close with their parents.

It seemed like Hailey was a good little soldier, doing her part. But Blair? No. He was taking her behavior personally because she'd let him down.

"We're leaving," he stated when he drew within hearing range of the group.

"No thanks." Her smug smile said, *You can't make me go*.

"Who are you?" one of the boys asked. The kid's sneer informed Luke that he didn't care about anything and wasn't threatened by adults. Luke knew the mindset well. It was the type that would land the kid in jail one day.

"I'm her brother," Luke answered.

That got their attention. "The guy from the earthquake?" the girl asked.

"Yep," Blair replied. "This is the brother who lived, though he does a pretty good job of acting like he's dead."

In one sentence, she'd summed him up perfectly. "You're leaving now with the brother who lived," Luke told her.

"No—"

"You can walk out of here with me, or I can carry you out of here," Luke said.

"Go ahead and try to carry her out of here," the future felon threatened.

Blair put a restraining hand on the boy's torso as he moved to stand, keeping him in place. "So," Blair said casually, glancing at her friends, "the brother who lived just finished a seven-year sentence for felony theft. I wouldn't fight him if I were you." She pressed to her feet, brushing off the back of her ripped jeans.

Future Felon rose, too. "I don't care. I'll take him on."

"I hope you do. I hope all five of you take me on." Luke meant it. He'd been in a bad mood since kissing Finley yesterday. Fist fights were better than workouts at the gym. He'd feed off the struggle, the adrenaline, the pain.

"I'm coming with you," Blair told Luke.

"You don't have to," Future Felon said to Blair.

"It's fine," she said firmly. "I'm going. I'll see you guys later."

Her friends murmured good-byes as the two of them walked away.

Intervening to protect her friends from a fight with him was the first intelligent thing he'd seen Blair do.

"No smoking in my truck," he said.

She glared at him. He glared back. After a few seconds, she tossed the cigarette on the asphalt and stubbed it out with the toe of her combat boot.

She was such a poser. It was embarrassing.

They climbed into his truck, and he drove toward their parents' house.

"I don't know what you were trying to prove just now," she said. "I'll be back out there with them tomorrow."

"Unless we strike a deal, and you hold to your side of the bargain."

"What kind of deal?"

"I'll work on your car if you stop smoking, vaping, and getting drunk at parties."

A few blocks rolled past. She looked out the passenger side window with a pouty expression. "I should've known that you wouldn't work on my car just to be nice."

"Right. You should've known."

She didn't respond.

"Well?" he asked. "I thought you wanted to be able to drive your car when you turn sixteen."

"I do."

"How bad?"

"Bad."

"Then the deal I'm offering is your only option. So do what needs to be done to get what you want."

"You're a jerk."

"That's not relevant. What's relevant is whether you're willing to put your actions where your mouth is when you say you want a car."

"If I agree, how many hours a week are you going to spend working on my car?"

"Eight hours every weekend."

"Do I have to be there with you, to work on the car?"

"I prefer that you not be there."

"Such a jerk!" This time she said it on a breath of disbelieving laughter.

"Still not relevant. Are you going to take the deal?"

She drew one knee toward her chest and moved as if to place the sole of her boot on the seat. "I guess."

"No boots on my upholstery. And 'I guess' is not an answer."

She set her boot on her opposite knee instead of his seat. "Fine."

"Fine what?"

"I agree to your deal."

"If you break your end of the bargain, I'll know. I'll be checking up on you."

"Your trust in me warms my heart." She spoke in a mocking sweet voice.

"I wouldn't even trust you to hold my cup of coffee."

She snorted, then ran appreciative fingers across his sparkling clean dashboard. "The best thing about you is your truck."

He pulled up in front of his childhood home. "I'm going to stay here and watch until you enter through the front door."

"Lovely." She exited.

He watched her disappear inside the house where he'd once lived. The house where he no longer belonged. The house he'd been desperate to get away from. The house that held some of the very best and very worst memories of his life.

Finley would like for you to join her in the play yard," Kat said to him the next morning when he arrived at work.

Without a word, he stalked toward the play yard. He wasn't surprised that she'd asked to see him. No doubt, she wasn't happy with the way they'd left things day before last and wanted to beat a dead horse.

His reaction to her kiss had been desperate. Which embarrassed him. He was not a man who gave up control for passion. With women in the past, he'd calculated how much he'd been willing to give.

With Finley, he'd simply responded. At first he'd been powerless not to respond. Then powerless to stop responding.

Since he'd left her house on Saturday, he'd tried to cut himself some slack. He'd been in prison for a long time. It had been even longer since he'd been with a woman. It wasn't surprising that he'd slipped. When she'd kissed him, biology had taken over.

He just wished biology had been the only thing in play. That would have been easier to write off. But the largest part of what he felt for Finley had nothing to do with her physical appeal. He genuinely cared about her. He liked her more than he could afford to.

He wouldn't let down his guard like that again. He had to count on himself because he wasn't sure if he could count on her not to make another move.

When he reached the play yard, Finley shot him a bright smile. "Good morning."

Equal parts infatuation and resentment roiled inside him. How could she look so happy after she'd wrecked his sleep for two nights straight? "Morning."

Her oversized sweater had slipped off the edge of one creamy shoulder. Her hair was messy in a sexy way.

For the thousandth time, he wondered why she couldn't have been a woman in her fifties, like what he'd been expecting, based on Ed's age.

Or why couldn't she have been plain?

Or have a personality as unlikable as Kat's? Why?

On this first morning in February, a strip of misty clouds hovered at the base of the mountains. Above, green slopes reached upward to form peaks. Then more white clouds obscured the sky.

"Tire trouble?" she asked Dawson, the dog with wheels functioning as his back legs. Finley adjusted a harness strap. "There you are, darling."

He licked her hand and rolled off.

Two dogs started barking over the same toy, and Finley quickly intervened, using nothing but her body language and a *tsk* sound. Making communication with animals look easy, she picked up the toy and placed it on a hook, putting it in time out.

Luke reached down and threw a ball for Arthur. Then another for Harry.

"I know that my suggestion that we try dating each other offended you," Finley said.

He straightened and buried his hands in his jacket pockets.

"And I understand why," she went on. "After thinking about it, it must have seemed like I had plans to use you in the short term because Chase isn't here in the long term."

He envied Chase with so much white-hot heat, he didn't allow himself to say anything.

"I'm sorry," she said. "I'd never use you. The truth is that I like you. And that's why I wanted us to try dating. Simply that. I like you."

After a few seconds passed, he said, "Okay."

"Am I forgiven?"

"Sure."

"Really?"

"Finley, yes. Drop it."

"Pardon my uncertainty, but if that's your forgiveness, it looks a lot like irritation."

He looked right at her. "This is my forgiveness."

"Thank you."

He could make out each of her long eyelashes and the kaleidoscope of blue in her irises. He needed to change the subject, complete the hunt, and drive to Montana. "What are we going to do about the latest clue?"

"I thought I might ask Kat about the number my dad provided.

She does crossword puzzles every day. A clue like this could be right up her alley."

"It's fine with me if you ask her as long as we don't tell her that the number is connected to the hunt."

"Agreed."

They made their way to the workroom, where they found Kat stationed in front of the fax machine.

"I wonder if you could help me with something," Finley said to her. "I received this clue in a brain game thing I'm working on, and I'm stumped." She jotted *306.8752* onto a nearby piece of paper.

Kat, who considered herself an expert in everything, looked pleased to have been asked. "This was the full clue? Just this number?"

"Correct."

"Hmm. I don't think it holds any particular mathematical significance. It's not pi, nor any of the other famous numbers I know. The decimal is interesting. If you're looking for a real-world correlation, I'd associate a number with a decimal first with a dollar amount. But this has four decimal places rather than two. My next guess would be that this number represents a temperature. For example, the temperature at which water freezes or boils. Body temperature. However, this number doesn't represent any of those."

It would be great if Kat's superior attitude, which he had to put up with for hours a day, would prove useful for something.

"Decimal, decimal," Kat muttered. Then snapped her fingers. "Dewey decimal system. Could this be a Dewey decimal number?"

Finley's face lit. "You know, that just might be it."

"Type that into your brain game and let's see if I'm right," Kat said. "I bet I'm right. I bet the answer's the Dewey decimal system."

"I bet it is."

When Finley didn't race off, Kat asked, "Are you going to check it?"

"Sure." Finley slipped toward her office.

Kat followed.

Finley blocked the door. "I need to return an email, then I'll check it."

"I'll wait here."

"All right." Finley closed the door. Kat positioned herself an inch from the threshold with self-satisfied body language, waiting for the chance to say *I told you so.*

Luke went to work. He'd start with the idiotic "*It's a great day to have a great day!*" social media captions so he could get them out of the way.

It could be worse. He could have a psychotic puppy to worry about.

After a few minutes, Finley's voice carried through her closed door. "You were right, Kat! The answer was the Dewey decimal system."

"I told you so!"

"Thanks a bunch. You're the best!"

Kat gave him a look that said *Top that, buddy* as she settled behind her desk.

His phone buzzed, alerting him to a text.

Finley
I told Kat she was right to make her happy and throw her off the scent. I don't actually know yet whether this number correlates to a book, but I think it's as good a guess as any.

Luke
If it does correlate to a book, do you think your dad would be referring to a book at the Misty River Library?

Finley
I do. Though he might also be referring to a book at the Hartwell Library he took me to when I was young. I say we swing by the Misty River Library during our lunch break.

The woman who fielded their request for help at the Misty River Library was young, redheaded, named Dakota, and had great taste in pets. She'd adopted a puppy named Loretta (three-month-old Maltese mix, licks air) from Furry Tails a year prior.

Finley had been chitchatting with her since they'd arrived at the customer service desk. Currently, Dakota was showing Finley glamour shots of Loretta on her phone.

"She looks like she's thriving in her forever home," Finley said.

"She is. I adore her."

"Wonderful. That's the outcome I hoped for."

Luke had remained quiet during the exchange. Except for his magnetism, which spoke loudly. Dakota had repeatedly shot him speculative looks, none of which he'd appeared to notice.

He'd yet to show much improvement in response to the conditioning of outings like this one.

"What can I help you with today?" Dakota asked.

"I came by to see if a particular Dewey decimal number is linked to any of the books here at the library."

"Certainly. What's the number?"

Finley relayed it.

Fake nails tapped against the keyboard as Dakota typed the digits into her computer. "Yes! This call number belongs to a book entitled *Brothers: Twenty-Five Stories About the Ties That Bind*. It looks like a compilation of nonfiction stories."

Hallelujah! "Excellent." She'd never heard of that book, but it sounded like the kind of thing her father would have liked. He'd always enjoyed reading both fiction and nonfiction. "Where should we look for it?"

"I'll show you." Dakota was halfway out of her chair, her focus still on the computer screen, when her progress abruptly stopped. "Oh, wait." She returned to her chair. "This book is still in our catalog, but it's no longer available. There's a note here that says that it was withdrawn."

"Oh?" Finley's exultation began to flatten. "What does it mean when a book is withdrawn?"

"It means that we decided to take it off the shelves and out of circulation."

"Does it say how long ago it was taken off the shelves?"

"It was removed three years ago."

Three years? The exultation flattened so much that it became a canyon. "What becomes of books that are withdrawn?"

"Our Friends of the Library group typically sells them in their annual sale."

She tried to get a read on Luke. He looked like a poster child for the brooding leading man in a romantic movie. Scruff covered his granite cheeks. If he was experiencing disappointment, it didn't show. His regard was level, steady. In fact, the only time he'd let his mask slip was during their kisses. At this moment, it was hard to believe that he'd revealed as much desire as he had.

She focused on Dakota. "I have reason to think that my father, who passed away in the fall, might have left something inside that book for me."

"Oh dear. What do you think that might be?"

"I'm not sure. But it would mean a lot if I could get my hands on the book. Any ideas how I might be able to do that?"

Dakota pushed her lips to the side. "We send out a weekly e-newsletter to our patrons. There's a News and Notes section at the bottom. We could add a note, asking people if they happen to have purchased that book at the sale. And, if so, to contact you." She pointed toward the hall leading to the bathrooms. "We also have a community bulletin board. You're welcome to pin a request for information there."

"Thanks."

Dakota picked up a pen and scribbled down information. "Here's the book's title and author. Here's its ISBN number, publisher, and date of publication. It looks like it was first released fifteen years ago." She lifted a binder from her desk drawer, flipped several pages, then began writing again. "Here's a name, number, and email for the man who handles our weekly emails. And, just in case it's useful . . ." She flipped several pages. "Here's the name, number, and email of the president of our Friends of the Library group. It might be worth giving her a call. Who knows? It's possible this book wasn't purchased at the last few sales. In that case, I'm pretty sure they store the books that don't sell and put them out again the next year."

Finley accepted the piece of paper with thanks. After wishing Dakota and Loretta her very best, she and Luke returned to his truck.

He immediately turned the heater up and steered them toward Furry Tails. The cab of his truck had become something of a mobile treasure hunt headquarters.

"I'm going to start," she said, "by calling the Friends of the Library president. If by some chance the book is still in their inventory, then there'll be no need to post on the bulletin board or in the email newsletter." With cold fingers, she typed in the phone number Dakota had given her.

When the president answered, Finley introduced herself.

"Finley! I know exactly who you are. I'm the owner of the Buttercup Boutique."

Recognition slotted into place. This was why Finley loved living in a small town. Forget six degrees of separation. Approximately one and a half degrees of separation existed between Misty River's residents. The owner of the Buttercup Boutique, a clothing store, was a fashionable woman in her late forties. She had several kids and fabulous hair. "Of course!"

"I'm crazy about reading, and so I said yes when they asked me to volunteer with Friends of the Library."

"That's so kind of you." Finley explained that she was seeking a book that held special significance. "Dakota at the library suggested that you may store leftover books until the next sale."

"That's correct. We set up a booth at the Apple Festival every year and sell books. The community is very supportive, so we never have many books left. At the moment, I believe I have two cardboard boxes full. I stuck them in the storage room in the back of my shop, so feel free to come by anytime during business hours. I'll take you back there and you can go through them."

"Would it work for you if we headed in that direction now?"

"Sure! I'll see you when you get here."

They disconnected. "Are you up for a stop downtown?" Finley asked Luke. "Friends of the Library books are stored at the Buttercup Boutique."

His U-turn showed his willingness to make the detour. "You mentioned the Hartwell Library earlier," he said. "Do you think it's worth giving that library a call to see if they have the book in circulation?"

"Yep." However, her call to the library in Hartwell revealed that they'd never had a book associated with that call number in their system.

Luke pulled to a stop in front of Sugar Maple Kitchen.

"What's this?" she asked. "The boutique is one block down."

"I don't want you to miss lunch."

"That's thoughtful of you, but I can make do with the power bar and apple I have at Furry Tails."

"They have a to-go line here. I'll be in and out in a few minutes. What would you like?"

"The vegan veggie wrap, please."

He left her in the truck, engine running.

The Luke who'd told her he didn't want to get involved with her had just stopped at a restaurant to ensure she didn't go hungry.

True to his word, he came out minutes later. She peeked inside the sack he handed her. In addition to the veggie wrap, he'd bought a package of nuts, a bag of chips, and a turkey sandwich for himself. "Thank you."

"You're welcome."

"I absolutely love this restaurant. I either eat here or get take-out twice a week." She set the bag between them. "Did you know that Sam, the owner of Sugar Maple Kitchen, is engaged to Genevieve Woodward?"

"Ben told me."

"I've seen them together at the restaurant a few times. Word on the street is that they're very happy." She motioned toward a cute storefront. "This is the boutique. Just up here."

They parked, and the owner showed them to her storage room. *Books for Friends of the Library* had been written in Sharpie across two cardboard boxes in the back corner of the space. Luke took one box. Finley took the other. Dust and the scent of old paper rose into the beams of winter light slanting through the windows as they took books out, looked at each one, then stacked them on the floorboards.

Not the right title.

Not the right title.

They reached the bottom of their boxes within seconds of each other.

It wasn't here.

Brothers: Twenty-Five Stories About the Ties That Bind, the book in which her dad had hidden her next clue, had been sold at the community sale.

CHAPTER FOURTEEN

Two weeks passed without a lead in the treasure hunt. Two weeks during which no one would leave Luke alone.

At work, Finley asked him to bathe dogs with her, walk dogs with her, meet with her about the website redesign, and a million other things. She continued to deposit water, herbal tea, fruit, and snacks on his desk. She often steered conversations toward faith and asked him probing questions about his relationship with God that he did not answer.

She continued to lead the team in daily meditation sessions. No way would she ever convince him to sit on a yoga mat with his eyes closed. But during the sessions, he began leaning back in his chair, watching the view beyond the windows, and listening. There was no point in trying to work while she spoke about letting your heart float upward and setting an intention. It was relaxing, at least. He hated it less as the days went by.

Finley would have been easier to deal with if his fixation with her ended when the workday ended. It didn't. He thought of her when making morning coffee. When exercising. When meeting with his parole officer. When watching sports. When falling asleep at night.

Without his permission, his brain had chosen her as its screensaver setting.

He'd spent years focusing on Montana. He'd planned his business, the floorplan of his house, every single furnishing. Doing so had centered him and given his life behind bars purpose.

But strategizing his Montana life had never given him the enjoyment and peace he experienced when he thought about Finley.

That was unique to her.

When he tried one night to purposely walk through his future home in his mind, the way he'd done so many times before, he found it had begun to blur. Furious with himself, he spent long minutes building back the details in his imagination. Seeing the place—*his* place. He'd been picturing himself turning in a slow circle in the living room of his dream home when an image intruded—Finley looking at him with humor in her eyes—and the Montana house vanished like smoke carried away by wind.

The day of their failed visit to the library, Finley had requested that an announcement about her search for the *Brothers* book run in the library email. The day after that, she'd tacked a piece of paper to the library bulletin board.

She hadn't heard back from a single person.

A week later, she'd discussed a new tactic with him.

"It could be that my dad didn't leave a specific clue in the library book." She sat in her office with a pug named Clarence on her lap and her hair on top of her head. "Maybe the clue in the *Brothers* book is like the clue at the train depot. There for all to see, but for me alone to understand. If that's the case, any copy of the book might do the trick."

Luke had liked Ed in life. But in death, Ed aggravated him. His old friend had sent Finley to a book that had been sold to someone who could not be found.

Weren't you smart enough to anticipate, Ed, that the book might not be available at the library eight years after you created this hunt?

Apparently not.

"Or it could be," Finley continued, "that the decimal number Dad left isn't actually meant to lead us to the *Brothers* book at all."

If that was true, he'd never make it to Montana.

"I think the *Brothers* book is right, though," she hurried to add. "I really do think that it's the next clue. So I'm going to order a copy for myself."

She found the book for sale at a small bookstore in Maine. Apparently they were sending it by boat because it wasn't supposed to arrive until February sixteenth.

Another person who wouldn't leave him alone—Blair.

He'd always had a soft spot for 1970 Pontiacs. Considering how low Blair's car-buying budget must have been, she and Dad had purchased a great car. However, cars were like houses. You'd rather get one that hadn't been updated at all than one that had been updated badly. Blair and Dad's repair efforts had screwed things up worse than they'd been before.

The car was stored in a barn-turned-garage owned by a friend of his parents. When Luke holed up there alone, he lost himself in the job in the best possible way. Working on the car demanded his concentration, occupied his hands, and lowered his stress. After every session with the car, he could see his progress. He'd forgotten how much he loved the process of bringing a broken-down car back to life.

Only one thing sucked the enjoyment from the Pontiac—the fact that Blair kept barging in on him. She'd ruin the quiet of the garage by griping about people at school. Lecturing him about how wrong he'd been to abandon their family. Talking big about all the things she was going to do after she had her diploma. Complaining about their parents' rules. In general, she did her best to undo the contentment her car brought him.

Another person who wouldn't leave him alone—Ben. Ben came by the Center two afternoons a week to volunteer with the afterschool program. Every single time, he stopped by to talk with Luke.

Ben had always been a good guy. The least observant person on the planet would recognize that Ben was a good guy. And Luke couldn't bring himself to shut Ben out after the way he'd helped him with Agatha.

Another person who wouldn't leave him alone? CeCe. Ben's plump, feisty mother kept showing up at Luke's apartment with food.

He would've pretended not to be home if her food hadn't been so delicious. If he had one weakness, it was Finley—

Strike that. That's not how he'd intended to finish that sentence.

If he had one weakness, it was food, and CeCe made some of the best food he'd ever tasted.

The last three times she banged on his door, he'd let her in. Then he'd put up with at least twenty minutes of her bossy conversation. She'd known him when he was a kid and she was a mother to one of the Miracle Five, so she seemed to think she had the right to give him advice he didn't want and had no intention of taking.

She kept going on and on about the Valentine's Day party that she and Genevieve's mother, Caroline, were planning. Caroline would be hosting it at her historic home in one of the oldest neighborhoods in town, and CeCe kept insisting that he had to come.

"I have an idea!" she told him three days before the party. "You can drive over in your truck on Sunday! I love your truck. We'll reserve space so that you can park it across Caroline's driveway. I'll make sure there will be lots of those giant balloons waiting for you. Just put them in the truck bed, okay? That'll make a great photo op when people come and go."

"No, thank you."

"I've brought you three meals now. You owe me this one little favor."

"I thought the meals came without strings attached."

"Well." She put her hands on her wide hips. "Now I want to add strings."

"I don't do parties."

"Two hundred people are coming to this party. All ages. Lots of them aren't social. My cousin Drew has hardly ever said two sentences in a row, but he's coming."

"No, thank you."

"I'm buying balloons for your truck."

"Don't buy balloons." He hadn't attended a single Valentine's Day party since the ones in elementary school. He set his teeth, wishing she'd leave so he could eat her pot roast.

"I'm buying balloons and that's final." She gave him a sly look. "Finley Sutherland is coming to the party and bringing a date."

Outwardly, he didn't so much as blink. Inwardly, a tiger leapt from sleeping onto all four feet.

"I went by Furry Tails the other day to help Ben with an experiment he'd set up for the kids," she continued. "I met Finley there and invited her. She said yes."

Finley had kissed him but was taking another man to a Valentine's party? How come she was now open to dating? Had she turned her attention to someone else because he'd indicated he wasn't interested?

CeCe stopped and looked over her shoulder at him on her way out the door. "So. Are you going to come to my Valentine's Day party?"

"No."

"See you there!"

Two weeks ago, Ben had asked Akira to come with him to his mom's Valentine's Day party as friends. In a weak moment, she'd said that she would. Which was probably the very *worst* decision she'd ever made because she was having the very *best* time and the party wasn't even set to begin for another hour.

They'd arrived early to assist Ben's mom with party prep. Akira hadn't anticipated how disastrously adorable Ben would be while helping his mother. He responded to her with patience. He showed his father respect and his siblings affection.

Akira's family was strong, but strong in a completely different way than Ben's family. Her two older sisters and parents were all tremendously driven. Quiet, focused, ambitious.

Growing up, they'd shared family dinners. Her dad discussed his job in strategic tourism and city planning. Her mom, a paralegal for the town's foremost attorney, discussed her cases. Her sisters discussed their impressive classes, extracurriculars, and upcoming tests. Akira hadn't been motivated by the things that motivated them, so she'd spoken about the things she cared about—kids, animals, and community service. They'd listened, but she'd understood that they found her odd. And perhaps a bit underwhelming.

After dinner, the rest of her family members had gone off to work intently toward their next goal. Akira had gone off to watch *Glee* or *Gossip Girl* or spend time with friends.

Where her extended family had been small, the Coleman family was large. Where her family had been subdued, the Coleman family was loud.

No fewer than twelve people had shown up simply to *prepare* for tonight's party: the owners of this home, Caroline and Judson; CeCe and her husband, Hersh; CeCe's other three kids and their spouses; and Akira and Ben.

Like a military general, CeCe barked out orders. Even so, amid the chaos, she'd made time to single Akira out.

Ben mixed punch ingredients in the enormous bowl on the dining room table while Akira helped CeCe move food from containers onto platters.

CeCe wore a white apron that said *Warning: Complaints to the cook will be hazardous to your health* over a sparkly purple pantsuit. She'd combed her graying hair tightly off her face and curled it into a low bun. Her long nails glittered with silver polish as she lifted deviled eggs onto a serving dish specifically made for deviled eggs. Who owned a serving dish specifically made for deviled eggs?

"Are you romantically interested in my son?" CeCe asked Akira, point-blank.

Akira continued positioning cookies on a heart-shaped wooden cutting board. She'd just met this woman minutes ago but could already tell CeCe appreciated candor. "I adore him," she confided. "But I'm very gun-shy."

"Because?"

"I almost died last year and—"

"Excuse me?" CeCe stilled, except for her eyebrows, which shot upward. "How did you almost die?"

Akira explained how her case of flu had deteriorated into life-threatening sepsis, which had resulted in ten days at the hospital.

CeCe sucked air through her teeth and returned her attention to her deviled eggs. "Praise the Lord you're okay. That must've been terrifying."

"It was. Recovery has been gradual. The whole thing—the most acute stages of the illness and the long road back—has forced me to reevaluate and get rid of things that aren't healthy for me. Falling in love is one of those things."

"Why?"

"In recent years, I've had three serious relationships. I ended up with a broken heart each time. I'm not strong enough for that at the moment. The euphoria, the sadness. The euphoria. The sadness."

"What happens if you meet the man of your dreams?"

"The odds of that happening are small."

CeCe whistled and shook her head. "You just met my son Ben, didn't you? The odds that Ben's the man of your dreams are high. I raised him. I know him better than anyone. So I can speak with authority when I say that you won't find a better man anywhere. He comes with a lifetime guarantee."

"He's incredible. So much so, I don't think I'm good enough for *him*. He'd never love me the way that I would him, which would plunge me back into the euphoria-sadness."

"Why aren't you good enough for him? Is there some fatal flaw with your personality that I should know about?"

"Either I'm shy with people or I spill my guts in the most awkward way, like I'm doing with you now. I've yet to find the middle ground."

CeCe looked unimpressed by her confession. "Are you loyal?"

"Definitely."

"A Christian?"

"Yes."

"Are you a zillion dollars in debt or secretly married to someone else?"

"No."

"Mostly unselfish?"

"I love that you qualified that with 'mostly.' Is wholly unselfish too high a bar?"

"Yes. Anyone who claims to be wholly unselfish is both selfish and dishonest."

"I do believe I am mostly unselfish."

"Then I think that you *are* good enough for my son, and I don't mind telling you that my opinion on the matter carries more weight than yours. Of course," she continued in a dangerously soft tone, "if down the line, you prove by your actions that you're disloyal, a zillion dollars in debt, or wholly selfish, then I'll retract my verdict that you're good enough for my son and you'll become my sworn enemy for the rest of your life."

"Good to know."

"Hmmph." The older woman set about opening packages of napkins that matched the pale pink, white, and gold color scheme of the flower arrangements, table linens, and professionally made three-tier cake.

Caroline and Judson's Colonial Revival home had been built in the 1800s, Akira had found out upon arrival, and it oozed charm and great taste. Swags of tiny hearts brightened the fireplace mantel, chandeliers, and mirrors. A tent had been erected in the backyard for the band and dancing. Even now, a team of family members was hanging a garland of opaque balloons down the center line of the tent's roof. The formality of it all made her glad she'd chosen to wear her gray dress with the beading around the V-neckline.

"Are you aware of the recent events in Ben's love life?" CeCe asked.

"No, I'm clueless." She sealed the Tupperware container that had held the cookies. "I've always known of him because of the Miracle Five, but I'm several years younger. We don't have many mutual friends here in town."

"For the last two-and-a-half years, Ben hasn't been dating anyone because he's fancied himself in love with a fellow teacher at the high school named Leah."

Disappointment sank through Akira, proving that she'd already gotten at least slightly wrapped up in Ben. Which was worrying. "Oh?"

"It turned out that Ben wasn't the right man for Leah. The right man for Leah was Sebastian Grant. Does that name ring a bell?"

"Another of the Miracle Five?"

She nodded. "And Ben's best friend." She waved a hand. "I consider Sebastian to be a son of mine and, between you and me, often find myself liking him more than I like some of my biological kids."

"I heard that, Momma!" CeCe's oldest daughter said from the far side of the kitchen.

"Good," CeCe shot back. "Let that keep you on your toes."

"If Ben liked Leah, then why did his best friend date her?" Akira asked.

"Sebastian didn't start dating Leah until Ben demanded he do so. And thank goodness he did. Sebastian was very lonely, before Leah. The two of them fell in love and they're perfect for each other, and Ben knows it and supports them. But now it's high time that Ben moves on. I only have six grandkids."

"Six sounds like a lot."

"Well, it's not! I gave birth to *four children*. I've spent the last forty years parenting, and that sucked most of the spunk right out of me."

If CeCe had any more spunk, she'd be a Chihuahua.

"Six grandkids isn't a good return for four kids," CeCe stated. "I want and deserve more."

"Yeah," her big husband said as he walked by and stole a cookie. "More grandkids."

"Steal another cookie, Hersh," CeCe said to him, "and you'll lose a hand."

"I really hope my mom isn't talking to you about wanting me to procreate," Ben called from the punchbowl.

"She is," Akira called back.

"Mom," Ben said, "this is the first time Akira's agreed to go anywhere with me. To get her to come, I had to assure her that we're just friends. I don't think she's ready for you to pressure her to go forth and multiply."

"Keep an open mind," CeCe told her. "It doesn't make a bit of sense for you to push away a man who *will* be good for you because you're afraid he won't be good for you."

Ben entered the room. "The punch is done."

"Did you add twice as many frozen sherbet balls than the recipe calls for?"

"Mom. I wouldn't dream of adding the amount the recipe calls for. I've known since I was five that pink party punch needs twice as many sherbet balls."

"See?" CeCe said to Akira. "Lifetime guarantee." She then handed them two brooms and commanded them to make a final sweep of the hardwood floors.

"It's a good thing this isn't a date," Ben said as they progressed into the living room. "Sweeping the floor and a sermon from my mom would have made me really hard to resist."

"You're so right. We're not vacuuming next, are we? I can't help but have a crush on men who ask me to vacuum."

"Then I definitely won't ask you to vacuum. I'll stick to asking you to scrub tables and wash dirty dishes."

They'd reached the foyer when all the lights suddenly dimmed. Since the sky outside on this Sunday evening was rapidly darkening, the effect emphasized the votive candles flickering on every surface. The atmosphere instantly turned romantic.

"Ten minutes before showtime," CeCe hollered.

"I can no longer see the dust," Ben said.

"Neither can I. How come we just swept if they planned all along to make the dust invisible with mood lighting?"

His smile threatened to obliterate her defenses. "A word to the wise—that kind of logic won't serve you well with my mother."

She snorted.

The front doorknob turned. A handsome dark-haired man and a blond woman entered.

"Once again you've managed to arrive after all the work is done," Ben said teasingly to the man.

"CeCe didn't give birth to me. She'll harass me a little, but she won't take my head off." He extended his fist to Ben.

Ben bumped it with the hand not holding a broom, then glanced at her. "Akira, this is Dr. Sebastian Grant and Leah Montgomery."

Oh! These were the two people CeCe had just been talking about. Ben's best friend and the woman Ben had been in love with. How uncomfortable! How fascinating. "Hi."

"It's nice to meet you," Leah said.

"You too."

"I've been volunteering with the after-school program at Furry Tails Animal Rescue Center," Ben told them. "Akira's the director of the program, and she's great at what she does."

Ben had said encouraging things to her about her work before, but this particular compliment was as welcome as sunshine in winter. She worked hard and strove for excellence with the kids. But she did so in obscurity, receiving job satisfaction through the kids' well-being and accomplishments. That a teacher of Ben's caliber thought well of her efforts meant more to her than any box of chocolates could have on this Valentine's Day. "Thank you, Ben."

Sebastian and Leah both asked her follow-up questions and Akira observed the dynamic between them and Ben as she answered.

Leah had styled her long bob in loose waves. Observant gray-blue eyes were the centerpiece of her lovely face. She'd combined her 1930s-inspired high heels with a simple off-the-shoulder dress made of a pink fabric so vibrant it verged on neon. She had the demeanor of a woman comfortable with herself.

Akira noted an underlying carefulness in the way Ben, Leah, and Sebastian interacted. They were all likely trying to navigate the territory they found themselves in now that Sebastian had ended up with Ben's heartthrob. No doubt Sebastian and Leah would be thrilled when Ben found a girlfriend. That would assuage any lingering guilt they might be feeling.

How bizarre that Ben had ended up as the odd man out in this trio. In no way did she perceive Ben as second-best or inferior. On the contrary, she viewed him as unattainably awesome.

Leah and Sebastian must have been destined for each other. Soul mates. That's the only thing that could explain why Ben hadn't ended up with the girl.

"Mom's expecting Luke to come tonight," Ben said during a break in the conversation.

"Luke's coming?" Leah asked with surprise.

"According to my mom," Ben answered. "Luke told me he wasn't coming. So I'll believe it when I see it."

"I'd love to meet him," Leah said.

"Don't get your hopes up," Sebastian told her. "Either about Luke showing up or about having a conversation with him if he does—"

"Sebastian!" CeCe's imperious voice carried from the back of the house. "If that's you, get in here *right now*. I want to give you a piece of my mind!"

Ben chuckled. "You've been summoned, man. Good luck."

"I'm not going in alone."

"I think you should," Leah said.

"No way. Our best hope of survival is the buddy system." Sebastian took Leah's hand, then the pair excused themselves.

Akira and Ben drifted toward the laundry room to put away their brooms.

"I heard you had your heart set on Leah for a while," Akira said quietly. "Is it painful for you to see her with Sebastian?"

"It's getting easier, but it's still a little hard."

Compassion tweaked within her. "I can imagine. For the record, Sebastian might be good-looking and, okay, a doctor. But he's no match for you in my eyes. As far as I'm concerned, you're the most eligible bachelor in Georgia."

Luke had been on edge all day. More so as the time of the Valentine's party neared.

He wasn't going. So why did he keep checking the clock?

Jiggling his knee, he told himself to put all his concentration toward his computer. He was reclining on the chair in his living room with his laptop. Over the past several days, he'd been hunting the Internet for information on the people Finley had told him were connected to her dad. Ed's family, friends, enemies. Carla and her family.

Today, he'd been researching Rosco Horton, Ed's attorney. The State Bar of Georgia's website was open before him, and Luke had just learned that Rosco had been disciplined twice over his long career. Once for violating the ethics of lawyer-client confidentiality. Once for how Rosco had dealt with client money.

Ed's attorney wasn't squeaky clean.

Luke's next step? Get a read on Rosco. To do that, he'd need to meet him.

He dialed Rosco's office and left a voice mail. "Hello, this is Luke Dempsey. I'm interested in hiring an attorney to prepare my will and would like to schedule a meeting with Mr. Horton." He left his number and disconnected.

The party's start time had come and gone.

See? He wasn't going. Now he could relax.

Except the fact that he'd missed the start time only intensified the unsettled feeling in his gut. His chest was tight and prickly. He couldn't shake the sense that he should be at the party.

Finley would be there. With another man.

Who? Who was he? Could her date have gotten close to her because he wanted to try to gain information about the hunt?

His gaze returned to the time. It had been ten minutes since he'd last checked. He'd spent all ten minutes arguing with himself.

He didn't like the idea of CeCe's balloons waiting on the driveway for a truck that wasn't coming—

Who cares? He told her not to buy any stupid balloons. But he was certain she'd gone ahead and bought some anyway.

Which wasn't his problem.

Yet it bothered him that she'd asked for a favor and he'd left her hanging.

Setting the computer aside, he rose.

Inside his closet, he considered the few items he owned that were formal enough to wear to CeCe's party.

He didn't want to go.

He wasn't going.

With a groan, he raked his fingers through his hair. Then he peeled off his T-shirt and reached for a sweater. He could stomach the party for a short time. Going would give him a chance to come through for CeCe, meet Finley's date, and keep an eye on the crowd to see if anyone appeared to be watching Finley.

Those were good reasons to go.

He definitely wasn't going because he was jealous.

CHAPTER FIFTEEN

Finley swirled her glass, then sipped in the raspberry that had been bobbing around in her fizzy drink. She chewed its squishy sweetness while scanning the packed living room. The party was in full swing—

Her vision collided with Luke.

The sight of him so astonished her that she nearly choked on the raspberry. Conscientiously, she swallowed. What in the world was Luke, *her* Luke, doing at a party? She would have sworn that *Luke* and *party* were mutually exclusive. But here he was.

He must've just entered, because he stood near the entrance. Oblivious to her, he was in conversation with Ben. He'd chosen a beautifully cut dark gray sweater and narrow black suit pants. It looked as if he'd used a wide-toothed comb and a little gel on his hair, which gleamed subtly under the lights. She loved the tousled way his hair usually fell. But this more severe style suited his bone structure. He'd never resembled an Italian prince more strongly than he did tonight.

Excitement tingled from the soles of her feet, up the backs of her knees, to the tip of her scalp. She'd been having a very nice time, but now that Luke had arrived, her enjoyment had quadrupled. She felt the way she had when she was in high school and her long-time crush, Benton Nichols, had appeared unexpectedly at her friend Dorrie's Fourth of July party.

She adjusted her dress—a cream floral design on a backdrop of red. It had fluttery sleeves and a gathered waist that flowed to a short breezy skirt. Holding her glass in one hand, she threaded her way through people toward Luke. She checked to make sure her three gold necklaces hadn't tangled. They had a little, so she straightened them.

Since the day she and Luke kissed, she'd done a lot of thinking about whether the time had come to try dating again. She'd prayed. Talked about it more with Meadow and Bridget.

God's will wasn't always the easiest thing to discern. In this case, it was subtle—a gentle invitation to lay down her shields and regard relationships with an open mind. She'd been shoving even the thought of romance aside for a long time. She needed to quit doing that out of habit. And cautiously put herself back out there.

That much, she'd deduced.

She couldn't date Luke, but to her chagrin, her body hadn't gotten the memo. She was more and more drawn to him every day. Lately, when they made eye contact, her senses jumped with electric awareness.

Luke, of course, had remained very much in control of himself. Reserved. Not cold, just distinctly out of reach.

Yet he'd shown up here. Here! Which proved her five-step plan was working better than she'd thought.

Some of the guests were stealing covert glances at him. In fact, a pulse of interest seemed to be traveling through the room. *Is that Luke Dempsey?* she imagined one person saying to the next, like a game of telephone.

She greeted several acquaintances as she passed. Running an animal shelter in Misty River ensured that she could attend any type of gathering and find people there she knew.

A redhead came into view, standing beside Luke.

Finley stutter-stepped. Wait. The redhead was Dakota, the beautiful librarian who'd helped them research the Dewey decimal number.

Surely, Luke had not brought Dakota as his date. Luke and

Dakota had been strangers the day of the library visit. Finley had introduced them. . . .

Vividly, she recalled the smitten looks Dakota had sent Luke.

Finley watched Dakota and Luke separate from Ben and walk together toward the fireplace.

In her whole life, she'd never experienced jealousy more powerful than a mild twinge. Until now. It began to simmer like acid in the center of her torso.

Finley had kissed Luke, and he'd kissed her back. Very thoroughly! Then he'd closed the door to the possibility of more between them. She'd thought he'd done so because of his inability to let himself care about anyone, because of his guilt, his issues. She might have gotten that wrong. Maybe it hadn't been about him so much as her. Maybe he was able to care, he just didn't want *her*.

She was still at least ten feet away from Luke. Even so, his chin turned in her direction as if she'd called to him. They looked at each other, his chiseled face inscrutable.

She pasted on a smile and approached. "Happy Valentine's Day!" Her words sounded so merry that they rang false. If she didn't tone it down, they'd think her tipsy.

"Same to you," answered Dakota, who wore a tight navy dress that accentuated her curves.

"Thanks again for your help when we came by the library a few weeks ago," Finley said to her.

"You're welcome. I just wish I could have done more."

All the things Finley wanted to say to Dakota, but wouldn't, filled her head in a rush. *I understand why you'd set your sights on Luke. Handsomeness and intrigue flow from him. However, I've spent more than a month talking to him, pulling hard-won smiles from him, getting to know him. You can't possibly understand as well as I do how broken he is inside.*

Derek appeared next to Finley. She startled. Upon seeing Luke, she'd temporarily forgotten about her date. "Have you both met Derek Upshaw?" she asked Luke and Dakota.

Luke's hazel eyes turned to chips of ice.

"I don't think we've met." Dakota introduced herself to Derek.

"Luke and I went to high school together," Derek said, shaking Luke's hand. "Can you believe so many years have passed?"

"I can."

"Have you been doing well?" Derek asked.

Luke gave a single nod but didn't reply.

See, Dakota? This is what I've put up with from him for weeks.

Thank goodness she'd brought Derek. He was good-looking, flirtatious, and loved animals. Derek reminded her of a mirrored garden orb. Shiny. So what if he had a habit of speaking in questions? That really wasn't annoying at all. It showed his willingness to involve others in discussions.

"What do you do, Derek?" Dakota asked.

"I'm a physical therapist. I'm really fortunate to get to work with patients, you know?"

"His patients are the fortunate ones," Finley responded dutifully.

"How do you two know each other?" Dakota asked.

"I drove one of my friends to therapy appointments with Derek when she was recovering from surgery," Finley answered. "We met then."

"I've been trying to convince her to go out with me ever since," Derek said. "And here we are. How did I get so lucky?"

A tendon in Luke's neck hardened.

"Love's in the air tonight." Dakota smiled.

Derek had expressed interest in Finley several times and had taken it well when she'd told him that she still wasn't over Chase. After all, Derek had no trouble in the dating department and certainly hadn't sat around, crying into a hankie, waiting for her.

Earlier this week, Bridget had encouraged Finley to invite him tonight. "*Valentine's Day is so much more fun with a date!*" she'd said. "*If you're going back on the market, who better to start with than Derek? He'll do great in a party setting. He's nice and he likes you, and we already know he won't be upset if you decide you don't want to go on more dates with him.*"

Derek asked about Dakota's job. She told him about her love of books and her responsibilities at the library.

Finley and Luke painstakingly avoided looking at each other. Even so, the air crackled with tension.

"Where are you working these days?" Derek asked Luke.

"I'm at the Center with Finley."

Derek's head pulled back. "What?" he said to Finley. "You didn't tell me that you'd brought Luke on board, did you?"

"It must've slipped my mind."

Derek slung an arm around her shoulders. "Finley runs the best shelter in the country. How do you like working there, Luke?"

Slight pause. "It's not really my thing."

Not his thing? *Not his thing!* Frustration shot her body temperature up precipitously.

"Weren't cars your thing," Derek asked, "back in the day?"

Was Derek innocently referring to Luke's affinity for cars in high school? Or was the comment a barb, referencing Luke's years working at a chop shop in Atlanta?

Luke's restraint did not crack. "Yes. Cars were my thing."

"Do you still work on them?"

"At the moment I'm working on my sister's 1970 Pontiac."

Hmm? Luke had told her nothing about this.

"A Firebird?" Derek asked.

"Yes."

"Awesome car, right?" Derek took a sip of his drink.

"My grandfather owns a 1957 Plymouth Fury," Dakota told Luke. "I have the best memories of driving around with him in it. I'd love to hear more about your interest in cars."

"We'll leave you to it," Finley interjected before Luke could reply. She rested her hand on Derek's forearm. "There's a band outside, and we haven't done any dancing yet. Want to give that a try?"

"How could I say no?"

They reached the tent. A band wearing matching white shirts with pink ties played fifties and sixties songs. The music invited couples to slow dance, two-step, and twirl.

If not a good dancer, Derek was, at least, a good sport. It should've been fun to dance a portion of the night away. The couples around them appeared to be having a marvelous time.

Finley pretended the same. Inside, however, she felt rattled. Hurt.

Her mind chewed on thoughts of Luke the way a child chews on a stolen piece of candy—secretly and relentlessly.

Luke cursed himself to hell and back.

He'd decided to come here.

He'd known Finley was bringing a date. But he hadn't known that seeing her with Derek would be so sharply painful. Possessiveness had twisted together with wanting someone he couldn't have to the point that he'd been unable to take a deep breath since she'd walked up to him.

He was mad. At the world. At Finley. Most of all . . . at himself.

For decades now, he'd been an expert at punishing himself. When they'd released him from prison, he'd told himself he was done with that. But apparently not.

He should have stayed home.

He felt sick to his stomach.

"I see my dad across the room," Dakota said. "Want to head over and say hi?"

"You go. I'll catch up with you later."

"'Kay." She moved off.

Dakota had approached him seconds after he'd entered the house. He didn't have anything against her. She was attractive and friendly. However, she wasn't Finley. So it was a relief not to have to keep making conversation with her.

He crossed to the bar. What were the chances they had tequila?

Zero, it turned out. They had regular and pink champagne, rosé, and a beer called The Love.

He picked up a beer and drank half of it down.

"Luke." A feminine voice spoke his name.

He turned to see three of the Miracle Five. Natasha and her sister, Genevieve, both carrying small plates of appetizers. Plus Sebastian.

He swallowed a curse word.

"I'm so glad that you came tonight," Genevieve said to him.

"Who managed to coerce you into attending tonight?" Natasha asked. "I'm going to send them a bouquet of flowers."

"Was it CeCe?" Sebastian guessed.

"Yes."

"In that case, CeCe will be receiving a bouquet from me," Natasha stated. "It's not easy to entice you into a public setting."

"Maybe we can ask her if she'd be willing to give us lessons," Genevieve said to her sister, "on how to be persuasive. The ability to persuade people to do what you want would be a fabulous life skill."

"CeCe's methods can't be taught," Sebastian said. "They're in her DNA."

Luke could see Ben on the other side of the space. He was pretty sure this was the first time all five of them had been in a room together since the ruined basement in El Salvador.

Uninvited memories carved into his thoughts.

Ben, hanging on to his optimism even though they were stuck in a dark hole. Natasha, stepping into the mom role, treating the cut on Genevieve's arm and assuring Sebastian that his head injury would be fine. Genevieve, praying out loud over and over. Sebastian, threatening him if he refused to drink water. Ethan . . . dead.

"Would you mind grabbing me some punch, Sebastian?" Natasha asked. "Dickens liked to drink punch at the holidays with his family."

"I'd be honored," Sebastian said dryly, and left.

"Luke looks rightfully confused." Genevieve gestured to her sister. "Tell him what Dickens has to do with anything, Natasha."

"A few years back, I kicked off a year of living Austenly. During that time, I tested out a lot of Jane Austen's habits. Last year, I completed a year of living C. S. Lewisly. And this year I'm doing a year of living Charles Dickensly."

Luke had no idea what she was talking about. Everything she'd just said sounded like a foreign language.

Sebastian returned with a glass of pink punch. Natasha lifted it. "Cheers."

"Cheers," Genevieve echoed.

Luke found Ben and Natasha the easiest to take. Sebastian and Genevieve were harder.

He and Sebastian had butted heads when they were trapped in El Salvador and every time since, whenever they crossed paths.

His reason for disliking Genevieve had nothing to do with her personality and everything to do with the fact that she was the one who should have died—would have died—if Luke hadn't sent his brother to the back of the line. Because of Luke's actions, Genevieve had been second to last walking through the basement hallway when the 7.8-magnitude earthquake hit. Luke had pulled her to safety. If she'd been last in line, Ethan was the one he'd have saved.

Genevieve had become a successful Bible study author and speaker. She'd taught hundreds of thousands of women. Her fame made things worse, not better, because Luke knew that some people would look at what she'd achieved and say that she'd survived for a reason . . . that she was destined to make an impact. The implication?

That Ethan had been more disposable than Genevieve.

Which was the opposite of true for Luke and his family.

Ethan had never had a chance to show the impact he could have made as an adult.

When they'd gone on that mission trip to South America, Ethan and Genevieve had been the same age. Twelve. Ethan was a goofy, talkative sixth-grader. The opportunity to become anything other than that had been crushed along with his body by the weight of an entire building.

"I know I speak for all of us," Genevieve said, "when I say that we'd really like for you to hang out with us while you're living here in Misty River, Luke."

He sincerely doubted that she was speaking for Sebastian.

"We get together at least once a month," Natasha added, "and it would mean a lot if you could come now and then."

"Seeing one another has been good for us." Genevieve set a half-eaten cookie on her plate. "It's my hope that seeing us might turn into something that's good for you, too."

"I'll think about it." Luke didn't plan to think about it.

"No gathering that the four of us have ever had," Natasha said, "has felt complete without you in it."

Luke never mentioned his affiliation with the group. Even so, the people in his life had occasionally found out. When they did, they immediately asked him about the other four. He could guess what it had been like for the rest of them, who didn't hide their past and were out in society much more than he was. They'd probably had to field countless questions about him.

Two more people, who were introduced to him as Leah and Sam, walked up. Sam was engaged to Genevieve.

Sebastian's girlfriend, Leah, was the sister of the kid who'd been feeding Luke information on Blair. "Thanks for setting things up between me and Dylan," Luke told her.

"You're welcome. When it comes to the teenagers in our lives, we adults need to have each other's back."

Sebastian's face softened with tenderness as he looked at Leah. Luke had never imagined that the tough, miserable foster kid he'd known would fall for someone. But he had.

As they talked, Natasha's redheaded husband also joined them.

Apparently they'd been married for several years and had two kids together.

Three of the Miracle Five seemed content in their relationships. More than content. Happy. They'd accomplished what he never had. They'd moved on.

As soon as possible, Luke made an excuse and separated from them.

Dakota intercepted him. Great.

She steered him to the heated tent.

Once there, he spotted Finley immediately. She and Derek were slow dancing to Elvis's "Love Me Tender."

Futility and longing clawed at him.

"You like Finley, don't you?" Dakota asked.

She'd caught him staring. "No," he lied.

"I'd be the happiest girl in the world if you didn't like me as much as you don't like her."

He remained silent.

"Finley's awesome," she said. "If she's into you—"

"She isn't."

"—then I think you could be amazing together. How about we dance over to them and then you cut in? I'll occupy Derek while you talk with Finley."

The song concluded. A few seconds later, "Unchained Melody" began.

"Fine." At the least, her plan would temporarily separate Derek from Finley. He took Dakota in his arms and expertly moved them across the dance floor until he tapped on Derek's shoulder. "I'm cutting in." No way was he going to ask the clown for permission.

"By all means," Derek said good-naturedly. He let go of Finley and began dancing with Dakota.

Without a word, Luke drew Finley's body against his. As they swayed together, he bent his head toward her hair, which smelled of shampoo. Her dress was as light and thin as air. Her waist, defined and feminine.

This was the best kind of torture.

"You can dance," she said with surprise.

"There's a lot of things you don't know about me."

"And whose fault is that? I'd like to know you."

"Trust me, you don't."

She met his gaze, eyes narrowed. "Yes, I do. In case you haven't noticed, I've been trying very hard to know you."

He'd been angry since he'd gotten here. Irrationally, he was pleased to see evidence that she was angry, too.

Keeping ahold of her hand, he led her off the dance floor and out of the tent. He followed a brick path that curved through flower beds and past trees until they came to a fence at the farthest corner of the backyard. Landscape lighting made the place feel like a king's garden.

She pulled her hand from his.

"You're upset," he said.

"I merely told you that I've been trying very hard to know you. Which, by the way, is perfectly true."

"I can tell by your expression that you're upset."

"No."

"Yes. Why?"

She rubbed her hands against her upper arms. Winter nights in the mountains held an icy edge.

In one motion, he stripped off his sweater, which left only the white, long-sleeved shirt he wore beneath. "Here." Most of the evening, his sweater and his train of thought had combined to make him feel almost overheated. He welcomed this temperature change.

"I can't take your sweater."

"Please." He held it closer to her. "There's no reason for you to be upset and cold at the same time."

With a great deal of pride, she put it on. It fell almost to the hem of her dress.

"Are you irritated because I came here tonight?" he asked.

"Of course not. I was delighted when I saw you."

He didn't like it when people made him guess at the source of their frustration. "Then what is it?"

Her skin was white as a statue, yet everything about her pulsed with life. She was maddening. Persistent, even when persistence made no sense. A defender of lost causes. Principled.

She made his demolished heart want to dream.

"I expressed my interest in you," she said, "the day we found the clue with the Dewey decimal number. You turned me down. I assumed that was because you weren't interested in anyone. But then I saw you with Dakota, and I thought, 'What if it's just me . . . that he's not interested in?'"

"Dakota and I didn't come together."

"Oh?"

"And I'm not interested in her."

"Oh." She pushed her inky hair behind her shoulders. "Now you go. What's your problem with me? And before you say that you don't have one, I can tell by your expression that you're upset." She'd turned his own words back on him.

"I can't stand Derek. I knew him in high school, and he's a womanizer. Not the kind that has one-night stands with random people. The kind that would make a girl fall in love with him, sleep with her for a while, then break up with her for another girl."

"Ah." She lifted her chin to a challenging angle. "And you were a choir boy in high school?"

"I never said I was."

"Have you changed since graduating high school?"

"Yes."

"How so?"

"For one, I never plan to break another law for as long as I live."

"Admirable. So you'll understand why it's possible that Derek might have changed, as well."

"He's not a pug that you can rehabilitate—"

"*If only* I could rehabilitate men as easily as I can rehabilitate dogs." The look she gave him spoke volumes.

"I don't want rehabilitating," he growled.

"Which is the crux of your issue."

His eyebrows drew down.

"I'm enjoying my time with Derek tonight," she continued, "and I plan to spend more time with him. You declined to date me, so I fail to see how you have the right to criticize the men who *do* want to date me."

They glared at each other.

Luke moved forward, wrapped an arm around her waist, and kissed her. One of his hands went to the back of her head, the other drew her against him. Her palms settled on his shirt, uncertain. But then she was kissing him back.

He wanted her with him forever. So long as there was a universe, that's how long. He'd go anywhere she went. Do anything she asked.

The kiss drew out, demanding, dangerous, impatient—

Without warning, she stepped back. She wasn't smiling.

His breath and hers jerked in and out, their exhales visible puffs in the night air.

"You are the most confusing man I have ever met," she said hoarsely. "What did that just mean?"

He'd carry his brother's death on his conscience his whole life. He cared about her far too much to want her to have anything to do with him. "Nothing."

"It meant nothing? Excellent! Thanks for making that clear." She whipped off the sweater, which left her hair crazy, and tossed it at him.

He caught it one-handed against his abdomen.

She stalked away.

He wanted to call her back—to explain, to apologize, to tell her how he felt about her.

But he did none of those things. He remained exactly where he was.

Silent.

CHAPTER SIXTEEN

The last time she'd kissed Luke, Finley had come through the experience feeling charitably toward him.

This time? Not so much.

After she returned home and tended to her pets, she flipped through the records she'd brought here from her dad's collection. This moment called for Janis Joplin. She placed the needle on the vinyl and turned the volume high. Then she walked purposefully to her bedroom. After diving stomach-down on the mattress, she clasped a pillow to her face and screamed.

Following Chase's death, this was the healthiest way she'd found to vent destructive feelings. She screamed again. Then again.

After a time, she sat up.

Take deep breaths. Relax your muscles.

It was very unlike her to leave a conversation on a jagged note, the way she'd done earlier with Luke. She typically maintained a sense of calm, even with demanding and difficult people. During their tense conversation in the garden, she'd repeatedly told herself, *Remember step two, Finley. Show extreme patience. Show extreme patience!*

Then, when they'd been kissing, the most heavenly sensations had swamped her. She'd ended the kiss not because she hadn't wanted it to continue for hours but because she didn't understand why the man who wasn't interested in her *was* interested in kissing her. Then he'd had the nerve to say that the kiss meant nothing to him.

She punched a text message into her phone, then sent it to Meadow and Bridget.

Finley
I kissed Luke again.

Bridget
On Valentine's Day! I'm not surprised. I have a really good feeling about you guys.

Meadow
A GOOD FEELING? What's the mantra we've been practicing, Finley?

Finley
Do not fall for emotionally unavailable men. I had no intention of kissing him tonight. We were arguing. And then we were kissing, which was divine. And then we were fighting again, which was lousy.

Meadow
I'm familiar with that roller coaster. It eventually crashes. Men! Grrr.

Bridget
I think Luke's in love with you.

Meadow
That's a destructive conclusion! If a man tells you he's not open to a relationship, no woman should interpret that to mean he's in love with her.

Bridget
Nonetheless, I think Luke loves Finley. He just hasn't admitted it to himself yet. He's been alone for a long time. He's afraid.

Finley
I don't think he loves me but I do think it's possible that his feelings for me are in the same galaxy as my feelings for him. The difference between us is that I'm willing to

discuss my emotions and follow where they lead. He's not.

Meadow

Case closed. Until a man tells you he likes you and shows you through his actions that he likes you he's not worth your time.

Music pounded through the house.

What was she doing? What was God doing? Why would He give her these feelings for Luke if He didn't intend something good to come from them? How had she toppled from her serene single existence into this—this *vat* of turbulent emotions?

So much unnecessary drama! And for what?

"I'm sorry," she whispered. She couldn't hear the words over the din, but it didn't matter. She was talking to Chase, and he could hear.

What she and Chase had shared had been beautiful. No way would she now settle for stolen kisses with a man who didn't value her. If she opened her heart to a man again, it would be to someone who respected her. Someone she could trust.

Luke had been right when he'd said playing with their physical attraction was playing with fire.

She performed another pillow-scream for good measure.

That's it! No more. Luke wasn't open to a real relationship, so it would be damaging to continue kissing.

Padding to the living room, she turned the volume low. Joplin became an undercurrent instead of a storm surge. She continued to the kitchen to make tea.

"*Staying committed to Chase is easy,*" Luke had said to her. "*He'll always remain perfect in your memory, and he'll never let you down. The relationship you didn't have with him can stay on its pedestal.*"

Luke, of all people, understood things about her she'd not only never said to another living soul but hadn't even acknowledged *to herself*.

She viewed herself as brave. People often complimented her on her bravery. She wore bravery like a medal around her neck.

Yet, when she got brutally honest with herself, she could admit that she wasn't brave about relationships anymore. If she let herself love someone new, she'd be vulnerable to the exact same devastation—which had lasted years and years—that she'd endured when she'd lost Chase.

She blew on her tea before taking a sip. "You can't live scared, Finley." In which case, why not go on more dates with Derek? He acted like a gentleman. He seemed to think she'd hung the moon. He did not send bolts of desire through her veins. In other words, he was exactly what she needed.

So she'd go out again with Derek. But what should she do about Luke?

Their responsibilities at Furry Tails bound them together for eight hours a day, five days a week. The treasure hunt bound them together for additional hours outside of work. She couldn't avoid him, nor could she give him the cold shoulder. She was an adult woman, and so she'd deal with him like an adult woman. With straightforward grace.

Even though she was still—*still!*—angry.

Luke spent Valentine's night stewing over Finley and sleeping little.

He showed up for work the next morning with no idea what to expect from her. She'd proven that she preferred to talk through conflicts. But it could be he'd pushed her over a line this time and now she'd freeze him out.

Before he'd taken a seat at his computer, the door to her office opened and she filled the doorway. Bell bottoms, black top, and a hat he hadn't seen before. Made out of black, white, and red wool plaid, the hat looked like a beret, except it had a very short brim at the front. Beneath that brim, her eyes were incredibly blue, like a candle glowing through sapphires. "Can we talk?" she asked.

He nodded, entered her office, and closed the door behind him.

They took the same chairs they usually occupied in this small room. This time, though, something new spiked the air. Hostility?

"Emotions were running high last night." She crossed her legs. "I said and did things I regret. Same for you?"

"Yes."

He struggled to read her mood. She was saying the usual Finley things but not in the usual Finley way, because hurt lay beneath every word. She wasn't freezing him out, but he *had* pushed her over a line.

"In the past, you tried to explain why it wouldn't be wise for us to follow through on physical attraction. At this point, I see the wisdom of that, too."

"Good." He felt anything but good.

"I think you were right, too, about the fact that God may not have intended for me to go without romantic relationships for the rest of my life. I'm going to attempt to open myself up to romance."

"Hmm?"

"I'm going to go out with Derek again."

He imagined connecting a right hook to Derek's smug, smiling face. "Great."

"I know. It's progress!"

They stared at each other like two generals across a battlefield. Buzzing dominated his thoughts. He couldn't swallow because regret cinched his throat.

"I'm hoping we can move on without any grudges between us," she said.

Impossible. He was going to hold a grudge against her. Mostly for invading his life and mind. For draining Montana of its power. For taking his advice and using it to start a relationship with Derek.

"Can we do that?" she asked.

"What?"

"Move on without any grudges?"

"Yes." It was the only answer he could give.

"Wonderful. Thanks, Luke."

Silence.

"I was really pleased to hear," she said stiffly, "that you're working on your sister's car. I hadn't realized you were in contact with your family."

"I communicate with my parents. It's only lately that I've been in contact with Blair. She'll turn sixteen soon, so she asked me to get her car running."

"What's your other sister's name?"

"Hailey."

"Everything I know about your family I learned through the town grapevine. I'd love to know more."

"There's not much to tell."

Her mouth tightened. "Isn't your mom a fitness instructor at the community center?"

"Yes."

"I'm going to email her and invite your family to stop by here so that I can give them a tour."

"I don't think they'll want to come."

"I disagree. I think they'll jump at the chance to see the place where you work."

More silence.

"Well," she said, "I won't keep you."

He stood. "I'm really sorry, Finley."

Her chest rose and fell. "I believe you."

"Good, because it's true."

"You're forgiven." She studied him. "I wish you could internalize just how forgiven you are."

She was talking about God now. "Why would He forgive me?"

"Luke. Your faithlessness doesn't affect God's faithfulness at all. Not at all. He is faithful. Always. That's part of His character. You believed in Him when you were young. Which means, when you ask for forgiveness, He forgives you. Period."

"I haven't done anything for Him."

"None of the love He has for you is conditional. It doesn't hinge on your actions or my actions. And *thank God* for that. You're loved by Him. And you're forgiven."

No way could he deal with a spiritual intervention right now.

He left her office. At this moment, to continue breathing, he only needed one person's forgiveness.

Hers.

That night, Ben and Akira reclined in the back of a truck bed in preparation to watch a drive-in movie.

"I'm glad this isn't romantic at all," Akira said.

Ben looked across at her and grinned. When he was with Akira, he often caught himself smiling. When they were apart, he looked forward to the next time he'd see her. Their personalities clicked effortlessly. She was funny and self-deprecating. He never had to guess what she was thinking or feeling because she was always quick to tell him.

"These thousands of stars glittering in the heavens." She swung a hand toward the sky. "These cozy blankets you brought. This delicious hot chocolate I brought." She lifted her travel mug. "Your face. I'm not finding any of that in the least bit romantic, which is a real relief, seeing as how we're merely friends."

"A great relief," he said wryly.

"Whew."

They saw each other a few times a week at Furry Tails, and they'd started hanging out once or twice a week in addition to that. They texted daily. He'd learned she had a thing for bonsai trees, mechanical pencils, and *Gilmore Girl* reruns. She also had a knack for sending him funny GIFs and memes right when he needed something to brighten his day.

The previews hadn't started, so there was nothing to distract him from looking at her graceful, lively face. His eyes traced the slopes of her cheeks, the firm curve of her chin. "The popcorn isn't great," he pointed out. "It's kind of stale and too salty. So that further detracts from the romantic atmosphere."

"I'd agree with you, if there was such a thing as not-good popcorn."

"Exhibit A." He tapped the rim of the popcorn tub.

"No matter what, it's crunchy kernels popped in oil, then sprinkled with salt. So—still good."

"In that case, you can have my share."

"I wouldn't hear of it. Then I'd gain ten pounds, and you'd become even more fit. If you were any more fit, I might feel romantic feelings."

He huffed with amusement. "My current body leaves something to be desired?"

"*So* much to be desired. And thank goodness for it. Your dad bod is my safety net."

"Uh-huh." He was in the same shape now that he'd been in back in college when he'd played baseball.

"Speaking of romance, how are things progressing for you on the recovering-from-heartbreak front?" she asked.

He took a sip of the hot chocolate. Delicious. Thick and rich with a crown of whipped cream. "I realized a while back that I'm not the best at letting myself feel negative emotions. It's not my M.O. to be the moody, pessimistic guy."

"Ah."

"Everybody counts on me to be the upbeat guy. Not that I'm blaming anybody else. I stay the upbeat guy because that's what I count on myself to be. I'm always fine. Always. So, if something makes me feel uncomfortable, I just shove it away and go on being fine."

"I understand." Her fingers toyed with the fringe on her throw blanket. "Back when I was sick, I did everything I could think of to distract myself from feeling scared. Bad decision. It would've been much better to talk with somebody about my fears and work through them. Instead, I didn't mention it to anyone and so anxiety kept bubbling up and then devouring me."

"What helped?"

"Addressing the root problem. Fear."

"My root problem is sadness. I've been trying to give myself permission to be bummed." He leaned back, angling his face to the stars. "I assured Sebastian that I could deal with pain. But it turns out, not so much."

"Talking about it with friends, like we're doing now, helped me."

"I've been talking about it with my brother and another of my friends. I've also been listening to 'I Can't Make You Love Me' by Bonnie Raitt on repeat."

She snapped her fingers and sat upright. "My heart has been broken three times. I have a whole playlist of songs to listen to when recovering. In addition to that song, I prescribe regular listening to 'Sandcastles' by Beyoncé."

"'The Dance' by Garth Brooks."

"Yes! 'Ain't No Sunshine' by Bill Withers."

"A classic."

"I'll share my playlist with you. I cried out more toxins listening to those songs than I've ever sweat out while exercising."

How come you're so uptight, anyway?" Blair asked Luke the following night.

Why? Why couldn't she let him work on her car alone?

He'd spent a lot of time here in the barn lately. He loved working on this car. But not even the Firebird had the power to distract him from Finley. He couldn't stand spending hours a day just inches away from her, smelling her light citrus perfume. Wanting to touch her. Then coming here in search of a few hours of peace and finding none.

Regrets, condemnation, anger over what had gone sideways between him and Finley on Valentine's Day . . . he'd wrestled with all of it.

And now, on top of that, he was having to deal with his sister.

Blair sat on the garage's counter, swinging her combat boots. A knit cap covered her head. She wore ripped jeans and a huge black T-shirt that said *Smashing the Patriarchy Is My Cardio*.

"I'm not uptight." He was leaning over the engine, working on the carburetor. "Hand me the needle-nose pliers."

She hopped down and brought him the pliers. "You're actually very uptight, which seems weird in a guy who's gone to jail."

"Only law-abiding citizens are allowed to be uptight?"

"Are you admitting that you *are* uptight?"

She was painfully frustrating. "I'm admitting that I'm uptight enough to want solitude in this barn."

"If only, bro." She peered at the engine critically. "Are you going to work on the crankshaft?"

"I am definitely not going to work on the crankshaft just because a fifteen-year-old—"

"—sister of yours—"

"—tells me to. Back away from the car."

"It's *my* car."

"If you want it to run, back away from it."

She retreated, palms lifted.

He liked her twenty percent more when she stood on the other side of the room and thirty percent more than that when she wasn't speaking.

"Fair warning," Blair murmured. "I can see through the windows that Mom, Dad, and Hailey just parked outside. They're about to come in here and ambush you."

Luke's shoulders sagged as he emptied his lungs in a slow stream.

"Son?" His dad's voice.

Luke turned.

Bruce Dempsey, now in his late fifties, was bald on top with gray hair shaved close on the sides and back of his head. Measured, thoughtful, and full of integrity, his job as an insurance agent suited him well. He was a Midwesterner who earnestly loved his wife and who somehow came out of every grocery store with more condiments than the family could consume.

His mom held the homemade coffee cake that had been Luke's favorite when he was a kid. Thick blond hair framed a face that was long and narrow, pretty and approachable. She showed genuine interest in every person she met. She wasn't competitive and typically lost when their family played games. So when they'd installed a pool table in the basement, the rest of them had been shocked when she'd easily beaten them all.

His parents had hardly changed in years.

The girl standing next to them *had* changed.

Luke's pulse thumped in his ears at the sight of her.

It was as if he were seeing a ghost. Ethan's ghost.

She was just a few years older than Ethan had been when he'd died. She had the exact same shade of dark blond hair. The same oval face. Same nose. Very similar mouth. Light freckles. But it was the sight of her eyes that punched him in the stomach. Her warm, friendly hazel eyes were set beneath expressive eyebrows. *Ethan's eyes.*

Was this a joke? Blair looked and acted like him. Hailey looked like his brother and, if what Ben had said was true, acted like him, too.

The three of them came forward. His dad hugged him with the same strong arms that had embraced him when he was a kid. "I love you," he said.

Emotion trapped Luke in a vise.

His mom came next. "Love you, Luke." She gave him a tight squeeze and pressed a kiss to his cheek.

"Hi," Hailey said self-consciously. He didn't blame her for feeling uncomfortable around him. They were practically strangers. They exchanged a stiff side hug.

"How come I didn't get a hug out of you during our touching reunion?" Blair asked.

"Blair," Mom said disapprovingly.

"You didn't get a hug because you didn't move in for a hug," Luke told her.

"I didn't move in for a hug because you looked like you were going to bite my head off."

This was the daughter the nicest parents in Misty River had received after one son had died and the other ran away?

"Do you still like cinnamon streusel coffee cake?" Mom asked.

"Yes." He could smell the doughy scent of it.

"It makes me happy to hear that. I hope you'll enjoy this." She set the cake on the counter, then appeared unsure what to do with her hands. Finally, she interlaced them in front of her waist. "You look wonderful. How are you?"

Mom, Dad, and Hailey were all trying so hard that it was difficult to watch.

"I'm doing well."

"Thanks for agreeing to help Blair fix up this car," Dad said.

"You're welcome."

"Blair, you're providing a lot of assistance like we talked about, right?" Dad asked.

"The only thing he'll let me do is hand him tools. He's told me more than once that he'd rather I not come by at all."

Blair had thrown him under the bus, of course. "She's a headache," he said, "as I'm sure the three of you have noticed."

A moment of tense quiet followed. Dad broke it with an affectionate chuckle. "Yeah. We've noticed." He softened the teasing words by wrapping an arm around Blair and drawing her against his side.

"Do you think you'll be able to get the car running?" Mom asked.

"I know I can." His family members gathered around as he explained what needed to be done and how he would go about it. As far as he knew, only Dad and Blair had an interest in car mechanics. But they all watched him with what appeared to be deep interest. Maybe because they'd never heard him say so many words in a row before.

"Wow." Dad looked impressed. "Blair and I worked on it some, but everything you just described is definitely above our pay grade. We're fortunate to have your help."

Luke didn't point out that nothing about their association with him had been fortunate. He hadn't forgotten the years of struggle when they'd laid down rules he'd repeatedly broken. His feelings toward his parents were complicated . . . and he could only imagine how complicated their feelings were toward him.

Hailey smiled shyly at him, and his chest ached.

"Welcome back to Misty River," she told him. "I'm glad you're here."

"I wish Ethan could've been here instead," he said, speaking words he'd never have given himself permission to say if he'd thought about them first.

"Not instead," Dad said quietly. "We never wanted him here instead of you. We always wanted you *both* here. We always will. We love you, Luke. Just like we love him."

"And always will," Mom finished, tears in her eyes.

Luke had to look away. He gestured toward the engine. "I'd better get back to work."

"By all means," Mom said. "We're here to assist, so please tell us what we can do."

An hour and a half later, Luke's family finally left.

Lowering onto the ground, he sat against the Pontiac's front fender. His arms rested on his bent knees.

Since his release three-and-a-half months ago, he'd broken no laws. He'd stuck to the goal he'd made for himself in prison and cleaned up his life. Yet his outwardly good actions weren't enough to fix what was still messed up inside him.

He was miserable.

Finley and his parents had dealt with hardship, too, but they weren't miserable. The one big difference between them and him was that they'd hung on to their faith.

"*Your faithlessness doesn't affect God's faithfulness,*" Finley had said to him. "*None of the love He has for you is conditional.*"

Was it worth trying to pick his faith back up at this point?

How, though? Was he just supposed to snap his fingers and resume his relationship with God?

He'd been through some of the worst things life can deal a person, and nothing should scare him. But two things did: trusting in God, and the fact that something inside him still wanted to be loved and needed.

He felt unworthy of love, yet the longing to be loved hadn't left him despite everything he'd done to suffocate it, and all the years of isolation in prison.

The scaffolding holding him up inside was cracking, and he didn't know what to do about any of it.

Mr. Dempsey?" A tall brunette who looked to be about thirty came to a halt in the reception area.

"Yes."

"Mr. Horton is ready for you."

Luke rose and followed her. When he'd told Finley about the disciplinary actions the state bar had taken against Rosco Horton, she'd supported Luke's plan to meet her father's attorney and told Luke to take as much time off work today as he needed. He knew she didn't expect him to make up the time it would take to drive to Hartwell, meet with Rosco, and drive back. But he'd stay late at the Center tonight and make it up anyway.

Rosco's office was old-school. The green carpet and dark wood gave the place an eighties vibe.

The brunette knocked on Rosco's door, then opened it for Luke.

"Thank you, Julia," Rosco said as he stood. The door clicked softly behind Luke as the older man came around the desk with a smile. They shook hands, exchanged introductions, and took their seats.

Rosco appeared to be in his early-to-mid seventies. He had the body of a mall Santa Claus, without the beard. He wore red suspenders and a tie that looked uncomfortably tight.

"Let's talk about how I might be able to help you," Rosco said.

"I'd like to have my will drawn up."

"Yes. Very wise. We can certainly handle that for you."

Rosco explained the steps involved as Luke studied him. The older man was polite and outgoing. Confident and kind.

When Luke met Robbie, he'd been able to see that Robbie had the capacity to conceal. He didn't see that here. Rosco seemed like someone's trustworthy grandfather, which was disturbing, seeing as how the disciplinary actions against Rosco called his trustworthiness into question.

Luke put more pressure on Rosco, asking him questions about the mission of his one-man firm and the level of confidentiality Luke could expect.

Rosco showed no sign of agitation as he patiently fielded Luke's questions.

Rosco might be a good man who'd made a few mistakes over the course of his career. Or he might be an excellent actor . . . Santa Claus on the outside, a snake on the inside.

Either way, this meeting had not brought Luke the clarity he'd wanted.

When Finley arrived home from work the following evening, she discovered a package stuffed into her mailbox. She retrieved scissors from her desk and cut the top of the envelope off. *Brothers: Twenty-Five Stories About the Ties That Bind* slid into her hand.

For the next two hours, she interrupted her power reading only to heat leftovers for dinner and to give Sally and Dudley the hedgehog their evening play session. Every time she encountered a reference or word or detail that reminded her of her father, she noted it with a highlighter and placed a strip of paper between the pages to mark it.

The beautiful stories examined many different facets of brotherhood, confirming her initial impression that this was a book her father would have enjoyed.

However, reading it had not illuminated her next step. At no point had she experienced a spark of rightness like when she'd seen the song lyrics at the train depot museum.

It could be that any old copy of *Brothers* would not do. Perhaps only the copy that had once belonged to the Misty River Library would provide the next clue.

In which case, her father's final treasure hunt would inevitably end here.

I read the entire book, and none of the potential clues I found stood out with any significance," Finley said to Luke the next day over lunch.

The two of them occupied a table in the corner of Sugar Maple Kitchen. He'd agreed to share lunch with her here because this setting, away from Furry Tails, gave them a degree of privacy.

She savored the taste of her salad—spinach, currants, green apple, and walnuts. "I've been pondering the places in the book I marked, but honestly, it feels like a reach to call any of them clues."

Her feelings toward Luke were thorny, thanks to his rejection of her. Since the Valentine's party, she'd been having a hard time falling asleep at night. And then every morning when she woke up and remembered the state of things between herself and Luke, disappointment washed over her.

Spending time with him at work and sitting across from him now filled her with an uneasy combination of pining and animosity. The important thing, she kept reminding herself, was to take the high road. She refused to abandon her five-step plan for Luke because of her resentment. No, indeed. She was made of sterner stuff than that.

Sugar Maple Kitchen was currently providing him with food. Step one of the Restoration of Luke—check! And it offered additional conditioning to the town, its people, and the social practice of a shared meal. Step four—check!

A plate of pork chops and veggies sat before Luke, though his attention was currently captured by the *Brothers* book in his hand. With his blunt masculine fingers, he made his way to each of the pages she'd noted. His dark head bent as he read, and she longed to reach out and run her fingertips through the brown strands of his hair, which curled slightly at the tips—

Geez, Finley! No.

His hazel gaze flicked up to hers. "Which of the places you marked do you think is most likely to hold a clue?"

The power of his attention affected her like a flame licking her belly. *After we kissed on Valentine's night, he said it meant nothing. Never forget that.* "I've narrowed it down to three that I think are most likely."

"I'm listening."

"In one of the stories, the author mentioned riding bikes with his brother when they were young. My dad often rode bikes with Robbie. In fact, Dad's childhood bike is hanging in the garage at his house. If we go there, and search the bike and its vicinity, we might find a clue."

Luke set the book aside.

"It feels unlikely," she admitted. "All of these feel unlikely."

"You said you narrowed it down to three possibilities."

"In another essay, the author talks about playing in an abandoned mine. My dad loved history. Over the years, he took me to every one of the old mines in northern Georgia that are open to the public. His favorite was the Big Cedar Mountain Gold Mine near Dahlonega. It's the only one we visited twice."

"You're thinking that if we go to the mine, something there will hold meaning for you."

"Yes. Again, it's a stretch."

He didn't look hopeful.

She gave a long-suffering sigh.

"What's with the sigh?" he asked.

"I was just thinking that you don't look hopeful. But then I thought, *When has Luke ever looked hopeful?* And that made me sigh."

"At my despair?"

"Cut me some slack. I'm a heroine for putting up with your despair as well as I do."

"What's the third possibility you found in the book?"

"One author wrote about pancakes. Buttermilk pancakes were special to my dad and me. Holidays, birthdays, long weekends . . . pancakes were our go-to celebration breakfast."

"Where should we look for a clue associated with pancakes?"

"My dad's kitchen."

"We can test both the bike and pancake clues at your dad's house, so I vote we try that first."

"I second that."

"Can we go Saturday?"

"I have plans Saturday."

His jaw set. "Sunday?"

"I'm headed to church Sunday morning. But after that, yes."

Finley's Saturday plans amounted to one very important event. A visit to the Carla Vance Memorial Auction.

A short road trip through the Blue Ridge Mountains brought her to the town of Toccoa. Carla, her father's deceased girlfriend, had grown up in the historic town of about eight thousand, where her three brothers still lived.

Every year, Carla's brothers and mother honored her with a fundraiser at their church. They kicked things off with a potluck lunch, followed by bingo for the adults and kid games for the littles. Then they held silent and live auctions. They finished with a concert by local musicians. All the money raised went to support the church's food pantry and soup kitchen.

Finley, who'd timed her arrival for the start of the auction, slipped in the back of the fellowship hall and took an empty seat at one of the round tables. She'd stay for a handful of minutes, then leave before anyone recognized her.

Carla's ninety-year-old mother had grown wobblier since last year but made her way to the podium on stage unassisted. Behind her hung an enormous sign emblazoned with *In Loving Memory of Carla* next to a picture of Carla's smiling face. Mrs. Vance thanked everyone for coming and led a prayer.

Finley bent her head as guilt, sorrow, and sympathy jumbled inside. Her father had accidentally killed Carla, and there was no way anyone could ever make that right, because the only way to do that was to bring Carla back to life. Finley's annual pilgrimage to this fundraiser didn't assuage the responsibility she carried on her father's behalf. But it did enable her to do the few paltry things she felt honor-bound to do. Pay her respects. Remember Carla. And support Carla's family's excellent cause.

All four of the Vance children had been close in age. Ken was older than Carla. Dennis and Jeff were younger. It was Ken who took the mic next, to share memories of his sister's life.

Finley pulled the ball cap she wore low. She'd only met the brothers in person once, at a party her dad and Carla had hosted.

They looked a lot alike. Big-boned, hearty men with square faces and thick dark hair. They'd been kind to her at the party, and after Carla's death, she'd been unable to get them and their poor mother out of her mind. She'd started checking on them every so often via their Facebook feeds, which was how she'd found out about the first memorial fundraiser.

Dennis opened the live auction bidding.

Finley's gaze centered on the giant photograph of Carla. *I'm so sorry.*

She extracted an envelope filled with cash from her purse as she made her way toward the exit. A donation box waited at the start of the potluck table. In one quick movement, she deposited two thousand dollars inside.

Late Sunday afternoon, Finley set her hands on her hips and blew a wayward strand of hair out of her eye.

She and Luke had been searching her dad's house for three hours. The entire time, the tension that existed between them now had been snapping like a downed electrical cable. She'd been much too aware of the scent of his soap. The strength of his movements. The musculature of his torso beneath his shirt.

They'd tackled the garage—examining every inch of her dad's old bike and the space around it. Nothing.

Then they'd gone through his kitchen. Nothing.

At that point, Luke had suggested that since they'd come all this way for the second time, they search the house in general. Even if the clue that was supposed to be found next after the *Brothers* book wasn't here, maybe they'd find a clue her dad had left for later in the hunt. If that occurred, they could leapfrog the clue.

They combed the house room by room. They peered under rugs and furniture. Peeked behind art. Opened every drawer. Ran their hands down the back of the closets.

They worked well as a team. They'd been fast and thorough.

"There are no clues in this house," Finley stated.

Luke hunched in front of the cupboard beneath the laundry room sink. He shut its door and straightened to his full height. After scrubbing his scalp for a few seconds, he dropped his arms.

She really did think she could make her peace with leaving the treasure hunt unsolved. She could even spin that ending fancifully in her mind. *You father will never be completely gone, Finley, because his final treasure hunt clues will always remain at large. Magical. Mythical. An open-ended resolution is sometimes better than a resolution in which every* i *has been dotted and every* t *crossed.*

Luke, however, would never be content with that outcome. He wouldn't feel he'd been released from his promise until they brought this to a clear-cut close.

Why were her emotions such a frustrating tangle? She wanted Luke to experience the freedom of a promise fulfilled. Yet she didn't want him to leave Misty River. Yet she *should* want him to leave Misty River, because her life would be far less confusing with him gone.

"I think it's time for us to call it a day," she said. "We gained valuable information because now we know that this house holds no more secrets and, as such, we should not sink more of our time here."

He frowned.

"Let's head home," she said. "We can visit the gold mine next weekend."

The whine of wind against the creaky walls of the house answered.

His shoulders braced. She'd noticed that sounds like that made him nervous. No doubt, that was an aftereffect of the earthquake. As was the window he kept ajar at work, the generator he stored behind his truck's bench seat, and the fact that he charged his phone the whole time he was at his desk.

Desperately, she wanted to lighten his mood.

His mood is not your responsibility, Finley!

Could she get away with hugging him?

No.

Though she felt compelled to hug him, she could not trust herself to do so.

CHAPTER SEVENTEEN

Late in the afternoon on Tuesday, Ben entered the workroom with his usual smile. "Hey, man."

"Hey." Luke rose, and they exchanged a fist bump.

"Where are your two sidekicks?"

"By sidekicks you can't mean Kat and Trish."

Ben chuckled. "I do, though. You three are a trip together."

"We're oil and water together. The only time I can think straight is when they're outside the building, like now, doing home visits."

"Any word on Agatha?"

"No."

"Do you miss her?"

"No." That wasn't exactly true, but there was no way he'd admit that he did think about the puppy. Sometimes. Hardly ever. "I'm just glad Agatha's family hasn't returned her and filed a suit for emotional damage."

"She was a cute little thing."

Luke slanted his head to the side a fraction. "Ben, is it tiring to view everything in its best possible light all the time?"

"Less tiring than viewing everything in its worst possible light," Ben said cheerfully.

He had a point.

"Listen," Ben said, "Sebastian, Natasha, Genevieve, and I are getting together for lunch on Sunday. Can you join us?"

"I might already have plans Sunday. I'm not sure."

"Is that true," Ben asked with a humorous expression, "or are you just blowing me off again?"

"Both." He didn't yet know if he and Finley were going to the gold mine that day. But even if they weren't, he'd probably rather blow Ben off.

Finley exited her office, and his idiot heart lifted at the sight of her.

"You should go to lunch with the others," she said to Luke.

"Were you eavesdropping?"

"Yes. Sure was." She beckoned for them to follow. "C'mon. Luke's family is here for a tour."

"Huh?" Luke said.

"I told you they'd jump at the chance to come."

Sure enough, when they reached the foyer, Luke's family waited inside.

"Hello! I'm Finley, and I'm so delighted you're here. Thank you for coming." Her face lit up as she shook hands with his parents and siblings.

Ben greeted them with familiarity and affection.

Finley asked his parents a few questions, and in no time, Ben helped her find common ground with them through mutual friends and activities.

Finley and Ben were exactly as comfortable with his family as he was uncomfortable.

"Your son is unbelievably talented with computers," Finley was saying. "He completed the website redesign for Furry Tails, and now he's creating a system that will match prospective families with available pets. He's also teaching the other employees how to upload each of the currently adoptable animals onto the site and how to manage the system."

"That's fabulous," Mom said.

"Way to go," Ben said to him.

It had been forever since anyone had called him out publicly for doing something good. He wasn't at ease listening to Finley brag on him. But he didn't hate it, either.

"He streamlined payroll and automated all of our administrative practices," Finley said. "We no longer need a physical filing system."

"Wow," Dad murmured.

"He's also helped us tighten security," Finley added. "At one particularly memorable staff meeting, he terrified us all with crime stats. We now follow his guidelines to the letter."

Mom beamed. No doubt she was glad to hear about his work but probably even more glad to see evidence that he had two friends.

"I hadn't realized he'd accomplished all that here," Dad said.

"Luke's not very forthcoming," Finley admitted.

"That's the truth." Ben grinned.

Blair snorted. "He's pretty forthcoming with me."

"That's because you make me mad," he said.

"And Finley doesn't?" Blair asked.

"I do sometimes." Finley smoothly saved Luke from having to answer. "But I try not to."

"I wish *you'd* try not to make me mad," Luke said to Blair.

At the exact same time, Blair said, "I've given up trying not to make him mad."

On Wednesday evening, Akira sat in the wooden bleachers at Misty River's community baseball diamond, watching the closing minutes of practice for Ben's league team.

She and Ben had planned to meet here, then go to the school supply store to pick up some items for the after-school program's next science unit. She'd purposely arrived fifteen minutes early, in hopes of seeing him in action on the field.

Ben was the picture of athletic grace. She watched his bat crack against a pitch. The ball sailed into the outfield. Another pitch. *Crack*. Hitting the ball was as easy for him as picking up flu germs had been for her.

He turned, met her eyes, and smiled.

Her heart actually contracted.

"Be there in two minutes," he called.

"No hurry." *I could sit here for hours.*

Watching him interact with his teammates was slaying her. Sometimes he smack-talked with them and made them laugh. Other times he complimented them or clapped them on the shoulder. She'd bet that if she asked any of these men who their closest friend was on this team, they'd all say Ben. He was magic with people. Others couldn't help but respond to him with warmth.

She was legitimately crushing on him, which terrified her.

She didn't view herself as the type of woman who had what it would take to win the heart of Ben Coleman. She wasn't like Leah Montgomery. She wasn't confident enough, or beautiful enough, or impressive enough. It would be so, so much safer for her to find contentment in her friendship with Ben. She *would* find contentment in it. And why not? Their friendship was superb. An unexpected gift!

She didn't want to risk either their friendship or her heart by attempting more with him. Yet these swoony feelings were growing every time she saw him.

Too soon, the practice finished. He tossed his equipment into a duffel bag that he hauled over his shoulder. Once he'd said goodbye to the others, he approached her.

She clambered down from the bleachers. "You'll be pleased to know that I didn't find anything about that practice the slightest bit romantic."

His eyebrows shot up. "No? What about now? I'm going to give you my smolder." He imitated a male model's serious face. "How ya doin'?" he purred.

She shook her head. "I'm impervious to that."

"How about this?" He extracted a bat from his bag. Turning to the side, he slung it over his shoulder, struck a pose, and held eye contact with her.

"Nope." The syllable emerged high-pitched because the eye contact was rearranging her insides into the shape of a heart with an arrow through it.

"That's great to hear." He broke character and they walked toward the parking lot. "It sounds like we're safe from romance."

"Nothing to worry about. At all."

Midmorning on Saturday, a tiny train drew Luke deeper and deeper into the tunnels of Big Cedar Mountain Gold Mine. Finley had recommended they retrace the steps she'd taken with Ed when they'd visited together. Today they'd start with the train tour, then mine for gold, then finish with the gift shop. Luke had agreed because he'd assumed he'd be okay with this tour. This glorified toy train was like a kiddie ride at an amusement park. This wasn't a basement. They weren't underneath a building.

Turned out, he wasn't okay with this. Maybe he'd never be able to go underground again—not in any way—after the earthquake. His heart was pounding, and he was having trouble getting enough air.

He sat next to Finley in an open-topped train car so small it barely fit two people on its wooden bench. Finley's thigh and upper arm pressed against his. The rounded roof of the tunnel zipped by inches from the top of his head. The cars in front of theirs held an older couple, a mom and dad, their three kids, and the engine where their driver/tour guide sat. The only light beamed forward from the front of the train. It brightened the tracks ahead but left him and Finley in shadow. He'd made the mistake of glancing back once into the black hole behind them.

What if the train lost power? They'd come to a stop in blackness.

Memories of El Salvador overwhelmed him.

Cold sweat gathered on his forehead. Angrily, he used the sleeve of his jacket to wipe it away. He was pretty sure they'd said this tour would last twenty minutes. How long had it been so far? It felt like seventeen minutes, but he had a sinking feeling that it had only been seven.

He thought of the cubic tons of mountain above them. The weight of it. The depth—

Concentrate on Finley. She was warm and comforting. She was close. Because she was close, he would be fine.

Over the clatter of metal wheels on track, the tour guide talked into a headset that broadcast to speakers mounted inside each car. An older lady, she had short hair dyed an unnatural shade of caramel and a huge overbite. Occasionally, light bounced off the veneers on her upper teeth.

She finished providing information about the Cherokee who'd once inhabited these mountains. Unfortunately for them, gold had been discovered in their homeland.

"A deer hunter named Benjamin Parks is recognized as the first to discover gold in these parts when he tripped over a rock, picked it up, and saw that it was full of gold," she said in a thick Georgia accent. "Rain had been washing gold off the mountainsides for centuries, you see."

How much time had now passed? Luke was having to think hard about his inhales and exhales.

He looked at Finley. Not only did she appear relaxed, she seemed to be enjoying this. Her lips were curved, and her hair sailed behind her. She wore her denim coat over one of the long dresses she liked. This one was brown print with a full skirt.

"News of Benjamin's find quickly spread, setting off a gold rush in the year 1828, twenty years before the California gold rush began. Some fifteen thousand people flooded into the region, hoping to find gold. The first ones who arrived were the lucky ones—they harvested it by simply picking it up off the ground. Once they'd collected all they could that way, they started panning for gold in rivers and streams, then directed water flow to create mudslides that brought material containing gold down into sluice boxes."

They sailed past tunnels snaking away from the main tunnel, then underneath wooden supports. Was he supposed to believe that splintery pieces of one-hundred-and-fifty-year-old wood would keep this thing from caving in? What if an earthquake hit?

"A robber baron named Milton Lawrence, who'd made his fortune in steel, sent geologists and surveyors to this area. They reported back to him that these hills were marbled with veins of quartz containing gold. Most veins of that type are an average of two-to-three inches thick. But here, they found an area where several large veins converged into a vein that was approximately *twenty-two feet* wide. They called it the glory hole. Milton Lawrence promptly bought up five thousand acres and built the Big Cedar Mountain Gold Mine."

The train slowed, then stopped. To the side, a room-sized area had been carved out of rock. It gave way to a narrow passageway. A few battery-powered lanterns built to look old-fashioned lit the space.

They climbed out of the cars. Damp ceiling hovered just above his head. His balance was off, and the whole place seemed to be tilting to one side and then the other, like a ship.

He took up a protective position behind Finley, legs braced, arms crossed over a chest that had gone tight with pressure. Panic edged his thoughts. What had he been thinking, bringing her down here? If this thing started to come down, he'd throw his body over hers. Were the walls closing in? It felt like they were closing in.

"The glory hole," the tour guide continued, "is one of the largest veins of quartz carrying gold that has ever been discovered anywhere in the world." She pointed out the area where it had been mined, explaining how long it had been and at what angle the vein had traveled.

He bit down on his molars, gritting it out.

The tour guide asked if anyone had questions. No one did, except the middle child of the family—a boy. He raised his hand again and again while his sisters played in the terribly small passageway. Every time one of them darted out of sight, Luke winced. If the tour guide tried to make him walk through that, he'd flat-out refuse.

The boy was proving the idea that there was "no such thing as a stupid question" wrong.

Luke wanted to strangle both the guide and the kid.

"Any other questions?" the tour guide asked.

Just as the boy brought his hand up to his chest in preparation to raise it, Luke caught the kid's eye. He gave him a scowl that said, *You ask another question and you die*. The kid's arm shrank back to his side.

Finley peeked at him. Her forehead tweaked. "You okay?"

"Fine."

She studied him.

He knew she was seeing more than he wanted her to see.

She came to stand beside him and interlaced her hand with his. She didn't speak as the tour guide led them back to the train for the trip out. She didn't need to speak. He knew what she was saying through their joined hands.

I'm here.

The mine tour had been painful for Luke, and Finley was kicking herself because *of course*. Of course! Dark underground places would stir up old trauma for him.

She should have been more thoughtful. She should have anticipated the problem before they'd bought tickets. She could have gone on the train alone and met up with him aboveground. She would have offered that, had it occurred to her.

She hadn't realized the error of her ways until they'd arrived in the underground space and she'd seen Luke's pale, drawn face. Instantly, her reasons for keeping distance between them evaporated in a wave of compassion. The simple, comforting connection of their hands had felt more right than anything had in days. His strong fingers. Her strong grip. Interlaced.

For the remainder of the tour, she'd held his hand, willing it to end as quickly as possible for his sake.

"I'm sorry," she told him as soon as they returned to open air. She released his hand as they were ushered onto a covered patio marked with several shallow metal chutes. "I know that was awful for you."

His lips firmed.

"The underground tour would have felt more worthwhile," she continued, "if I'd had a revelation about the treasure hunt. But because I didn't, it feels like I put you through that for no good reason."

"I don't blame you. You couldn't have known whether or not you'd find anything before we started."

"How are you doing now?"

"Better."

His skin was still too white against his beige shirt and black jacket.

"Who wants to pan for gold?" their tour guide asked.

"No, thank you," Luke said.

Simultaneously, Finley said, "We do!"

They looked at each other.

"I'd love to pan for gold," Finley said before Luke could shoot the idea down. At the very least, it would buy him time to decompress.

The guide handed Finley two pans and explained the process. Water burbled down the chute that she and Luke had to themselves. "What's not fun about this?" She submerged her pan.

"It's fifty-three degrees out here."

"And this water is freezing," she acknowledged. "But that only makes it more invigorating." She shot him a challenging look, then nudged his unclaimed pan toward him with her elbow.

Grudgingly, he took it and mimicked her actions.

"I'd like to know more about the years following your departure from Misty River," she said.

"No."

"Yes." Finley knew he planned to run away to Montana, but he'd already left Misty River once before, and it hadn't healed anything. Talking with Luke's wonderful family the other day had inspired her to learn more about his past. "Where did you go, exactly, when you left home? You were only an eighteen-year-old kid."

"I rented an efficiency apartment. It was near the industrial part of Atlanta where there were several body shops."

"With what money did you rent an apartment at that age?"

"When I was sixteen, I sold the car my dad and I had fixed up for a profit. I used that money to buy another car, which I fixed up and sold for a profit. By the time I turned eighteen, I'd sold four cars. I used that money to rent my apartment and pay for food until I got a job and started earning a paycheck."

"Who hired you?"

"A guy named Ronaldo who owned a body shop. He paid me minimum wage, but he taught me a lot."

"His business was legal?"

"Yeah. But one of their customers wasn't so legal. He was a kid around my age who kept bringing in the most rare and expensive cars I've ever seen or worked on."

Finley plucked a pink gem from his pan and put it on the grooved lip of the chute. "Did anyone ask this kid where he was coming by all of these rare and expensive cars?"

"Ronaldo had a strict don't ask, don't tell policy. I should've stuck to that. The kid's name was Kyle, and we became friends. His situation was like mine. He was into cars. He'd also left home early."

"Why had he left home early?"

"Abusive father. Eventually, Kyle's boss invited me to come and work for him."

"At the chop shop?"

He nodded.

"And you said yes because?"

"The pay was ridiculously good, and I got to work with incredible cars."

"Stolen cars."

"At that point in my life, I didn't care that they were stolen. I figured the people who owned them were so rich they could cash in the insurance and buy another."

"What about the danger involved?"

"That was the best part."

He'd been careless. More than that. It was almost as if he'd *dared* God to take him down. "I don't know much about chop shops. Did you basically just steal cars and then change their appearance and resell them on the . . . black market?" She whispered the last part. Saying *black market* made her feel like she was impersonating a movie character.

"That was a part of the business. Most of the time, though, it was safer and more profitable to break the cars down and sell them for parts."

"What happened that landed you in jail?" She knew the answer in general but wanted to hear it in his own words.

"I stole a brand-new Mercedes S-class."

"How?"

"It's called relay theft. Kyle and I went to a fancy restaurant in Atlanta and watched people park their cars. We knew which types of cars we were looking for, and it was easy to see which ones had keyless entry systems. We decided on the Mercedes, and Kyle followed the driver inside. I went to the car. As soon as Kyle got near the driver's key fob, he captured its signal using a device. I received the signal on my device and the car was fooled into thinking its key fob was nearby. At that point, its doors unlocked, and it allowed me to start the engine."

"No hot-wiring necessary?"

"No."

"What went wrong that night?"

"We'd hit that restaurant twice before. It was a mistake to go back a third time, because it turned out the police had planted the Mercedes to catch us. I tried to outrun them, but they anticipated my escape route. They put down spikes that blew out the tires. After they took me in, they offered to downgrade the charges if I'd turn on the guys at the shop and provide information on them."

"Which you refused to do." It wasn't a guess. She knew him well enough to know how he'd have reacted to that.

"Correct. At the time, I considered those guys to be my family. They were like me, they understood me."

She could imagine how much they'd meant to the kid who'd left his biological family behind. "So, after your arrest, they had your back and ensured you had a good lawyer?"

He stopped panning. "No."

"No?"

"When I got out on bail, I went to see them. They'd cleared out the shop. There wasn't even a wrench left. They'd moved out of their homes. I couldn't reach them on their phones."

"But they knew where you lived. Did they get in touch with you?"

"I never saw or heard from a single one of them again."

"They let you take the fall? Without any support or communication or anything?"

He shrugged, but she could sense the betrayal. When he'd been facing a trial and jail time at the age of twenty-six, they'd abandoned him.

"I'd like to—to go find Kyle," she said, "and spend some time shouting in his face."

He gave her a bona fide grin. Crooked and weathered and glorious.

Her chest flooded with adoration. The shell-shocked boy had been to hell and back and emerged a man.

"I thought you were a pacifist," he said.

"I have my limits!" She captured her wind-tossed hair, twisting it into a coil as she drew it forward over one shoulder. "Did you use a public defender?"

"No. I made a lot of money during my years at the shop. I had a good attorney. It's just that every jury member could see that I was guilty. Which I was."

"Did you spend all your savings on your attorney?"

"No. I spent some of it on my legal fees and invested the rest."

"Oh. So . . . that money continued to appreciate while you served your sentence?"

"I have plenty," he said evasively.

"Define plenty."

"No."

"You're saying that your ill-gotten gains have grown in value?" she asked, trying not to let the horror show on her face.

"That's usually how investments work."

"You shouldn't keep ill-gotten gains!"

"Watch me."

Green and red gems sparkled as she captured them in her pan. "How did prison change you?"

He didn't answer.

"I'd really like to know," she added.

"How did it change me for the better or for the worse?"

"Start with for the worse."

The sound of distant thunder rolled over them. Dark gray clouds smudged one corner of the sky.

"I distrust pretty much everyone I meet," he said after a time. "I hold myself . . . apart, because it's easier to hide my emotions that way."

"Is it necessary to hide your emotions?"

"It was in prison."

"Go on."

"I don't have much tolerance for fake people or manipulators.

I'm more paranoid about my surroundings than other people. And it's hard for me to stop remembering some of the stuff I saw and experienced."

She wanted so badly to fix his past for him, to reassure him the way she reassured abandoned puppies that everything was going to be okay. But she couldn't. Finley set her pan aside, dried her hands on her jacket, then stuffed them into her pockets. "And how did it change you for the better?"

"I'd made so many bad decisions that I don't think I would have found my way out of my situation on my own. Prison took me out of my situation. Inside, I couldn't run away or sleep around. I couldn't drink alcohol, do drugs, or steal cars. The thing I could do . . . was change." He shrugged—a tight gesture that attempted to minimize the enormity of what he'd been through. "I had to figure out who I was and find the strength to get through."

"You also pursued college degrees while you were on the inside."

"That's true."

Their tour guide poked her overbite between them. "If you're finished here, I'll escort you to the gift shop."

They'd decorated the large gift shop with gold rush flair. Slowly, Finley made her way down the first row of goods, Luke following.

Ill-gotten gains indeed. He was going to get a piece of her mind about that. But not today. He'd unburdened himself more than she'd expected. She didn't want to immediately make him regret confiding in her.

She came to a display of glass vials containing gold nuggets. Memories flickered at the back of her mind. She picked up a vial, recognizing its old-fashioned black-and-white sticker. Her dad had purchased one of these for her. She'd played with it in the woods, pretending to be a rich princess ruling a kingdom of animals. "I think I know where we'll find the next clue."

A man watched Luke's Chevy turn out of the gold mine in the direction of Highway 115.

He eased from his parking place. He'd tail them as long as he could, until he determined where they were headed. Or until he ran the risk of raising suspicion. Whichever came first.

CHAPTER EIGHTEEN

"I have keepsake boxes," Finley announced when they arrived at her home after leaving the gold mine.

Luke waited while she greeted her weird hedgehog, enthusiastic dog, and grumpy cat. Then he followed her to her hall closet. Inside, several large boxes with lids rested on shelves.

"One contains mementos from my baby years," she explained. "Another from when I was a child, another from my high school years, another from my college years. I kept my vial of gold nuggets, and I *think* it's in this one." She pointed to a box above her head.

He lifted it down.

In her kitchen, he set it on the table. She slid out of her coat, folded it over the back of a chair, and began digging through the box.

Luke worked to remain neutral because he was afraid to let himself hope that this hunch of hers might pay off. Once, he'd been very good at remaining neutral because he honestly hadn't cared about most things.

Why did he find neutrality so hard to come by with Finley? She had a way of ripping that source of security from him and leaving him vulnerable.

She released a soft gasp. "Will you look at this," she breathed. Straightening, she showed him the item she held between her thumb and forefinger. The exterior of the vial was identical to those they'd seen earlier at the gift shop. The inside was different, though. At the shop, he'd been able to see straight through to the nuggets inside. This time, all he could see on the other side of the glass was white paper with black markings.

She unscrewed the cap and tipped nuggets onto the table. Once she'd slid the rolled-up paper free, she smoothed it flat.

Luke stepped closer, eyes narrowing.

"It's a page from a calendar," she said.

It looked as though it had been ripped out of a desk calendar. The rectangles for all seven days of the week were empty. How could they know if this had been placed here by Ed? Wasn't it just as likely that Finley had stuck the page inside the vial when she was younger?

Finley turned the paper over. Words filled the space for Saturday, April 20.

Finley,
Ask Robbie about this day. After you talk to him, take June aside privately and tell her you'd like to see my poem. Don't mention to either of them that your questions are motivated by your birthday treasure hunt.
I love you, Dad

Finley blinked at him. "This is a clue . . . which means that, by the skin of my teeth, I was right when I speculated that the mine in the *Brothers* book was of importance. Which totally amazes me, to be frank. In the original book, I'm guessing that Dad had tabbed down a page or underlined something. He might have even left a note for me that would have led me directly to this vial in my keepsake box."

"Probably. Without access to the original book, we were at a disadvantage."

"Yet we emerged victorious."

She'd voiced her doubts about her theories regarding her dad's clues. But she was smart. Her instincts were often right. "If your dad could see you now, he'd be proud."

She stared at him, eyes soft. "That's a very nice thing to say."

"If I was nice, it was unintentional."

She made a sound of amusement but didn't look away. Intensity leapt to life between them.

"*In the past,*" she'd said to him the day after their last kiss, "*you tried to explain why it wouldn't be wise for us to follow through on physical attraction. At this point, I see the wisdom of that, too.*"

Wouldn't be wise was an understatement. His hunger ran so close to the surface that if he reached for her now, he wouldn't let go until this whole house turned to ash.

She's probably dating Derek now, he told himself. But that dark thought didn't bring logic. It shredded it.

"Intimidating Luke Dempsey is never nice," she said.

"Never."

"I understand. You're like Lady Gaga. You—"

"I'm *nothing* like Lady Gaga."

"—have an image to maintain. No need to worry. Your secret niceness is safe with me."

"I have no secret niceness."

"That's because it's secret even from you. Don't be alarmed." She lifted her hands in front of her like a person showing the police they held no weapons. "I'm not going to make any sudden movements, but I *am* going to give you a hug. A friendly one."

He wanted to feel her body against his so badly that it made him angry at himself.

"May I?" she asked.

He tipped his chin. She wrapped her arms around him and laid her head against his chest.

His arms had a mind of their own. They banded around her.

His chin rested gently on the top of her head. She was warm, her body fit and soft at the same time. He closed his eyes, trying to memorize the feel of her.

They breathed together, and a hard knot inside of him loosened.

Holding her like this was less sexual but more emotional. Back in the day, he'd been able to compartmentalize sex. This, he couldn't.

"I'd been worried," she murmured against his shirt, "that the Dewey decimal number was a dead end . . . that we wouldn't be able to finish this hunt. And I couldn't stand the thought that you wouldn't receive closure."

"Me? This is your hunt."

"This is *our* hunt."

"This is *your* hunt."

"Fine. This is *my* hunt. But the completion of it fulfills *your* promise. It's important to me that you have the chance to make good on what you told my dad you'd do."

They stood there for a few more minutes. He heard dog nails on hardwood and the ice maker dropping new cubes in the freezer.

Eventually, Finley parted from him and returned her attention to the calendar page on the table. "April twentieth fell on a Saturday almost nine years ago. I know that because Sunday, April twenty-first, is a day that will always be seared into my consciousness. That's the day Dad shot Carla and his whole world came tumbling down."

She'd easily transitioned from hugging him back to the treasure hunt. He had no ability to transition from holding her to anything else. The contact between them had dazed his brain.

She chewed the edge of her lip. "This day, this Saturday, should have been the last normal, uneventful day of Dad's life. But he's asking us to go to Robbie and inquire about it. Why?"

"Because whatever the two of them did on that day will remind you of something from your past with your dad and lead you to the next clue?"

Finley picked up her phone and selected a song from one of her playlists.

Great, more wind chimes.

"Thinking music," she said.

He'd already tried to explain to her why this wasn't music. No point in wasting more breath.

"Do you have any idea what Ed was doing the day before Carla died?" he asked.

"No. The day before she died, I was studying for finals, dating Chase, and living my life as if I didn't have a care in the world. I'm ashamed to say I was focused on myself and oblivious to what was going on with my dad."

"I think most daughters that age are focused on themselves and oblivious to their parents."

"Even so, in retrospect, it seems incredibly self-absorbed."

They both looked down at the calendar page.

"It's strange that he's asking you to do two things," Luke said.

"Right, because in every other clue, he asked me to do one thing."

"If Robbie is the one with the clue, why didn't he just ask you to speak with Robbie?"

"And if the poem holds the clue, why didn't he just ask me to speak with June?"

He held his silence instead of trying to answer an unanswerable question.

"Is there significance to the fact that my dad is requesting I talk to Robbie first and ask June about the poem second? Is he telling me, by ordering it that way, that the conversation with Robbie is where the clue will be found?"

"I don't know."

She toyed with a lock of her hair. "It could be that Dad wants me to ask Robbie about the day before everything fell apart for a reason separate from the hunt. Perhaps he simply wants me to know that day was a good day. Or it could be that he wants me to ask June about the poem for a reason separate from the hunt. Maybe that poem's about me? Or maybe it's one he's particularly proud of?"

"How soon can we visit them?"

"I'll ask." She dialed her uncle. Lowering to a chair, she scooped Sally onto her lap. "Hello!" she said into the phone. "It's your favorite niece."

Luke leaned against the counter, hands curved around its edge.

"I miss you and June. I was thinking about driving down and swinging by for a visit. Would you be up for that?" As she listened to his reply, she shot Luke a thumbs-up. "Awesome. I'll drive over after work Monday. In fact, how would you feel about me bringing Luke? He strikes me as a little lonely and somewhat underfed. He could use company and a good meal."

He scowled.

She winked. Her slender fingers scratched beneath Sally's ears. "Perfect. Great! We'll see you then. Bye." She ended the call. "We're all set for dinner at Robbie and June's house day after tomorrow."

"Good." This hunt was finally regaining momentum. "Though I'm not lonely. Or underfed."

"And yet I stand by my statement. You could use company and a good meal. We all could."

He pushed away from the counter. "I should go."

"You don't have to. You could stay and hang out."

"So we can . . . what? Repot your cacti and talk about the sad fate of the whales?"

"We can also sip herbal tea, don't forget."

"And make dreadlocks in our hair."

"I don't think you make dreadlocks. I think you just stop brushing your hair and they naturally form."

"Whatever. I'm not doing it."

"Spoilsport." She picked up the calendar page. "I'll just stick this in the safe with the other clues, then walk you out."

He stopped in the doorway of her office as she slid open a desk drawer.

She went completely still. "Wait." She pulled the drawer out farther.

From his position, he could see the safe inside the drawer.

"This isn't how I left it," she said slowly. She looked up at him. "I keep the safe sideways, so that the keypad on top faces me when I'm sitting in my desk chair. Now the keypad is facing the front of the drawer."

Cold spread through him like ice. "Are you sure you didn't leave it this way?"

"I mean . . . I'm ninety percent sure."

A warning of danger prickled the skin at the back of his neck. "Are the clues still inside?"

She typed in her code, and the door popped open. "Yes. But . . . I really don't think I left it this way, Luke." She swallowed. "Do you think someone's been in my house?"

Someone might still be in the house. His muscles tensed and his senses jumped to high alert. "I'm going to search the house. You stay here."

"No. I—I've never had a burglar in my house, and I'm freaking out a little, which will only get worse if I'm in here alone. Also, this is *my* house. You need me with you because I'm the one who's familiar with all the places where a person could hide. And I'm the only one who'll know if something's out of place."

"Fine." He went to the door of the bathroom beneath the stairs. "Stand back."

She did. He pulled the door open. The small room was empty.

He made his way to her bedroom, which held the scent of her. Orange blossoms. "Stay near the doorway, please."

She did so. "Everything looks totally normal in here." Her voice was thin, shaken. "I don't store anything under the bed, so a person could fit under there. They could also fit in my closet."

He looked under the bed. Then the closet.

They made their way through every square foot of the house, her talking him through it.

They finished in the backyard, where he searched under the deck and in the small garden shed on the side of the house. Nothing.

The sliding glass door made a rasping noise as they reentered the living room. They faced each other. The intruder was gone, but that only eased his mind slightly. "When we arrived here after the gold mine, I don't remember you turning off the house alarm."

"True." She scratched her temple. "I've been very consistent about setting the house alarm every night before I go to bed, but I don't always set it when I leave during the day."

"*Finley*."

"I know, I know. You asked me to set it, and I did a really good job of that at first. But sometimes when I hurry out the door, I forget."

"Did you lock both the sliding door and the front door this morning?"

"Yes."

"I didn't see any evidence of a forced entry. So, if the doors were locked, how did someone get in?"

"I'm not sure."

"Tell me you keep your windows locked."

"I do. That is to say, I open them often when I'm at home. For fresh air. But then I close them and lock them."

He began checking the windows. Locked, locked, locked.

When he reached the window nearest the kitchen table, it slid upward. Unlocked. Fury mounted in him like water flooding a room.

"Shoot," she whispered. "I must have accidentally left that one unlocked."

He shut it, locked it, and straightened to his full height. "Finley, we both know that someone else is after the treasure. Someone who might be willing to hurt you to get what they want."

"Yes, and I didn't consciously decide to be negligent. It was unintentional."

"The intention doesn't matter. All that matters is the result, which is that someone was in your house."

"You're right. I messed up." She looked torn . . . as if she had another confession to make but didn't want to make it.

His stomach turned to lead. "What are you not telling me?"

"When I came home from work the day we rescued Agatha, a strange feeling came over me."

"What do you mean?"

"My animals' behavior was a little . . . off. It worried me for a bit. But nothing had been disturbed."

"How come you didn't tell me that at the time?"

"Because it was pretty easy to write off. My animals *do* act oddly at times for harmless reasons."

His self-control felt as thin as a spiderweb. "When your father was dying, your safety was the *one thing* he cared about. It's the one thing *I* care about." *Shut up, Luke. Don't say anything else.* But he couldn't hold the words back. "Do you think that I could live with myself if something happened to you?"

"If something happens to me, it won't be your fault—"

"The answer's no. I will not be able to live with myself." He'd failed to protect Ethan. There was no way he could fail to protect Finley. No way he could survive that a second time.

She searched his features. "I'm sorry."

Strain grew between them, so strong it seemed to suck the air from the room. He strode to the doors, staring out, trying to make sense of the chaos inside his head and heart.

"Do you think the burglar left fingerprints on the keypad of the safe?" she asked.

"No. I think anyone careful enough to cover their tracks when they tried to breach my computer would also be careful enough to wear gloves."

"But not careful enough to put the safe back in the drawer the same way they found it?"

He shrugged. "Maybe they did make a mistake. Or maybe they put it back that way on purpose."

"Why?"

"To rattle us."

"In the hopes of?"

"Making us rush. Get scared. Get sloppy."

He could almost hear her mind turning. "Is there any point in calling the police?" she asked.

"To report what? That nothing was stolen but that you think—but aren't certain—that your safe is facing a different direction?"

She exhaled tightly.

"We have no evidence," he said, "that a crime was committed here."

"So how do you suggest we react?"

"I'm going to call your security company and pay whatever it takes to get someone out here today to install exterior and interior cameras, as well as window sensors."

"All right. But you won't pay for it. I will."

"What's the number for your security company?"

She pulled out her phone and read off the digits. He input them into his phone one by one.

"I'll be in the bedroom," she said. "I need a minute to regroup."

Finley shut herself into her room, then sank onto the chair in the corner, hands covering her face.

At first, when she'd seen the position of the safe, shock had swept over her mind like a cloud. Confusion and dread followed closely, making the cloud even more dense. Now that cloud was thinning, which was almost worse because it had acted as a buffer.

Indignation crept in. Someone had had the nerve to break into her house. Her beloved, defenseless animals were here! This was her haven. Her safe place. She felt . . . violated.

Guilt crept in. Why hadn't she been more careful? She wasn't suspicious or anxious by nature. But, obviously, in this case, she'd been too relaxed.

Doubt crept in. What if *she'd* been the one who'd turned the safe that direction? She really didn't think so, but she wasn't absolutely sure.

Her insides were shuddering.

Dad was gone. Chase was gone. They weren't here to comfort her and so she wished, with every cell, that Luke could give her another one of those all-encompassing hugs like they'd shared earlier. She hadn't experienced a hug like that from a man in a long, long time. It had wrapped her in closeness and security—all the things she longed for now.

However, another hug was the last thing she could ask Luke for at the moment, seeing as how he currently wanted to strangle her.

Someone had, she was almost certain, been in her house.

"Lord God," she whispered.

Who had been in her house?

CHAPTER NINETEEN

"If you don't do everything in your power," CeCe stated in the type of ringing tone Abraham Lincoln might've used when delivering the Gettysburg Address, "to sweep Akira off her feet, then you're a fool. And we both know I didn't raise any fools."

After church, Ben had gone home to change clothes. Then he'd stopped by his parents' place. When his mom had learned that he, Sebastian, Natasha, and Genevieve planned to ambush Luke with lunch today, she'd volunteered to make a cake for them. He was only here to pick up dessert, but, of course, she was also serving up her opinions.

"Akira's great," he said calmly. The more fired up his mom got, the more patient he became. He'd learned that tactic early.

"And do you agree that you need to do everything you can to sweep her off her feet?"

"She's been hurt in the past. Pretty badly. At this stage we're just getting to know each other without an agenda."

"But you like her?"

"Yeah. A lot, actually." Enough that he was getting worried. He didn't want to end up back in the same boat he'd been in—the one where he invested himself in someone who didn't like him back.

"And you believe you could be good for each other?"

"I do."

CeCe sucked air through her teeth. "Then don't wait! I'd known your father three days when I decided I was going to marry that man. But now everybody thinks they need time. Time, time, time!"

"I specifically remember you telling Joel and Rachel not to rush into relationships."

"That's when Joel was trying to date that older girl in high school who was much too experienced. And when Rachel wanted to date that awful man who was living off the government's charity and was named after a Hawaiian island."

"Same principle applies here, though. It's good to take time."

"This is a completely different circumstance than with Joel and Rachel. I can see with my own eyes, as clear as day, that girl is perfect for you. If you wait too long, someone else is going to snap her up."

He hated the idea of Akira with another man.

His mom lifted the cake from the entry table and pushed it into his hands. "There's a fine line between biding your time and becoming a little old man at the old folks' home who doesn't have any visitors."

Ben didn't see that as a fine line. He saw that as a gigantic line, fifty years thick in his case.

"How many of the women that you've dated have I liked?" she asked.

"None."

She could raise one eyebrow and narrow her stare better than anyone. "Well. This one, I like."

When Luke left prison, all he'd wanted was a quiet, simple life.

His life had been getting less quiet and less simple ever since he'd started work at the Center.

With a groan, he answered the knocking on his apartment door around one p.m. on Sunday.

Ben, Sebastian, Natasha, and Genevieve stood there. The women were each holding a handle of a picnic basket. Sebastian had a cooler. Ben carried a circular container.

"Surprise!" Natasha said.

"Mmm."

"We couldn't get you to commit to having lunch with us," Ben explained, "so we brought lunch to you."

"Mmm."

"The good news is that we have excellent food here," Ben said. "My mom's chocolate cake."

"Sam made chicken curry salad sandwiches," Genevieve added.

"Fruit." Natasha gave him a persuasive lift of her brows. "Potato chips. Cashews baked with my own rosemary salt blend."

Luke sighed.

"Step aside," Sebastian ordered, "and let us in."

Luke held the doctor's gaze. "I'm not your patient."

"If you were, I'd have given you a heart that actually worked by now."

For a moment they faced off, but then Sebastian startled Luke by grinning.

Since Luke had discovered yesterday that someone had been in Finley's house, anxiety had been crawling over him. Through the night, he'd struggled with nightmares.

At this point, he was willing to try just about anything that might distract him. Including this.

He moved back and held the door for them.

Finley's bachelor father had not harbored a deep and committed brand of love for very many people. His parents. Robbie and Robbie's wife and kids. Finley. Just those. Nonetheless, the people he'd loved, he'd loved and protected fiercely.

Memories of her history with her aunt and uncle swam through

Finley's mind as she and Luke walked toward their front door on Monday evening.

Her dad's parents had passed away before Finley's birth, at which time Robbie's family of four had relocated to the Sutherland farm. Robbie and June had sold off the farming equipment and continued their long-held jobs—Robbie as an accountant and June as a full-time mom.

When Finley was small, Aunt June had been her dad's backup caregiver. Whenever Dad needed time to himself to work, run errands, or go on a date, Finley had come here to Robbie and June's.

She remembered standing on a chair next to her aunt, both of them wearing pink aprons and making sugar cookies. June had let Finley choose the cookie cutters and drop food dye into the white frosting to create the most fantastical colors.

June was the one who'd introduced her to Sesame Street and kept fresh Play-Doh on hand. She'd brought her daughter's old dollhouse down from the attic for Finley, who'd spent hours concocting lives for the dolls and their pets. Together, June and Finley would walk down to the pond on the property, June's gray cat prancing along behind them with its tail held high.

Back then, Robbie and June's kids—Eric and Leslie—had been in their early twenties. At every family gathering, they'd been Finley's good-natured playmates. Occasionally, luxury of luxuries, she'd had one of them all to herself when they'd served as her babysitter.

In her eyes, they'd been incredibly cool. Young, energetic, great-looking. Eric took her out for ice cream in his sports car, rode bikes with her, beat her at card games. Leslie put makeup on Finley and painted her nails.

Before Finley started kindergarten, she'd served as flower girl at both of their weddings.

Robbie and June were now eighty and seventy-eight, respectively. Eric was fifty, with a college-aged daughter. Leslie, two years younger, also had a college-aged daughter, plus two high school–aged sons.

Finley had never met her mother, so the Sutherlands were the entirety of her family. All she'd known. All she had. She'd been fortunate. They were gracious, loving, supportive.

Finley rang the doorbell, then glanced up at Luke. Just that—the two of them looking at each other without words—caused the air to turn hot.

His eyes glittered. She'd experienced his passion through his kisses but what she saw in his eyes was even more compelling. This . . . this desire that hovered between them was growing unbearable—

June answered the door and enveloped Finley in a hug that smelled, as it always had, of Shalimar perfume. A pretty woman with a pillowy body, June had the type of personality that would have been perfect for a TV chef famous for cooking Southern food. She'd styled her short dark gray hair in a flattering style. She had on knit pants, a turquoise top, pink-rimmed glasses, and an enormous, chunky necklace.

Robbie approached with a smile, wearing a V-neck sweater over a button-down. He motioned them into the foyer. "Come in, come in."

They passed the front office and sitting room and made their way into the open-concept living room, dining room, and kitchen space.

In the 1920s, Finley's great-grandparents had built the original clapboard farmhouse. With gingerbread porch trim and redbrick chimneys, it oozed charm, if not square footage. By the time Robbie and June inherited it, it had been crumbling at the edges.

Right around the same time Finley had received her nest egg from her dad, her aunt and uncle had renovated the farmhouse. They'd added three thousand square feet in a way that beautifully complemented the original style and architecture. Nowadays, every inch of this place was in excellent shape.

A Jeep Grand Cherokee, Lexus sedan, and a sports car from the 1960s occupied the new garage. They'd purchased a vacation cottage on the Gulf Coast and went on two cruises annually.

Given that the increase in their standard of living had occurred right when Finley had received a monetary gift from her father, and given that Robbie's job had remained the same up until his retirement, she strongly suspected that she had not been the only beneficiary of her father's lucrative investment in Apple. It would have been very much like her dad to give money to both of the people he cared about most.

The group settled onto the overstuffed furniture. Soon, they had drinks in their hands and were snacking on the appetizers arrayed on the coffee table. Robbie and June's current cat—the fourth gray cat they'd owned during Finley's lifetime—curled into a donut on her lap.

There was no reason to rush the conversation she'd come to have with her uncle. In the most recent clue, her dad had specified that she should not alert Robbie to the fact that her questions were connected to the hunt. To pull that off, she needed to act as normally as possible and raise the subject of the day before the murder as organically as possible.

She amused herself by observing Luke in the habitat of her relatives' home. He'd chosen clothing more formal than usual—a simple navy sweater and gray pants. He was on his best behavior. Quiet, but polite. Charming in a reserved way. She could tell that Aunt June was already in raptures over him.

After a time, they transitioned to the dining table. Robbie and June carried over ham, biscuits, salad, and potatoes. Finley helped herself to everything except the ham, which most definitely wasn't vegan.

June, bless her, brought up Finley's dad while they ate. "I miss him so," she said. "Just the other day, Robbie and I went to Skyline Diner, where we used to eat breakfast with your father. I couldn't think of anything but him the whole time."

"It's like that for me, too," Finley said. "Certain foods or places bring him to the front of my mind." She set down her fork. "Songs, too. In fact, the other day I heard John Denver's 'Take Me Home, Country Roads.'"

June nodded. "He couldn't listen to that song and not sing along to it."

"Exactly. After it came on, I started thinking about my dad's arrest."

Luke sat directly across from her, hands resting on his thighs.

"It troubles me that I wasn't around at the time of Carla's death," Finley continued. "I really don't know anything about the days leading up to it."

"I understand why that would be upsetting," June said. "What would you like to know?"

"Carla died on a Sunday. Do either of you know how he spent his time the day before that? Or the day before that?"

"I'm afraid that I don't," June said. "Robbie? I know the two of you went somewhere together a day or two before Carla passed away."

"Yes. The day before." He finished slicing a sliver of ham. "Ed had come across a horse he was interested in acquiring. So we drove down, took a look at it, and drove home. He didn't end up buying the horse, but we had a great time. We laughed, we ate barbecue, we talked. When we were in Ed's truck, we listened to that talk radio he liked so much."

"Do you remember where you drove for the horse? And what kind of horse it was?" Finley asked. "I'd like to be able to picture his last free day."

"It was a bay quarter horse. Down near Macon."

Macon was more than two hours from Hartwell. Finley pulled thoughtfully on her earlobe. "Where did you guys eat barbecue?"

"Satterfield's."

"Are you a fan of barbecue, Luke?" June peered at him like a freshman girl peers at the high school quarterback.

"Yes, ma'am."

"Good," June said warmly, "then I guess I won't have to revoke your citizenship in the state of Georgia."

Unfortunately, none of the details Robbie had provided seemed clue-worthy, and she couldn't think of any other questions to ask about Dad and Robbie's whereabouts that wouldn't make her line of questioning seem suspicious.

An hour later, the coffee maker happily percolated decaf as June slid cobbler from the oven.

Finley had told Robbie about Luke's fondness for classic cars. As expected, Robbie had offered to show Luke his sports car. They'd gone to the garage, effectively providing Finley a private moment with June.

"Talking about my dad earlier jogged another memory," Finley said to her aunt.

"Oh?"

"One of the times I visited him in prison we talked about his poetry. He mentioned that you had one of his poems."

"Yes! As you know, I was always a fan of his poetry."

"May I see the one you have?"

"Absolutely." June slipped off her oven mitts and gestured for Finley to follow. "I tucked it away for safekeeping."

They made their way upstairs to the reading room connected to the master bedroom. June knelt before her bookshelf and slid her fingers along the spines of her journals, which were arranged by year. For as long as Finley had known her, her aunt had kept her household well-organized. Winter accessories in labeled bins. Pictures in scrapbooks. Prayer requests and mementos in her journals.

She pulled out the journal belonging to the year of Dad's arrest and flipped through it until she located a folded sheet of paper. She handed it to Finley.

The poem was titled "Carla."

You.
A woman of feelings. Deep and
rich.
Of songs. Loss and hope.
Of dreams. Found and faded.
Of passion. Unashamed and bold.
Of creativity. Mystical and awe-
inspiring.
A woman of love. True and loyal.
You.

This poem, like many of his others, gave evidence of his romantic soul. He'd written the words on a simple sheet of unlined paper. She turned it over, exposing a sketch. Her father had often doodled scenes like this when deep in thought. This time, he'd drawn mountains, a stream, a pond.

"June?" Robbie called from downstairs.

"Be there in a minute," June called back.

"May I take this home with me and return it to you the next time I see you?" Finley asked.

"Be my guest."

"I'd like to have it photocopied so I can add it to my collection."

"Of course." June squeezed Finley's hand. "Your dad told me that he wrote it for Carla before her death. He wasn't quite happy with it. He'd wanted to edit it, but then she died in such a sudden and tragic way. He never had the chance to show the poem to her. He gave it to me later, when he was out on bail. He said he wanted me to have it so that it could serve as a reminder not to postpone things because you're hoping for perfection. If he were here, I think he'd encourage us to go ahead and do and say the things we feel led to do and say."

Tears stung the back of Finley's eyes. "Amen."

The drive home to Misty River cocooned Luke and Finley in shades of black as they racked their brains and talked in circles regarding possible clues stemming from their evening with her aunt and uncle.

Robbie had told them that the day before Carla died had been filled with horses, barbecue, talk radio.

At this point, they couldn't see how talk radio might prove relevant.

Horses? Maybe. She'd had a horse when she was young, but they'd housed it at a friend's stable. Her dad sold the horse during her high school years, and their friends sold the stable a few years later.

They could drive to Satterfield's Barbecue to look for another public clue. But doing so would require the better part of a day, and she didn't feel enthusiastic about that possibility, since she and her father had never been there together.

She scrutinized the sketch. She read the words of the poem out loud to Luke three times. They tried assembling the first letter of every word to see if it spelled out a clue. No. Then they tried stringing together the first letter of every line. No. Then they tried the first letter of every sentence. No.

"Why did your dad warn you not to tell Robbie or June that you were asking questions in connection to the hunt?" Luke wondered out loud. "To me, that means he didn't trust them."

"No," she said immediately. "He trusted them. I think he said that because he intended this hunt for me and me alone because that was our tradition."

"If so, he broke that tradition when he pulled me into the hunt."

"True. I can't explain that." She pressed her thumb against the edge of the paper. "My dad sometimes did spontaneous things that he regretted later. He once bought a seven-night trip for the two of us to the Swiss Alps because he ran across a great deal. It was only later that we realized we were booked to go in March, but not during my spring break week. Not only was it very cold in Switzerland at that time of year, but I also had to work on school assignments the whole time. I have to wonder if this treasure hunt was like that. I can picture him getting swept away by the excitement and drama of it all when creating the hunt."

"But then, over the years, it occurred to him that this might not be the safest thing for his only child?" Luke sounded annoyed.

"In a word . . . Yes."

"Then why didn't he scratch the whole thing? He created this hunt years ago. He could have contacted Rosco Horton from prison and asked him to amend the will and throw away the first clue."

"He must have still wanted me to have whatever he's left for me at the end."

"If so, he could have told you where to find it one of the times you visited him."

"You're right. He could have." She sighed. "I don't have any answers, and all of this speculating is making my head hurt." She wanted two Advil and a cup of tea.

"Do you think your dad asked you to read the poem about Carla because Carla herself is the clue?" he asked.

"It could be. Are you thinking we should research Carla?"

"Yeah."

"The idea has merit. I'm willing to do a little digging into Carla."

"Same." He adjusted his position, settling his left hand atop the steering wheel, resting his right hand down. "Did anything your dad wrote about Carla in that poem surprise you?"

"No, not at all. That poem was textbook Dad. I knew he cared about Carla deeply. His relationships were all zero to sixty. He *always* cared deeply about the women in his life . . . for a time."

"For a time?"

"Never longer than eight months or so. After that, his ardor would cool."

The headlights of an oncoming car highlighted the elegant, masculine lines of his profile. Pirate prince.

Wait. Was the car coming much, much too fast? She stiffened, her fingers curving against the upholstery.

"It's okay," he murmured reassuringly.

And, just like that, it *was* okay. She relaxed. The car whizzed by, returning him to darkness.

Luke seemed very comfortable in the dark.

Which made perfect sense. Darkness had been wrapping its tentacles around him for almost twenty years. "*For our struggle is not against flesh and blood . . .*" The famous verse whispered through her memory. "*. . . but against the rulers, against the authorities, against the powers of this dark world and against the spiritual forces of evil in the heavenly realms.*"

Today was March first. Over the past two months, she'd spent a great deal of time with Luke, but she'd not made as much progress with him as she'd have liked. Then again, broken souls did not mend on established timetables. Some took more time than others.

He *had* improved. He talked more easily. She'd seen him smile. He was spending time with his family, restoring his sister's car. He interacted with Ben every time Ben volunteered at Furry Tails. He'd attended a Valentine's party.

So, see? She needed to focus on the good.

Personally, selfishly, she wished he'd opened up to her more. Been willing to risk a dating relationship with her, even. But that was her issue. Just because he'd been unwilling to do that didn't mean he wasn't healing.

Two months of knowing him. Two months of working with him and tracking down clues with him. Numerous sessions of prayerful meditation. Countless prayers prayed for him. An untold amount of time thinking about him. They'd danced together at the Valentine's party. Twice, they'd kissed.

The past two months had jolted her out of her status quo.

They'd changed things for them both. But one thing remained exactly the same as the day she'd met Luke.

She staunchly refused to surrender Luke Dempsey to darkness.

Luke could no doubt defend himself. He'd spent years dealing in stolen cars. He'd been to prison. His body was roped with muscle.

Even so, protectiveness toward him was a storm inside her.

If given the chance, she'd fight for him, intercede for him. His history was paved with people who'd tried to defend him—his family, his friends. She might fail at defending him, too. But at least she'd go down swinging.

Just ten miles to go and they'd reach her house.

"Can we talk about guilt?" she asked.

"It's not my favorite subject."

"And yet guilt is the thing that's defined the bulk of your life." No adult, but especially no child, was equipped to bear the guilt of their sibling's death. "You screwed up," she said, "when you told your brother to go to the back of the line in El Salvador."

He cut a shocked glance at her beneath hooded brows.

"I'm sure everyone who's talked to you about this has tried to tell you that what happened to Ethan wasn't your fault, but they were wasting their breath. You were there. You lived it. And you'll never accept that it wasn't your fault."

"That's true," he said.

"After Chase died, I dealt with a lot of guilt."

"Why?"

"He rarely wore seat belts. He found them restrictive and uncomfortable. It was a sensory issue with him. So what did I do? Did I research? Did I figure out how he could overcome this sensory issue? Did I talk seriously with him about this? No, I did not. I accepted that he didn't wear a seat belt. And then he was thrown from his Jeep and died. And I—the person who was supposed to love him above all others—had done nothing to prevent it."

Several seconds pulled thin.

"Guilt doesn't respond well to reason," she continued. "Stating that it doesn't have a right to exist only increases its power." The tires rolled quietly beneath them, a steady undertone. "I spent years in therapy. A fortune in therapist's bills boils down to this fact: Addressing guilt is about acceptance and forgiveness."

"I'm aware. My parents put me in therapy after the earthquake."

"Luke Dempsey, every therapist's dream client," she teased.

"Finley Sutherland," he countered seriously, "every therapist's dream client."

"That's true. I really am a dream client. I love talking through these issues."

"I do not."

"I'm guessing you've had enough time to accept what happened to you."

"A hundred times over."

"It's the forgiveness piece you can't get past. Had Ethan lived and you'd been able to apologize, and he'd been able to offer you forgiveness, things would have been different."

"Everything in my life would have been different if Ethan had lived."

"Same for me, with Chase. I couldn't ask for his forgiveness, either. My therapist had me write letters to him. He was dead, but it still helped to tell him about my mistakes and express how sorry I was. Have you written about what you went through?"

"No."

"Over time, I developed greater compassion for myself. I started talking to myself about my failings the way I'd talk to someone I loved about theirs. Would you hate Blair if she'd told Hailey to go to the back of the line right before an earthquake struck?"

"Is that a trick question? I don't like Blair to begin with."

"Yes you do. You love Blair. And the answer is no, you wouldn't hate her. You'd have compassion for her. She's older now than you were back then, so why not give the kid you were the same compassion you'd give Blair?"

He sighed impatiently.

He was not responding with gratitude to the phenomenal insights she was providing.

"Instead of beating myself up," she pushed on, undaunted, "I'd acknowledge that I messed up and reassure myself that I'll do better next time. That I *am* doing a lot of good in the world currently."

"I didn't buy this type of psychological jargon then. I don't now."

She shifted her weight onto her hip as she turned toward him. "Did you know that people who are more prone to guilt are also more trustworthy? Guilt is a marker of empathy. It shows that you feel a responsibility about how your actions affect others."

"Right. I was really trustworthy and empathetic when I was stealing cars from people. I don't like it when you sugarcoat who I am."

"You're imperfect." She was growing more impassioned, her volume rising. "We're all imperfect. We've all made mistakes. Yet Jesus paid for *every single one of them*."

"Ah. So now you're moving into a sermon?"

"I'm just getting started." For a little longer, Luke was shut inside a car with her, a captive audience. It seemed the Holy Spirit had been storing up a tide of words within her. "Your salvation is certain. Your future is certain. His love for you is certain."

He didn't speak.

"His economy isn't about works. It's about grace, which is the best news ever in your case. Yet you refuse to accept it."

God's grace. It never, never lost its power for her. Her thankfulness over the magnitude of it was a waterfall inside, a pressure against the backs of her eyes.

"As far as the east is from the west—that's how far He's removed your sins from you," she continued. "Death has no claim on you. Neither does guilt. Every single chain has been broken. They're all lying shattered at your feet." Her voice wobbled, and a tear spilled over her lashes. "It's as if you haven't noticed.

You're still standing in the jail cell of guilt instead of living like someone who's free."

He pulled to a stop in front of her house and faced her.

"You're free," she repeated. She *needed* her words to penetrate his hard heart. "Every chain is broken."

He reached out and caught her tear on his thumb. Gently, he wiped it away. "I'm not worth your tears."

"That's where you're wrong. I see your worth so clearly. I only wish you could see a fraction of what I see." Quiet bound them in the warm interior of the truck. She felt God's presence—between them, within her. "Will you think on that?"

He stared at her, dashboard light illuminating one side of his face.

"Will you?" she asked again.

"Yes."

The full-blown sermon he'd predicted she'd give collected in her throat. However, like those red flags at the beach that signal danger, his hazel eyes warned her away. They cautioned her that she'd said enough. They told her to resist grabbing his hand or hugging him or setting her fingertips on the side of his face.

She'd said earlier that her dad had cared deeply about the women in his life . . . for a time. Panic circled around and around her ribs because, unlike her father, she was not wired for temporary affection. She'd only cared deeply about one man in the past. And she'd remained faithful to that man for five years after his death.

And now . . .

Now she cared deeply about Luke. She had not succeeded at talking herself out of it. The hurt he'd caused her had not vanquished it. She had a steadfast heart and it wanted, against all that was sensible, to give itself over to Luke.

"I'll walk you to the door," he said.

"No need." She'd lived alone for ages and would continue to do so when he left.

She treaded through moon shadows toward her cabin.

What about Derek?" Bridget asked the next night. The three friends occupied a table at the Green Eatery, where they'd met for a quick dinner after work. "Didn't he invite you to go out with him after the Valentine's Day party?"

Harmony, Meadow's daughter, sat at the next table over. She was supposed to be doing homework and, indeed, had a book open and a pencil in her hand. But from what Finley could tell, she was spending most of her time watching YouTube on her phone.

"Yes," Finley answered. "Derek did ask me out, and I told him that sounded great. But since then, I've been stalling. I haven't let him pin me down on a day and time."

Meadow swallowed her bite. "Keep stalling. Nothing good can come out of dating him."

"That's not true," Bridget said mildly. "Something good might come out of it. She won't know until she tries."

"Trying with men is exhausting." Meadow flicked a hand. "It's freeing to give up on the trying."

Meadow had a point. Finley's life had been less stressful when she'd been closed to the possibility of men.

Bridget picked up a crumb with a fingertip and deposited it in the napkin in her lap. "How come you're stalling with Derek?"

"Because I like the idea of dating him more than the actuality of dating him."

"Why?" Bridget asked. "Because of Luke?"

"Luke's part of my hesitation. I'm doing a good job of keeping a barrier up between us. Even so, to be completely honest, I really, really like him."

"Don't you dare pine for Luke," Meadow said.

"Since things aren't moving forward with Luke," Bridget said diplomatically, "I don't see any harm in going out with Derek. He's handsome and outgoing. You'll have fun with him. Derek's a good gateway back into the world of dating."

"No way am I handing over my passport at that gateway." Meadow plunged a veggie spring roll into peanut dipping sauce.

For years, Finley and Meadow had both been off the market. No doubt part of Meadow's grumpiness regarding Finley's decision to open herself to romance sprang from the fact that Meadow was losing an ally.

"Do you view me as a defector to the dating side?" Finley asked her.

"Of course I do."

"Does that make you feel lonely?" Bridget asked, thoughtful as always.

"I couldn't care less if I'm the only woman in America left on the non-dating side. I'll still wave that flag proudly."

"We love you," Bridget said.

"We really do," Finley agreed.

"And I love you two, which is why I don't like seeing you set yourselves up for disappointment. But you're grown-ups. So do what you gotta do. I'll be here to pick up the pieces, even though I wouldn't make the same decisions in a million years."

"Was that Meadow's version of encouragement?" Finley asked Bridget.

"I think so."

"Men are trouble," Meadow declared.

"Well," Bridget said with a straight face, "thanks for letting us do what we gotta do."

Luke certainly did spell trouble for Finley. It's just that he was the most tempting brand of trouble. Delicious, irresistible, intriguing trouble.

"If you decide not to go out with Derek," Bridget said to Finley, "do you think he'd be interested in dating me?"

CHAPTER TWENTY

Like an actor striding to center stage in advance of her first line, spring made a bid for preeminence ahead of its official start date. Slightly warmer, sunnier days interspersed more and more with the cold and rainy ones. Finley admired the early wildflowers, white and yellow and bright blue, which bravely opened their petals.

Days passed—three, then four, then five—as she and Luke pondered her father's most recent clues. However, they came up with no other lines of inquiry other than those they'd brainstormed during the car ride home from dinner at Robbie and June's.

When the weekend arrived, they drove to Macon to visit Satterfield's Barbecue. The patrons and employees must have thought her very strange, since she'd spent an hour studying every nook and cranny of the establishment. No clues there.

In case Dad's poem about Carla was meant to spur them to investigate Carla, they scoured every bit of information they could find about her online.

Carla Virginia Vance had remained at home after high school for two years while she'd pursued her associate's degree. After that, she'd relocated to Nashville and attempted to forge a music career. While she'd never accomplished that on a big scale, she'd sung backup for some notable names and accumulated a few songwriting credits. At the age of forty, she'd moved to Hartwell to open a store. At the age of fifty-two, she'd died of a bullet wound to the chest.

Finley was glad for the chance to learn more about Carla, but nothing they learned translated into a usable treasure hunt clue.

At the time of her death, Carla had lived in a historical building that had been refurbished and divided into apartments. Finley's dad would've known that Finley couldn't gain access to Carla's old apartment. Thus, if a clue was to be found at Carla's building, they surmised they'd find it on the exterior or in the lobby.

The weekend after they'd trekked to Macon, they trekked to Hartwell. She and Luke carefully studied the building and lobby. Both—perfectly ordinary.

No clues in Carla's biography. No clues in Carla's building.

One foggy Wednesday morning in mid-March, Luke recognized Finley's footsteps entering the workroom. Moments later, the scent of her soap reached him.

His mind told his body to resist her, but his body had its own ideas. She put him at war with himself. So much so that by the end of every workday, he returned home exhausted.

He'd never liked or respected a woman as much as he did Finley Sutherland. He'd never wanted a woman as much as he wanted Finley Sutherland.

"Look who came by for a visit," she said.

He swiveled his chair and saw that she was holding Agatha in her arms.

Dumb affection for the puppy clutched him. "Is this a nightmare?"

"More like a dream come true."

"Did the Gomez family return her?"

"No!"

"Because if Agatha were an automobile, she'd be a lemon."

"I can see through your gruffness. I know you're happy to see her, and look"—she extended the wriggling animal in his direction—"she's incredibly happy to see you."

Like a wind-up toy that starts thrashing before it lands on a surface, the dog's tiny legs started moving before Finley set her on the floor. Agatha charged to him. Placing her front paws on his ankle, she panted up at him with what he could swear was the canine equivalent of a smile.

Agatha hadn't forgotten him. For some reason, that made his throat tight.

He scooped her up and placed her on his lap. She'd grown, but she was still the smallest dog he'd ever seen. Her hair stuck out like a lion's mane around her face, interrupted only by her giant ears. She rolled into a ball against his abdomen, and he supported the piece of fluff with one big hand. She licked his wrist.

Finley beamed at them. "Mrs. Gomez is on a school field trip with her kids today. She reached out to say that she was more than willing to put Agatha in doggy daycare but wanted to ask if coming here was a possibility. The whole family seemed to think that time spent with you would do her good. And they were right. *Aww*, look. Agatha's on cloud nine."

The puppy was still enthusiastically licking his wrist. "She's only acting like this because she wants me to hand-feed her before she embarrasses me by forcing me to be seen with her in public."

"Luke. I hereby give you permission to feel love toward Agatha."

"The only thing I feel is annoyance that I donated several days of my life that I can't get back to this animal. And now the Gomezes are hitting us up for free babysitting."

"This isn't the Gomezes taking advantage of us. This is our charitable organization gladly giving support to one of our excellent adoptive families."

She smiled at him with so much tenderness that he found it hard to breathe. Finley appeared to know everything he was trying to hide. How he felt about her. How he felt about Agatha. All of it. The conflict and desire and longing and regret.

For the rest of the day, Agatha refused to let Luke out of her sight. When he was at his desk, she sat in his lap or napped on his shoe. When he walked around the Center, she ran beside him. When he took her outside, she eyeballed him while she peed.

"It's best not to allow dogs to get accustomed to sitting on your lap while you're trying to work," Kat informed him near the end of the day.

He continued typing.

"It's better if they self-soothe and learn to rest quietly on their mat or in their crate."

"I wish I could take all your advice," Luke said calmly, "strap it to a firework rocket, launch the thing into the sky, and then watch it explode."

"Excuse me?" Kat demanded in an offended tone.

Luke met her eyes. "You heard me."

Just as he'd known she would, she immediately backed down.

"May I hold her for a minute?" Trish asked sweetly.

He passed the puppy over. The older woman attempted to cuddle Agatha, who scrambled to get back to Luke. Not even Trish's quivering Christmas tree earrings or the humming of "Away in a Manger" satisfied the dog.

"The puppy is not responding to lullabies," Kat told Trish in a superior tone.

Trish stopped singing. "In that case, 'Twas the night before Christmas and all through the house . . .'"

Agatha was having none of it.

"Oh my," Trish murmured. "You really are partial to Luke, aren't you, little sweetheart?"

"It's best not to encourage such obvious favoritism when you're training a puppy," Kat announced. "You want them to show affection toward all—"

"Firework rocket," Luke warned her, which shut her up.

He accepted the dog back from Trish.

When Mrs. Gomez and her daughter arrived to pick up their puppy, Luke gave Agatha an expression that said, *I hope I never see you again.*

Agatha, who went to the Gomezes happily enough, gave him a decisive look in return. It said, *I'll be back.*

Luke received a text from his high school informant, Dylan Montgomery, near ten thirty on Friday night.

Dylan
I'm at a party and your sister is here, too. You asked me to let you know if I saw her smoking, vaping, or getting drunk. Sorry to say this, but she's pretty drunk.

Luke cursed and texted Dylan back.

Luke
Thanks for telling me. Party address?

He'd been watching sports after finishing a take-out meal from the Junction. Trust Blair to ruin a perfectly good evening.

In his closet, he pulled on Nikes and a hoodie over his track pants and T-shirt.

Dylan texted him the party's location before he reached his truck.

Fifteen minutes later, he arrived at a large piece of property set out in the country. The ground around the house had become a parking lot, packed with at least seventy-five cars.

Once again, Luke's parents had their hands full with a headstrong child. In some ways, they were too kind to know how to restrain a kid like Blair.

Luke did not have that problem.

He entered the house, ignoring the confused and questioning looks of teenagers. The whole thing was so stupidly stereotypical. Kegs of beer. Liquor bottles covering the dining room table, surrounded by shot glasses and spilled alcohol. Thumping music. Kids dancing with their arms in the air. Other kids making out in corners.

He wasn't interested in shutting down this party or in calling the police. He was only interested in extracting one very frustrating person.

He walked through downstairs rooms jammed with people and the smells of perfume and sweat. Kids darted out of his way. He didn't see Blair, so he let himself out through French doors that led to the back deck—

There she was, in the corner, wrapped in the same blanket as a teenage boy who had his tongue down her throat.

Luke's temper shot upward. "Blair," he said loudly as he approached.

The two of them jerked apart. Blair looked at him with glassy eyes. For a long moment, neither teenager moved nor spoke, then Blair had the nerve to giggle. "Hey," she slurred, throwing out her arm. "Look who's here, everyone! My older brother. He's *a lot* of fun. The party can really get rockin' now."

He was not amused. "We're leaving. Same choice I gave you in the alley. Do you want to come with me on your own two feet, or am I going to have to carry you out?"

Exaggerated eye roll. "Are you kidding? I'm not going anywhere. This guy . . ." She patted the side of the boy's face. Her forehead wrinkled with confusion. "What's your name again?" she whispered to him.

"Carson."

"This guy Carson here is a really good kisser."

"We're leaving," Luke said.

Her expression turned pouty. "I'm having fun."

"Will you be walking out of here? Or will I be carrying you?"

"Why are you even here? You don't care about me."

"Sounds like you're choosing for me to carry you out." Luke hunched over and tapped his shoulder. "Jump on."

She tossed aside the blanket. "I'll walk, you . . . you . . . monster!"

If she remembered this in the morning, she'd be mortified that she'd called him such a lame name.

Her ability to walk in a straight line had deserted her. Instead of trying to get her through the house, he led her down the deck stairs. Twice, he had to save her from breaking her neck.

He cut a path through the cars while she zigzagged behind him singing, "Luke sucks." It took effort, but he finally got her secured in his passenger seat.

The full moon turned the landscape silver as they drove.

"You think you had it *so* hard," she said after a time, her syllables rounded.

"Because I did."

"And you think I had it *so* easy."

"Because you did."

"You don't know what it was like for me, growing up in Ethan's shadow. Mom and Dad sent me to a counselor once, and he told me that I have survivor's guilt."

"No," Luke said tightly. "*I* have survivor's guilt." The words Finley had spoken to him surfaced. "*You're still standing in the jail cell of guilt instead of living like someone who's free.*"

"I have survivor's guilt, too," she said stubbornly. "You're so consumed with your own problems that you can't see that anyone else is struggling."

Spare him. "You never even met Ethan."

"I don't *need* to have met him to have survivor's guilt. I grew up with him, even though he wasn't there, and he was *so*, *so* perfect—"

"Say anything negative about Ethan, and I'll toss you out of this car."

"If you don't listen to me, I'll throw myself out!"

Great. His sister was a confrontational drunk.

"Do you know what they call children born after the death of a sibling?" she asked. "Replacement children."

Luke drew on every bit of patience he had. "You and Hailey were a surprise. Mom and Dad weren't trying to replace Ethan when they had you."

"As soon as they had us, we became his replacements."

"No. I watched Mom and Dad in the years after Ethan died. They grieved, but they also put in a lot of work toward healing. It made their relationship stronger. You're not going to convince me that they didn't love and accept you for who you are in your own right."

"I knew they were comparing me to him in their minds!"

"No. *You* were comparing yourself to him in your mind."

"They hyper-idealized Ethan, which is so messed up—"

"No," he said. "If anyone hyper-idealized him, it was you."

"And you," she accused.

The two words struck deep, carving through the center of him.

"How am I supposed to live up to the perfection of my dead brother?" she asked.

"You're not. Ethan wasn't perfect. And no one expects you to be anything like him."

"My counselor said I have unexpressed anger."

"Really?" Luke asked wryly. "Seems to me like you're doing a pretty good job of expressing it." He pulled up in front of their parents' house. "Are you going to ring the doorbell, or am I?"

"I'm not going to ring the doorbell! I'll just climb up the chimney and sneak into my bedroom."

He had no interest in arguing with her when she was sober. He definitely wasn't going to sit here and argue with her when she was in this state.

He walked to the front door and pressed the bell. His dad answered, wearing sweatpants and an Ohio State T-shirt. "Luke?"

"One of Blair's friends told me she was drunk at a party. I went and got her."

"What?" Lines of concern grooved Dad's face. "She was supposed to be at her friend's house for a sleepover."

"She wasn't."

"I'll put my shoes on and be right out."

Luke neared his truck. All was dark and still. No sign of Blair. He found her hiding on the passenger floorboard.

"Will you please keep what happened tonight secret from them?" she asked.

"No. Dad's already on his way out."

She muttered a string of swear words.

"We had a deal, Blair. I work on your car, you stop smoking, vaping, and getting drunk at parties. Remember?"

"I can't believe you told Dad."

"You broke our deal."

"So . . . what? You won't work on my car anymore?"

"No." Disappointment tasted bitter in his mouth. Not just because she was such a selfish rebel without a cause. But because fixing her car had been his therapy. It was the first tangible thing he'd been able to do for his family. It was his way of apologizing, of communicating how he felt about them in a way that didn't require words.

"The deal's off," he said.

This isn't romantic, is it?" Ben asked Akira the next morning as they browsed the spring bazaar in Misty River's central park. He leaned in close, looking at her seriously beneath his eyebrows.

She had to mentally restrain her arms from flinging themselves around his neck. "Not romantic in the least!"

"I'm trying to give off a Michael B. Jordan vibe."

It was absolutely working. "Not a single flutter."

Akira handed the woman at the fruit stand a selection of strawberries, peaches, and plums. Once she'd paid, Ben picked up the fruit bag. He was already carrying her bag containing honey and another sizable purchase of handmade soap.

"It's also not romantic at all that you're carrying my bags," she said as they set into motion.

"Am I carrying bags for you right now? Their weight is so light and my muscles so large that I actually hadn't noticed."

She laughed. The weather was perfect. And Ben was beside her.

The more time they spent together, the more they understood each other, and the deeper their friendship grew. Ben was quickly becoming very important to her—which both thrilled and scared her.

What-ifs kept rumbling around in her head.

What if he met someone, and she had to watch him fall in love with another woman? She'd be crushed, and yet she'd have no right to feel that way. From the start, she'd specified that she and Ben were friends, and he'd been respectful of that boundary.

What if, miracle of miracles, it turned out that he wanted to date her? And she said yes (because, hello . . . she daydreamed about kissing him every spare moment), but then it didn't go well, and she lost him? She'd lost boyfriends before, and it had been devastating. Somehow, though, the thought of losing Ben seemed even more horrific.

What if she and Ben started dating and it *did* go well? That prospect was, in some ways, the hardest of the three because it stirred in her a hope so sweet it was painful.

Akira, you're friends! Be grateful for that, and don't let premature dreams of happily-ever-after steal your common sense.

She pointed to the storefront of the smoothie shop. "I'd love a mango smoothie."

He got there first and held the door.

"The fact that you always hold open doors for me?" she asked.

"Yeah?"

She passed by him into the interior of the shop. "Also not romantic in the least."

Blair had accused Luke of hyper-idealizing Ethan.

After gnawing on that for most of Saturday morning, he'd concluded that's not what he'd done. Okay, he might have done a little of that. But, for the most part, he remembered all of Ethan's strengths and all of Ethan's weaknesses. Thing was, when you stacked those up, Ethan had been a pretty great kid. A pretty *ideal* kid. Remembering him that way didn't mean Luke was making him something he wasn't.

The treasure hunt had stalled, which was giving him too much time to think.

Restlessness scratched at him from the inside. He needed to *do* something productive to get the hunt going again, so he sat down at his laptop and continued doing the only thing he could—sifting through information online about the people Ed had known.

A sunset-orange sky filled his windows by the time he pushed his chair back. Nothing had tripped his suspicion. Nothing fit together in a way that provided a new lead.

He ran a hand through his hair, then texted Finley.

Luke
I'd like to take a look at all the clues in order.

Maybe seeing them that way would shake something free. That hope felt desperate, but he was desperate.

Finley
Sure! Come on over. The animals and I are enjoying a relaxing Saturday night in.

By the time he reached her place, she'd clothespinned every

written clue, as well as items representing the unwritten clues, to a strand of white lights she'd hung across the only blank wall space in her living room.

Her hair was piled on top of her head. She wore bell-bottom jeans and a short, wide, fuzzy sweater. Slippers. Rings on every finger.

She considered the clues. "Does it help to see them all lined up like this?"

He jerked at her words, realizing he'd been staring at her instead of the wall. "It does." *Put her out of your mind, Luke.*

It wasn't possible to put her out of his mind. She was all he wanted, all he could think about.

Focus on the clues for her sake. He forced himself to study them, to remember the details of each one and try to picture them from Ed's perspective.

Finally, he reached the two newest clues. On a blue sticky note, Finley had jotted down the things Robbie had told her about the day before Ed killed Carla. Next came Ed's poem about Carla.

He freed the poem and walked a few steps so he could hold it next to a lamp. Slowly, he read it. Then turned it over to the side covered with a picture.

"What does this look like to you?" Luke asked.

"One of my dad's drawings."

"I'm a car guy. You want to know what this looks like to me?"

"Yes."

"A map."

CHAPTER TWENTY-ONE

A *map?* Finley thought, arrested.

He pointed. "What's this?"

"Grass?"

"Look closer."

She bent over the page, straining to decipher what he'd seen. Two of the many blades of grass Dad had drawn had been connected with a horizontal line at the base, creating a shape that looked like a rectangle without a top. Three trees formed a triangle around it.

"Could it be a symbol?" he asked.

"A symbol?"

"For treasure?"

Her chin whipped in his direction. "I'll . . ." She cleared her throat. "I'll go get my computer so we can try to figure out if that shape has a meaning."

Once she returned with her laptop, she indicated the sofa and waited for him to sit first. Had they been negotiating, she would've let him throw out the first number. Same principle here. Allowing him to sit first gave her an advantage because, as soon as he'd landed, she plopped down *right* next to him. So close their thighs touched.

She pretended not to notice that he'd tensed. She also pretended not to notice how heavenly this felt. He looked especially handsome tonight in a pair of weathered jeans and a dark gray long-sleeved crewneck, pushed up at the forearms. It was dangerous to imagine a string of future nights—so many that the succession of them would bring them into old age—spent pressed up against him on this sofa.

The initial search she ran made it immediately apparent that a great number of people in the world were interested in symbology. She refined her search, rewording it a few times. In took less than ten minutes to locate what she sought—a list of American symbols used to indicate treasure.

Slowly, she scrolled through the content. Could Luke be right? Was this drawing—and not her conversation with Robbie or the poem—the real clue? Were they looking at a treasure map?

"There," Luke said, pointing to a replica of the symbol he'd spotted.

"'This particular shape represents treasure below,'" she read aloud. Goose bumps raced down her shoulders. She twisted to him. "You were right. This is a treasure map."

Excitement lit the depths of his eyes.

"This is the first symbol Dad has ever used in a hunt," she said.

"Probably because this is the first thing he's given you that's worth a lot of money."

She set the map on her laptop's screen so they could study it. "If that's the case and this drawing had fallen into the wrong hands, Dad wouldn't have wanted his gift to be marked with a red X or a picture of a treasure chest."

"Exactly." A few seconds passed. "I wish there were some words on this map."

"I do, too. He hasn't named the pond, the hills, or anything else. We're going to have to figure out the location of the treasure using these landmarks alone."

"Do you recognize anything here?"

Dad had sketched a few lines through the trees that might be roads or might be trails. "No."

"Is this a map of the property where you grew up?"

"No."

"A map of the land surrounding this house?"

"No."

"Your aunt and uncle's house?"

She shook her head. "No. I'm sorry. I wish I recognized this. But I don't."

"Which means your father hid the treasure on a piece of land that you and Robbie don't own. He's expecting you to trespass, locate the treasure, and get away carrying diamonds or cash or a Fabergé egg."

She laughed.

He cocked a questioning eyebrow.

"It's just that a Fabergé egg is the last thing I would've expected you to mention."

"It's the last thing I planned to mention. Forget I said that. It's not manly."

She'd trade a year's worth of herbal tea for permission to slide her hand into his silky, overgrown hair. "Just you watch." She placed the map on the side table. "We'll find the treasure, and it *will* be a Fabergé egg."

"You were supposed to forget I said that."

"Never." She brought up a Google Earth image of northern Georgia on her computer. "Historically, my dad doesn't plant clues farther than a three-hour drive from my house. It's a safe bet to conclude that the treasure is buried somewhere inside that radius."

She zoomed in so that even small country roads came into view.

Starting with her home and working outward, they hunted for a configuration of stream, roads, and pond that matched her map.

After thirty fruitless minutes, her eyes started to cross from a combination of strain and impatience. "This might take a lot of time. Maybe even days. While I'm very enthusiastic about this new development and incredibly impressed by you, since it turns out you're a bit of a mastermind—"

"I am not a mastermind."

"I'm thinking we should table this for tonight and pick it up tomorrow. Squinting at my computer for the rest of the evening wasn't exactly what I had in mind for my Saturday night."

"Okay. I'll head back to my apartment—"

"No." She may have responded a little *too* vehemently. It seemed she'd unintentionally placed a hand on his leg just above his knee to hold him in place. She kept it there because touching him was like receiving a transfusion of pleasure. "Sally, Rufus, Dudley, and I were planning to start a movie. Will you please stay and watch it with us?" *Say yes. Say yes.*

"What movie?"

"*The Sisterhood of the Traveling Pants*, but I'm willing to switch to something different. What type of shows do you like?"

"Sports and documentaries."

Just when she'd pegged him as an action-thriller movie type of man, he'd surprised her. "I could go for a high-quality, informative documentary. Which one?"

"I'm watching Ken Burns's documentary on World War Two."

"I'm open to that."

He looked skeptical. "You want to spend your Saturday night watching episodes in a seven-part series on a bloody and depressing war?"

"My dad was the history buff in our family. It would be edifying for me to learn new things."

"Go ahead with the movie you picked out."

"Only if you'll watch it, too. I'll make us vegan peanut butter chocolate chip cookie bars." She interlaced her hands in front of her chest into a begging position.

"I'll stay because I can't say no to vegan cookie bars."

They bantered while they mixed cookie dough. Once she slid

the pan into the oven, she rounded up her pets and they all settled in for the movie.

"Is this a thirty-year-old TV?" Luke asked.

"Dad bought it for my college dorm room, so it's twelve years old."

"You're watching a twelve-year-old thirty-two-inch TV that doesn't have high def and can't stream apps like Netflix?"

"I'm not interested in the latest technology. I typically only buy a new phone or computer when the old one gives up the ghost."

"This TV is so small it's making me think I need to schedule a visit with an optometrist."

She laughed. "It's not that bad!"

"Do you have to get up to manually change the channels?"

"Hold this." She placed Sally on top of his lean torso. "Maybe she'll distract you from my television's shortcomings."

She'd last watched *The Sisterhood of the Traveling Pants* in middle school. She remembered liking it, but it turned out that watching the most girl movie of all girl movies with a very masculine man made the experience one hundred times better.

He muttered dry, funny comments through the whole thing. He poked fun at the guys' haircuts, the romance plotline, her taste in movies. She reminded him that he was the one who'd chosen this option over an educational documentary.

They ate gooey cookie bars.

When a dog came on the screen, he said, "Knowing you, you're probably now more interested in the dog's story than any of the humans' stories."

"Aww! Yep. He's gorgeous."

"I'm not an animal lover, and *I'm* more interested in the dog's story."

Later, when she got teary-eyed over a sad turn of events, he regarded her with disbelief. Then he offered his forearm so she could use his shirt to wipe her eyes.

At the conclusion of the movie, she broke into spontaneous applause. It had been a long time since she'd felt so incandescently . . . light. Some of this lightness could be attributed to the discovery of the map. But much more of it could only be attributed to the man beside her. Wonderful, heartbreaking Luke with his hawkish nose, hard cheekbones, scuffed boots, and leave-me-alone aura.

Both of them were leaning back, resting against her sofa. She rolled her face toward him and found that he was already watching her. A pulse of connection joined them. Awareness.

"I enjoyed it," he said.

"You hated the movie."

"But you liked it. And I was here with you. So I enjoyed it."

A huge admission, coming from him.

Her body physically ached with yearning. The chemistry between them was a force of nature. Stronger than the river running relentlessly through her property. It could not be stopped. Nor diverted. Nor diminished.

"Are you and Derek together?" he asked.

The question took her aback. She hadn't expected him to go there. "No. He asked me out, but I've been procrastinating."

"Good."

"Good?"

"That's the best news I've heard in a while."

What did that mean? She tried and failed to read his mind. "I'd like for you to tell me something, Luke."

He waited.

"I want to know how you feel about me," she said.

Time passed. Right when she was sure he wouldn't answer, he said, "I'd do anything for you."

Her heart tugged upward like a helium balloon.

His eyes went smoky, but then he pushed to his feet. "I should go."

She scurried in front of him, blocking his exit route. "No. I think you should stay." She sensed the importance of this moment.

Whatever happened next would impact their future. For better. Or for worse.

God, she prayed, *please*. If they were going to have a relationship, she needed his dam to break. "Did you just say you'd do anything for me?"

A battle waged in his face. "Yes. I'd do anything . . . sacrifice anything for you. Your well-being is the most important thing to me."

"Luke."

"The fact that you're in this world makes this place worth living in. For me."

She'd . . . she'd suspected he felt that way. But to have it confirmed was blowing her mind. She needed to be careful. How she handled this meant everything. "I feel the very same way about you."

"You're the patron saint of lost causes. If you're into me, it's because you pity me."

"No. I have sympathy toward a lot of people, including you. But I haven't wanted to date any of those other people. Not for five years. I do want to date you. You're trustworthy and straightforward and loyal."

He shook his head and looked ready to disagree.

"Most of all, you . . . fit with me," she said. "It's mysterious. I'd never have expected it, and I can't explain it. We're totally different, and yet we fit."

"You can't let yourself care about me. If you do, you'll only end up hurt."

"I don't believe that has to be true. But even if it is, I'm willing to pay that price." After Chase, she hadn't been ready to open herself up to the kind of pain she'd endured when she'd lost him. Until now. This step scared her. But she wanted this even more than it scared her. She moved closer, reaching up to intertwine her hands behind his neck. "Will you give a relationship between us a chance?"

"I want to be with you, but I can't."

"Why?"

"If I let you down the way I did my brother, I won't be able to go on."

"'It's better not to love anyone new than have them taken from you,'" she said, mirroring the words he'd spoken to her weeks ago. "I understand. We have the same fear. I'll face it for you if you'll face it for me."

"If I'm going to keep my promise to your dad, I have to be able to concentrate. I can't let anything, including you, distract me."

"As we figure out where this treasure is buried, I will not distract you."

"You can't help but distract me."

Her lips twitched up at the edges. "If that's the case, is the level of distraction I present really going to change whether we're together or not?"

He exhaled raggedly. She could feel his coiled control.

"We've lost people we loved. We've learned that life is short. Too short not to give this a try." She outlined his ear and charted a delicate trail down the side of his neck. It was glory to touch him. "No matter what happens, I think we'll be okay so long as we communicate honestly."

"I don't know what your dad was thinking when he asked me to make that promise. I'm definitely not good enough to be your protector."

"My dad was crazy smart. I think he knew exactly what he was doing." Her vision slid to his lips and paused there while her heart thundered. Under heavy eyelids, she met his gaze.

Desire sharpened his expression. Color rose on his cheeks. In the next instant, his strong hands sank into her hair, and he took her mouth in a kiss.

Joy vaulted inside her.

With a groan, he pulled her close.

Hunger. Devotion. Rightness.

It went on and on. A few minutes. Then more. And more.

She couldn't get enough of exploring his contours and textures. The ridge of his spine. The layers and feel of his hair. She kissed her way along his jaw. She inhaled his leather-and-soap scent. She listened to his sawing breath.

The intuition of belonging swamped her. She'd said to him that they fit, and they did.

When he lifted her off the ground in a fluid motion, she broke the kiss to lock an elbow behind his neck. "Don't stop."

"I'm not stopping." He bent his head, and they continued kissing as he walked.

Why was he moving them to a different location? The bemused question sailed through her fuzzy, wildly infatuated brain like a butterfly. "Are you . . . taking me to my bedroom?"

"Yes."

She giggled. "You can't take me to my bedroom."

"Kitchen table?"

She grinned at him. "You can't take me to a bed or a kitchen table."

His motion stopped. Luke, with her finger tracks mussing his hair, was officially the most gorgeous thing she'd ever seen. Which was saying something because she'd seen thousands of puppies.

"I'm not having sex with you tonight," she explained. "In fact, I've never had sex with anybody."

She remained suspended in his arms. "You've never had sex?" he asked.

"No."

"Never?"

"Never."

"Were you and Chase waiting until after marriage?"

"Yes. And that's still my plan."

He surveyed her with grave consternation.

"I know it's countercultural," she said. "So much so that most people view me as hopelessly strange. But I don't care."

A lopsided smile slowly overtook his mouth. "Could we elope tonight?"

"Tempting! Maybe they have a twenty-four-hour wedding chapel in Atlanta, complete with a faux stained-glass window and pink carpet."

"I lived in Atlanta for years. I'm pretty sure they don't have anything like that."

"Crying shame."

Carefully, he set her feet on the floor.

They faced each other across a space of inches that sang with heat. He hadn't tried to persuade her to sleep with him. He'd respected her stance, even though it was different than his own.

"Despite the fact that our plans for elopement are probably foiled," she said, "you're welcome to stay longer."

"I want to stay so much that I need to go."

She absorbed that, taking a snapshot of him in her mind so that she could go back and revisit it for all her days. "I get it." She gave him a kiss as light as silk. "Good night, Luke."

"Good night."

By force of will, she separated from him, then watched his broad back as he crossed to the front door. Quietly, he closed it behind him.

In a trance of swooniness, she locked the door, then walked onto her back deck. The night wind cooled her overheated cheeks and raked through her hair.

Sally stopped beside her with an expression that communicated, *You kissed that man!*

"Yes I did," Finley replied. Boy, had she kissed that man.

She pulled out her phone and texted Meadow and Bridget.

Finley
Something integral shifted between Luke and me tonight. He finally told me how he felt about me, and I told him I felt the same way. I'm giddy. And a little frightened. But really happy.

Bridget
Oh, Finley! I knew it. I'm delighted for you two.

Meadow
You deserve all the happiness in the world. However, I'm speaking on behalf of your best interests when I advise caution.

Bridget
Let's get together ASAP to discuss the details.

Meadow
Definitely.

Finley
Agreed.

A full minute passed before Bridget followed up with another text.

Bridget
Is this a sign from God that Derek and I are destined to be together?

Meadow
The short answer is no.

Not surprisingly, Meadow had responded to tonight's turn of events by urging caution. Finley saw the value in that. Luke had agreed to nothing, after all. Best to temper her expectations.

Yes. Well and good. Expectations tempered!

That said, a little bit of celebration was merited. Luke Dempsey had created a trapdoor in his defenses just big enough for her to slip through. That trapdoor represented a sacred trust she could never betray.

Luke steered his truck through dark mountain roads. He'd probably live to regret the things he'd said and done tonight.

But when it came down to it, he'd been unable to stop himself from saying and doing them.

He replayed it all. Then replayed it again and again. He worked to adjust to what had happened. To make himself believe it. To get used to the unfamiliar satisfaction . . . or hope . . . or happiness that had stolen over him.

Until a few minutes ago, he'd taken for granted that she'd had sex with Chase. They'd been in a serious relationship for years, then been engaged. He'd also assumed that she'd had sex with people before Chase.

He'd defaulted into thinking that her past was similar to his own. A mistake, because Finley was nothing like him. She was a quirky animal activist, a hippie for Jesus. Based on everything he knew about her, her view on sex made sense.

He came to a stop sign. Turned.

He'd never been with a virgin. Even the girls he'd slept with in high school had been experienced. So how come kissing Finley . . . just kissing her and nothing else . . . had been the most powerful physical experience he'd ever had?

He wanted to tell himself that he didn't know the answer, but that wasn't true. The power of kissing her had nothing to do with how worldly he was or how worldly she wasn't. It was because of *her* and how he felt about her.

It seemed impossible, but she liked him back.

He couldn't screw this up. She meant too much to him to screw this up. Yet he couldn't imagine how this could go well. His little brother was in the grave, and he was an ex-con—so what right did he have to happiness? The score between him and Ethan seemed closer to settled when Luke was lonely and cut off from connection. Also, he still suspected that Finley was in love with Chase. He couldn't compete with Chase.

A relationship between a man who had no right to happiness and a woman who was in love with her dead fiancé wasn't going to work. Right?

Finley would continue loving Chase, which meant he could never be happy. And since he had no right to happiness, that was how it would be.

There was a horrible perfection to it—

Stop.

He couldn't think about the future.

All he knew was that here in the present, he *could not* screw this up.

Uneasiness circled inside him like birds of prey.

CHAPTER TWENTY-TWO

Midmorning the following day, someone knocked on the door of Luke's apartment. For the first time since he'd moved into this place, the sound didn't cause him to frown, because his immediate thought was, *Finley?*

He had no reason to think that. She'd never come to his apartment. Still, he couldn't help but hope.

In recent weeks, he'd finally let go of his prison schedule. He still preferred for his days to have structure, but he didn't need that structure to be as strict as it had been. This morning he'd slept in and was wearing pajama pants. He shouldered into a T-shirt, then crossed the living room in bare feet.

Let it be Finley.

Opening the door, he saw that it wasn't Finley.

It was Blair.

Disappointed, he swung the door shut.

She stuck a combat boot between the door and its casing, entered, then looked everywhere but into his face.

"I came by to apologize," she said to his area rug.

"Did Mom and Dad force you to do this?"

Amusement tugged at her mouth. "Mom and Dad don't really have the ability to force me to do anything."

He crossed his arms. "I'm waiting."

"For?"

"Your apology."

She hauled her focus to him. He was used to seeing cockiness in her expression. Today, the cockiness was still there but so was remorse. "I'm sorry I got drunk at the party and broke our deal." She pulled her knit cap lower. "I'm also sorry that you had to come and get me and see me like that. And I'm really sorry that you spilled the beans to Mom and Dad because now they're mad at me, too."

"What do you care? They don't really have the ability to force you to do anything."

She folded her fingers into her palms. "I care because even though I get in trouble with them a lot, I don't like to upset them."

"Huh."

"Isn't this when you're supposed to say that you forgive me?"

"That's not how apologies work. The person who's been wronged isn't obligated to forgive the other person."

"Fine, but will you come back and work on my car?" The next word came out the way a rusty nail comes out of a plank of wood. "Please."

"No." He walked toward his kitchen table. "You can let yourself out."

Sitting, he continued reading a *Wall Street Journal* article online.

Her boots approached. The chair across from him squeaked under her weight. After a few seconds, she caught the top edge of his laptop and carefully lowered it. "I made a mistake," she acknowledged. "It won't happen again."

"I don't believe you."

"I promise you that it won't happen again. From now on, I'm going to stick to our agreement. Will you give me a second chance?"

His conscience pricked. He'd done a hundred things wrong in his life, yet Finley hadn't hesitated to give him a second chance. She'd hired a parolee. She'd let him into her work and life and treasure hunt. It would be hypocritical to refuse to do the same for Blair, even though he didn't expect her to change. Nobody could compel Blair to make good decisions, and he highly doubted she was ready to start making good decisions for herself. "If I do start back to work on your car, I'm warning you that if you step out of line again, I'm done. Nothing you say or do at that point will convince me to help you out again."

"I understand."

"People don't like it when they place their faith in someone and then get burned."

"I understand."

"Also, if I do start back to work on your car, you need to cut out your derogatory comments and your rude attitude toward Mom and Dad. I won't put up with that."

"Okay."

"And you need to make sure that I'm alone at least three-quarters of the time I'm in the garage. There's been way too many people in my business."

"Got it."

Silence settled. "You went on and on the other night about how you're a replacement child for Ethan. You complained about trying to live up to his standard. Was that just the booze talking?"

A blush rolled up her cheeks. It encouraged him to see she could still feel embarrassment.

"That was mostly the booze talking," she said.

"The way I see it, Mom and Dad did a great job with you. They didn't expect you to take his place. Right? Be straight with me."

She fiddled with the table's edge. "Right. Mom and Dad are cool."

"But?"

"But that doesn't mean it's been super easy to grow up with a dead brother."

"Life isn't easy. If you want to find out how hard it can be, then mess up as much as I have. If you want to save yourself a lot of grief and jail time, then start taking responsibility for yourself."

"But—"

"No buts. Don't blame anyone else for your mistakes. Especially not Ethan. He doesn't deserve it."

She set her chin at a defiant angle, but then her shoulders relaxed. "Fine. Does this mean that you'll fix up my car?"

"On a trial basis."

"Really?"

"Yes."

"Thank you." Her face brightened and she lifted a hand for him to high-five.

He didn't reciprocate.

"Fine," she said. "Leave me hanging. Can I give you a hug?"

After a reluctant sigh, he nodded.

She came around the table and leaned down to wrap her arms around him. "Thank you, Luke."

Several miles south of Luke's apartment building, Finley pulled to a stop on the side of a country road. This location would look unremarkable to the rest of the drivers who passed it today. Yet this particular spot, bordered on both sides by nature, had so profoundly impacted her life that her knees were already quivering. It was anything but unremarkable to her.

A Nissan zoomed by. She couldn't make out much about the driver, except that he was male and didn't look her way.

She took a fortifying breath and exited her car. Picking her way around shrubs and beneath trees, she reached the place where Chase's car had crashed to a halt.

His Jeep had left a path of destruction. It had gouged the earth and cracked one young tree clean in half.

Numerous times, she'd come here. Sometimes on Chase's birthday. The anniversary of his death. The anniversary of the day he proposed.The anniversary of what would've been their wedding.

The first several times, it had looked as though the damaged young tree would not survive. A large section of it had, indeed, died. Gradually, though, the remaining section recovered. It gained height and breadth.

Finley rested her palm on the dark fractured piece of its trunk. Anyone who cared to look closely would always be able to see the harm that had been done to the tree. Her vision traveled upward. But anyone who cared to look closely would also see *life*. A canopy of brand-new spring leaves arched above her.

She would always bear the mark that Chase's death had left on her. But that didn't have to stunt her future. It didn't have to mean that scars couldn't become a part of a beautiful whole. God held life in His palms, and He was calling her to continue living and growing.

She approached the patch of land where Chase's body had come to rest after he'd been thrown from the vehicle. Today, wild blue violets blanketed it. They weren't fully blooming yet, but soon they would.

She sat cross-legged as cleansing tears drifted over her eyelashes.

She cried for him and the tragic way his life ended. For how young and wonderful he'd been. For all the things he hadn't had a chance to do and give. But she also cried from a place of thankfulness. She'd had the opportunity to know him and love him. Their relationship had made her life richer, and thank goodness they'd experienced all they had before his death.

She'd put up a shield to protect herself from love. It had done its job; it had kept her safe. But the time had come to move out from behind that and walk forward.

It's what Chase would've wanted for her. It's what God wanted for her. It's what she wanted for herself.

In all earnestness, she'd planned to rehabilitate Luke. However, it seemed the reverse had happened.

To her astonishment, Luke was rehabilitating her.

A server dressed in traditional German garb approached the table where Ben, Akira, and Mr. Wrigley sat. "*Guten Tag!*"

"Guten Tag," Ben answered gamely. Poor thing. Dressing in a costume for work every day had to suck.

"Will you be having the *Wiener schnitzel* or the bratwurst?"

Ben politely let the others order first. They opted for the schnitzel. He went for the bratwurst.

The woman scribbled on her notepad.

The water main that serviced both Misty River High School and East Side Elementary had broken in the middle of the night. Crews were still at work, so administrators had canceled school today. Akira's kids had the day off, but their parents did not, so she'd scrambled to organize a daylong field trip. She'd asked Ben to come along because she needed more chaperones than herself and Mr. Wrigley, the elderly gentleman who volunteered with the after-school program. This morning, Ben had driven everyone to the town of Helen in Furry Tails' van.

More than fifty years ago, Helen had reinvented itself as a Bavarian village. They'd painted frescoes of dancing German people, hung flower boxes, opened beer gardens, and plastered everything with old-fashioned German lettering. The town felt like a German theme park, which had turned it into a tourist magnet.

They'd taken the kids zip-lining before stopping to eat lunch on this covered patio. German pennant flags curved in the March breeze.

"Would anyone like a stein of beer?" their server asked.

The adults declined but of course one kid shouted, "Me!"

"Water for the kids, please," Akira said.

"*Danke schön!*" the woman replied before moving to her next table.

"What do you have planned for us after this?" Ben asked Akira.

"A short walking tour of downtown. We'll be stopping at the Alpine Bakery at one fifteen for a Black Forest cake tasting. After that, we'll let the kids do some shopping." Her pale blue sweater complemented her skin tone and dark hair. Hoop earrings swung against her neck as she talked. "I'm afraid that the cake isn't going to be enough to make up for all the indecision and drama of the shopping. Inevitably, the kids try to buy things they don't have enough money for. I apologize to you both in advance."

"Budgeting," Mr. Wrigley observed, "is a valuable life skill."

"And a skill these children do not yet have."

Ben had been to Helen several times in the past for Oktoberfest, the Christmas market, and to tube the river in the summer. Even though he was partly responsible for ten kids today, this was his favorite trip to Helen so far because he was here with Akira. He watched her now, entertained by her experessive face.

Lately, she was always on his mind. He was embarrassed to admit how often he checked his phone to see if she'd texted him.

They'd started off as friends. They were still friends, because that's what Akira needed. But they were also more than that now. The chemistry between them hadn't been platonic for quite a while. Which might or might not be a good thing. The last time he'd liked someone this much—Leah—he'd been set on her for years.

He'd had months to get over Leah, and for the most part, things were normal between them now. He'd walked through the worst of his sadness, yet the confidence he'd once had when it came to dating had taken a beating.

After eating a bratwurst on a crusty white roll with lots of spicy mustard and sauerkraut on the side, he followed Akira down the sidewalk. She played tour guide, trying to interest the kids in historical facts about Helen and eagerly pointing out landmarks. At the scheduled time, their group crammed into the small interior of the Alpine Bakery. To give everyone more breathing room, Ben and Akira stepped outside the glass door. They kept an eye on the kids while the baker explained how they made their most famous dessert.

"Can you put me out of my misery about something?" Akira asked him.

He looked into her upturned face. "I can try. What's bringing you misery?"

"You."

His brows shot up. "Me? I make people happier. Ask anyone."

"To my dismay, I'm starting to have romantic feelings toward you." She pretended horror.

"No kidding?" So she was finally willing to shift them out of their holding pattern? The wave of hope that hit his brain made him dizzy. "Is that because I'm wearing this backpack full of water, emergency snacks, wet wipes, and confiscated electronics?"

"Yes. It was the backpack."

"Sorry about that, Akira. It really wasn't fair of me to wear such a sexy backpack around you."

"Can you please assure me that you're not interested in me romantically? That should put a stop to this immediately."

"I would if I could." He propped a shoulder against the rough-textured wall. In the quiet, their teasing drained away and the atmosphere turned serious. He gathered his courage. "The truth is, I am interested in you. Very."

Her eyes widened. "I, too, am interested in you. Very."

His mouth curved into a smile. He was surprised by how good it felt to hear her admit that. "Really?"

"Really. I'm worried, though. I don't think I'm the kind of girl who can hold your attention."

"You're wrong."

Her expression informed him that she wasn't sure if she could believe him. Her former boyfriends had cut down her self-image, which made him crazy.

"You're amazing," he told her. "Those other guys couldn't see it, so they were either stupid or visually impaired. I'm neither of those things. You have my full attention, and I see exactly how amazing you are."

"Thank you." She made a wobbly sound of uncertainty. She

shook out her arms like a basketball player trying to release stress before shooting a free throw. "I'm worried," she said again.

"Nobody's rushing you, and nothing has to change between us today. We have time."

"Is this when you announce that you're actually a prince in disguise?"

"No," he answered on a chuckle.

"An angel?"

He shook his head.

"A knight who touched a sacred stone and time-traveled forward to this year?"

"I'm nothing fancy. I'm just a guy who likes teaching and baseball."

"Do you know that guys like you are as rare as wholesome food choices at a five-year-old's birthday party?"

"Guys like me aren't that rare—"

"Yes. You are."

"Your perspective is skewed because you've been unlucky lately in the boyfriend department."

"Lately? I've been nothing *but* unlucky in the boyfriend department. I'd forsaken my tendency to fall for guys at first sight. And then I saw you. And every single time I've seen your face since that first day, I've been trying *not* to fall." She resettled the angle of her smart watch. "Without success."

The bakers must have brought out the cake because the sound of the kids' excitement reached them.

"Did you actually just say that you're romantically interested in me?" she asked. "And you weren't joking?"

Anticipation flowed between them.

"I actually said that. And I wasn't joking."

Luke returned to his desk as usual on Monday. Despite Trish telling him that Finley would be out of the office all morning for back-to-back meetings with donors, he kept glancing toward the workroom door. He was so busy listening for her, he couldn't concentrate.

It was almost two. Where was she?

He hadn't contacted her yesterday because he didn't want to seem overbearing. He wasn't sure why she hadn't contacted him. Nor was he sure what their new dynamic was supposed to look like. Everything had changed. Right? But how? He couldn't guess her mindset. He didn't know how to act with her or how to get rid of this underlying anxiety.

"Today's social media captions aren't upbeat enough," Kat complained. "Your Instagram caption just says, 'Good day to you,' and on Facebook you wrote, 'Best wishes.'"

"You know, Luke," Trish interjected, "there are some lovely and inspiring Christmas poems out there that are so old they're copyright free. You could quote lines from those in your captions."

"If this job requires me to read and quote old Christmas poetry, I'll have to quit."

"Quitting might be for the best," Kat said.

"No!" Trish laughed nervously. "She's joking. We wouldn't want that. Finley and the rest of us love having you here."

Kat tsked. "I think even Finley can tell he's not cut out for a career in animal rescue."

"People I've *never met* can tell that I'm not cut out for a career in animal rescue," Luke said.

"That's not true," Trish insisted. "You're wonderful at this. So gifted."

"He's strong with technology, but his animal care skills are lacking, which is no surprise since he spent the last several years . . ." Kat appeared to think better of continuing.

"In prison," he finished.

"Even Jesus Christ," Trish said desperately, "was arrested—"

Finley glided into the room. "Hello, everyone."

Immediately, every detail of his surroundings—other than her—dropped away. She wore the blue patterned robe-thing over a white shirt, leggings, and clogs. Her hair was very straight today, her eyes ocean bright as they met his.

A charge filled the air.

Trish was too clueless to notice, and Kat had the social awareness of a turtle.

"The meetings took longer than I expected," she said as she crossed into her office, carrying her purse and a few file folders.

"Finley," Kat called, "today Luke used 'Good day to you' and 'Best wishes' as social media captions."

Finley reappeared in her doorway, this time without the folders and purse.

"I tried to tell him that's not the Furry Tails way," Kat said.

Finley looked at him warmly. "I'm fine with it."

"Excuse me?"

"Luke's doing such a great job overall—"

"I beg to differ," Kat said.

"—that I'll let the less-than-cheery social media captions slide just this once."

Kat sniffed. "It's never a good idea to lower standards."

If Finley wanted to be with him, she was lowering her standards.

"Luke, can I borrow you for a bit?" Finley asked. "I'd like to inventory the supply room and could use an extra set of hands."

"Sure." He followed her into the hallway.

"In case it wasn't obvious," she whispered when they were a few doors down, "inventorying the supply room is a ruse. I made it up because it feels like a week since we've seen each other even though it hasn't been two days. I want time alone with you."

Thank God.

She wrapped a hand around his forearm and pulled him inside the small room. Right away, he pressed her against the back of the door.

"Hello," she breathed, smiling as her hands snaked behind his waist. "I just showed you blatant favoritism despite shoddy social media captions. I was in the same room with you, so I was too blissed-out to care."

His mouth was on hers, insistent and demanding.

"Don't expect to get away with shoddy social media captions in the future," she murmured between kisses, their lips millimeters apart. She was already breathing hard.

"I don't."

"It's not the Furry Tails way."

They were kissing again. Desire turned every molecule of him liquid, greedy. They'd picked up right where they'd left off Saturday night and he'd never been so relieved.

"How come you waited so long to inventory the supply room?" he asked.

"There was no waiting involved. There was only me, rushing through my meetings this morning as quickly as humanly possible."

For Finley, a wonderful Monday gave way to greater and greater happiness as the workweek unfolded. She and Luke ate takeout at his apartment for dinner. The next morning, they met for breakfast before work. The following day, she convinced him to ride bikes. They shared dinner at an outdoor restaurant next to the river. They bathed Sally, which devolved into a war of suds, which morphed into a storm of emotions when he took her in his arms.

When he wasn't nearby, which wasn't often, she *missed* him.

He was the first person she sought out every morning when she arrived at work. She made up reasons to talk to him throughout the day about the treasure hunt or the animals. Every time she tackled a Furry Tails task that called for two people, she chose him as her second.

Only one dark cloud hovered over her perfect week: Luke's unfailing productivity.

Now that he'd completed the initial tech to-do list she'd given him, she struggled to keep him occupied. She pretended to be passionate about pursuing better search engine optimization and adding more social media platforms to their portfolio. She claimed she wanted him to grow their email subscription numbers. She declared that she needed him to run more ads.

During his after-work hours, he combed images of North Georgia with the fervor of Sherlock Holmes, searching for landmarks that matched her dad's map. Worse, he expected her to do the same. He'd divvied up Georgia and asked her to search the northwest corner. He'd taken the northeast corner. Each evening when they returned to their respective homes, they studied the terrain, working their way toward the middle of the state.

It was like trying to find a thumbtack at a garage sale, and for the first time since opening the initial clue, Finley wanted to embrace her father for making the treasure hunt so difficult.

Because here's the thing. Luke's technological contributions to Furry Tails were of value. The treasure hunt was of value. But *his presence* was of far greater value. If the end of the hunt meant he'd move away, then she wasn't ready for the hunt to end. She'd lost Chase with the suddenness of an axe falling. An emphatic *no* filled her every time she contemplated losing Luke with the same swift finality.

She needed more time with him. His family needed more time with him. She began praying that God would give them more time.

But on Friday night . . .

Time ran out.

CHAPTER TWENTY-THREE

Luke had become so used to staring at online maps and finding nothing that when he finally did view a body of water shaped in a familiar way on Friday night, it took him several seconds to recognize what he was seeing.

He leaned toward the computer, his boredom and tiredness vanishing. Had he found something that resembled Ed's drawing?

He had.

Lake Trahlyta was written in the center of the blue mass. A narrow lake, it rested in a diagonal direction. Round like the head of a club at the top, jagged at the bottom.

It was nine thirty. He'd been reclining on the sofa, feet on the coffee table, laptop balanced on his abdomen. Now his bare feet hit the floor as he sat up and reached for his photocopy of Ed's map.

He compared the page to his screen. A match.

Adrenaline pumped through his body, giving him a taste of what it must've felt like for Finley when she'd figured out each clue.

He zoomed in and out on the digital map until the other elements included in Ed's drawing came into view. The roads, check. The streams, check.

He'd found the location of the treasure.

He pushed the heels of his hands against his eye sockets, then dragged his hands down his face and dialed Finley. He couldn't wait to end this hunt. Only by ending it would he be able to ensure her safety.

"I found it," he told her before she could even say hello.

"You found the location of the treasure?"

"Yes."

"Luke! You rock star!"

"It's at Vogel State Park." Which was located just under an hour away. "Pull up a map of that area and tell me if you think I'm right."

"Will do. Hang on."

He smiled at the muffled noises on the other end of the line. He liked being on the phone with her, even when they weren't saying anything. In the same way, he liked being in a room with her at the Center. It didn't matter if her attention rested on something else. Her nearness meant his breath could ease, his heartbeat could steady.

"You're absolutely right," she whispered. "It's exactly like Dad's drawing. You know . . ." Her words drifted to nothing.

"I know I'd like to be making out with you right now," he said.

She laughed. "Then drive over."

"I can't." Which actually meant, *I won't*. He was way too into her. So much so it was dangerous, and he knew it. He was trying to protect himself from her, and he was also trying to protect her from him.

"I was going to say . . . *you know*, I'm pretty sure my dad and I visited this state park. Is it the one with a waterfall at one end of the lake?"

"I have no idea."

"Let me check." She made cute thoughtful sounds. *Mmm*. And *oh*. "This *is* the park with the waterfall. He took me there once during my college years. We stretched out on the beach for a whole afternoon, reading. Then we got back in the car and drove to a more remote section of the park. We hiked off-trail until we found a spot on the hillside where we could eat the dinner we'd packed and watch the sunset. The view was stunning."

She paused. He didn't speak because he didn't want to interrupt her memories.

"We had a great conversation," she continued. "It was one of those rare moments in time that was absolutely and completely perfect."

"If you felt that way about it, your dad probably felt that way, too."

"He probably did. Goodness. Recalling that day makes me miss him."

"He loved you."

"I loved him, too. And now I'm getting weepy. Here. I have a napkin to use on my eyes. I'm fine!" Her voice trembled a little. "Everything's fine!"

"Do you think he buried the treasure at the location of your picnic? Then marked that place with the symbol on his map?"

"That would make sense." He heard Finley take in a deep breath. "If we overlay the hand-drawn map on a digital map of the same scale, we should be able to drop a pin onto the digital map on the spot of the treasure symbol."

"Yes."

"Then we hike to the spot of the pin using GPS and simply . . . start digging?"

"Let's think this through." Pressing to his feet, he began to pace. "I do not want to dig up—"

"—a Fabergé egg?"

He snorted. "I don't want to dig up a valuable treasure of any kind in broad daylight. Anyone could see us. But if we go after dark, it'll be hard to hike through the woods."

"We'll need to arrive when there's still some light left because the GPS might not be precise. It might take me a while to visually confirm whether the GPS led us to the place I remember."

"So we'll get there shortly before dark," he said, "and start digging after dark."

"I agree."

"The quicker we get in and out of there, the better. We'll be digging on state property."

"I'm not a fan of disturbing nature. We'll replace all the dirt and pine cones and everything, right?"

"Right."

"I can work on trying to drop a pin onto a digital map," she said.

"Okay. I'll get supplies."

"Once those two things are in order . . ."

"We'll be ready to claim the treasure."

Immediately after ending the call, Finley began adjusting the dimensions of an online map of Vogel State Park until Dad's map lined up with it exactly. The treasure symbol appeared to fall in the middle of a wooded area removed from trails and roads.

The map Dad had drawn was a game changer. Had he given her a clue simply directing her to return to where they'd shared the sunset picnic, she'd never have been able to find it. He'd been driving that day. When they'd left the lake, she'd paid no mind to the roads he'd taken. After they'd parked, he'd searched for a viewing spot using nothing but his compass and instincts.

At the time, the path he'd taken had been untraveled. But it appeared he'd traveled that path a second time when he'd returned to the spot of their picnic to leave her the final gift in a lifetime of gifts.

On Sunday, they parked at six thirty p.m. on one of the roads curving through state park land.

Finley surveyed the items in the back of Luke's truck with admiration. He'd brought two shovels and two bulky high-beam flashlights with square faces. Two headlamps. Two backpacks. Bottled water, granola bars, nuts, apples.

She'd done her part by dropping an electronic pin into Google Maps on the projected location of the treasure. Then she'd sent that pin to her phone. She planned to lead them on a straight course from here to there.

Luke's T-shirt rode up when he reached forward to draw the gear closer to them, revealing the side of his hard, smooth abs. *Lord, have mercy.*

They stuffed equipment and additional layers of clothing into the packs. Currently, the weather was sunny and sixty-three degrees. But in late March, night could fall quick and harsh in the North Georgia mountains. The temperature was forecasted to drop to forty overnight, and they had no way of knowing how long they'd be out in the elements.

She'd paired the same hiking boots she'd probably worn the last time she'd come here with leggings and a white long-sleeved athletic shirt. When she put on the backpack, it came down almost to the backs of her knees. She peeked up at Luke and found him watching her with amusement.

"I would've bought smaller backpacks," he said, "but I have no idea how big this treasure might be."

"If it's so large that I have to fill this entire backpack, we're in serious trouble. Not even a pack mule could carry the volume of this thing."

His eyes twinkled. "I'll be the pack mule. You don't have to carry anything you don't want to."

"Not to worry. I believe Fabergé eggs are only about this big." She held her fingers four inches apart.

He grinned.

Why did he have to look like a model for Patagonia? He was a car-loving ex-con. He shouldn't look so comfortable in his navy fleece, rugged pants, and lace-up boots.

Was there enough time before sundown for her to twine her hands through his hair and press her body to his—

"Ready?" he asked.

She shook herself from her reverie. "Ready." She dropped another pin in their current location and labeled it *Luke's Bad Boy*

Truck. She didn't want them to get lost in the dark on their return hike.

They set off, making their way around brambles, over fallen limbs, through drifts of old leaves.

"Not even a horse cart could carry the volume of this backpack," she stated.

"Uh-huh."

She entertained herself with more and more far-fetched scenarios. "Not even a Mack truck could carry the volume of this backpack." Crunching twigs. "Not even a train car." Birdsong. "Not even a Learjet." Cool breeze. "Not even a rocket ship."

The sun's rays danced against textured tree bark. The air smelled of pine. Typically, nature relaxed her. Today, its relaxing properties were directly at odds with the nervousness that had been growing within her all day.

It should take just under thirty minutes to reach the site. She had *no idea* what to expect. Would they find the treasure? If they did, would Luke leave? If he stuck around, how long would he stay?

She'd opened the first clue almost three months ago. Mentally and emotionally, she'd had time to prepare herself to finish the last hunt her father would ever plan for her. Now that the moment had come, however, she didn't feel prepared. This final stage came wrapped in more questions than answers, which gave her imagination permission to drum up all kinds of scary scenarios.

What treasure did you bury for me, Dad?

She could picture him as he'd been the day of the picnic, in his lightweight hiking pants and National Model Railroad Association T-shirt. His white-gray curls had framed a tan face made even more striking thanks to the grooves that gave it character. She imagined him looking back over his shoulder at her and smiling.

"Hold up," Luke murmured in an undertone of warning.

She stopped.

He nodded to the right. Straining her eyes, she spotted movement through the trees. A trace of red and brown, followed by a feminine voice and a chuckle. Several yards away and heading toward them, a friendly-looking mom and her teenage son came into view. With a sigh of relief, Finley continued forward. Clearly, these two were not a threat.

Attempting not to look like someone en route to excavate treasure, Finley greeted them. They cheerfully returned her greeting as they passed.

Luke was always vigilant, but the fact that he'd registered the mom and son before Finley informed her that he was on high alert.

As they progressed deeper into the forest, they could no longer hear the sound of cars on the road. They encountered no other humans.

Just a quarter-mile left.

"Almost there."

Less than seven hundred feet left.

The topography began to open, allowing glimpses of sky ahead. The GPS counted down the remaining feet to her destination. *Yes*. In general, this felt right. A few more steps, and the terrain dropped downhill, providing an iconic North Georgia landscape of mountains undulating to the horizon. Lake Trahlyta nestled below like a sapphire cushioned in green velvet.

Coming to an abrupt stop, Finley consulted her phone. "This is where I dropped the pin." She took in her surroundings. "This isn't exactly where we had the picnic, though. It wasn't steep like this. It was level and ended in a cliff."

"Do you think we're close?"

"Yes, I do think we're close." It was time for her to do what her dad had done when he'd found the spot the first time. Follow instincts. She walked to the right. Farther.

She looked up. Nope.

She looked down, then went still. "That's it," she whispered reverently, pointing. Several yards below and to the side, on an outcropping of ground, was the site of her long-ago picnic with her dad.

"Good job," Luke said.

Gratification buzzed around her like fireflies. She'd found it.

When they reached the picnic spot, they set down their backpacks. After drinking some water and surveying the view, she slowly pivoted, taking it all in. Her vision tracked past a large tree—

She noticed something she hadn't expected to see. The letter *F* had been carved into the trunk. "Luke."

"Yeah?"

She approached the tree and gestured to the carving. "Do you think this *F* is for Finley?"

"Maybe."

The *F* was about two inches tall. The lines that formed it had been cut deep, straight, sure. "Dad was good with pocketknives. Whittling was one of his hobbies. But if this is a clue, why did he use an *F* here instead of the symbol he used on the map?"

"Maybe because any stranger could have come along, seen that symbol, and done what we did—look it up."

"At which time, they'd have realized the symbol meant treasure."

"And then they might have started digging."

"And made off with my treasure. So, instead, he left my initial. If someone saw an *F* here, they'd shrug and go on about their business. I see carvings in trees when hiking and never think twice."

Luke cocked his head. "Is he telling us to dig under this tree?"

"I don't know." She scanned the area. "Look." Another *F*, carved into a different tree. "And look." Yet another *F* carved into a third tree.

"There might be more."

They parted, searching for additional carvings on trees.

They couldn't find any others.

Coming back together, they faced their backs to the view and considered the three trees.

"They form a triangle," Luke said.

He was right. Two of the trees stood to the left and right of the picnic spot, near the cliff. The other grew exactly between those two, but sat farther back. "He drew three trees on the map and the treasure symbol right in the center of them."

"He's helping us pinpoint where to dig."

"Yep. Where does the center of the triangle fall?" She glanced back and forth, positioning herself in the middle of the three points. "Here."

"Is that approximately where you and your dad sat that night?"

"As far as I can remember, this is precisely where we sat." The wind blew a strand of hair against her lips.

Luke followed the motion, his attention dropping to her mouth.

Warmth flushed across the skin of her chest, neck, face. There was much that had gone unspoken between them. But this—their physical chemistry—was a mighty communication all its own. It was as if their souls and bodies had already settled on things their words had not.

She tugged the piece of hair away, sliding it over a shoulder. "I say this is where we dig."

"I agree."

She created a marker by stacking two stones on top of each other on the spot. "Do you want to start now? Or do you think it still makes the most sense to wait until its darker?"

"I'd like to wait until it's darker."

"Fine by me." They sat, snacking on the food, chatting, joking, and doing what she and her dad had once done—watching the sunset. It wasn't a bright marmalade color this time. It was mellower. Dusky blues and warm golds.

She leaned her head against Luke's shoulder. He lifted her hand and kissed the inside of her wrist.

"I learned the name of this mountain when I was looking at the online map," she told him.

"Yeah?"

"Before white settlers arrived, a terrible war was waged near here between the Cherokee and the Creek tribe. Because of it, they called the site of the war Slaughter Gap and this place Blood Mountain."

"Happy story."

"The history behind the name of the lake isn't any more cheerful. Legend has it that a Native American princess named Trahlyta was gifted with beauty from a spring. She was kidnapped by a rejected suitor. As soon as he took her away from the magical spring, she began to lose her beauty. In the end, the rejected suitor promised to bury her back here in her homeland. Down below, people leave stones on what is said to be her grave for good luck."

"How's a person supposed to get lucky by placing a stone on the grave of a very unlucky person?"

"Legends aren't known for their logic."

The sun slipped behind the mountains, shooting its dying rays against the underbellies of the clouds. Opaque air crept over the rising and dipping Blue Ridge Mountains.

Luke stood and pulled his shovel free. She did the same. He motioned toward the ground where she'd left the stacked stones. "Do you want to do the honors?"

"Sure." She wedged the sharp edge of the shovel into the dirt. It didn't delve very far. The elements had hardened the earth of this exposed ledge.

They got into a rhythm, taking turns shoveling, pausing every now and then to rest. Her shoulders were already complaining, and they'd only dislodged a circle about a foot wide and a few inches deep.

When the hole grew to six inches deep, they added headlamps. By the time full darkness arrived and stars began to wink in the ebony above, they paused for more water and an additional layer of clothing. A plum-colored fleece for her. A padded black vest for him.

"How much deeper do you think we'll need to dig?" she asked.

"I don't think your dad would've buried it more than a foot belowground. But I'm not sure."

"I hope we chose the correct place to dig. It's going to be grueling if we have to shovel more than one hole."

"I'm not sad that I didn't become an archaeologist."

They set the flashlights on boulders so that their beams pointed at the dig site, then continued. Night sounds pressed close—the low foghorn call of a bullfrog, the song of an owl.

Their hole was now about ten inches deep. What if someone had come upon this area shortly after Dad had been here, seen freshly turned earth, and gone digging out of curiosity? Maybe a stranger had already taken the item that had once been here. Or maybe the nameless, faceless person Dad regarded as a threat had figured out the hunt and beaten them to it—

The clashing sound of metal striking metal rose from the tip of Luke's shovel.

Their eyes met.

Her pulse burst into a gallop.

"Did you just . . . hit something?" she whispered, questioning the obvious.

"I did."

She laid down her shovel and sank to her knees.

Carefully, Luke pressed his shovel back down and cleared more dirt. Then down again. Then again.

She swept loose clods to the side, revealing a flat, shimmering surface.

"Want help?" Luke asked, lowering to his knees across from her.

"Yes, please."

His hands joined hers, dislodging dirt.

Letters and numbers began to appear, imprinted into the surface of the metal. "'Fine. 1863,'" she read aloud.

Had her father left her . . . bars of gold? That's what this looked like. Bars of gold. Her brain cartwheeled, and for a few disorienting moments, she could not determine which way was up and which way was down.

Luke continued to work, finally freeing a rectangle of metal and handing it to her.

A gold bar. From 1863.

"Are you okay?" he asked in a concerned tone.

"No. Yes. Undecided."

He pulled off his headlamp, his expression grave.

She eased into a cross-legged position, holding the bar in her lap. "I know what this is. Do you remember me mentioning that Dad raised me on bedtime stories of unsolved mysteries?"

He nodded.

"This is some of the Confederate gold that went missing at the end of the Civil War. He told me all about it. Many times."

Artificial light lit the few feet of space between them. Dark forest encroached on every side like a crowd of avid witnesses. The wind ruffled Luke's hair. His long-lashed eyes gleamed bright.

She cleared her throat. "When Richmond, Virginia, was about to be overtaken by the Union, the president of the Confederacy, Jefferson Davis, received an emergency message from General Robert E. Lee, urging him to evacuate. Late that night, two trains left Richmond. One with Davis and other leaders. One with the Confederate treasury—gold, silver, coins. A fortune estimated to be worth millions." She turned the gold bar over. Then right side up again. "Some of the treasury money was used to pay troops and buy supplies. But most of it was still present when the train arrived in Washington, Georgia. Washington's less than an hour's drive from where I grew up. Davis decided to disband the Confederate government and asked two of his trusted men to smuggle a huge portion of the treasure out of the country, to Great Britain."

"It never got there?"

"No. They think some might have been hidden and some stolen. What's certain is that when Davis was captured six weeks after leaving Richmond, *none* of the treasure remained. My dad and Robbie . . . read books and articles written by people who'd tried to track the missing gold. They concocted theories about its whereabouts." Memories dawned. "The two of them went hunting for it across our region of Georgia with their metal detectors."

"And one of those times, the metal detectors led them to this?"

"It appears that way." The gold in her hands seemed to pulse with menace.

"Do you think that sending us to a gold mine was your dad's way of hinting at the final prize?" Luke asked.

"Yes. In fact, let's think back through the clues." The gold bar was giving her the creeps. She set it aside. "The first clue contained a picture of Dad and me in front of the bookshelves at the house where I grew up. That picture and that place reminded me of how much he loved me."

"We found the next clue on a record cover."

"The name of the band that made that record was The Civil Wars." Tingles raced down her spine. "He was using the clues to tell a story about me, and him, and this treasure."

"The record led us to a hollow tree."

"Which reminded me of the things he used to leave for me there, so that I could take care of the imaginary animals that lived in that hollow tree."

"The next clue took us to the train depot."

"A historic train depot ties into the missing gold because the gold came to Georgia on a train."

"Next came the Dewey decimal number."

"Which took us to a book about brothers." Her stomach lurched. "If my dad found this gold thanks to his metal detector, you can bet that Robbie was right beside him at the time."

"The *Brothers* book sent us to the gold mine and the gold nuggets."

"Which led us to a calendar page and a request that we talk to Robbie about the day before Dad's arrest. Also, that we ask June about a poem—which turned out to be about Carla." Suddenly, the cold seemed to invade her bones.

"The clues weren't just meant to take you from Point A to Point B," he stated.

"No. They were purposeful. It's almost as if he wanted to . . . explain." They'd uncovered a porthole-sized view of the buried gold, but they'd yet to uncover the full length of the stash. "What I don't understand is why he'd leave this for me."

"To provide for you?"

"He already provided for me in a law-abiding way. I have all that I need."

"Was he a . . . fan of the Confederacy?"

"He was a Civil War buff. He knew a lot about the war, but no. He was not a supporter of the Confederacy's ideals. In fact, the opposite."

"I'm guessing he didn't find this on his own land. If he had, he'd have left it buried there for you."

"Correct."

"Which means this was taken from someone else's property."

"Stolen." *Dad. What were you thinking?*

She forced her thoughts to organize. "Part of me is shocked that he would take this." She was loyal to her father. At this point, though, it wouldn't do her any favors to wrap herself in a blanket of denial and refuse to acknowledge his flaws. "The other part of me can admit that this isn't totally out of character for him. He was a bit of a maverick. He'd been pursuing the unsolved mystery of the gold most of his life, ever since his mother told him about it. When I picture him finding this, I can also picture why it would have been hard for him to go through the proper channels and hand it over." Sighing, she shook her head. "I really wish he had. I don't see how he could have thought I'd want *anything* to do with this."

He watched her, his brows drawn together.

This gold was no doubt worth a fortune. A mind-boggling amount of money. A frightening, soul-destroying amount. "I have integrity." Her voice quavered. "I would never want to take possession of anything that's not rightfully mine."

"I know."

She'd always yearned for someone to see her and value her, just as she was. Luke did, and that truth quieted some of the turmoil within.

"What do you want to do?" he asked.

She crossed her arms, trying to find comfort by lacing them tight. "I joked earlier about the size of the backpacks. But now I'm glad they're big. I suppose I want to carry all of this out of here and take it to the nearest . . . I don't know? Police station?"

"We don't know how long it will take us to uncover all the bars. Or how much the total amount will weigh." He scowled at the hole. "I say we call the police, tell them about the discovery, and let them come and handle the rest."

Instantly, she saw the wisdom of his suggestion. "That's a better plan. We might have to walk a ways, though, before we can place a call. On the way in, the GPS continued to work, but we lost all the bars about three-fourths of the way here—"

Luke abruptly raised a hand. He'd heard something.

She froze, senses straining.

She heard it, too. A motor of some kind.

Luke moved with incredible speed. He lunged to the first flashlight and extinguished it. Then to the second and extinguished it. She dashed for the headlamps, flicking them off.

Darkness fell over them, thick and sudden.

CHAPTER TWENTY-FOUR

When Luke was a teenager, he'd made a hobby of dangerous situations. When he'd worked at the chop shop, they'd come with the job. When he'd been in prison, they were part of the culture. He'd cultivated nerves of steel.

But Finley was with him this time.

And that changed everything.

The motor—which sounded to him like it belonged to an ATV—neared. The vehicle's headlights were off. Only someone who wanted to keep their presence secret for as long as possible would drive without them at this time of night.

He muscled past the fear threatening to immobilize him and led Finley to the side, cutting a path into the woods. Silently, he cursed the dark. Had they been able to see, they could have run. As it was, they had to balance speed with the need to move carefully over roots, bushes, rocks.

"Our stuff," she whispered to him, so quietly he could barely make out the words.

"Leave it."

"The gold."

"Leave it."

"I don't want it to fall into . . . the wrong hands."

"And I don't care about anything except you."

The ATV came to a stop, engine idling.

All at once, illumination brightened the area. Luke darted a look back. The ATV had a mounted light bar.

He tried to draw Finley behind the cover of a huge tree to shield them from view. Before he could, the beam of brightness turned, catching them in its crosshairs. The ATV's engine revved as it drove toward them.

The driver had seen them.

Horror shot through his limbs.

He and Finley plunged ahead. She tripped, but he was holding her hand and didn't let her fall.

The vehicle gained. Gained. Easily, it outran them. Dirt spewed as it fishtailed to a stop in front of them. Three men sat inside a four-seater Polaris all-terrain vehicle. They wore night-hunting gear and black ski masks with holes at their eyes and mouths. They carried semi-automatic AR-15s.

No. His breath rasped. *No, God.*

He'd worried about the danger Ed had predicted. But he'd never imagined they'd be so outnumbered and outgunned. Desperate, he changed direction, guiding Finley downhill.

"I wouldn't do that," one of the men warned in a deep voice. The sound that came next—the metallic noise of a rifle charging in preparation to fire—was worse than a nightmare.

If he and Finley continued to flee, they'd be shot. But if they stopped, they'd be at the mercy of the men.

Finley made the decision for him, coming to a halt.

Still holding her hand, Luke positioned himself between her and them.

The men, similar in height and size, closed in on Luke slowly. Their boots crunched the earth.

"What do you want?" Luke asked.

"I think you know what we want," the one in the middle answered. The others kept their weapons fixed on Luke. They stopped ten yards away. "Take us to it, and neither of you will get hurt."

"What assurance do I have of that?"

"None. With or without your help, we'll find what we're looking for. We sure would appreciate your cooperation, though."

They'd be more likely to let Finley go if they got what they wanted—the chance to collect the bars at their own pace and get away without showing their faces. "We'll take you to it," Luke said.

"Good choice."

He and Finley made their way back toward the ledge. Two of the men followed on foot, one followed in the ATV.

His brain had gone icy cold, but his heart was fiery hot. *How do I protect her? I can't allow anything to happen to her.*

It didn't take them long to reach the dig site. The one driving the Polaris killed the motor but not the lights. When the strangers came to stand next to the hole, Luke could feel their satisfaction and greed.

"Have you told anyone else about this?" the leader asked Luke.

He could lie and tell him they'd already called the police. But that might agitate them, and he didn't want to force their hand. "No."

"I don't believe you," one of the others said.

"It's the truth," Luke bit out.

"Is it?" the leader asked Finley, who was still shielded by Luke's body. "Who else knows about this?"

"No one," she said clearly.

Two of the men went to the ATV for boxes and shovels.

The leader drew closer. "Come out, Finley," he said mildly.

Foreboding knotted Luke's stomach. He let go of Finley's hand in order to reach toward his lower back.

"How do you know my name?" Finley asked.

"How would anyone know about this gold if they *didn't* know your name?" he countered. "Step to the side. Let me get a look at you."

"No," Luke said.

"You're not in a position to tell me no."

For a tense moment, no one moved. Then the leader tried to reach around Luke for Finley.

Luke drew a handgun from his waistband at the exact same time that the man raised his weapon. They pointed the muzzles at each other.

"Wait." Finley slipped forward, standing beside Luke. Out in the open. "Everything's all right. You can lower your guns."

Neither of them lowered their gun.

"Luke." There was anguish in Finley's tone.

She didn't want him to risk himself, but she couldn't know how little he cared about his own life in this moment. He hadn't saved his brother. He would die before he failed to save Finley.

"Lower your guns, please," she said.

They continued to face off.

"You're welcome to the gold," she told the leader. "In fact, we'll help you load it. Just let us go."

The leader kept his aim on Luke but drew a few inches nearer to Finley.

"Get any closer to her and I'll kill you," Luke promised.

"No." Finley reached toward Luke's forearm, distracting him for a split second—

The leader charged him, knocking Luke's gun upward right before Luke pulled the trigger. The sound of his gun firing boomed through the air as the man shoved him. Luke planted his feet to keep his balance, then drove his shoulder into the wall of the man's chest. A grunt sounded. Luke wedged an uppercut against his jaw. The man's head snapped back, and he faltered.

Another man collided with Luke from the side. The third wrenched his gun arm up and behind him, twisting the ligaments and tendons in Luke's shoulder. He lost his grip on the gun.

Luke kicked one man's knee. Swung and connected with a *crunch* against the other's cheek.

Finley cried out. Luke whirled in her direction. The leader had ahold of her waist and was yanking her away. One of her arms stretched toward Luke.

"Let her go," Luke yelled, pain exploding in his head as a gun struck him on the back of the neck. He stumbled but didn't go down. He tried to run to Finley, but the others gripped his arms.

She was struggling against her attacker. She reared back, spun, and pulled up his mask. "Ken," she gasped, then writhed as he dragged her toward the cliff. "*No*. What are you doing?"

Fury detonated inside of Luke. He headbutted one of the men and pushed him aside. Took a punch to the face from the other that rattled his brain. He buried a fist in the guy's gut and was free of them both. He grabbed his gun off the ground and aimed. He didn't have a clear shot. Couldn't shoot Ken without risking Finley. He sprinted forward.

Ken had forced her close to the edge.

"Stop!" Luke was almost to them.

Finley met Luke's eyes with a look that said a hundred things. Alarm. Love. Apology.

Luke lunged for her just as Ken shoved her off the ledge.

She fell out of sight.

He'd once seen concrete collapse the hallway where his brother had been. Watching Finley fall—just as terrible.

He rushed to the side of the cliff, where there wasn't a sheer drop. Here, he could run down.

"Freeze!" one of them yelled.

He didn't.

Gunshots rang out. He ducked, and the descent took him out of their line of fire. He turned, gun ready. As soon as one of them appeared above, Luke fired. The man wheeled back, out of sight.

"I have plenty of ammunition," Luke said loudly. "Every time you come into view, I'll shoot."

He could see Finley's body lying motionless a short distance away. It was about a ten-foot drop from the ledge to where the steep, rocky mountainside had caught her. By the look of it, she was unconscious. She might have broken bones. Might have a broken neck.

"I'd get busy taking the gold if I were you," Luke said. He needed them gone. *Now*. "People must have heard those gunshots. Rangers will be here soon."

He crossed to Finley, looking repeatedly for more signs of the men . . . who must be Carla's brothers. She'd had three of them. And the oldest was named Ken.

He heard them talking in urgent tones. He couldn't make out all of what they were saying, but it seemed they'd decided to load the gold.

He knelt beside Finley. She appeared fine, except for a bleeding scrape on one wrist. He gently swept her dark hair out of her face. "Finley," he whispered.

No response.

His fingers probed the back of her head. Warm, sticky liquid. *Blood*.

He feared moving her. But even more, he feared leaving her here, where Ken and the other two would have a clean shot at her. With extreme care, he lifted her and carried her behind two thick trees. The branches would shield her from sight and the trunks would provide some protection.

She was breathing steadily, but her skin felt cold. He laid her down just long enough to strip off his vest, which he pressed against her head injury. Screaming inside, he hugged her against him and willed his heat into her. His vision latched on the cliff above. His free hand gripped his gun.

With his mind, his body, his soul—he loved her. He loved her, and he should have stopped the hunt long ago. At the very least, he should have told others about the hunt and brought several people here tonight. He'd been an idiot, and he hated himself for not doing the things he should have done.

On this black mountainside, it was just him, doing a lousy job of keeping alive the person he cared about most in the world. He'd never been so alone. Never been so aware that he was not enough.

"God," he whispered raggedly.

It seemed as if the wind answered, blowing not just through the trees but through him, too.

I know I screwed up, but I need you now. Forgive me. Don't let her die. Don't. Please. Forgive me.

He carefully rocked her back and forth. Frantic. Praying.

Please. Please, God.

From a long way off, the wail of sirens drifted to him. His warning to the men about the park rangers had been accurate. They were coming to investigate the gunshots. If they saw his truck parked on the road, they might use that as a starting point.

It had taken him and Finley thirty minutes to walk here. If the rangers ran, it would take maybe half as long. Except it was dark now. Plus, the rangers didn't have GPS to guide them.

The men shut off the ATV's lightbar. A lesser light source remained. The ATV's headlights?

"Finley, wake up. Please, wake up. Are you okay?"

Nothing.

Why wouldn't she wake up? Did she have internal injuries in addition to the head injury? She needed medical treatment. Should he pick her up and take her toward the road? He didn't have his phone or a flashlight. He might injure her worse. He might miss the rangers in the woods and end up costing her even more time.

He'd stay here.

God, don't let her die.

Ken and the others had come for the gold. But not just the gold. They'd known who Finley was, and Ken had pushed her off the cliff because he'd wanted to hurt her. Why? Revenge? Revenge for his sister's death?

Eventually, Luke heard new voices approaching. Rangers.

The ATV growled as it raced away, taking the last of the light. Luke could see nothing but black tree branches and gray sky.

He needed to signal the rangers. He rested Finley on the earth, then felt his way back to the site. He lost his footing, slammed his injured shoulder, then scrambled the rest of the way. He switched on the flashlights they'd brought, pointing one in the direction of the rangers and one toward Finley's position.

He returned to her. "You awake? Finley?"

Still no answer.

He lifted her and climbed the embankment until he could lay her on the flat surface of the ledge. Then he hauled his arm back and threw his handgun as far as he could down the mountain. If he was caught with a weapon, he'd go to prison for five more years.

He picked up both flashlights and made Xs in the air in the direction of the rangers.

"This way!" he yelled. "A woman is injured, and we need help."

Carla's brothers had been forced to leave before they'd dug up all the gold. They'd taken most of it, but some of the bars remained at one edge, half-covered in dirt.

He looked down at Finley, pleading silently for her to come to. If something happened to her, his life was over.

"Here!" Luke called. "We need help."

People crashed through the foliage. Not rangers, as he'd expected. Police. Four of them. A thin, dark-haired, middle-aged officer ordered him to put his hands up.

Luke did so. "She's hurt and needs medical treatment. She has an injury to the back of the head."

Two knelt next to Finley.

"Ma'am," one officer said as she bent close to assess Finley's head wound. She didn't try to move the vest still pressed against it. "Ma'am?" When Finley didn't react, she rubbed her knuckles against Finley's upper chest to wake her. "Ma'am. Can you hear me? Can you open your eyes and let me know how you're doing?"

The middle-aged officer patted Luke down with the efficiency of a veteran. "I'm Detective Romano, Blairsville Police." He nodded as he stepped away, letting Luke know he could lower his arms.

The officer beside Finley checked her airway, then reached down and wrapped a hand around Finley's wrist, feeling for her pulse.

"She fell approximately ten feet," Luke said, "and has been unconscious since then."

"For how long?"

"I'm not sure. Twenty minutes? At least."

"Transporting her to the road will be difficult," the female officer stated, "and it might take a ground ambulance forty-five minutes to meet us."

"Call a medical chopper to evacuate her," Romano said. Then, to Luke, "Do you two have identification?"

"In the backpacks."

Another officer moved to search the backpacks.

"Your names?" Romano asked.

"I'm Luke Dempsey. This is Finley Sutherland."

"What's your relationship?"

"She's my . . ." *Everything*. "Girlfriend."

"We received several reports from people who heard shots fired. What happened here?"

"We learned that her father buried something for her here years ago. We didn't know what. We came tonight to dig it up."

Romano accepted the IDs the deputy handed him and turned away to radio their names to dispatch.

The female officer remained crouched beside Finley, monitoring her vitals.

"There are gold bars here," a deputy said.

Romano neared. "You're saying this woman's father buried gold bars for her?"

"Yes. We think it's Confederate gold that went missing during the Civil War. As soon as we realized what it was, we decided to notify authorities. Before we could make it to an area with cell service, three men drove up in a Polaris ATV with AR-15s. They threw Finley off that cliff, shot at me, took most of the gold. When they heard the sirens, they left, and I carried her back up here."

"There was more gold?" Romano asked.

"A lot more."

"Who were the three men?"

"They were wearing masks. We only saw the face of one. His name's Ken Vance. From Toccoa. I suspect the other two are his brothers, Dennis and Jeff." They needed to pay for what they'd done to Finley. "Did you hear the motor of the ATV as you were getting closer?"

"No."

"You'll find their footprints and the ATV's tire marks there." Luke indicated the area. "There should be fired casings from their guns, unless they collected them all."

A muted voice spoke through Romano's radio. He listened. "Are you out on parole?" he asked Luke.

"Yes."

"For what primary charge?"

"Felony theft."

Romano didn't react outwardly. But Luke knew that in the officer's eyes, his trustworthiness had just taken a huge hit. He'd told the truth. But the truth might not seem very true to Romano when spoken by a felon standing next to an injured woman and stolen gold.

"How did Ken know you two were coming here tonight to dig this up?" Romano asked.

"I don't know. Maybe one of them followed us to the road? And another brought the ATV on a trailer? Was anyone else parked on the road?"

"No."

"Finley will corroborate my story."

"She's unconscious."

"Which is why I want her taken to a hospital," he snapped. "When will the chopper get here?"

"As soon as it can."

Luke's frustration and fear ratcheted higher. "It's taking too long."

After a long moment of silence, Romano began to ask Luke a

series of questions. Luke told him about the treasure hunt. About Ken's sister, Carla, and her connection to Finley's father. About Ken, Dennis, and Jeff. Their possible motive. He told him that someone had been in Finley's house and tried to hack his computer.

Every second that he waited for Finley to wake—and she didn't wake—turned to agony. Every minute that he waited for help that didn't come grated like knives on his skin.

Finally, he registered the drone of a helicopter. Louder and louder. Deafening. It centered them in its spotlight. Luke's hair whipped in its downwash.

A litter, accompanied by a man in paramedic gear, lowered from the chopper. The man strapped Finley to a board with a neck collar while the female officer related what they knew of Finley's injury and status.

"*Finley*," Luke tried one last time.

Then she was lifted into the night.

CHAPTER TWENTY-FIVE

Three hours later, the staffers at Northwestern's ICU finally gave Luke permission to enter Finley's room. This hospital, located thirty minutes from Misty River, was the only facility in this part of the state large enough to receive patients by helicopter. He walked down the hallway, watching the numbers beside each doorway increase.

201. 202. 203.

This was it. 204. Finley's room.

Emotions gathered heavy in his chest as he let himself inside.

Everything about this hospital room was as expected. The automated bed. The dull wallpaper, windows, machines. One thing in this room, though, was so wrong that it jarred the air from his lungs.

The sight of Finley, lying unmoving. Still unconscious.

He came to a stop near her shoulder. Lines and tubes were attached to her. She looked pale, frail, and vulnerable.

He felt as if he were caving in on himself.

His love for her was a fire inside. Bigger than time.

Helplessly, angrily, he wished it were him with the brain injury. Him in the hospital bed. Never, never her.

"I'm here." His voice came out rusty.

He hadn't succeeded at the one thing he'd promised Ed and

himself he'd do: protect Finley. Everything about tonight had gone wrong.

If she recovered—*when* she recovered—he would get everything right. No more mistakes. He would do whatever it took to help her heal. He would be careful and patient. He had a lot of strength, and he would give it all to her. He would make sure the Vance brothers were brought to justice.

Finley had seen how difficult he could be. Now she would see how sacrificial he could be.

For long minutes, he remained at her bedside like a statue. Then he sent a text to Ben and moved to the chair in the corner. He hunched over, holding his head in his hands, silently begging God to heal Finley.

Around midnight, someone rapped on the door, then opened it.

Ben had come, but he hadn't come alone. Sebastian, Natasha, and Genevieve flanked him.

A Miracle Five reunion.

Feeling wasted and one hundred years old, Luke pushed to his feet.

They regarded him with concern.

"Can you tell us what happened?" Ben asked.

Luke did so, as quickly as possible.

The officers had viewed his story with suspicion, yet not one of these four questioned it. Ben, Genevieve, Natasha, and Sebastian had no reason to have faith in him. But they did.

"What can we do to help?" Genevieve asked.

"I need an understanding . . ." A lump lodged in his throat. "I need an understanding of Finley's diagnosis and condition. Because of privacy regulations, they wouldn't tell me anything."

"I'm on it," Sebastian said. "I have privileges here because I occasionally consult on cases." He left the room.

"What else?" Ben asked.

"Finley will want someone to go by tonight and take care of her animals."

"I'll do it," Genevieve said.

"I know Akira has a spare key to Finley's house," Ben said to Genevieve. "I'll call her and arrange a way to get you the key."

"Great. How many animals does she have?"

"She has a dog, a cat, a hedgehog, and a fish," Luke answered.

"I don't know how to care for a hedgehog, but I'll figure it out."

"Ask Akira." Luke turned to Ben. "Please also ask her to notify the people close to Finley about her injury. Her friends, Meadow and Bridget. The employees at the Center." He purposely didn't mention Robbie and June because they might be somehow involved in this, somehow guilty. Until he knew if that was true, he didn't want them near Finley.

"Are you planning to stay here?" Ben asked.

"Yes."

"I'll go by your apartment and get whatever you need. I'll also bring food, so you'll have something to eat."

Luke didn't bother telling him he had no appetite. Instead, he focused on Natasha. "If the police interrogate the Vance brothers, and if the brothers say I'm the one who stole the gold and hurt Finley, then I might need an attorney."

"I've been on hiatus since I had kids," Natasha told him. "But I've kept my license current, and I'll come out of hiatus for you. I'm good and my services are, in your case, free."

"You're hired."

Sebastian returned. "Finley's CT scan showed mild traumatic brain injury. They've put her into a medically induced coma, which will slow down the metabolism of the brain and also slow down the swelling. Essentially, they're giving her brain a rest, which is the best way to help it heal. As soon as they decide it's safe, an anesthesiologist will reverse the coma, and they'll bring her out of it."

Coma. "I need a timeline," Luke said.

"No one can give you an exact timeline. It'll depend on how quickly the swelling subsides."

"Are we talking a few hours or a few days?"

"A few days, I'd expect."

"And how will this affect her?"

"Hard to know. In cases like these, age is one of the strongest indicators of a good prognosis. She's just thirty years old, which is in her favor. They're hopeful that she'll make a complete recovery."

"How long will it take her to recover?"

"They can't predict that but, best case scenario, I'd say at least two to three weeks."

"What can I do to help her?"

"Some patients in a coma have nightmares. Some have visions. Some are aware of elements of their surroundings. I recommend that her visitors talk to her. If she knows familiar people are here with her, that will bring her comfort. Just make sure the conversations in this room are positive and encouraging."

After they left, Luke paced. Then he stretched his frame onto the pull-out futon with an elbow bent over his eyes.

He was up and pacing again when two women rushed into the room. One short with pink hair. One slim and blond. Both looked as though they'd woken from sleep, thrown on clothes, and rushed here as quickly as they could. Worry pinched their faces.

The blonde introduced herself as Bridget and the other as Meadow. They talked to Finley for a long time in hushed tones. Then Meadow held Finley's hand while Bridget walked over to Luke and asked a string of soft questions.

Yet again, he retold the story because he knew that's what Finley would want. She loved these two and talked about them often.

When he finished explaining, Meadow finally spoke. "You can go now," she said to him.

"I'm not going anywhere."

Her head swung around and they locked eyes. He let her see exactly how determined he was, and she eventually looked back to Finley, choosing to ignore him.

Medical staff came and went. Luke prayed. Scowled through gritty eyes at the wall.

What he did not do throughout that awful night?

Sleep.

When he finally did leave Finley's room the next morning, it was with a purpose.

He needed to make a house call.

Around nine a.m., Luke knocked on Robbie and June's front door.

Robbie answered. "Luke," he said with friendly surprise. "How are you?"

"Not well. Can we talk?"

The older man's smile dropped. "Certainly. Here." He motioned to the office off the foyer. "Right this way."

"Honey?" June called from the back of the house.

"Finley's friend Luke is here to discuss something with me," Robbie called back. "We'll be in the office."

She made a happy sound of acknowledgment, then he and Robbie were shut inside an office that resembled a movie set for the office of a comfortably rich man. Dark wood desk. Full bookshelves. Windows letting in golden morning views of his acreage.

"Care to have a seat?" Robbie asked.

"No."

"All right." He wore the same type of tidy, classic clothing he'd worn the other times Luke had seen him. A striped blue-and-white button-down shirt under a maroon V-neck sweater. Khaki pants. He half-sat on the edge of his desk. "What's wrong?"

"Your niece is in the hospital."

He flinched. "What? Why?"

Luke told him about his promise to Ed as Ed was dying. The treasure hunt. How Finley had been injured.

Robbie had an excellent poker face. However, Luke was now certain that Robbie was hiding something.

Light tapping sounded on the office door. "I brought coffee," June said.

"Come in," Robbie replied.

June set a tray on the desktop containing two mugs of coffee and a plate of powdered donut holes. When she saw Luke's body language, she stilled. "Is something the matter?"

"Finley's been injured," Robbie answered. "She's in stable condition at Northwestern Hospital in a medically induced coma."

June rested her palm over her heart. "Oh no."

"Luke was in the middle of explaining what happened," Robbie said. "I'll be out in just a minute, and I'll relay everything to you."

"Do the doctors think she'll make a full recovery?" June asked Luke.

"They hope so. But they're not sure."

"This is heartbreaking. Robbie, I'll call Eric and Leslie and the four of us can drive over to see her."

"Absolutely."

"Thank you for letting us know about this, Luke." June hesitated on the room's threshold. "I'll get things ready out here so that we're prepared to leave." The door clicked behind her.

"When Finley and I came here for dinner," Luke said, wasting no time, "we came because Ed sent us. Through a treasure hunt clue. He told Finley to ask you about the day before Carla was shot."

Robbie reminded Luke of a house hit by a hurricane. Too late, its owner was trying to protect it by shutting all the doors and windows.

"Finley and I realized that Ed was telling us a story through the clues. One of the clues was a book. It was called *Brothers: Twenty-Five Stories About the Ties That Bind*. As soon as Finley saw that gold, she knew the two of you would have been together when the discovery was made. So I don't buy the story that Ed spent the day before Carla died driving to Macon with you to check out a horse. What actually happened on that day?"

"It . . . it was just like I told you."

Luke moved forward. Getting right up in Robbie's face, he fisted his hand in the fabric of the older man's sweater. "Tell me the truth. Right now."

Robbie stiffened with fear.

"Do you understand me?" Luke asked in an ominously quiet tone.

"Yes."

Luke removed his hand.

Robbie put several feet of space between them. He went to stand by the bookshelves, then smoothed the clothing Luke had wrinkled.

"What happened nine years ago on April twentieth?" Luke demanded.

"Ed and I . . ." He cleared his throat. "Ed and I went out on one of our expeditions, as we liked to call them. With our metal detectors. Carla, Ed's girlfriend, had come with us on our expeditions a few times. She enjoyed them, and so she came along with us that night, too. The three of us went out to eat. Then, after dark, we drove to a piece of land east of Washington. It was a crisp, clear, beautiful night." He pushed his hands into his pockets. "We'd done a great deal of reading over the years about the Confederate gold. We'd learned from the experiences of other treasure hunters and formulated our own theories about where portions of the gold might have ended up. We had good reason to think that if someone had buried the gold, they'd buried some of it in that general region. We'd gone over other sections of that piece of land with metal detectors in the past." His words ended in prolonged silence.

"And you returned that night to check a section you hadn't before," Luke supplied.

"Yes. The gold had been lost a hundred and fifty years before.

We'd been searching for it for most of our lives without success. It was mostly *the thought*, you see, of discovering something so elusive that we liked. It kept us going."

As if his knees had gone too weak to support him, Robbie lowered onto a wingback chair. "That night, we walked back and forth with our detectors for an hour or so. Then we took a break. We sat around a camping lantern, eating the brownies Carla made."

"And?"

"Then we resumed the search. Fifteen minutes or so later, Ed's metal detector started going off. I brought mine over. Carla came with the shovel. It wasn't unusual for us to find things. Tin cans. Belt buckles. Knives. Coins. We started digging."

"And ended up finding the missing Confederate gold."

Robbie gave Luke a look that asked for understanding. "To our astonishment, we did. Our mother had raised us on legends of that gold, so it was like coming face-to-face with Santa Claus or the Easter Bunny. Surreal. Euphoric."

"The land where you were digging did not belong to you."

"No."

"The ethical thing would have been to call the police and notify the landowner."

"It's very unlikely the landowner would have been able to profit off the find. Have you heard of the Archaeological Resources Protection Act?"

Luke shook his head.

"It passed in 1979. Anything deemed an archeological resource, and the Confederate gold certainly qualifies, belongs to the government."

"Then why didn't you turn it over to the government?"

"That question is harder to answer."

"*Answer it.*"

"The gold was the most precious thing any of us had seen in our lifetimes. And Ed and I had found it. We'd found . . . a miracle, through our own efforts."

He wanted to tell Robbie he'd been an idiot for stealing the gold. But after all the cars Luke had stolen, saying so would make him a hypocrite.

"Ed was open to the idea of turning the find over to the authorities," Robbie said. "Carla and I weren't. At least, not in that moment. We decided to give ourselves time to think. There was nothing we could do with it that night anyway. Gold is heavy. We didn't have the means to transport it all. We covered the area with dirt and made plans to come back the following night with wheelbarrows and supplies, then split it three ways between us. We vowed not to tell anyone else."

"But Carla must have told at least one of her brothers."

"After hearing what occurred last night, I'm afraid that's true."

Luke's brow knitted. "The day after the gold was found, Carla was killed."

Robbie's mouth formed a thin line.

"I don't believe that Ed accidentally shot her while cleaning her gun," Luke said. "How did she die?"

"I'm not willing to say."

"But you *will* tell Finley when she wakes up." It was an order, not a request. "She deserves to know."

Robbie paused. "If Finley wants to know, I'll tell her. But her alone."

"Who have you told about the gold?" Luke asked.

"No one."

"Not even June?"

"No. No one knows."

"I'm guessing the gold Finley and I found last night was Ed's share."

"Yes. Have the police arrested Carla's brothers?" Robbie asked.

"I don't know. If not, I'm going to do my best to make sure that happens." Robbie was Finley's next of kin. His opinions and wishes would hold weight with the police and the DA. "If the detectives call you, I need for you to tell them that you think I'm innocent—because I am. And that the statement I gave them is accurate—because it is."

"All right. Whatever you might think of me, Luke," Robbie said sadly, "I do love my niece. I want her best."

After exchanging phone numbers and parting from Robbie, Luke drove in the direction of Carla's hometown.

He hadn't been able to breathe well when he'd been inside Finley's ICU room. But being away from her was five times worse. He needed to get back to the hospital. Soon. But he had a stop to make first.

Forty minutes later, Luke parked a few feet from the window-lined front wall of the business Ken Vance owned. The brightly lit interior of the Feed Supply Company revealed customers milling around inside. A man Luke recognized as the same one who'd pushed Finley last night sat behind the register.

Ken was going about his day. Free. Normal. As if there wasn't a woman lying in a hospital because of his actions. The anger that had been swirling inside Luke mounted higher and higher, throbbing against his skull like a migraine.

He didn't feel glad about anything, but he recognized in a dull sort of way that he should be glad that Ken was still in town. He hadn't made a run for it. Yet.

Both he and Finley had seen Ken's face, but Finley was unconscious. If Ken and his brothers had denied Luke's account to the police, then it was Luke's word—the word of a felon—against the word of three men who were seen as upstanding members of the community.

When Finley woke, she'd confirm the story Luke had given the police. But only if she remembered what had happened. She might not remember. Even if she did, she'd sustained a blow to the head. He wasn't sure how clear or legally binding her memories would be.

What would the Vance brothers do next? Possibly try to keep Finley from waking? He'd see if Robbie could get the DA to approve a restraining order against the brothers so that they couldn't get into her hospital room. He'd also make sure one of her friends or family members was with her in the ICU at all times, like Bridget was right now.

No doubt the brothers had already stored the gold in a secure location. They might be preparing to leave the country, but that was likely their last resort. They had families, jobs, and deep ties to this town. They'd want to stay here if they could.

Luke needed evidence against them.

Ken moved around inside the building, tidying up.

You underestimated me when you decided not to flee this country, Luke thought, his eyes on Ken, as his truck rumbled to life beneath him. *And now you've given me time to take you down.*

He steered the truck toward Northwestern Hospital. Using the voice controls on his phone, he called his mother. She answered with a pleased "Luke?"

He let his eyes sink closed for a split second before refocusing on the road. He told her that Finley had been hurt and was currently in the hospital.

"I'm so sorry. Is there anything that I can do?"

"I wondered if you could work out a schedule so that there's always somebody with Finley in her hospital room while she's in the ICU. Around the clock."

"I'd be happy to do that."

"I'll stay through the night tonight and most of the day tomorrow, so don't book those times."

"Got it."

"Call Ben. He knows the people who work at the Center with Finley. I'll send you the phone numbers of Finley's two best friends and her uncle."

"I'm on it."

"Thank you."

"You're welcome. This community is small, Luke. Helping is what we do for one another. I'm glad for the chance to do something tangible for Finley."

What she didn't say but what he understood clearly was that she was also glad for the chance to do something for him. This was the first time in decades that he'd asked her for anything.

"Luke?"

"Yeah?"

"I love you."

For years, when she and Dad had said those words to him, they'd bounced off as if he were wearing a suit of armor. But Finley's injury had ripped away his defenses. This time, when she said the words, they penetrated. So much, he found it hard to reply. They exchanged good-byes and he disconnected.

He directed his next phone call to Ben's mom, CeCe Coleman.

"I'm fired up," she said instead of answering with a normal hello. "I just found out about Finley's accident at the beauty shop. The beauty shop! Not from my son or from you. Which just isn't right—"

"I need information." Luke had no time for CeCe's drama, even on his best days.

"What kind of information?"

"Information on the Vance brothers." CeCe knew more people in their region of Georgia than a phone book. Somehow, the Vance brothers had learned about the treasure hunt. And somehow, they'd followed him and Finley to the dig site in an ATV. In order to accomplish those things, they'd most likely had help from friends or family. The more Luke learned about those close to the Vance brothers, the more likely he'd understand how they'd gotten away with what they'd done.

"Do the Vance brothers have something to do with Finley's injury?" CeCe asked.

"They caused it."

She released a furious whistling sound.

"I've already researched everything that's available online about the brothers. Now I need you to discover all the things that aren't online about Ken, Dennis, and Jeff Vance."

"Are you looking for anything in particular?"

"A family tree that lists the brothers, their wives, and kids would help."

"You bet."

"I'd also like to know who their friends are. Where the brothers live. Where the brothers work. Plus any other information you can find."

"I'll work on it and get back to you. When it comes to the town grapevine, I'm a better detective than Magnum P. I."

Finley hovered, weightless, inside an ocean of fog.

She couldn't make sense of anything . . . except that voice. That deep, masculine, familiar voice. It was a voice she knew, filtering in from a great distance.

"I'm here," he was saying. Luke. "I need you to come back to me soon. I miss you."

Her heart answered, expanding.

"I can't be here without you," he said. "It almost killed me when I lost Ethan. I can't do that again."

Luke. The safety of him caused sunlight to find her in the fog, to bathe her skin with warmth.

"I don't care if you'd rather go and be with Chase and your father. Please don't do that to me. Do you hear me, Finley?"

She rose out of the depths and walked along the white sand beach of her Caribbean island. She'd spent hours and hours here. Resting on this beach. Admiring the hills, the lush green vegetation, and the monkeys dangling from the vines. The first dog she'd ever owned, Rajah, ran up to greet her, then trotted beside her like always.

"I'm selfish enough to demand that you stay here with me." Luke's voice broke. The force of his emotions sent the palm trees swaying. "I'm going to make it right," he said. "Everything that happened with the treasure hunt and the gold and those men. You don't have to worry about any of it because I will handle it. I promise you."

He hadn't left her.

"Please come back to me. Finley. Please."

I'm coming.

He hadn't left her, and she wouldn't leave him.

CHAPTER TWENTY-SIX

Around noon the following day, Luke looked up from the chair in Finley's hospital room to see his mother enter. Like that night at the garage, she'd brought coffee cake.

"Wow," she said, coming to a stop. "She's received a lot of support."

"Yeah." Since word had gotten out about her injury, a stream of visitors had come through. The ICU only allowed five visitors at a time, so Luke often stepped into the waiting room so that someone else could take his spot. At this point, flowers, balloons, and cards occupied most of the flat surfaces in the space. The kids in Akira's after-school program had hand-drawn a banner for Finley. Trish and Kat had made a poster with pictures of all the dogs currently living at the Center.

"How is she?" Mom asked.

"The same."

She placed the cake on the side table, then stood next to Finley, murmuring encouragement. "We're praying for you. You're doing great, you know. Everything's all right here. Just keep fighting. You'll be back to feeling like yourself in no time."

Everyone said the same things to her. It always came out awkwardly, because no one was used to talking to someone who couldn't talk back.

Light-headed with exhaustion, Luke rose to his feet. He swayed, then propped a shoulder against the window's wood trim to steady himself. The hours had hollowed him out, so it took him longer than it should have to realize Mom had quit talking. Instead, she was studying him with so much compassion that he honestly couldn't take it.

"You look tired," she said.

"I am." Since returning to the hospital yesterday, he'd only been home for twenty minutes to shower.

"How about you go to your apartment and get some sleep?" she suggested. "I'll sit with her for the next few hours, and then your dad will take the next shift."

His worry about Finley and his regrets about how the treasure hunt had ended kept him awake most of last night. Yet the idea of going home caused resistance to sharpen within him. How was he supposed to trust other people enough to leave her? He'd prefer to remain here 24/7.

Mom came over and rested a gentle hand on his shoulder. It brought back a flood of memories from when he was a kid. All the times she'd hugged him, felt his forehead when she suspected he had a fever, ran her fingers through his hair.

"Finley would want you to take care of yourself," she said. "She's depending on you not to fall apart, so you need to rest."

She was right. If he continued like this, he'd be of no use to Finley. "You'll contact me immediately if they decide to bring her back to consciousness?"

"Immediately," she confirmed.

"And you'll give my number to all the people who are taking shifts through the night and tell them to call me if that happens?"

"Already have."

"And the whole night is covered?"

"It is. Everyone in Misty River loves her. It wasn't difficult to fill every slot."

That night, Akira answered the doorbell to find Ben standing in the hallway outside her apartment, holding a bouquet of flowers. She pulled him inside, kicked the door closed, and hugged him.

Almost two days had passed since he'd called to tell her about Finley's injury. It had been a wretched two days.

Fear had been stalking her. So had disbelief. How could healthy, vibrant Finley—whom she'd seen at work just a few days ago—be lying unconscious in an ICU bed?

A year ago, Akira had been a patient in that same ICU, fighting for her life. That time, she'd been so sick that it had been hard to pray. This time she could pray, and so she had been.

She basked in the comfort and steadiness of Ben's hug. This evening, they were scheduled to spend time with Finley from ten p.m. to one a.m. But they had a few more hours before they'd need to leave for the hospital.

When she pulled back, they quietly measured the nuances of each other's faces. She'd developed the ability to look beyond his exterior to his character. And what she saw there lit a candle of hope within her.

He was kind, easygoing, humble. He had integrity and strong faith. He was trustworthy and, if she needed it, he would give her the shirt off his back. He liked kids, same as she did. He lived a life firmly centered in things that mattered. Instead of a destructive presence, Ben promised to be the opposite. He was everything his mother had told her he was, and more.

She was the unremarkable little sister. Unlike her family members, she had not racked up towering achievements. Her ambitions were modest. But this man who really was too good to be true found her valuable and beautiful. She could see that he did, in his eyes. And it made her want to cry.

"For you," he said, extending the bouquet.

Her dad gave her flowers every Valentine's Day, but no other man ever had. Reverently, she accepted the bouquet from him.

Pale pink primroses. Branches of lightest green. White peonies. "Thank you."

"You're welcome."

She inhaled gratitude and the fragrance of the flowers. "Are we marking a special occasion?"

"Nah. Just because."

Once she'd placed the bouquet in a vase, they took seats on the two tall rattan bar stools that fronted the island. She spun toward him until their knees touched. "Finley's accident has me thinking," she said.

"Yeah?"

"My bad boyfriends, followed by my slow recovery, made me reluctant to risk dating. But it strikes me now that there's a different takeaway."

"Which is?"

"I should grab the good while I can. In dating and in everything else." She tucked her hair behind her ears. "Are you still interested in dating me?"

"One hundred percent interested."

"In that case, I think I need to get over my hang-ups and take hold of this opportunity with both hands." *Courage, Akira*. She was done with letting potential heartbreak suppress potential joy. Maybe, just maybe, things would work out beautifully between them.

He edged nearer, setting one foot on the floor. "Sure that you're willing to take a risk?"

"It is a risk," she acknowledged. "But you're worth it."

"And you won't change your mind?"

She hadn't forgotten that he'd been hurt by Leah. This wasn't easy for him, either. "I won't change my mind." She scooted to the front of her barstool. "Are you willing to take a risk on me?"

"Yes. I'd risk a lot for you, Akira."

She rested tender, unsteady fingertips on his cheek. In doing so, she pushed past the boundary of their safe friendship to something that felt less safe but infinitely promising.

Her heart pounded—

He pressed his lips to hers and she lost herself in the fireworks he set off within her.

She'd made the right choice. She didn't want to miss this. She'd put her heart back on the line again because she wanted to *live*. This was scary and heavenly, but most of all, this was living.

She flung herself at him, locking her arms behind his neck and very nearly knocking him off his stool.

They both laughed, and then they were kissing again. Deep, sweet kisses that tasted like destiny.

Luke wrenched from sleep to a sense of panic. How long had he been out? It felt like days.

What if he'd slept too long? What if he'd missed calls and they'd brought Finley back and he hadn't been there?

Sheets twisted around his body as he grabbed his phone off the bedside table. It had been right beside him all night, ringer on.

Five a.m. Wednesday, March 31. No missed calls or texts.

He let his tight lungs release and collapsed back onto his pillows. His dim room closed around him. Eyelids sinking shut, he tested to see if he could sleep for another few hours.

No use. His body was having none of that.

He'd told his mom that he'd start his shift at nine. There was no way he could stay away from Finley that long, but he also couldn't arrive at five thirty. That would insult the people who'd lost sleep to take that shift.

He went to his computer and searched through photo after photo of ATVs. He started with this year's Polaris models, then worked backward in time.

At last, he found an image of an ATV, currently for sale in California, that was the same color combination and style as the one Ken had driven.

Luke took a screenshot of the photo and typed the pertinent information about the Polaris into an email. He directed the email to Detective Romano and hit Send.

When Luke arrived at Finley's hospital room, he found his sisters inside, arguing over a TikTok video that Hailey loved and Blair hated. Their conversation jerked to a stop when they spotted his frown.

He went to the bed. Someone had recently brushed Finley's hair. It flowed, shining, over her shoulder. Other than that, he saw no change. She was still trapped in her coma. Injured, unreachable, fragile.

Powerlessness turned his stomach to acid.

He'd do anything to change this. But he couldn't. Not for her and not for Ethan. How was it possible that he was still standing, when he would've traded places with either of them?

He turned to his sisters. Hailey curled on the chair. Blair sat on the small futon, legs extended, combat boots crossed on the upholstery.

"Get sleep?" Blair asked.

"Some."

"Then how come you look so grumpy?"

"Because I regret that Finley's had to listen to you two fighting about TikTok. You do know, right, that we want to motivate her to wake up?"

Blair laughed. "Your brooding silence is going to motivate her to wake up?"

"I talk to her." For hours and hours, in fact. "Why are you two here on a school morning?"

"I have PE and Hailey has ceramics first period. We got here at seven, and Mom gave us permission to stay until nine. It's pretty rare for Mom to let us skip. You're here early, even though I was counting on you to come at nine so that we'd get to miss all of first period."

"I wouldn't count on me for anything."

Blair's boots hit the floor with a thunk. "But I am counting on you. To finish fixing up my car."

"Your sensitivity is amazing."

"I wouldn't count on me for sensitivity," she shot back.

"The world doesn't revolve around you, Blair. Your car is not my priority right now."

"Okay, but remember: When Finley was giving us the tour of Furry Tails, she said she thinks it's great that you're going to get my car running before our sixteenth birthday. FYI, that's on April twenty-first." She stood. "I have to pee." With a flap of the flannel shirt she'd tied around her waist, she was gone.

Hailey gave him a shy look of apology she'd probably given a million times before in regard to Blair.

He lowered to the sofa and crossed an ankle over the opposite knee. He had no idea how to talk to tenderhearted teenage girls, but since this was the first time he could ever remember being alone with Hailey, he felt obligated to speak. He heard himself say, "I wish you could have known Ethan."

"I really, really wish that, too. I've always felt connected to him. I don't believe in reincarnation or anything. I mean, I know I'm *not* him. I just think he and I have a lot in common." She rubbed her lips together as if trying to spread her pale lip gloss. "I relate with everything I've heard about his personality. And, of course, Blair's my sister. Everyone says she's a lot like you, so maybe I know a little bit about what it's like for Ethan to have you as a sibling."

He rolled that statement over a few times. "Blair's similar to the person I became after Ethan died. The sibling Ethan knew wasn't like that."

"I—I guess what I'm trying to say . . . is that I might know something about how the Ethan who's in heaven feels about having you as a sibling."

Her words struck him mute.

"If that Ethan were here," she said, "I think he'd want me to tell you some things."

He met the eyes of this sister who looked so much like his brother that it gave him chills. "Okay."

"He'd want you to know that he doesn't blame you. He forgives you. You're his brother, and you would've protected him if you'd known the earthquake was coming. But you didn't know it was coming." A few seconds passed. "God was the one who took him. Not you or anyone else."

His heart was thrashing. He had nowhere to hide.

"Here's what you can do for Ethan now," she continued in her quiet voice. "You can move forward. He doesn't want you to feel guilty. He loves you, and he wants you to have a good future. A happy future." She bit her lip. "We all do."

Hailey, this sister he hardly knew, had seen him. Maybe everyone saw him . . . and saw through him.

"I'm sorry that I haven't been there for you," Luke said. Finley had told him again and again that she wanted him to be there for his family. "I'm going to try to do better."

"And I'll keep praying for Finley. I've been asking Ethan to put in a good word for her with God. I have a feeling that Ethan is going to insist that she come back. For you."

His throat went dry.

Blair reappeared. They gathered their things.

"We need to call Mom and tell her we're done early," Hailey said.

"*Or*," Blair suggested, "we could just stay at the hospital until nine because what Mom doesn't know won't hurt her. There's a donut shop on the first floor."

Hailey made a skeptical noise.

"Honestly. You're as obedient as a ventriloquist's puppet, Hailey." Blair knocked Luke in the upper arm with her fist. "I want you to know that, seeing as how this is a really lousy time for you, you don't have to worry about me breaking our deal by drinking or smoking. I might do a little weed. But that's all."

He scowled.

She laughed. "See how sensitive I can be?"

They left.

He dragged a chair to Finley's bedside, held her hand, and watched the steady rise and fall of her chest. The movie screen in his brain replayed the image of her falling out of sight. The image of her lying on the rocky hillside. The image of the chopper drawing her into the air.

Older memories played. Ethan asking him question after question as they'd walked toward the building to store sports equipment. His brother's face when he'd told him to go to the back of the line. The hallway caving in with slabs of concrete too heavy to survive.

"*He'd want you to know that he doesn't blame you,*" Hailey had said. "*He forgives you.*"

Sorrow built inside Luke.

"*He loves you, and he wants you to have a good future.*"

He bent an elbow onto the mattress near their joined hands, then rested his forehead on his arm. He made no sound as the scaffolding that had been crumbling since he'd met Finley fell. Hot tears filled his eyes.

Fine, he thought fiercely. He'd outgrown the old methods of coping. They weren't doing him any favors. When Finley came back, he needed to be better than he'd been.

He'd asked for God's forgiveness back on the side of Blood Mountain. If Finley could be trusted, and she could, then all that was left was for him to forgive himself.

He imagined the scene Finley had described in the car the night they'd driven back from dinner with Robbie and June.

Him, standing in a jail cell.

He saw chains, cracked, broken, useless at his feet. He saw a figure, a man, made from nothing but light. The figure pushed open the cell's door and beckoned Luke to follow.

Luke hesitated. The figure walked forward, toward the prison's exit. The air around Luke in the cell darkened, but Luke didn't move.

The figure returned and the light returned. He waited for Luke, expectant.

Luke nodded.

The figure began walking again.

This time, Luke followed. He put more and more distance between himself and the cell. The figure swung open another door and they were out of the prison. Walking down a path in the woods.

Free.

When Luke at last sat upright, new and unfamiliar hope had taken up residence in his chest.

He reached for the journal and pen someone had purchased so that visitors could leave notes and prayers for Finley to read later. He ripped several pages from the back.

When he was alone here with Finley and wasn't talking to her, he often played music on a portable speaker or movies on the room's TV. Sebastian had said she might have some awareness of her surroundings. If so, he wanted her to have awareness of things she liked. Today, he used his phone to select a musical track that made it sound like they were canoeing through a rainforest.

He stared at the blank pages.

"*Have you written about what you went through?*" Finley had asked him.

She'd been trying to communicate something important to him that night. He'd dismissed it then.

He was listening now. Taking it seriously now.

He'd never written a letter to Ethan, but there was nothing he wouldn't do for Finley.

Dear Ethan,

You gave me the best start in life I could have had. You were my brother, and we shared everything. A family, a history. Bikes, clothes. The walk to school and home. The last two Hershey bars in the pantry. Almost every childhood memory I have includes you.

You didn't do anything wrong the day of the earthquake. It wasn't unusual for you to follow me around. You did it a lot, and you were just excited that day. That's all. Just asking me questions. I'm your big brother, and I've wished every single day since that I was nice to you in return. Instead, you got on my nerves, and the one who should have been looking out for you let you down.

Telling you to go to the back of the line is the worst choice I've ever made in my life. I can't undo it. I'm so sorry. I hate that I said that. I hate that, when the world started shaking, I couldn't pull you out.

You were just a kid. A kid who deserved a long, happy life.

I hope Grandma Dempsey makes pie for you up there and that Granddad wraps you in his big *hugs and throws a football with you. You liked throwing the football.*

Mom and Dad are doing well. They talk about you often. No one could ever replace you, and you're still at the center of our family. They had a sculpture made of a boy playing in a puddle. It stands near a playground in town and has a plaque next to it saying how much they love you.

The town of Misty River holds so many reminders of you. So does our neighborhood and our house, where they all still live. You impacted every one of us who knew you.

I'm not sure when I'll join you, but I will one day.

When I get there, I hope your face is the first one I see.

Luke wrote and wrote and wrote.

The pages poured out of him. The words had been rumbling inside of him, it seemed, waiting to be said.

The following afternoon, a nurse poked her head into Finley's room. "Mr. Dempsey?"

He looked up. "Yes?"

"The doctor has decided that it's time to bring her back to consciousness."

CHAPTER TWENTY-SEVEN

People were speaking to her. Finley crimped her brow because the words were hard to understand. Vague and fuzzy.

No. Too difficult.

She rolled her head to the side and gave herself permission to return to her beach. When Luke was with her there, it was cozy. Peaceful.

"Everything's fine." Meadow. "You're safe."

"You're doing great." Bridget. "We can't wait for you to come back to us."

"Finley?" Her uncle. "We're here."

"We love you." Aunt June.

"Can you open your eyes?" *Luke*. He had the best voice. It always sounded as if he needed to use it more in order to oil it.

She began to sink down, down, down again.

"Can you talk to us?" Luke's question found her, caught her, and drew her forward. "Can you tell us how you're feeling?"

She didn't want to open her eyes or talk. That would take much more energy than she had.

"Can you let me know you're okay?" Luke asked. Worry marked his words.

She really couldn't allow him to worry. So . . . she'd do her best. Her eyelashes were heavy, but she managed to crack them open.

Immediately, she was rewarded with a blurry outline of Luke's body. She blinked. Why weren't her eyes working?

"Finley?" he asked.

"Yes," she tried to say. Her throat didn't cooperate. She swallowed, concentrating on him. Blessedly, like a camera lens finding focus, he slowly became clearer. Not totally clear. But close.

He was near. Standing next to her bed? In a . . . hospital room? Meadow, Bridget, Robbie, and June were here, too. As well as strangers . . . medical staff.

Where had the island gone? Dread trickled into her groggy thoughts.

Concentrate on Luke. He didn't scare her. He calmed her.

Luke leaned closer, his hazel eyes glowing with intensity. His dark hair was tousled, his face unshaven. The hawkish features that always reminded her of a pirate prince had aged since the last time she'd seen him. Beneath his gray T-shirt, his powerful shoulders held tension.

Had she been drugged? She felt drugged. Exhausted. Her head ached, and there was a faint ringing in her ears. But this . . . this view of him was the best of her life. A sound halfway between a sob and a laugh escaped her. "Luke," she said hoarsely.

"Finley." He spoke her name like a prayer.

"Hi," she said to the rest of them.

"Are you okay?" Meadow asked.

"I'm great," she lied. Luke was holding her hand. When had he taken hold of her hand? "How are my animals?"

"They're fine," Bridget said.

"I'm Dr. Ellis," said a middle-aged man with gelled blond hair. He stood on the side of the bed opposite Luke. "Can you tell me your name?"

"Finley Sutherland."

He asked if she knew what year it was. She did.

"What month is it?" Dr. Ellis asked.

"March."

Memories slotted into place, like the cells of a spreadsheet filling one by one. She remembered the last walk she and Luke had gone on with the shelter dogs. How the spring sun had danced through new green leaves as he'd kissed her. "Is it still March?"

"It was when you were last conscious," the doctor answered. "It's now April first. You've been unconscious for four days."

She'd been unconscious? *For four days?*

"Do you know who this is?" He indicated her relatives.

"Uncle Robbie and Aunt June."

"Very good," the doctor said. "And these people?"

"Meadow and Bridget."

"Excellent," the doctor said. "Can you move your arms?"

She could, though they felt like they weighed twice as much as they should.

"And your legs?" he asked.

She moved her legs. "What happened to me?"

"You sustained a mild traumatic brain injury," the doctor said, "but you're doing very well."

God, she prayed.

God. That one word was the longest prayer she had the ability to form. "How—how can an injury be both mild and traumatic?" she asked Luke.

His lips twitched. "I'm not sure."

"I've been out for four days?"

"Yes," Luke confirmed.

"To give your body the best chance to heal," the doctor said, "we put you in a medically induced coma. If you're feeling disoriented, that's normal."

"I'm *so* disoriented."

"Do you remember the events that led to your injury?" the doctor asked.

She opened her mouth to answer, and . . . no answer came. She couldn't remember.

She'd been hurt. Why couldn't she recall how?

Anxiety scratched up her throat.

"You doing all right?" Luke asked. Clearly, he'd read her expression.

She shook her head and began to cry.

Luke's grip on her hand communicated warmth and steadiness.

"What's the matter?" Bridget asked gently.

"Am I dying?"

"No," the doctor answered.

"You're going to make a full recovery," Luke told her. "I won't allow it to go any other way."

Finley didn't care if he was making a promise he couldn't keep. His words—spoken with such certainty—were exactly what she needed to hear.

"I can't remember how I got hurt," she admitted.

"Not to worry," Dr. Ellis said. "That's to be expected. What's the last thing you can remember?"

She groped around in her mind. "Luke's truck. Getting in Luke's truck to drive to the state park."

"Good job, Finley," Bridget murmured.

She and Luke had been going to the state park. To find her dad's treasure. They hadn't told anyone about that. Was it still a secret? Had something gone wrong with the treasure?

"When we were at the state park," Luke said, "you fell several feet down a steep mountainside and hit your head. You were brought here for treatment."

Her chin was quivering and her lungs were shuddering. She didn't understand what was going on. She had a brain injury? Coma? She'd lost time. "I . . . might need to cry awhile longer."

"Of course," Bridget soothed.

Fear gathered around her like evil black smoke, but . . .

Luke was here. And he'd promised her she'd recover. She clung to his promise and his presence until the smoke began to fade.

Hospital staffers wheeled Finley on a gurney down hallways for scans. Once she returned to her room, they helped her sit up and dangle her feet over the side of the bed. The simple motion stirred a cyclone of dizziness.

They returned her to a reclining position, then physical therapists arrived to work with her. A speech therapist administered a swallow study, to test if she could swallow water without choking. She had to concentrate on swallowing more than ever before but she passed the test.

Through it all, Luke remained. He watched with vigilance. He asked questions and defended Finley's opinions and demanded they back off when he could tell they'd pushed her too far or asked her to do something that caused her pain.

She wished she could cut them all off and loudly announce, *What I need, in order to feel better, is time alone with Luke*. They were trained health professionals. Their sole aim was to help her. She knew this. Yet what she earnestly wanted was for everyone to go away. She had so many questions for Luke. She wanted to ask them all, then she wanted him to lie next to her in the quiet so she could throw an arm over his chest and rest her head on his shoulder and sleep for a long, long time. *That* was the medicine she needed.

But time alone with Luke she did not get. When the staffers finished with her, Meadow and Bridget were on hand. Then Robbie and June reentered. Then her cousins. Akira. More. Five people were in the room with her when she started nodding off for the night. *A good hostess shouldn't fall asleep in front of her guests*, she thought fuzzily.

Then she was out.

God had brought Finley back.

Luke was certain of it. He'd prayed and prayed that God would bring her back and He had. Now it was Luke's job to follow through on what he'd determined he'd do the night of her injury.

Get things right. With how he treated Finley. With his pursuit of the Vance brothers.

He'd folded out the futon in her room and was lying on it, one knee bent up. He wedged his forearm between the back of his head and a pillow so that he had a view of her.

The machines hummed. An IV dripped medicine and fluid into her veins while Finley slept peacefully. No longer in a coma. Simply sleeping.

He knew she cared about him. Beyond that, he wasn't sure of her feelings. She was very open. She'd said soon after they met that she'd give him her treasure if he wanted it. She'd once told him, "*I'll love Chase forever.*" She'd once asked, "*Are you interested in dating me?*"

If she loved him, she would've told him. Right?

He didn't think she loved him, and so the thought of telling her he loved her scared him. But nothing would ever again have the power to scare him as much as her injury had. So down the road, when she was completely herself again, he would tell her how he felt.

At that point, she would no longer need to lean on him. She'd be strong enough to hear him say *I love you* and, if she didn't feel the same, to tell him so truthfully.

At the moment, she was dazed and not in her right mind and at a disadvantage. In the days to come, the highest priority for them both had to be and would be her health.

He'd given up on ever being good enough for her, but he would show her that he could, at least, be good.

In the middle of the night, a nurse woke Finley while doing her rounds. Across the dim room, she spotted Luke, sleeping on a futon that looked much too hard and much too short for his frame. His position revealed the firm underside of his jaw. His hands rested on his flat abs.

He was still here.

And she was still alive.

The God who'd carried her through trauma before had carried her through it again. *Thank you, God, for saving me. For sending Luke. Praise you, Lord.*

God had given her a second chance. She recognized the value of that, and she planned to take it and run with it.

Of course, she could barely sit upright at the moment, let alone run.

But when she was better, watch out, world.

The sight of Luke stoked a glow of contentment in her while the nurse bustled around. When the woman finally left, one of Luke's eyes slid open.

"You're awake," Finley said.

"I'm awake."

"Come here."

He did so.

It took some doing, but she managed to scoot over. She patted the open space she'd created on the bed in invitation.

"I'll take up all the room," he said.

"I hope so."

He lowered the rail on his side, then stretched out beside her. His arm drew her close against him. Just as she'd imagined, she placed one arm across his chest and rested her head on his shoulder. At last, something about this difficult day had gone her way. The reality of this was far, far better than she'd anticipated.

"I want to know what happened when we went to Blood Mountain to dig up the treasure," she said.

In a darkness penetrated by glowing machines, he unwound the events for her. He stopped only to answer her questions.

She could picture herself and Luke, kneeling on either side of that hole in the earth, astonished by what they'd uncovered. *The missing Confederate gold*. She could imagine the fear they must have experienced at the sound of an ATV approaching and the sight of three men standing before them with guns.

It was bizarre to have been an active participant in something so dramatic that she could not remember. She willed herself to recall what Luke was describing. But only emptiness occupied the space where those hours belonged.

"There are things I need to find out," he said.

"Like?"

"How the Vance brothers knew about the hunt. I also need to know how they got an ATV to such a remote site. I asked Detective Romano if he saw a trailer on the road near where we parked. He said he didn't."

"Maybe they followed us and parked the trailer with the ATV on a different road nearby."

"Maybe. But they wouldn't have known they needed an ATV until they trailed us to the state park. They live in Toccoa, an hour away. At that point, they wouldn't have had time to drive home, get an ATV, and drive back."

She closed her eyes in order to better hear his heart, smell his soap, feel his strength.

"I also need to know," he said, "where the brothers are keeping the gold. If I can learn that, the police will have the evidence they need to arrest them."

"Do you think they've put the gold in a storage facility somewhere?"

"Probably not, because that would create a paper trail. Bills. A record of payments made."

"On someone's property, then?"

"To me, that's what's most likely. I wouldn't expect them to store it on property they own, because that's where police would look first. But maybe on the property of someone they trust." His fingers gently wove through the strands of her hair. "I'll figure it out."

But what if he didn't? Could Luke make peace with that outcome? She cared far more about Luke's well-being than about punishing the Vance brothers. "Answering those questions is important. But not so important to me that it's worth putting you in danger. The Vance brothers are ruthless." It was hard to square in her mind that the brothers who held a fundraiser in their sister's honor were the same brothers who'd tried to kill her and Luke. But they were. "I think we should let the police handle it."

"I agree. I'm just going to . . . help the police along."

"I'm not as feisty and emphatic as I will be when I'm healthier. But really, Luke. I need you to hear this." She lifted her head and adjusted his face until their eyes met. "I don't want you to get hurt, and I don't want you to do anything that will end up getting *you* sent back to jail. Okay?"

"Okay."

"Promise me you won't risk yourself or break the law."

He hesitated.

Worry clenched painfully within her. "*Luke*."

"I promise."

She resettled her cheek against his shoulder.

"I had a talk with Robbie while you were unconscious," he said. "He told me what really happened the day before Carla's death."

"I'm listening."

He provided the details of her dad and uncle's miraculous find.

"Did Robbie tell you what happened the next day?" she asked. "When Carla died?"

"No. He said he'd speak to you and you alone about that."

"Will you ask him to come visit me tomorrow?"

"Sure you're up for that?"

No. At the moment, she didn't feel up for anything except this. Just this. Resting here with Luke. "I'm sure."

Minutes passed during which she tried to convince herself that she could trust Luke's promise not to risk himself.

"I'm sorry, Finley," he whispered all of a sudden. "I hate that I didn't keep you safe."

"But you did." Against the odds, he'd kept her alive. He'd gotten her help. "If it weren't for you, they'd have killed me."

"They almost did kill you."

"Almost. But not quite."

She could feel just how much he wished he'd been able to do more.

"I'm grateful to you," she told him.

"No," he said. "Don't be grateful."

"I can be grateful if I want to be. And I do." She toyed with the collar of his T-shirt. His palpable anguish broke her heart. "I don't blame you at all for what happened. What I'd like, very much, is for you to find a way not to blame yourself."

Luke was incredibly loyal. But how much of this devotion could now be attributed to obligation? To pity? To a misplaced sense of responsibility over her injury? She desperately wanted him beside her . . . but not for those reasons. Not because he had a PhD in carrying guilt.

"The Vance brothers aren't going to get away with what they did," he vowed.

Apprehension pierced her.

She and Luke had come so far. She couldn't stand to come this far only to watch vengeance tear him apart.

Trish and Kat's voices stirred Finley awake the next morning. Luke was gone. When she asked after him, they said he was at his apartment and would be back soon.

Her employees offered her the herbal tea they'd brought and chatted until a police officer arrived. He introduced himself as Detective Romano and said he'd come to take her statement.

"I'm very sorry," Finley told him when they were alone. "I wish

I could remember the things that happened that night, but I can't. My doctors tell me this issue is common for someone who's experienced a head injury like mine."

"I understand." Romano was of medium height. He had a wiry frame and a still, observant manner. The front middle of his brown hair looked like it wanted to remain on his forehead, but the sides had given up and receded. "Can you tell me what you do remember about the treasure hunt and the days leading up to Sunday?" he asked.

She recounted every detail until the point when her memories abruptly cut off.

"Ken Vance and his brothers admit that they were on the side of the mountain that night. They say they were out there for fun, enjoying a drive." He scratched his cheek. "They saw Luke push you off the cliff and then place the gold in a backpack. They say they tried to intervene, but that Luke shot at them to protect the treasure."

Fury swept hotly up Finley's face. "That is a pack of lies."

"How can you be sure?" he asked calmly.

"Because I know Luke."

"He's out on parole for felony theft."

She wanted to scream. Her hands fisted in the hospital sheets. She'd never felt such a primal need to defend another human being in her life. The need was so all-consuming that it blotted out everything except one diamond-bright revelation, simultaneously earth-shattering and simple.

She loved Luke.

Heaven help her, she did.

"Are you all right?" Romano asked.

"Yes." She had no idea how long she'd been silent as her thoughts reeled. *Think, Finley. Tell him about the evidence that points to Luke's innocence.* "Did Luke signal you the other night when you were responding to the reports of gunshots?"

"Yes."

"If he was the one who'd injured me, he'd have taken off with as much gold as he could carry as soon as he heard sirens. He didn't. He stayed, and he signaled to you, because he wanted you to reach us as quickly as possible." Her words gathered steam. "How likely is it that Carla Vance's brothers would be out on a joyride and just happen to drive their ATV past the exact spot where Luke and I were unearthing a treasure of historic proportions? Totally unlikely. Luke told the truth when he told you what happened. I trust him. So please focus all your energy on investigating Ken Vance and his brothers."

"Rest assured, we are investigating them, miss."

"Do you have any leads?"

"Luke sent us information about the type of ATV he says the Vance brothers drove. I called the dealerships in this area, asking for their cooperation. They gave me a list of names of the people who've purchased ATVs matching the description Luke provided."

"Was Ken, Dennis, or Jeff Vance on the list?"

"No."

Shoot.

"We found a spent shell casing from an AR-15 below the ledge, near the blood from your head injury."

"That casing proves the Vance brothers shot at us."

"That casing proves that someone fired an AR-15 at some point in time," he corrected. "We ran it for fingerprints and came up empty, so the casing can't be definitively connected to the Vance brothers' guns."

Finley's shoulders sagged. She needed the police to close this case. Not because she wanted revenge on Ken for injuring her. Not because she couldn't live with the Vance brothers keeping the gold for themselves.

Because she feared Luke would not rest until this was settled.

CHAPTER TWENTY-EIGHT

When Finley's CT scan showed no blood issues, Dr. Ellis informed her that, following her PT session, he'd have her transferred out of the ICU to a neuro floor. According to him, she'd been very fortunate. However, he said she needed to honor the fact that her body had sustained a hard knock and give both her physical and mental function time to recuperate.

They wheeled her to the PT suite, this time in a wheelchair instead of a gurney. The therapists coaxed her—with a great deal of support—to stand and take a few steps.

More dizziness.

Be patient with yourself, she told herself again and again. *Give yourself grace*.

When they finally brought her to her new room, Luke was waiting there for her. She'd only been apart from him for a couple of hours. Regardless, tenderness exploded in her like a shower of golden sparkles at the sight of him, framed by the rainy sky beyond the window.

Good grief, *of course* she loved him.

"Hi," she said.

"Hi."

Luke came over to assist as the orderly prepared to move her into the bed.

"I'd like to sit in the armchair for a bit, please," she said.

The two men helped her into the chair. Maybe she was becoming more lucid, because, for the first time, she was slightly mortified by the realization that Luke was seeing her in this condition.

She was nowhere near the best version of herself. She'd been stripped of her funky clothes, her accessories, her entourage of animals, the work that gave her days purpose.

He was gorgeous and fit.

She was weak and muddled.

"You're worn out," Luke said after the orderly left.

Correct. Her energy was zapped. "So are you." His eyes were red, and he looked dead on his feet.

"Your uncle's waiting down the hall, but I can tell him to come back another time."

"No," she said stubbornly. "Don't you dare."

He smiled. "If you're bossing me around, you must be feeling better." He pulled the blanket off the bed and handed it to her.

She smoothed it over her legs. "I'm ready for him."

He left, and soon she heard their footsteps approaching. They entered and her uncle bent to delicately hug her. "How are you?"

"Improving."

"Can I get you something to drink?" Luke asked her.

"Yes, please. They've promoted me all the way to vegetable broth."

"I'll be back."

With that, she and Robbie were alone.

Finley considered her uncle. Her father's brother. She'd grown up with him, spent an untold amount of time with him, been on excellent terms with him. Because of that, she'd always assumed she knew him well. For the first time in her life, she doubted that. The mild, gentlemanly version of Uncle Robbie she'd known wouldn't have been capable of stealing gold.

He sat in the remaining armchair.

It struck her that she had more faith in the man who'd just gone to get her vegetable broth—the man she'd met three months ago—than this relative of hers she'd known since birth.

She moved to tuck one foot beneath her opposite thigh and realized that required more strength than she possessed. "Luke relayed to me everything that you told him."

"I figured as much. I'm sorry, Finley. I'm so very sorry about all of this. Your dad never would've wanted any harm to come to you."

"I know." Inwardly, she gathered herself, trying to psych herself up to hear the truth. "Please tell me how Carla died."

His mouth pursed.

"Go on," she said, a trace of steel in her words.

"The night after we . . . found the gold, Ed, Carla, and I returned to the site with supplies. It took us a few hours, but we dug up every bit of that gold. Then we drove to Carla's apartment and helped carry her portion upstairs. We had to go down and back to the truck a few times. After we finished setting the last of it on her living room floor, I remember looking up at her and realizing something was wrong."

"How so?"

"She was visibly nervous. Pale. Fidgeting. The worst feeling came over me."

Finley registered the hum of employees chatting down the hall. The siren of an ambulance nearing the ER. "What did she say?"

"She said that if we wanted her to stay quiet about the gold, then we had to give her half of it."

Oh no. Finley waited for the rest.

"She'd done none of the work," he continued. "She hadn't researched the path of the stolen gold. She hadn't read account after account or studied historic maps. She'd never used a metal detector in her life. Yet she wasn't satisfied when we divided the gold three ways. She was greedy and wanted more."

He was conveniently overlooking the fact that *none* of them had a rightful claim to the gold.

"Ed loved her, in his way." He pinched his thumb with the fingers of his opposite hand. "When Carla turned on us, she betrayed Ed. She cared more about that treasure than she did about my brother."

"What did you do when she said she wanted half?"

"I tried to calm her down. I couldn't see how we'd be able to live with giving her half. On the other hand, I couldn't see what we'd do if she went public and told everyone about our discovery. I hoped we could reason with her and figure it out."

"How did Dad respond?"

"He went silent, which is how I knew he was boiling inside. The more I tried to get Carla to speak with us, the more agitated she became. She reached over and pulled a gun out of a drawer. Then she tugged a blanket off one of those old-fashioned cassette tape recorders. The spokes were moving. She'd been recording us. She told us that if we didn't go down and bring up more gold until she had half of everything we'd found, she'd dial 9-1-1. At that point, Ed called her bluff. He told her that he'd rather dial 9-1-1 himself than let her have half."

"And?"

"She started yelling. She pointed the gun at us with one hand and grabbed her phone with the other. Her hands were shaking. She was punching numbers into her phone and demanding that we go and get more gold. I admit, I panicked. When she looked at her phone, I rushed her. I grabbed the hand holding the gun. I tried to point it upward and take it from her. She had a death grip on it. Ed pushed his way between us. He took hold of the gun, too, then shoved me to the side. Ed and Carla struggled over the gun. One or both of them ended up pulling the trigger. The bullet went through her chest."

For nine years, Finley had believed that her dad had killed Carla while cleaning her gun. She'd believed it because that's what he'd told his attorneys, his jury, his judge.

Purposely, he'd misled them all.

Was Robbie misleading her now?

"Is that really what happened?" Finley asked. "If Dad killed

Carla in cold blood so you two could keep all the gold . . . just tell me. Don't sugarcoat it."

His expression took on a twinge of hurt. "Ed had no intention of killing her. They were wrestling over the gun and it went off."

She stared at him doubtfully.

"Finley. You know your father couldn't kill anyone in cold blood."

Did she know that?

She supposed that she did. He'd shown her steadfast love all her life. When angry, he kept his temper. He was one to talk things out bluntly. He was not one to resort to violence.

"Ed and I didn't want to give Carla half the gold. But we didn't want to kill her. We never would have wanted that. In fact, I couldn't believe it as I watched her fall. Carla herself looked stunned, lying there on the carpet. The whole situation had escalated extremely fast. One minute, I was carrying gold up the stairs for her. Moments later, she was bleeding out."

Finley tried to twist one of her rings around her finger and comprehended for at least the twentieth time since waking in the hospital that she didn't have her rings. "How did you and Dad respond?"

"Ed administered CPR. I felt for her pulse. There was nothing we could do. She died very quickly."

"And then?"

"Ed and I sat there. We were horrified. Shocked."

"I know you called the police soon after she was shot. Why not tell them the truth?"

"If we'd done that, we'd have had to explain why Carla drew a gun on us. In which case, we'd have needed to come up with a plausible story that didn't include the gold."

"Or," she said tiredly, "you could have told the officers the whole truth. About the gold. About all of it. I bet Dad was willing to do that. It was you. . . . It was you who wanted to keep it a secret."

He inclined his head. "That's fair. I did want to keep the gold a secret. But not just for myself. If we'd told the authorities about the gold, we'd have been charged with stealing it. Plus, it would have been hard to make anyone believe, once they knew about the treasure, that Ed had killed Carla accidentally in self-defense."

"So you two invented the story about Dad killing her while cleaning the gun. Instead of a guilty person who'd stolen gold and rushed at Carla, you became an innocent eyewitness."

He nodded apologetically.

Her father had a long, long history of protecting Robbie. Through the *Brothers* book, her dad had given her a glimpse into the bonds that tied him to his younger sibling. It was as if he was saying to her, *This book shows a facet of who I am and what makes me tick. Can you understand?*

"It's now clear," Finley said, "that Carla told at least one of her brothers about the Confederate gold before she died. When she was suddenly shot in the presence of her two accomplices, there's no way her brothers would have believed it to be an accident."

"I'm afraid not."

"Which is why Ken tried to hurt me. As retribution for what Dad did to Carla."

"Yes."

"Then you and Dad . . . what? Hid the gold? Destroyed the cassette tape? And later split the treasure fifty-fifty?"

"We did."

"And eventually you found a way to sell your share?"

"Yes."

"Which lifted you from financially stable to financially affluent. You added on to your house, bought cars, started taking trips."

He didn't answer, but he didn't need to. She could see the affirmative answer on his features.

"Do you still have any of the gold?" she asked.

"No."

"How come the Vance brothers didn't go after you and your gold?"

"They tried. Early on, after Ed's conviction, they attempted to hack into my computer. They followed me. They threatened me. They never could find any evidence that I was in possession of gold. Eventually, I was able to get a restraining order against them. That stopped them."

"I wish you'd warned me."

"I assumed Ed had gotten rid of his gold long ago."

"You never asked what happened to his share?"

"I asked, but he'd only say it was safe. Nothing else."

"I can't imagine why he gave it to me."

A pause. "Can't you?"

Her curiosity was piqued. "Can you?"

He leaned toward her. "I believe he was giving you an opportunity to do what he felt he couldn't do, for fear it might incriminate me."

"Which is?"

"Make it right. As soon as you found that gold, did you plan to give it up?"

"Yes."

"Your dad knew you well enough to know how you'd react. He trusted you to do the honorable thing."

Emotion knotted in her throat, because yes. That made perfect sense to her. Her father trusted her to do the honorable thing.

"Are you going to tell the police everything?" he asked. "June doesn't know about this. My kids and grandkids . . . They don't know."

"I'm not going to volunteer information about your involvement. But if and when they ask me how Dad came into possession of the gold, I'll answer their questions truthfully. Lies have done more than enough damage." She pulled in a painful breath. "When the police catch up with the Vance brothers like Luke thinks they will, the Vance brothers will have to answer for their actions. You may have to answer for your actions, too." Her words rang with compassion and determination both. "My dad's no longer here to protect you, Robbie."

Immediately after Finley woke from her coma, Luke had promised her that she'd be okay. It was proving harder to convince himself of that.

Days passed. Two, then three, then four of them. Finley's progress was so impressive that they transferred her from the hospital to a rehab facility. Yet he still felt foolishly protective of her. On edge.

Every night since the one when they'd had their middle-of-the-night conversation, she'd insisted he return to his apartment to get quality sleep. What she didn't know was that quality sleep was no longer an option. Nightmares infested his dreams. In them, Ken dragged Finley closer and closer to the cliff. Luke fought to reach her in time, but he never did. Each time he failed, he watched her fall.

At most, he got five hours of sleep a night. Which left him with a lot of time, alone and awake. He no longer watched TV or read news on his computer. He spent every free hour chasing down information on the Vance brothers, their families, their friends. Or writing about what he'd experienced before, during, and after the earthquake in El Salvador. Or praying.

Near seven o'clock on a Wednesday morning, six days after Finley regained consciousness, Luke received an email from CeCe.

It included a long list of all the people connected to the Vance brothers and every detail about them she'd unearthed. She'd even attached a photo of a drawing she'd created that showed the Vance family tree.

Luke increased the size of the drawing until it filled his computer screen. Hungrily, he searched the image for information.

One of Dennis Vance's daughters worked at a law firm. Reading the name of her law firm was like slotting a missing puzzle piece into place.

When Luke reached Finley's room at the rehab center two hours later, he found her sitting cross-legged on her bed, wearing a soft yellow sweater and leggings. She'd piled her black hair onto her head. He'd brought her jewelry box to her days ago, and now several rings glittered on her fingers. Yesterday, he'd caught her speaking passionately to one of the staffers about the need for more managed feral cat colonies. The day before that, she'd started asking the nursing and PT staff if they felt called to adopt a dog, foster a dog, or volunteer at her non-profit.

She was more and more herself all the time. So how come he couldn't stop worrying that her health would backslide?

She beamed at him. "Good morning."

"Morning." He cradled her face in his hands and kissed her. "I missed you."

"I missed you, too."

"Then let me sleep on the sofa in here tonight. Please."

"No. You're running ragged even though I'm sending you home to sleep. I can't imagine how worn out you'd be if you slept on this sofa every night."

"I'd be better if I was near you."

"You're near me now."

"Thank God. Can I get you anything?"

"More ice water? That kiss gave me a hot flash."

He took her glass and refilled it with the jug an employee had left on the side table. "I have information."

"Oh yeah?"

He handed the glass to her.

She took a long sip, then gave him a look that said, *Spill all your information immediately*.

"Turns out Dennis Vance's daughter Julia started working as an administrative assistant at a law firm in Hartwell soon after her aunt Carla's death. Which law firm do you think it was?"

Finley considered him for several seconds, swirling the ice in her glass. "Horton and Associates? Where my dad's will was on file?"

"Exactly. I saw Julia the day I met with Rosco. She was the one who checked me in and showed me back to his office."

"Is she tall? With dark hair?"

He nodded.

"I remember her," she said. "I saw her, too, the day I went to Rosco's office for the reading of the will. She's Dennis's daughter?"

"She is."

"Which probably explains how the Vance brothers learned of the treasure hunt."

"Right. They knew Carla, Ed, and Robbie had found gold. But they didn't know what had become of it. Julia was graduating college right around that time. She needed a job, so I'm guessing her father encouraged her to apply for a job with Ed's attorney."

"Free two birds with one key. She'd be earning a paycheck, and she'd also have opportunity to snoop through my dad's legal documents." Finley's sweater slipped off one shoulder. She tugged it back in place. "Dad mentioned the treasure hunt in his will. If Julia told her father about that, it wouldn't have been a stretch for him to correctly conclude that the treasure hunt was leading me to Confederate gold."

"Exactly."

"The will also included the first clue and Dad's instruction to open it on my next birthday. The brothers would simply have waited a few months for my birthday to roll around. Then they tried and failed to hack into your computer. They succeeded at getting inside my house and searching it once or maybe twice. And they tailed us places."

"I still don't know how they did that. I can say for sure that no one car ever followed us from point A to point B during the treasure hunt. A couple of times, a car took some of the same turns that I took. But whenever that happened, it was never the same make and model as the time before. I was paying attention."

"I know you were." She set her glass aside and interlaced her fingers with his. "We didn't realize we were up against three separate men. Between their wives and kids, think of how many cars Ken, Dennis, and Jeff have access to. All three of them might have taken turns following us on a single trip. Then, on the next trip, all three might have been driving three different cars than the time before."

Still. It sickened him that the Vance brothers had successfully followed them on his watch.

"Luke."

"Mmm?"

"Will you tell me honestly how you're holding up?"

"I'm fine."

"I'm worried that you're not. Your pursuit of the Vance brothers has formed this . . . dark cloud that hovers over you. I'm recovering. But sometimes I'm afraid that you're deteriorating."

"No. So long as you're good, I'm good."

"I'm good. See?" She stretched out her free arm. "Look at me. All good!"

He gave her a tender, uneven smile. "Then I'm good, too."

She released a sound of frustration and squeezed his hand. "Look. I know you're brooding about what happened to me. Please don't. When you were in El Salvador and trying to find your brother in that hallway, your actions, unfortunately, didn't affect the outcome for Ethan. But this time—for me—they did. This time, your actions made the difference. That's what I've chosen to focus on." She looked at him fiercely. "That's what I want you to focus on, too."

Maybe a healthier man, a man who hadn't lived through the death of his brother, would be able to focus solely on the positive. His reality was more complex than that. Finley had lived—and he was more thankful for that than he'd ever been for anything. At the same time, he wasn't willing to release the Vance brothers.

He was a man who held on to things. At times, that was a flaw. At times, a strength because it meant he would love Finley with everything he had until his death.

Since the day he'd written the letter to Ethan, he'd been working to forgive himself and trust God. But a lifetime of patterns couldn't be cured with a single prayer. They demanded unlearning. Daily, he was doing his best to release his mistakes and forgive himself.

He still wasn't great at that. But he was trying.

She slid her legs over the side of the bed and moved to stand.

He assisted her to her feet. "How's the dizziness?"

"Better. Almost gone now." She moved into his arms, sliding her slim fingers into the hair at the nape of his neck.

Their eyes met and just that—one heated look from beneath her dark lashes—undid him. He lived for moments like this when they were alone together.

"I know better than to ask you to give up your pursuit of the Vance brothers," she said. "But maybe you could take a week off? Do some self-care?"

He snorted. "I'm not a girl. I don't do self-care."

"Therein lies the problem." She smiled. "To clarify, the fact that you don't do self-care is the problem. The fact that you're a man is one hundred percent not a problem."

He kissed her.

They shared an intense type of intimacy he'd never before allowed himself. It sent his blood rushing. Yet he never let himself lose his head with her. He was extremely careful with Finley these days.

His heart beat, *Mine. She really is all right. Mine. She really is all right.*

He'd built a dream of a life in Montana while in prison. It hadn't been wasted. It had served its purpose. It had given him a destination to visit in his mind when he'd been caged. He'd needed that then. And after his release, he'd continued to need it because it had provided him with a plan.

He hadn't thought of Montana in quite a while because he no longer needed it.

His reality—*this reality*—had become his dream.

Late the next night, Luke printed out CeCe's email and the sketch she'd made of the Vance family tree. He set them next to his computer and pulled up the Union County Assessor's Office website.

He'd thought a lot about how the Vance brothers could have accessed an ATV on short notice. The only scenario that made sense to him? That one of their family members or friends lived in the vicinity of Blood Moutain and had made the ATV available to Ken.

The state park was located in Union County, and the county's website enabled visitors to search their records based on property owners' names. Days ago, when he'd found this site, he'd tried the Vance brothers' names without success. But now he had dozens of names, thanks to CeCe.

He started at the top of the list. By the time he'd typed in every surname CeCe had provided, he'd compiled three possibilities.

Ken's daughter was married to a man named Cody Ollenburger, and a couple named Cliff and Stacy Ollenburger owned property in Union County.

Jeff had a close friend named Thomas Smith, and a T. Smith owned property in Union County.

And Dennis's wife's sister was named Connie Collins, and a woman named Dorothy Collins owned property in Union County.

Luke's pen scratched across paper as he wrote down the address of each of the three properties.

He opened Facebook and located the profile associated with the first name. Cody Ollenburger posted often and wasn't touchy about privacy settings. After several minutes of scrolling, Luke found a picture from Father's Day last year of two men who resembled each other, though separated by a few decades in age. In the post, Cody wrote about how much he appreciated his dad. He'd tagged only one person in the post.

Cliff Ollenburger. His father.

CHAPTER TWENTY-NINE

Shortly after dawn the next morning, Luke followed his GPS along a dirt road that carried him upward through dense forest toward the Ollenburger property. He'd expected to follow the address to a neighborhood, but this wasn't that. He'd call these structures vacation cabins, not houses. As he continued, the cabins became fewer.

No streets connected this area directly to Vogel State Park. But as the crow flies, it was probably only about six miles from here to Blood Mountain. Ken and his brothers could have crossed that distance in an ATV in thirty to forty-five minutes.

He passed by Ollenburger's address, taking a long look at the small, brown-shingled cabin set far back from the road. No cars parked there. No lights on.

After reading more of Cody and Cliff's Facebook posts last night, he'd learned that Cliff and Stacy had moved to the Middle East for a year for Cliff's job.

As soon as the road widened, he parked his truck, then doubled back on foot through the woods until he reached the structure. It appeared to be thirty or forty years old but had been kept up well.

Cupping his eyes against a window, he saw that the interior had been updated. Vacuum tracks marked the rug. A folded throw blanket rested over an armchair that looked new.

He moved to the next window and the next, peering in each one. He didn't see a stash of gold bars. Then again, he hadn't expected to. What he did see? A large gun safe spanning one wall of the second bedroom. Had Ken and his brothers borrowed hunting gear and semi-automatic guns from here? It seemed likely.

He went to the free-standing garage. A gap in the wood gave him a view of the odds and ends that surrounded a rectangle of empty floor space. The empty floor space was approximately the size of a four-seater ATV. To cover their tracks, Ken had probably moved the ATV used in the attack. But no doubt it was usually parked in this exact spot.

Luke turned and studied the backyard, hands on his hips.

A picnic table. A firepit. Lots of pine needles and a few fallen branches.

Taking his time, he walked forward.

His eyes narrowed. What was that?

Set to the side under the cover of trees, a small pipe sprouted from the earth. It was topped by a conical roof. Luke knelt next to it. This was a ventilation duct. Unlike the house, this had been built in recent years. Maybe around the time of the renovation.

What were they venting way over here?

And then it struck him.

They were venting something underground.

He yanked his phone from his pocket and ran a search. *What does a ventilation pipe for an underground bunker look like?*

The first image populated. His pulse and his focus intensified as he held up the image on his phone's screen, comparing it to the scene before him.

It turned out that a ventilation pipe for an underground bunker looked just like . . . *this*.

What better place to store stolen gold than in a bunker, on a remote property, owned by someone not named Vance?

Certainty flooded him.

He drove to the nearest town. A friendly local directed him to the only pay phone still in operation. He pushed a quarter into the slot and dialed.

"Blairsville Police Department," a female voice said.

"Is this Detective Romano's station?"

"It is. But I'm afraid he's not in just yet."

Excellent. He'd hoped for that because he didn't want to risk Romano recognizing his voice. "No problem. A friend of mine told me yesterday that he saw an article about missing Confederate gold. It mentioned that the police are searching for it and listed Romano's name. I have information for him."

"I see. I can transfer you to his voice mail—"

"Actually, can you take down a written message and hand it to him when he arrives?"

"Certainly." Paper rustled on the other end. "I'm ready."

"I thought Romano would want to know that I have a place near Blood Mountain. About a week and a half ago, I was out smoking a cigarette and saw three men unloading gold from an ATV into my neighbor's cabin."

"Do you know which night that was?"

"Sunday, March twenty-eighth."

"And where is the cabin located?"

Luke rattled off the address. "It's owned by a guy named Cliff Ollenburger, but Cliff wasn't one of the guys unloading gold. Cliff has a son named Cody, and one of the men looked to me like Cody's father-in-law, Ken Vance. Are you getting this down?"

"One second." Then, "Yes. Go on."

"Cliff has an underground bunker below the house."

"May I have your name and number?"

"I'd prefer to remain anonymous. I wouldn't want to stir up any trouble with my neighbor. Will you make sure that Romano gets this message?"

"I will."

Before she could say more, Luke hung up and texted Finley.

Luke
I'm going to arrive late today. Can I pick up anything for you?

Finley
How about some vegan cinnamon rolls from Sugar Maple Kitchen?

Luke
Done.

He swung past Sugar Maple Kitchen for cinnamon rolls, then drove to Ken Vance's Feed Supply Company. He parked half a block down and made himself comfortable.

He'd waited days for this.

He could easily wait a few more hours.

That afternoon, Luke rested a wrist on his steering wheel, gaze trained on the feed store as Detective Romano and another officer entered.

Minutes later, Ken ran out the back entrance and climbed into his Jaguar convertible. He tried to start it. No luck. Again and again he tried.

The engine wouldn't turn over.

The policemen flowed out the back, surrounded Ken, and arrested him.

"Gotcha," Luke whispered.

Justice had caught up with Luke because of the bad decisions he'd made. Now he'd ensured that it caught up with Ken, too, and retribution tasted very, very sweet.

Once Ken had been secured in the back of the squad car, Romano strode over to Luke's truck.

Luke rolled down the driver's side window.

"Good afternoon, Mr. Dempsey."

"Good afternoon, Detective."

"What a coincidence to find you here."

"Wild coincidence," Luke agreed.

"Someone left us a tip this morning saying they'd seen Ken unloading gold at a property owned by relatives of Ken's daughter. You wouldn't know anything about that, would you?"

"Nope."

"It took some doing to get into the underground bunker. But we managed it. And what do you know?"

"You found the gold."

"We did."

"Glad to hear it."

Romano shielded his eyes from the sun and looked toward the Jaguar. "Ken Vance's car wouldn't start just now."

"Oh? That was unlucky for him."

"You're pretty knowledgeable about car engines, are you not?"

"I am."

"Probably enough to disable one."

"Yep."

"Huh."

Luke shrugged. "You can't count on cars that weren't manufactured here in the USA."

Romano smiled. "You have firsthand experience with the inner workings of a chop shop, correct?"

"Yes."

"And, from what I hear, hacker-level computer skills."

"I have strong computer skills, but they're not hacker skills. They're law-abiding skills."

Romano took a step back. "You know, we could use a consultant like you."

Luke cocked an eyebrow in disbelief.

"We'd only call you in from time to time. To give us your viewpoint."

Life was strange. He'd once used his knowledge of cars, criminals, and computers to commit crimes. Now he was being invited to use the same knowledge to solve crimes. "I might be willing to help out. As you said, from time to time."

"Excellent." Romano extended his hand and Luke shook it. "I'll be in touch."

Across town, Finley received a text from Luke saying he was on his way. She hurried to the foyer of the rehab center in time to watch his truck arrive out front.

He walked toward the entrance carrying a white box. The scruff on his cheeks was thick today, his hair touseled. He wore a pair of jeans she loved with a light brown henley and his black jacket.

Her heart executed a jubilant spin-and-swoon maneuver. Since she'd woken from the coma, he'd never arrived this late in the day before. He was certainly entitled to time away, and she'd already determined that she wouldn't pry. But now that she was seeing him, it became clear that refusing to pry was going to require effort.

Immediately, she took hold of his hand and led him toward the door to the garden. "Meadow and Bridget just texted to say they're about to stop by, so we don't have much time alone."

"When they get here, I'll leave to give you guys privacy."

He did that a lot, she'd noticed. She was fortunate to have a large number of visitors. But when others came by, Luke often slid out. In the case of Meadow, it was, she suspected, a dual motivation. One, he didn't want to intrude. Two, he could only take Meadow in small doses.

"I don't want privacy from you," she said. "I want privacy with you."

She drew him toward the two-seater wooden swing positioned beneath the shade of a sugarberry tree.

When they reached it, he handed her the white box. "Cinnamon rolls."

"Thank you." She peeked inside. Gooey delicious sweetness

stared back. It was a testament to Luke's appeal that she was far more interested in him than the cinnamon rolls in this moment. She placed the box on the grass, then practically pushed him into the wooden swing.

He landed with a soft "*Oof.*"

She climbed onto his lap. Stretching her legs along the wooden seat, she sat upright, placed her palms on his shoulders, and studied him. "Busy day?" she asked lightly.

"Yes, because . . ." Dramatic pause. His eyes glittered in a way that slayed her.

"Yes?" she prompted.

"Today, the Confederate gold was recovered."

Her jaw sagged open. "What!"

"One hour ago, Ken Vance was arrested for attempted murder and armed robbery. Dennis and Jeff Vance were arrested for armed robbery."

She saw it then, the change in Luke. The dark cloud had gone. His forehead was smoother, his posture lighter. *Praise God.*

"You did this," she said.

"I helped."

She kissed him. Grinned at him.

"Happy?" he asked.

"I've been happy ever since the night we made out after watching *The Sisterhood of the Traveling Pants*—"

"I want to point out that *The Sisterhood of the Traveling Pants* had nothing to do with why we made out."

"Now, today, the Vance brothers have been arrested and you're here with cinnamon rolls. So I'm tremendously happy. Are you happy?"

"Very."

"Tell me everything."

He did so.

Just like she'd always known, he was a hero. A genius! "You kept your promise and didn't break any laws."

"I kept my promise."

She kissed him again, and it was a slow, excellent, soul-stirring kiss. However, he kept it very . . . controlled.

She pulled back to study him some more. Her jubilation began to melt like spilled ice cream.

Ever since her injury, he'd handled her as if she were a Ming vase. She hadn't noticed at first, maybe because she'd needed very cautious handling during the early days following the coma. Now the cautious handling was beginning to feel less like a compliment and more like a wall between them.

It was uncharitable of her to find fault with him. His behavior was exemplary. He'd been trustworthy, steadfast, good. He'd just brought the Vance brothers to justice, for goodness' sake!

It was only that he was so perfect all the time that it was beginning to feel manufactured. She missed the imperfect, unscripted, blunt, sometimes surly version of him that she knew to be the true version.

He'd told her that he was taking the first steps toward regaining his faith and working through trauma. These past days, they'd endured a brutally hard trial together. They'd seen what the other was made of. And they'd gotten each other through.

She loved him. So many things were going well. Was it too much to ask to want to connect with the real him? "You know, right, that I'm regaining my strength? You don't have to tiptoe around me anymore."

"I know."

She gave him time, but he didn't offer more.

She leaned one shoulder and the side of her head against his chest.

He eased the swing into motion, and a few quiet minutes passed while she soaked in the feel of him and tried not to angst about how terrifying it was to love Luke.

Did he love her back?

He'd always said that he'd leave once the treasure hunt ended. The treasure hunt was now, very officially, at its end.

Would he leave?

She'd have no grounds to make him stay if he was set on going. The larger point was that she didn't want to *make* him stay, even if she had that power. She wanted him to want to stay.

Stop borrowing trouble from the future. It was premature to agonize over Luke's leaving. He was here now, and this line of thought dismayed her.

"What are you thinking about?" he asked.

She couldn't blurt out, *I'm thinking that my heart is on the line, which is unbelievably scary.* So she broached something else that had been on her mind. "I'm thinking about all the damage done because my dad, Robbie, and Carla took something they shouldn't have taken. It created a ripple effect that's still going. The Vance brothers lost their sister because of it. Nine years later, I'm in rehab because of it."

She felt him nod.

"Stolen things do harm," she said in a meaningful way.

"Why do I think we're now talking about me?"

"Because we are. You have quite a bit of money."

"From stealing things."

"And I wouldn't want stolen things to do *you* harm."

"If you want me to, I'll give it all away."

"I don't want you to do it for me. I want you to do it for you. It's your money. Your decision. It's not about me."

Her dad had known she'd do the right thing with the gold. But she couldn't force Luke to do the right thing with his money. His life had been rocky. His money likely gave him a sense of security.

"Your greatest occupational dream is not to work at Furry Tails," she said.

"No."

"What do you want?"

"When I got out, I was planning on a career in technology."

"And now?"

"Cars. Working on cars is the thing I like to do most. I want to start a business buying, restoring, and reselling."

She lifted her head so she could see his face. "I love that plan. It's what you're passionate about."

"It's one of the things I'm passionate about. But it's a far second to you."

Desire curled deliciously within her, and she lost herself in his gaze—

"Just so you know"—Meadow's loud voice broke the intimacy of the moment—"we see you, so don't move forward with PDA thinking you're alone."

"You don't have to be alone for PDA," Finley called back. She wrenched her attention to her friends, who were making their way across the garden. "That's why they're called *public* displays of affection."

"Fine!" Meadow gestured. "Go ahead and kiss him right in front of us."

"We'll use extreme self-control and resist." Finley climbed to her feet.

Luke also stood, exchanging hellos with her friends.

A blush darkened Bridget's fair skin. Finley had yet to see Bridget withstand Luke's presence without blushing. "I'm sorry we interrupted you," Bridget told them.

"You didn't interrupt," Finley said, even though they kind of had.

"I'm going to head inside and check something on my laptop." Luke moved off.

"Luke," Meadow said.

He stilled.

He was much taller, so Meadow had to tilt her chin way back. "I know I've acted sort of . . . suspicious of you."

"You have?" Luke asked with a straight face.

"I have. But that's because some men are toads, and I'm really protective of my friend. I was thinking that you were a toad, but you've proven that you're actually not. Now I think you're . . ."

Luke waited.

"Decent," Meadow proclaimed.

"Thank you," Luke said solemnly.

"You're welcome. But if you hurt Finley, I'll drop-kick you."

"If I hurt Finley, I'll drop-kick myself," he said, then continued toward the building.

"That was very big of me," Meadow said to Finley and Bridget.

"It really was," Finley concurred. "Group hug."

They embraced.

"Every time I see Luke, I think how ready I am for a boyfriend," Bridget whispered from inside the huddle. "I'm still wondering if Derek might be interested."

Two days later, two weeks after she and Luke had gone treasure hunting at Vogel State Park, Finley was cleared to return home.

Home!

Luke, Meadow, and Bridget helped her make the transition. They cleaned her already-clean house. Made her lunch. Asked if she was comfortable.

She kept assuring them that she was. It was lovely of them to dote on her. However, she'd had more than her fill of the role of patient. She couldn't wait to return to the much more enjoyable role she'd played all her life—caregiver to animals.

She sat on her deck with Sally, Rufus, and Dudley tucked around her. Her pets stared at her like she was a pastor giving a sermon. She cuddled them, talked to them, played with them, reassured them.

Home. She planned to delight in her bed, her bathtub, the view of the river, her kitchen, her cacti, and all the rest of her eclectic belongings.

She still struggled with post-concussive headaches. Her sense of smell had not fully returned. Overall, though, she was extremely pleased with her improvement. Only one thing was putting a damper on today's excellent mood.

Concerns about Luke.

How was it possible that she and Luke were simultaneously closer than they'd ever been and yet still so separate?

It was possible because he was still acting strangely well-behaved. She was more and more tempted to call him on the carpet for being . . .

Too good?

And he had been good. Wildly good. A five-star boyfriend. No one could have been more devoted. But how much of that was due to his guilt over her injury?

After the earthquake, he'd retreated from everyone who'd loved him. She couldn't bear it if he stayed in Misty River out of a mistaken belief that he owed her. On the other hand, it would break her heart if he followed his old ways and retreated from her now. Would he retreat if she pushed him for too much, too soon?

Dudley the hedgehog crawled toward her knee. She turned him over and gave him a belly rub.

Relax, Finley. Focus on the positive. Listen to your gut.

Right now, her gut was telling her to give Luke additional space to breathe and heal. After all, she wasn't the only one who'd been dealt a blow the night Ken had pushed her off a cliff. Luke had been dealt a blow, too. Like her, it was taking time for him to recover. She needed to be as patient with him as he was with her.

But even as she decided to postpone a confrontation, her conscience whispered an indictment. *You're being a coward*, it said.

CHAPTER THIRTY

Finley was hosting a party.

Her favorite time of year had arrived in the Blue Ridge Mountains. Spring breezes sent pastel wildflowers dancing. Birds sang from the trees. The sun fell gentle and clear. Her heart had been crying out for a tangible way to thank everyone who'd cared for her so well. Her backyard had been crying out for people and pets. A thank-you party seemed like the ideal solution.

She'd moved home two weeks ago. A few days after that, she'd resumed work—albeit shorter hours and less strenuous tasks. A few days after that, she'd floated her party idea to Luke, Meadow, and Bridget.

Meadow and Bridget had been in favor of it, but Luke had shot it down. Too taxing, he'd said.

She'd kept after it. She'd negotiated with him. She'd only invite a few people. Everyone would bring a dish. All she'd have to do was make tea, decorate, buy supplies, and choose which records to play.

Still, he'd resisted. At which time, she'd put her foot down and informed him that she was going to host the gathering with or without his approval. He'd grudgingly come on board.

The night of the party, she donned the new dress she'd purchased for the occasion. Its dusky blue fabric matched her eyes and set off her dark hair. She liked its off-the-shoulder neckline, full sleeves, and short hemline—which showed off legs that had turned tan during the hours she'd spent relaxing on her deck. She slipped on high-heeled wedge sandals moments before the doorbell started ringing.

Several guests had arrived when Luke walked over and murmured, "Hailey just called me. My family's about to pull up, and she asked if you'd be willing to come outside. They have something to show you."

"Of course."

No sooner had they reached the front of the house than she heard the deep rumble of a motor. A Pontiac slid into view, then came to a stop, Blair at the wheel.

"Luke." She reached over to grip his hand. "It's a work of art." Classy and gleaming.

"Thank you."

Blair stepped out of the car, even more pride and swagger in her body language than usual. The rest of his family followed. Finley hugged them all, then made a great fuss over the car. Such a fuss did she make that she suspected Luke of blushing.

He looked wildly handsome tonight in a slim white crewneck sweater and black jeans. He'd combed his hair off his face like he'd done the night of the Valentine's party. It turned her to *mush* when he did that.

"Why are there so many people?" he whispered near her ear as they made their way back inside. "You told me there would be a total of ten."

"That was my initial plan." She waved a hand breezily. "The plan grew in an organic way."

"*Finley*."

She laughed as she parted from him to deposit his mom's coffee cake on the food table.

The divine late-April weather had freed everyone to mingle outside, just as she'd hoped. Rented tables and chairs dotted the land between her house and the river. Kat had made tablecloths from patterned pastel fabric Finley had chosen. Arrangements of ivory and pink peonies served as centerpieces. Later, when darkness came, string lights would add character.

Gratitude and pollen drifted down on her.

She was flush with health. Flush with it! And tonight, she'd be surrounded by all her favorite people.

Happily, she made her way from one group of people to the next. No matter where she mingled, however, she was always conscious of Luke's position. Frequent glances in his direction proved that he was handling himself admirably. He'd had a great deal of practice at interacting with her friends and family members while she'd been in the hospital and rehab facility.

Eventually, she approached him from behind while he was in conversation with Trish and Kat.

Trish was singing the praises of the pimento cheese dip someone had brought. "You both have to try it."

Kat scoffed disdainfully. "I'm going to have a protein shake for dinner. I brought the ingredients with me."

"But this dip is wonderful. Addictive!"

"This morning I ran five miles in less than thirty minutes," Kat announced. "Fitness requires sacrifices."

"Luke," Finley interjected, "I'd like to introduce you to tonight's guest of honor."

He turned, and she showed him the puppy she held in her arms. Agatha. Finley had invited the Gomez family because they'd fostered Rufus and Gloria the fish during her convalescence. She'd expressly requested they bring Agatha tonight, and the grudging smile Luke gave the dog confirmed that she'd been right to do so.

Upon recognizing her beloved, Agatha wiggled furiously. Finley handed her over, and the puppy attempted to burrow under Luke's sweater.

Finley wouldn't mind burrowing under his sweater herself.

Luke patted Agatha's back. "She's grown."

"She has."

"She's now closer to the size of a rat than a mouse," he said.

"You must have a bad self-image, Agatha. And, honestly, it's justified."

Finley laughed.

Agatha's tiny, fierce expression communicated her willingness to bite any person who attempted to separate her from the man of her dreams.

Ben was a Baptist from the South, which meant he'd never met a potluck meal he didn't like. He surveyed his packed plate with pleasure. Fried chicken. Green bean casserole. Salads. One overachiever had baked homemade macaroni and cheese.

Akira sat next to him. "There's even Jell-O," she said with delight.

"That you're happy about the Jell-O proves that you're the woman for me."

"The proof is in the Jell-O."

"Where've you been all my life?"

"Waiting for you."

She'd spoken the comment teasingly, but he suspected that he really had been waiting all his life for her. Something rare and important was taking shape in their relationship, which made him feel like the luckiest man here tonight.

Natasha and Wyatt, Genevieve and Sam, Sebastian and Leah occupied the remaining chairs at their table.

"Your wedding will be here before we know it," Leah said to Genevieve.

"It's just a month away!" Genevieve replied.

"Are you ready?" Sebastian asked Sam.

"I can't wait," he said sincerely in his Aussie accent. "Had I known she'd want so many months between our engagement and our wedding, I'd have thrown her in the back of my truck and taken her straightaway to the justice of the peace."

"And deprive me of my moment?" Genevieve countered. "You owe me a big white dress and flowers and a wedding in a church."

"Is that all?" Sam asked wryly.

"No. You also owe me the sight of you waiting at the altar. And 'you may now kiss the bride' and everyone applauding as we walk back down the aisle together. And dancing. And everything else that comes with the reception."

"You don't care about all that fanfare?" Akira asked Sam.

"I just want to marry her."

"Marry me you shall," Genevieve told him. "And soon."

"Not soon enough."

Genevieve's long hair swung as she leaned over to kiss her fiancé.

"Where are you going on your honeymoon?" Leah asked.

"Australia," Genevieve answered. "We'll spend a week resting on the beach and snorkeling at the Great Barrier Reef. Then we'll head to the part of the country where Sam grew up."

"We'll have another ceremony—small and casual—" he gave Genevieve side-eye—"for my Aussie family and friends."

"I'm excited to see all the places he's told me about."

"You'll fit right in on the cattle station," Sam said.

"I expect to. I've already been assembling outfits that will hit just the right note of outback chic."

Ben chuckled. Genevieve was not a cattle station kind of person. But she loved Sam. She'd told Ben how much it meant to her to have the chance to experience the places that had shaped him, to spend time with the people who'd raised him.

"As I recall, you also have a big day coming up," Natasha said to Leah. "Your brother's graduating, right?"

"Right." Leah tucked her blond hair behind her ears. "There were days when I despaired that we'd ever get to this point. But here we are. He's looking forward to going to college in the fall to study art. In large part because he'll no longer have me peering over his shoulder."

"Then Leah will begin her PhD coursework," Sebastian said.

"Good for you," Akira told her.

"Thanks. I'm going to keep working full-time, so it'll be a lot."

"But worth the effort," Sebastian stated. "Soon we'll be attending Leah's graduation and calling her Doctor."

"A pair of doctors." Natasha regarded the couple with approval.

Sebastian glanced down his shoulder at Leah and grinned. "Yeah. Two doctors."

Sebastian was Ben's closest friend. For decades, Ben had wanted the best for Sebastian. It turned out that Leah was what was best. In her, he'd found the things he'd badly needed. A place to belong. Love and acceptance. A family of his own. Ben had never seen Sebastian love anyone the way that he loved Leah.

Leah had changed for the better, too. Sebastian's support had relaxed her. No longer was it Leah and her brother against the world. She had a powerful ally, now and forever.

It no longer hurt Ben to see them together. They were meant to be, Sebastian and Leah. Things were as they should be. And he could move on.

Someone asked Natasha about her Year of Living Charles Dickensly.

"I want to take a family trip to Chatham, England, this fall!" She explained her dream itinerary while her husband, Wyatt, listened good-naturedly.

When Ben spotted Luke walking up with a puppy asleep in his arms, he set down his chicken leg. They all quieted, looking at the newcomer as he stood in the gap between two chairs.

"Thank you," Luke said. "When I needed someone to be there for me, that first night in the ICU, you were there. Even though you had no reason to help me."

"We didn't need a reason to help." Genevieve faced Luke more fully. "But we did have one. You saved me, all those years ago, when you pulled me out of that dark hallway during the earthquake."

"And me," Ben said.

"And me," Sebastian said.

"And me," Natasha said.

"We haven't forgotten," Ben told Luke. "And we never will."

"We love you," Genevieve said.

"And it would mean a lot to us if we could be your friends," Natasha dared to say.

Everyone waited while Luke's intimidating gaze swept the group. *He's holding a puppy*, Ben reminded himself. *He's not as scary as he used to be.*

"Okay," Luke said simply. "Friends."

Genevieve and Natasha clapped. Sam asked about the puppy.

One by one, Ben took in the details of Misty River's famous Miracle Five. All of them together this evening.

The miracle of the Miracle Five wasn't just that they'd physically survived the earthquake. But that they'd all found ways to thrive despite the trauma they'd suffered.

The God Ben knew could be trusted to redeem the hardship He allowed.

He'd done just that for every single one of them.

In His time.

Luke was not a social person.

For Finley's sake, he'd done his best tonight. He'd helped set up. He'd talked as much as he could. He'd catered to Agatha. He'd refilled people's glasses and handed out vegan cake. He'd spent time with his family and hugged each of them—even Blair—when they'd left.

When only three guests remained, Luke gave himself a pass and started filling Finley's dishwasher. Everyone had done a solid job of cleaning things up and taking their dishes home with them. Even so, there was enough here for a full load, and he didn't want Finley stuck with it. She still tired easily, and the party must have drained her energy.

She drifted toward the front door, chatting with the stragglers. He finished loading the machine, then started it. When he straightened, he saw Finley walking toward him in bare feet. Her hair was loose. Her dress glided against the lines of her body.

"You look sexy when you clean," she said.

"That's why I do it."

She stopped a few feet away. "I had a chance to thank everyone tonight except you."

"You don't need to thank me." In fact, her thanks made him uncomfortable because he wanted so badly for her to love him . . . but not because of thankfulness.

"I do need to thank you. You've done far, far more for me than anyone else. I recovered as quickly as I did, in part, because you bent over backward to make it so. Thank you."

"You're welcome."

She moved to him, her feet positioned between his boots, her palms resting on his chest. "I want a million things for you. At the top of that list is for you to know that you're free."

His stomach dropped with fear. "Free? I don't want to be free."

"Free from constantly having to take care of me."

"I don't feel like I have to constantly take care of you."

"Really?" she asked gently. "Because it seems like you feel duty-bound to do just that. Tonight's party is an example. I did almost nothing and you did almost everything."

She was so close. He was inhaling her perfume and need was rising in him dangerously. "You did more than you should have. You were on your feet most of the night."

"I feel great."

"I'm just trying to be careful. Of you."

"And I'm trying to convince you that I'm totally fine." She gave him a stern schoolteacher expression. "You can stop treating me like a Ming vase."

"A what?"

"You've been so kind, which is fabulous. But now I need you to hear me when I say that *I am fine*."

Warning slithered down his neck. "I hear you, Finley. I just don't want you to push it—"

"When you say you don't want me to push it, you're telling me that you actually *didn't* hear me." She stepped back, looking to the side with a tight profile.

He had no idea how this had turned south. "Finley?"

Her chin swung toward him, and she drew herself tall. "It feels like you're harboring guilt about what happened on Blood Mountain, and treating me like I'm an invalid is your penance."

"What? No."

"You say that, but I think I'm right. It's as if . . . as if you won't admit I'm well enough to stand on my own two feet because you're not done serving your sentence." She stacked her palms over her heart. "Here I am, thrilled that the balance of power is equal between us again, and there you are, refusing to let that happen."

"I'm not refusing to let that—"

"Stop trying to earn forgiveness for your sins. They've already been forgiven. It's done!"

"I know."

"No, you don't."

"Yes, I do."

"And quit being so . . . so *reasonable*!" She flung up her hands.

"What?"

"Stop being so perfect all the time. Stop protecting me. Stop coddling me. Stop acting so composed and cautious around me."

Crap. He loved her, and he needed to make this right. "I . . ."

"Lose your temper, Luke!" Her eyes snapped. "I miss the man who carried me to my bedroom. Remember him? So carry me to the bedroom so that I can shoot you down and tell you that's not going to happen."

"No."

"*Right now*."

"No. You've had a brain injury and—"

"I'm fine!"

"You're recuperating—"

"Get out," she ordered.

"Finley, let's talk—"

"Get out of my house." She pointed toward the front door with a trembling finger.

His own anger answered, pushing aside some of the fear. She was kicking him out? After he'd dedicated every minute of the last month to her? Because he was still trying to put her interests first and not throw her progress in the trash?

He stalked from the house. As he crossed to his truck, he heard the front door slam behind him.

As soon as she was alone, Finley turned on her heel and screamed.

She wanted to strangle him and crush her mouth against his and force him to *be real* with her. Her hope that time would bring down the wall separating them lay in ashes at her feet. She hadn't handled that well just now, but if this was going to work, he had to open himself up to her! And maybe he never would. And what had she just done?

She loved him, yet she'd driven him away. She couldn't let him go—

Even right this minute.

She genuinely could not let him go.

She yanked open the door to find that he was already storming back toward her, the black sky his backdrop, features set. He entered her foyer, and she slammed the door for the second time in the space of a minute. This time, instead of shutting him out, she'd shut him in.

They faced off.

"Are you going to leave Misty River?" she demanded.

"What?"

"You're going to leave, aren't you?"

"I am never going to leave." He spoke each word distinctly. "If Misty River is where you live, it will always—*always*—be where I live, too."

Surprise stilled some of her inner chaos. "It will?"

"Yes. I love you," he said almost savagely. "I love you, Finley. You're my breath. And so I felt like I was suffocating when I thought that you might not wake up. If you die, I will die. So if I'm protective of you, that's why."

Her . . . her brain couldn't catch up with the pace of his words and the raw emotion surrounding each one.

"I don't deserve you," he said. "And I don't expect you to love me back. I know that you'll never love anyone the way you loved Chase—"

She pressed a fingertip to his lips. It seemed she was crying. She took a moment to inhale, then removed her finger from his mouth. "You're right. I'll never love anyone the way I loved Chase. But I *do* love Luke the way I love Luke. When I loved Chase, I was a younger, sweeter, more naïve person. A person unscathed by grief. I'm a different person now. And this person loves *you*. To the bottom of my heart. With everything I am. I love you."

His face smoothed with shock.

"From the time I was a girl," she continued, "all the way through to this present moment, I've been making my way to you. I'll love you for every single day I have left."

A pocket of silence.

Slowly, he took her into his arms and angled his gaze down to her.

"I love you." He said it like a promise, then communicated the depth of that promise through a kiss—vulnerable and endlessly passionate. Soon her heart was thundering.

At last, no wall between them. His control had cracked. Her worries had been vanquished.

"You love me?" she whispered when she came up for air.

"I do. And I always will."

"I love you, Luke."

The broken man had found redemption, and the wounded woman had moved past her fear. Despite their scars and heartbreak, new hope had come for them. Their history made that truth all the sweeter.

They loved each other.

The wonder of it spun like a ring of stars around them.

EPILOGUE

"Your eyes are closed, right?" Luke asked. He walked behind her, steering her forward.

"Luke. My eyes are closed. Plus, I'm wearing a blindfold. Plus, your hands are covering my eyes. Rest assured, I cannot see anything."

"Good."

She smiled, anticipation bubbling inside. It was her birthday, and he'd planned some sort of surprise for her. Two years had passed since she'd opened the first clue in her father's final treasure hunt, and she knew for certain that the treasure her dad had actually sent her, during that hunt, was Luke.

They'd celebrated Genevieve and Sam's big day. Then Sebastian and Leah's engagement. Then Sebastian and Leah's wedding. Then Ben and Akira's engagement. Then, this past June, she and Luke had married in a simple outdoor ceremony held on the lakeshore of her father's property. Her boho dress had swished as she walked. The lake glittered blue. Dogs available for adoption dressed in bow ties and tutus charmed the guests.

The thing she remembered best about that day, though, was Luke's face—sharp-boned, clear-eyed—as he'd gazed down at her and spoken his vows.

They'd taken a glorious honeymoon trip, and then he'd moved into her house. He worked restoring cars, and she worked rescuing dogs, and her heart could not contain any more happiness, of this she was convinced.

Luke drew her to a stop.

Her breath caught. "Is it time for the big reveal?"

"Yes. Are you ready?"

"Yes."

"You don't sound sure."

"I sounded extremely sure!"

"Because I can wait—"

"I am beyond ready for the big reveal," she stated emphatically.

He whipped the blindfold up and off.

She was standing in front of a large enclosure on this cold winter day. At a . . . zoo? She scanned the enclosure and realized that a lion—an honest-to-goodness *lion*—was sleeping on a raised platform.

A placard had been erected a few feet in front of her.

This habitat was made possible by a generous donation given in honor of Finley Sutherland Dempsey, animal activist, by the man who loves her.

Her mittened hands lifted to cover her mouth. She knew where she was. Georgia's big-cat rescue center. She'd been here before, but this habitat was entirely new and, no doubt, outrageously expensive. She swiveled to face her husband.

"I found a way," he said, "to spend my ill-gotten gains."

She flung herself into his arms.

Easily, he caught her.

"This is the best birthday present I've ever received," she said.

"You're the best gift I've ever received. I love you."

"I love you," she whispered.

"Happy birthday."

She'd been wrong just now because her heart *could*, she discovered, contain even more happiness.

". . . in love you have delivered my life
from the pit of destruction,
for you have cast all my sins
behind your back."

Isaiah 38:17 ESV

DISCUSSION QUESTIONS

1. The plot of *Turn to Me* was inspired by recent real-life stories of historic treasures discovered, as well as stories of treasures purposely left for others to track down. Becky could have written a romance novel without the treasure hunt element, but chose to include it. What did that element of the book add to the reading experience?
2. Did you learn anything new while reading *Turn to Me* about running an animal shelter or the challenges inherent in reacclimating to life outside of prison?
3. Becky considers Luke to be a "bad boy" hero type. If you fell in love with him alongside Finley, what was it about him that melted your heart?
4. Becky let readers know early on that someone was following Luke and Finley. Why do you think she let you in on that? Who did you think that person might be?
5. Where did the humor in this book come from?
6. The theme of *Turn to Me* is embracing new beginnings. At first, it seems that only applies to Luke because Finley appears to be thriving. Later, we (and Finley) realize it applies

to her, too. How did Becky explore this theme differently in Luke and Finley's journeys?

7. Did any scene make you emotional? If so, which one?
8. *Turn to Me* is the final book of the MISTY RIVER ROMANCE series, which is bound together by the "Miracle Five." Why do you think Becky chose to center her series on adults who'd suffered through a childhood tragedy?
9. For Becky, one of the challenges of writing a three-book series is attempting to incorportate the six main characters into the other novels just enough—but not too much. If you read the other books, do you think she struck the right balance? If so, what methods did she use to do that?
10. Every author has what we in the publishing world refer to as a "writer's voice," which encompasses the writer's style, tone, uniqueness. How would you describe Becky's writer's voice?

Becky Wade is the 2018 Christy Award Book of the Year winner for *True to You*. She is a native of California who attended Baylor University, met and married a Texan, and moved to Dallas. She published historical romances for the general market, then put her career on hold for several years to care for her children. When God called her back to writing, Becky knew He meant for her to turn her attention to Christian fiction. Her humorous, heart-pounding contemporary romance novels have won four Christy Awards, the Carol Award, the INSPY Award, and the Inspirational Reader's Choice Award for Romance. To find out more about Becky and her books, visit beckywade.com.

Sign Up for Becky's Newsletter

Keep up to date with Becky's news on book releases and events by signing up for her email list at beckywade.com.

More from Becky Wade

When pediatric heart surgeon Sebastian Grant meets Leah Montgomery, his fast-spinning world comes to a sudden stop. And when Leah receives surprising news while assembling a family tree, he helps her comb through old hospital records to learn more. But will attaining their deepest desires require more sacrifices than they imagined?

Let It Be Me • A Misty River Romance

You May Also Like . . .

Led to her hometown by a mysterious letter, Genevieve Woodward wakes in an unfamiliar cottage with the confused owner staring down at her. The last thing Sam Turner wants is to help a woman as troubled as she is talkative, but he can't turn her away when she needs him most. Will they be able to let go of the façades and loneliness they've always clung to?

Stay with Me by Becky Wade
A Misty River Romance
beckywade.com

Britt and Zander have been best friends since they met thirteen years ago—but unbeknownst to Britt, Zander has been in love with her for just as long. When Zander's uncle dies of mysterious causes, he returns to Washington to investigate. As they work together to uncover his uncle's tangled past, will the truth of what lies between them also come to light?

Sweet on You by Becky Wade
A Bradford Sisters Romance
beckywade.com

Willow Bradford is content taking a break from modeling to run her family's inn until she comes face-to-face with former NFL quarterback Corbin Stewart, the man who broke her heart—and wants to win her back. When a decades-old family mystery brings them together, they're forced to decide whether they can risk falling for each other all over again.

Falling for You by Becky Wade
A Bradford Sisters Romance
beckywade.com